This will give you an idea
of how much ground I covered

ALSO BY HÉCTOR TOBAR

FICTION

The Barbarian Nurseries

The Tattooed Soldier

NONFICTION

*Deep Down Dark: The Untold Stories of 33 Men Buried in a
Chilean Mine, and the Miracle That Set Them Free*

*Translation Nation: Defining a New American Identity in the
Spanish-Speaking United States*

The Last Great Road Bum

The Last Great Road Bum

Héctor Tobar

MCD
Farrar, Straus and Giroux
New York

MCD
Farrar, Straus and Giroux
120 Broadway, New York 10271

Copyright © 2020 by Héctor Tobar
All rights reserved
Printed in the United States of America
First edition, 2020

Grateful acknowledgment is made for permission to reprint lines from "My
Mother upon Hearing News of Her Mother's Death" (poem) from *Split*,
copyright © 2014 by Cathy Linh Che, Alice James Books.

Photograph on page 188 of Joe Sanderson in a hammock copyright © Susan
Meiselas / Magnum Photos.

Library of Congress Cataloging-in-Publication Data
Names: Tobar, Héctor, 1963– author.
Title: The last great road bum / Héctor Tobar.
Description: First edition. | New York : MCD/Farrar, Straus and Giroux, 2020.
Identifiers: LCCN 2020003424 | ISBN 9780374183424 (hardcover)
Classification: LCC PS3570.O22 L37 2020 | DDC 813/.54—dc23
LC record available at https://lccn.loc.gov/2020003424

Designed by Richard Oriolo

Our books may be purchased in bulk for promotional, educational, or
business use. Please contact your local bookseller or the Macmillan Corporate
and Premium Sales Department at 1-800-221-7945, extension 5442,
or by e-mail at MacmillanSpecialMarkets@macmillan.com.

www.mcdbooks.com • www.fsgbooks.com
Follow us on Twitter, Facebook, and Instagram at @mcdbooks

10 9 8 7 6 5 4 3 2 1

In memory of Gus Gregory

Contents

I. The Part About the Boy: Natural Histories

II. The Part About the World: Pax Americana

III. The Part About the War: Lucas

Some Introductory Remarks
from the Author

THE PROTAGONIST OF THIS NOVEL was a real-life person who lived in the United States in the twentieth century. He left behind several boxes of typed pages and handwritten letters in which he recounted the many humorous, surreal, tragic and grand adventures that fill the pages of this book. Joe Sanderson was the youngest son of an educated family, raised in a college town set amidst the bountiful farmland of the central United States; he was also lucky enough to live during a time when the U.S.A. was the most powerful and dazzling empire on the globe. But unlike most of the people he grew up with, he did not bask in the perks and the glory of a professional career, or sign up for multiple mortgages and marriages. He chose not to enjoy the privileges and creature comforts of the American middle class, even though such comforts were his birthright. Instead, Our Hero dropped out of college and roamed the world for twenty years, telling his mother and father he was gathering the raw material he needed to write the Great American Novel.

Put another way, the Protagonist of this book was a real person who tried to become a novelist by living his life like a character in a novel. Joe Sanderson did many bold things that were like the plot elements of the books he liked to read. He traveled as a "road bum" across the United States, Africa, South America, Southeast and Central Asia and the Middle East, rode ships across the seas and worked to heal the sick and feed starving children. And he carried firearms. Our Hero drank beer and wine, whispered sweet words to the women who fell in love with him, learned to fly airplanes and was detained by the police and local military forces in half a dozen different countries. He dodged bullets in three different wars (on three different continents), even though he was never actually drafted to fight in one. While doing these things, Joe Sanderson wrote thousands of pages of fiction—not a word of which was ever published. As you'll soon see, he loved books from an early age and believed so deeply in the power of the novel that he risked his life again and again trying to write one. Eventually, Our Hero talked his way into a guerrilla army in Latin America. When he died, he was carrying about four hundred pages of notes for his masterpiece: a novel about the civil war and revolution in El Salvador.

Unfortunately, Joe Sanderson was unable to complete, or even start, really, this last book. And to be perfectly honest, all the other novels he did finish are largely unreadable, in the unanimous opinion of those who've tried to read them. (While God blessed Joe Sanderson with all the brio and the daring of a great fictional character, He gave Our Hero very little writerly discipline.) The bulk of this book is based, then, on the letters Joe wrote home to his mother, Virginia Colman, his father, Milt Sanderson, his brother, Steve Sanderson, and to one of the many lovers with whom he corresponded, a woman who wishes to be identified only as Mafalda. I've quoted from his letters verbatim, except for changing a name here and there, and correcting his spelling. (Even though I'm as poor a speller as he was, I have the luxury of spell-check, and I'm not writing, like he was, from desert camps and bombed-out villages.) And I've done all the normal things novelists do in bringing true events back to life: I've imagined scenes, created composite characters and entirely fictional characters and I've spent a lot of time praying to the Muses to help me conjure Our Hero's world and enter his nicotine-fed brain.

The book that follows is, then, a work of fiction. But before we leave the rigorous realm of nonfiction, I'd like to say one last thing: During the many years I've spent writing this novel, I have not failed to notice the wrinkled brows that occasionally greet me when I describe the Protagonist to people I meet. Height: five foot eleven. Hair color: blond. Eyes: blue. Complexion: pale, waxy even, unless he'd been tanned in the sun, which he usually was. The unspoken but obvious question that follows is this: Why would I, a person "of color," want to write a novel about a man who isn't? Well, because it's a great story. And it just happens to reach a true-life climax in Central America, that beautiful and suffering isthmus where my own family history begins. More precisely, the final half of this book takes place in El Salvador, "the pinkie finger of the Americas" (as the Chilean poet Gabriela Mistral called it), a country that is home to a brave people with proud indigenous and mestizo roots. The Protagonist and I are therefore completing a circle together. To live this novel, Joe Sanderson left behind his Illinois homeland and learned Spanish and ate pupusas and drank atol de elote, and he climbed tropical volcanoes, and slept in hammocks under banana trees. And to write this novel I learned to appreciate the polite but emotionally reserved Midwestern way of being, and ate lots of mashed potatoes and buttered corn on the cob, and I allowed myself to be seduced by the unpretentious enchantments of Urbana, Illinois, and all its swell people.

In other words, dear reader, this is *our* book. A collaboration between central Illinois and Central America. The Protagonist lived it, and I wrote it, and I hope that wherever he is, Joe Sanderson appreciates my efforts.

The Last Great Road Bum

A STATEMENT FROM OUR PROTAGONIST

My name is Joe Sanderson, and you are about
to read the book that killed me.

One of the few things I still miss from my Midwest childhood was this weird, deluded but unshakable conviction that everything around me existed all and only *For Me*.

—David Foster Wallace, on growing up in Urbana, Illinois

I
=

The Part
About the Boy:
   Natural Histories

1.

Urbana, Illinois, U.S.A.

BETWEEN THE SWAY OF WIND-CATCHING WILLOWS, Joe Sanderson searched. He climbed over the knotty skeletons of old shrubs, and planted his feet into spongy soil. His sneakers snapped dead branches in two. These were the early days of autumn, and his arms and cheeks were still summer-bronzed and freckled over the last layers of his baby fat. He was eleven years old and an expert butterfly collector. Probably the top kid-lepidopterist in Champaign County, in his own humble opinion. At night his bones ached and added marrow, and each morning his limbs felt more sinewy and masculine, as if he'd somehow entered the body of Davy Crockett. Or Daniel Boone. Manhood was calling to him in the contracting muscles of his calves and his bulkier biceps, but not yet in his loins. For the moment, he was still a boy.

Joe's friend Jim trailed behind him. Above them, the Illinois sun streamed through the tree canopies and their leaves became emeralds and rubies. Joe looked down at the ground before him, which had been made wet by weeks of rain showers, and saw slugs, snails and hopping insects, creatures that were burrowing and slithering. An earthworm oozed over his foot. His new canvas tennis shoes were covered in mud and ruined. Mom's going to be heaping mad! Nah, that's a dumb thing to think. A scientist doesn't worry if his shoes are covered in mud. His father, Professor Milton W. Sanderson, was an entomologist at the University of Illinois and the world's leading expert on the June beetle. Joe had been trying to sound like his father when he invited Jim on this butterfly expedition. They had traveled from Joe's house on Washington Street on bicycles, down the straight and flat asphalt strip of Race Street to the edge of town, past the asterisk petals of yellow wildflowers, to this grove of university-planted trees. Nearby, the last patches of native prairie grass in Champaign County were catching the wind and drawing bugs, while the shallow stream whispered to the butterflies and dragonflies to come rest by its muddy shores.

Muddy shores. Muddy shoes. My mother will be angry at these muddy shoes.*

---

*So here I am, reading a novel about me. And for some reason, the fictional me is a little kid. Well, you can only expect strange things when you're in the hands of a Guatemalan dude, which is what the Author of this book is, despite the bald eagle on his passport, and the native English that flows from his tongue. My travels taught me that the Central American people are as friendly and romantic a lot as you'd hope to meet; they also possess a lovably dark sense of wit. And without those qualities, no writer would be able to tell my story.

TWO HOURS EARLIER, Joe's mother, Virginia Sanderson, née Colman, had watched Joe emerge from his bedroom in his pajamas. She felt, for what would prove to be the last time, the sensation that had often come over her when Joe was a cotton-diapered infant and milk-toothed toddler: that he had somehow stretched out, thinned out, and grown taller overnight.

On most days, Virginia sat behind a desk at the Champaign County Bank and Trust. She spent her workdays keeping ledgers and turning the crank on a machine whose gears could add up to $9,999,999.99. When she got home, Virginia kept on counting. One man, two boys (Joe and his brother, Steve), four steaks, one pan, four potatoes, one cup of milk, two teaspoons of butter, four hours till bedtime. Four feet eleven inches, size-eight shoes. With each new school year and season, her healthy, freckled son presented new puzzles. He had a mouth of mostly new permanent teeth, with perhaps one last baby canine or premolar still left to drop. His energy was boundless, protomasculine and unfocused, as evidenced by the ever-growing collection of bugs and other artifacts in his bedroom, filling his room with the sugary, unnatural aroma of preserved death; and some-times, the musky, fermented scent of the urine and wet fur of the living mammals he brought into the house from the wild. More than two hundred and fifty butterflies in his collection. The rescued baby rabbits she helped him feed with an eyedropper. Mom is the mother rabbit, Steve! Look at Mom! She kept waiting for him to grow out of his collecting and wandering stage.

FOR THE REST OF JOE SANDERSON'S LIFE, butterfly collecting will be a metaphor for curiosity and adventure. When he's on battlefields distant from Urbana and the United States, he'll jokingly call himself a "butterfly collector" and say his M16 rifle is his "butterfly net." At the age of eleven, he keeps picture frames with his captured and pinned butterflies, and also jars filled with snakeskins. He can identify the castes in his ant farm. He has a stuffed oriole, dried maple leaves and beetles. Intricate, startling and perfect things that remind him of the infinite variety of the living world. The wing of a monarch butterfly when he blows it up five hundred times in his father's microscope and sees rows of delicate scales, a feathery field of saffron-colored grass. The exoskeleton of a beetle, and the stacked-coin patterns in the snake's rattle.

Now, in this small ecosystem tucked between the city and the corn-fields, wounded sparrows died and putrefied, the caterpillars secreted smelly vapors, and the short-tailed shrews and meadow voles dropped feces. Cycles of living things. The mud inside his shoes made music as he marched. Swish, issh, swish, issh.

"This is a good spot," Joe told Jim. "There's water nearby. And all these shrubs down here. You catch them near what they eat."

A stiff breeze came rushing into the grove of willows, cottonwoods and oaks again, causing the branches and leaves over his head to fill with a sound that made him think of sand falling through an hourglass. The tall pillar of air around Joe shifted westward, then eastward, with him and Jim and all the other living things inside it moving in the same cadence, every leaf and every branch, every bird, every nest. The swaying stopped, and a warm air was born from the stillness, the final hot humid breath of a Mid-western summer. Joe saw a brown, beating stain in the shadowy light, a butterfly rising and falling on currents of air as if careening down some in-visible roller coaster. It passed a foot or so from his left ear and came to rest upon a shrub. Quickly, expertly, Joe plopped his net down and the fat but-terfly was his, spotted wings beating furiously in the white mesh. "It's a silver-spotted skipper," Joe said, and he held the net closed with one hand and reached into the pocket of his collector's jacket with the other, retriev-ing a jar and a wad of cotton, which he moistened with ether. The butterfly fluttered its wings in a final convulsion. So cruel to kill a living thing.

When they were done collecting, Joe and Jim marched out of the woods and heard the elephant wail of a passing train, and felt a tremor moving through the ground: the Illinois Central, on its diesel march between Chicago and New Orleans. The boys stepped out onto Race Street, into full sunshine, and they retrieved their bikes and pedaled northward through two parallel fields of harvest-high corn. A wind-wave rippled through the ears, the tassels and the silk. Urbana was surrounded by so much corn it made you feel like a castaway on an island in a corn ocean. They passed the sign announcing the city limits: URBANA: ELEV. 730 FEET. He could follow this road all the way to Chicago. Maps at the gas station with this highway and many others, and railroad lines. Danville, Bloomington, Decatur. The blue whorls of the Sangamon River.

Joe forgot about the butterflies and the dragonfly in his jacket. What next? What now? He felt the book shift in its pocket. Maybe I should write this down. Words made adventures live forever. His father was reading *Les Misérables* to him at night. They were almost finished. Dad said they'd read *Robinson Crusoe* next. When he visited his grandmother in Kansas, she read *Huckleberry Finn* to him. Books brought him joy, and books doomed him, because from an early age he believed every exciting thing that happened to him belonged in a book. Even now, as a fifth grader, he believes his story can fall onto a sheet of paper as easily as the rubber tire of his bicycle rolls onto the black asphalt. One day he'll write as many words as there are white dashes in the center of this road. You live something, you write it down with words, words, words. Men set off on ships to conquer new territories, across the ocean, wave after wave, word after word.

HIS MOTHER WASN'T HOME, and Joe stepped into the backyard and washed his shoes with the garden hose and left them out on a clothesline to dry. He slipped on some older leather shoes that felt like a vise around his ankles.

When Joe entered the kitchen and faced his mother, her eyes were drawn immediately to his feet. What's the story here, little man? But for the sizzling steak on the stove, she would have asked. Her boys moved toward the table, eager to take their seats and to eat, to grow, Joe growing fastest. The new boy Virginia saw in the morning, not the same one she'd seen the night before. These moments will stand out in the chain of her lived days. Suppers served here in Urbana, and on the Kansas farm where she grew up. Douglas County, North Fifteen Hundred Road, on high ground in the valley of the Kansas and the Wakarusa Rivers. The hay and the corn that fed the cattle; two horses, one sable, one ash colored, to pull the cart and the plow. Today, chuck eye, fifth rib of the cow, store-bought at forty cents a pound, blood browning in the heat of the skillet, blue kernels of flame, city-gas uniform and steady. A meal of marbled meat, flesh born from grass and the gnashing molars of the steer; a farm here in her skillet. Once upon a time, the cast-iron stove, the firewood and the coal, a singeing roar of orange flames. Fat curdling in the chuck eye, crystals of Morton salt in the blood juice, becoming salty vapor.*

"SMELLS GOOD, MOM!" Steaming string beans, like the ones they grew on the farm, by the barn, Virginia's "easy" girl-work to water and weed. Vegetables sold here in grocer's mounds under gray light tubes, filling up a pewter scoop. One meal, ten thousand meals, from the crushed apple, the dried milk, the boiled carrots for the toothless infant, to the potatoes in the

---

*To my salvadoreño brothers and sisters reading this: You see? My mother, your mother. No son tan diferentes. They cook, they worry, they work. Mine in the garden by the barn, walking past curtains of green corn; yours using a metate to grind the corn. My mother was from a farm town that had its own wars, its own massacres buried in its history, believe it or not. We had our Bleeding Kansas, you had your 1932. La misma mierda, the same burning merry-go-round, as far as I can tell.

saucepan for this supper, starch softening with butter and more salt and milk into mush. A bit of gravy from store-bought powder, because there was a limit to what one working mother could do. The gathering of the smells above the stove, scent of motherhood and mothering; a meal, here, from me, to you boys, patient boys, obedient, waiting, standing before my fancy new rubber place mats, just rinse them off and use them again and again.

Suddenly and without preamble, Milt said, "We might go to war in Guatemala. Over bananas." The boys chuckled at the sound of the word *bananas*. Earlier in the day Milt had read a story in *The Atlantic Monthly* about war rumblings in Central America. The United Fruit Company, based in New Orleans, was prodding President Eisenhower to protect its bananas from the left-wing government there. In the pages of *The Atlantic Monthly* and *Time*, Milt read stories about the assorted tin-pot dictators who ruled most of the globe. Like the generalissimo Trujillo in the Dominican Republic. Milt once collected carrion beetles in the mountains of that tropical country. The larvae grew inside the buried corpses of mammals and birds; to find them he traveled on roads past checkpoints manned by the dictator's soldiers, who wore low-slung belts and carried old M1 rifles. Carrion beetles burrowed into dead flesh to lay their eggs and Trujillo dumped the corpses of his enemies in the cloud forests. In the big, wet world there was always a new war waiting to metamorphose somewhere from mud and moist air. The last one was in Korea. Maybe the next one would be in Guatemala.

No one at the table asked Milt to explain the banana war. The Sandersons scooped from the plates of mashed potatoes before them, chewed and swallowed their steaks. Virginia saw a streak of mud on the back of Joe's neck and then another one on the underside of his arm, and later she looked out the kitchen window to the backyard and saw his new pair of tennis shoes hanging over the clothesline, their white laces colored orange by the dusk. A little mystery in the mud and the shoes.

Virginia was losing track of who Joe really was. Does every mom feel this, or is it just me? Have I neglected him in some way?* She decided not to ask Joe about the shoes, and she returned to the kitchen, alone, standing before the open door of the refrigerator, looking at the nearly empty bottle of milk that was waiting there. The boys had really polished that off. She poured the final half glass, and left it there on the counter near the sink, and picked up the bottle to take it to the porch, for the man in the black tie to pick up tomorrow morning. He comes pulling a wagon on a horse. A little bit of the country in this college town. Outside, on the neighborhood door-steps, more empty bottles awaited the milkman. Next door, and two doors down, where the Eberts and their son, Roger, lived. Empty bottles next to doors where other American boys were preparing for bed with milk in their stomachs, adding marrow to their bones.

---

*Interesting. I loved Mom, but I never made her a character in my books. When I wrote my novels, my heroes were all confident and bumbling American men (like me). I'll admit, now, in hindsight, to being a chauvinist pig. (A girlfriend or two did call me that.) I was a product of my age. We Americans are different, now, as a people. Better in some ways, and worse off in others.

2.

Champaign, Illinois

FALL ARRIVED, AND DEEPENED, and the ash trees on Washington Street outside Joe's bedroom window became skeletons that resembled pleading arms reaching to the sky. On the calm ocean of soil beyond the city limits, the crops were in. The local farmers, cleaned up in new plaid and old denim, their fingernails freshly scraped, drove into Urbana to visit the Champaign County Bank and Trust, where Virginia Sanderson worked. They brought their leather ledger books and made big deposits. Abundant applications of ammonium nitrate and the ordinary rains of summer had brought Illinois another bumper crop.

When winter arrived the outsiders transplanted to this college and farm town grew bitter and angry with the icy roads and the frosty, cutting wind; and the natives were stoic and silent as they scraped and shoveled away snow. The land was fallow. Like a man or a woman following the act of procreation, it was in a state of quiet repose.

Joe asked his father to take him hunting.

"With any firearm in your hands, you really can't allow your attention to wander, Joe. Understand?" They drove an hour outside town, past carpets of collapsed cornstalks turning gray in the rain, and past a stretch of woods where fallen, rain-moistened leaves were blackening into mulch. They reached a pastel prairie with jasmine-colored switchgrass, and the violet seed heads of big bluestem grass, and they stopped, squatted and waited. A single wild pheasant settled into the grass about twenty yards away. "Remember: shoot where it's going to be," Milt said, and he brought his cold hands together in a loud clap. The pheasant startled and took flight, and Joe took a half step forward and fired, and the pellets struck the bird about six feet off the ground. Feathers exploded into black confetti and the bird fell into the grass with a thud.

Thirteen months later, when Christmas came around again, Milt bought Joe a .22 Remington rifle. Joe lifted it from its box and took in the solvency scent of the rifle's lubricants, the milled ball of its bolt and the walnut grain of its stock. Milt thought it was as good a time as any to tell his son the family gunman stories again. Great-Grandpa Frank was very handy with a rifle. Ran away from home when he was twelve—left Maine and made it all the way to South Dakota. Lived with the Sioux for a while, and made friends with Wild Bill Hickok. Got a job on the railroad and went on strike with the socialists; he took Milt on his first hunt.

For target practice with his new rifle, Joe took long rides on his bicycle and hikes outside the Urbana-Champaign city limits. To the Mahomet woods and beyond. Rimfire cartridges, brass bodies and silver heads, re-membering his father's lessons. "A rifle is different from a shotgun. You point a shotgun, but you aim a rifle. Breathe three times and squeeze the trigger as slowly as you can. The rifle is going to recoil. You can't allow your fear of the recoil to make you jerk the gun." After he bought a telescopic sight Joe could hit a squirrel from seventy-five yards.*

The corpses of the squirrels oozed muscle tissue from the wounds his bullets inflicted on them. He saw an ad in *Boys' Life* and wrote to the National Rifle Association and joined as a junior member, and took a self-administered shooting test and passed it, and got a wallet-size card in the mail identifying him as a "marksman." He struck a crow from one hundred and fifty yards, and afterward he came home and told his father, "This rifle is my most prized possession." On television many years later, the actor Chuck Connors fired off a rifle too, a Winchester, in a new show called *The Rifleman*. Lucas McCain, as the benevolent hero was called, was an expert shot, and he used his rifle skills to right wrongs on the Western frontier. The show aired on Tuesday nights and Joe would watch many of its episodes.

UNLIKE GENERATIONS OF Midwestern fathers before him, Milt Sanderson had little reason to believe that his son would ever need to use his home-taught shooting skills in battle. The United States was at peace, more or less, except for the thousands of troops stationed in Germany to scare off the Russians, and the thousands more in Korea to scare off the Chinese,

---

*Sorry. I can't help myself. This writer, he's being too subtle for my taste. I was always pretty direct when it came to writing. So I'm gonna let you in on something that's pretty obvious to me, and to my Salvadoran friends, and anyone else who knows how my story turns out: All this shooting is going to come in handy later. One day when there's something bigger than squirrels to shoot at, and when the "squirrels" start shooting back at me, so to speak.

and the fleets of Stratofortresses waiting in airbases in the Great Plains, ready to deliver nuclear warheads over the Arctic Circle. The war in Guatemala had lasted only a few days: the U.S. Central Intelligence Agency orchestrated a coup to overthrow the country's leftist president, Jacobo Arbenz, with undercover American pilots flying P-51 Mustangs to bomb Guatemala City. The drama unfolded on the front page of the *Champaign-Urbana Courier*, which Milt read every day. "Anti-Red Exiles Mass on Guatemala Border," read one headline, next to an incongruous photograph of a local woman in a pioneer dress, celebrating the centennial of Loda, Illinois, population 550. "Casualties Heavy, Guatemala Capital Prepares for Raid," read another headline; on the same day the newspaper reported the city of Champaign would be installing new, fluorescent streetlights. Then President Arbenz fled Guatemala and the war was over, and as the weather warmed and summer approached the *Courier* reported on a heat wave and on a University of Illinois study on the ill effects of air-conditioning.

SOMETIMES JOE WENT OUT on expeditions with both his rifle and a butterfly net. In farm fields, in orchards, by streams. He caught a buckeye, with its six black onyx eyes on its wings to scare off predators; and an eastern comma, and a question mark, *Polygonia interrogationis*. He marched twenty miles with the Boy Scouts on the Lincoln Trail, and earned merit badges for botany, astronomy, shooting and citizenship. Soon he was a Star Scout. All these skills would serve him well later in life, when he became a professional road bum. At the Crystal Lake pool in the summer, he became a powerful swimmer, and he climbed out of the water feeling the muscle added to his arms by hundreds of strokes: his pectorals remained thin and boyish, but were home to a few pioneering strands of chest hair. A strange mammal was being born inside him. Tumescence. In the morning and in his sleep. Mysteries of male biology.

His father read to him from the pages of *The Atlantic Monthly*. Unbe-knownst to father and son, these articles were often about places Joe would visit in the next decade: *Real control [in Afghanistan] is vested in a royal oligarchy . . . It has no railways; its four thousand miles of rough, all-weather roads are used mostly by donkeys and camels; [The Indonesian] islands— draped around the equator like a girdle of emerald . . . —are quite mountain-ous, with many volcanoes.* When Joe grew older, and too restless to sit and listen to his father read, Milt gave him a leather-bound journal as a fourteenth-birthday present.

They moved a mile away to Mumford Drive and a newer subdivision where the streets were wider and curved gracefully past big front lawns. A local television station heard about Joe's butterfly and reptile collection, and in one of the first local broadcasts in Urbana of WILL-TV, channel 12, young "Joey Sanderson" appeared with his framed and pinned Lepidop-tera specimens, and assorted birds and reptiles. On that night, Joe was fa-mous. In Urbana. The *Courier* wrote a story about him being on TV. He liked being famous.*

ON HIS FIRST DAY OF HIGH SCHOOL Joe stood with the milling student body before Urbana High, in the small park across the street, and waited by the statue *Lincoln the Lawyer.* A pair of incoming freshman boys stood be-low the great Illinoisan, admiring the streaks of rust in his bronze suit. The school was integrated, and the few Negro students were gathered in clus-ters, awaiting the morning bell; like their white counterparts, they were dressed in wool sweaters, and the girls in long skirts that reached down to

---

*My brother still has the newspaper clipping: "On the program, Joey will display part of his collection of more than 400 butterflies." It's true, I liked being famous. It's this sort of tall feeling, very pleasant and light. The Author wants to be famous too. He hopes this book will make him famous. It's a powerful drug, and once you get a taste, it will make you do crazy things.

their calves. Everyone so formal and fresh. Aerosol hair spray and hair pomades, menthol shaving cream and lavender perfume. The measured vanities of the Midwest. Years later, when he'd seen more of the world than any other member of his Urbana High graduating class, Joe would remember the eagerness and earnestness of this moment—the United States in the middle of the twentieth century. The bell rang and the student body surged toward the small rectangular orifice carved into the brick-and-concrete building, and in this sudden collective movement, Joe felt the strides of the girls especially, the sway of their hips and the bounce of the cone of their skirts. Oh man, oh man, oh man. He was astonished by their variety. They were plump and they were statuesque; pimply and clear-faced; blue-eyed and hazel-eyed. They wore somber autumn oranges and blacks, and extrovert pinks and purples, and their hair was done up in dos that were full of parlor-styled and bathroom-ironed curls, so that many seemed to have storm systems of swirling locks floating about their heads.

Joe filled up the pages of his journal with his high school observations, and he left all the natural specimens in his room to gather winter, spring and summer dust. "This journal is now my most precious possession," he told his father. When his brother, Steve, brought home his first car, a royal blue 1951 MG-TD, cars became Joe's new obsession. He approached his father with a grim and serious face. "Dad, I don't want to collect any more butterflies and reptiles," he said. "I'm not interested in those things anymore."

"Okay, Joe," Milt said. "So what are you interested in now?"

"Cars and girls."

Two months later they gathered up Joe's naturalist collections. Milt gave the jarred reptiles and assorted snakeskins to a colleague in the biology department, and told Joe he would donate his butterflies and other insects to the Illinois Natural History Survey. "They're going to be really happy to get these, Joe, because you've got all the right data with each one." They drove to the Survey's offices and met the collections manager, who

led them into a room with a table. He began opening Joe's glassine envelopes. "Very nice," the collections manager said. "Impressive. Ah, the
question mark. Let me show you how we'll store them," and he guided Joe
and Milt into a room filled with rows of cedar cabinets with thin drawers.
He opened one and revealed a battalion of dead roaches, with wings the
texture of marbled chocolate, all lined up in rows, their antennae deployed
skyward, awaiting insect radio signals. A Hercules beetle from Peru that
had a horn that was four inches long, armed for a jousting tournament. Joe
Sanderson's butterflies joined this insect menagerie, with *J. D. Sanderson*
listed in the catalog as the scientist-collector.*

---

*And they're still there! My own little scientific legacy. Even the silver-spotted skipper I
caught at the beginning of this novel. See? The Author wasn't making that up. Not
entirely.

3.

Piatt County, Illinois

AT URBANA HIGH, Joe became the master of the solid B grade, though he was not above settling for the occasional C. When he got an A, a minus always seemed to trail after it. He could talk to you all day about Voltaire, and the bending of space-time, or how cool and easy Spanish verbs were next to English, but when it came time to take a test, he didn't see the point in studying. He felt a deep sense of moral superiority to everyone who earned an A, or who even cared about earning an A. Screw these nosebleeds following the script, regurgitating and reciting. My mind is pure. He began to think of himself as an outcast and outsider. One day at lunch, he decided on a whim to cross the cafeteria's informal racial divide, an imaginary pane of glass that walled off a half-dozen tables in the cafeteria.

"Hi, mind if I join you? Name's Joe." He sat on a bench next to two young black men, and extended his hand for a fraternal, introductory handshake.

"Yeah, I know," one of the young men said. "I'm in your English class. Ernest."

"Oh, yeah, right."

"This is Cory. Cory, Joe. I told you about this guy, Cory. He's the one who was talking about sex to Mrs. Henderson. *Romeo and Juliet.* 'Lie with her!' You're a cutup, man. That was too much."

The now multiracial trio laughed and they ate their ham sandwiches and pushed around their potatoes, and Joe talked about how it might rain, and other topics of friendly conversation. Ernest and Cory nodded, and the conversation died. In the quiet, from behind their sweaters and collared shirts, Ernest and Cory gave Joe the glances of young men sizing up a stranger, trying to determine his intentions. Earlier that day, Ernest and Cory had walked to school together, kicking rocks on unpaved streets, past homes converted from chicken coops and coal sheds. Champaign-Urbana was de facto a segregated town, separate and unequal, but also freer and friendlier than other places a black family might settle. Or, as Ernest's dad put it: "When I got to Urbana, son, a white man invited me into his house, and he offered me a sandwich. A really fine one too, with lettuce, tomatoes, and mayonnaise." And Cory's dad: "Next to Tennessee, this is a liberal place, son. You can walk down the street wearing one purple shoe and one green shoe and no one will say anything." But Ernest and Cory longed to move to Chicago, to be surrounded by street-cars and blues and bold women. What was there here in Urbana? A school day that was defined by the stiff politeness of the white students and teachers around them, and also a steeliness and a distance that was unmistakable.

Today this white boy had come to sit next to them. His unexpected presence had the odd effect of keeping their black friends away from them for the rest of lunchtime, making the deadening whiteness of Urbana High School all the more obvious.

"Got to get to class," Ernest said. Cory held out his hand and added, "Nice to meet you, Joe." Thus ended the first, boldest and final attempt Joe Sanderson ever made to encourage the mixing of the races at Urbana High School.*

WHEN YOU'RE A BOY, you fight your way into the world, and Steve and Joe grew up fighting, and since Steve was bigger and brawnier, Steve always won. "Ankle biter! Stop bothering me. Go catch butterflies or something!" More than once, he pushed his brother's face into the ground. "Runt! Insect! The dirt is where you belong. Slither like a snake, why don't you." Little brother, little oddball. Sick half the time. Fever dreams and cold compresses on my forehead. The mucus crystals falling from my nose. When he was six or seven, Joe had a serious ear infection, and a doctor treated it with radium, inserting two luminescent capsules filled with chartreuse radioactive dust up through his nostrils. He caught a glimpse of his board-flat chest in the mirror, and felt the need to bulk up, so he joined the wrestling team. At the first practice the middle-aged coach wore sweatpants and took crouched side-steps across the training mat, like a vaudevillian actor doing slapstick on a rickety stage. Joe began to ghost-wrestle at home and in the school hallways. "What are you doing, Sanderson? What a kook!" He lost himself in extended fantasies of his newfound indefatigability, of his spidery lateral shiftiness; he practiced the occasional evasive sideways movement in his classrooms, and at home before dinner when he stood before Steve in the kitchen.

*My brother told the Author that I always identified with "the underdog," which was maybe his polite way of saying people who were not "white." But I thought the point of a novel was to make the hero (me) look heroic. Where is this going?

"Get that MG working again?" Joe asked, taunting his brother, because Steve's car hadn't been running for several days.

Steve said nothing, but then he raised his arm, as he had done many times before, to grab his little brother around the neck. Joe ducked and made himself short, causing his brother to lose his balance and stumble forward. Wrestling lessons. Two quick steps to his left, and Joe grabbed his falling brother from behind and used his forward momentum to lift Steve up and flip him over and turn him upside down against the kitchen floor.

Joe's kitchen-wrestling victory made the brothers equals again, and not long afterward Steve helped Joe buy a car from a neighbor for three hundred dollars: a 1950 Chevy two-door coupe with whitewall tires and a body that was smooth and bulbous, like sculpted steely-blue clay. Steve gave Joe a few driving lessons out in the farm country where there was a perpendicular crossroad every mile, each going due east and due west, due north and due south on the invisible latitudes and longitudes of the corn-covered plain. "Take the wheel, sir. It's your car," Steve said. The Chevy moved with a massive gasoline-fueled glide across the asphalt, quiet for a moment, and then clanky and old, as if there were six fidgety goblins dressed in tin under the front hood, pounding at the Midwestern-made pistons with rubber hammers, making it go.

TO HIS CLASSMATES, Joe was becoming a lovable paradox. He was a smart kid who liked to read and talk about ideas, but who didn't seem to care about his grades; he was a funny guy who had lots of friends, but who often looked lonely. When he turned sixteen and drove his own car legally for the first time, he invited a girl named Betty Jo to go to the movies in his Chevrolet. On the second date he took her to the Widescreen Drive-In Theater, which occupied a stretch of asphalt on the edge of Urbana that abutted the ubiquitous fields of corn. She had a face whose color and shape suggested her ancestors braided their hair into blond crowns and gazed at fiercely frigid Baltic seascapes. As the lighthearted film *No Time for Sergeants* played out inconsequentially in black-and-white on the big screen, Joe turned and faced her on the front seat of his Chevy. She pulled him closer across the wing-shaped vinyl skin of the seat, and they joined their lips, slowly, and Joe tasted the beeswax of her lipstick.

My first kiss. Silly kiss. Sloppy kiss. But I am kissed.

After two more dates, his verdict on Betty Jo was that she was looking for someone to be a mister to her missus, and was in a hurry to do so because in the coming months everyone in the class of 1960 would be a senior and eighteen years old. He didn't call her again. He dated other girls and the word about him got around to the female half of the Urbana High student body, through anecdotes and observations shared in the cafeteria and in the stands at football games and at the Tiger's Den, an off-campus dance hall. Joe wasn't one of the serious ones. Yes, he was fun, kind, polite and respectful, but he wasn't going to get googly-eyed over you and make you feel you were his Guinevere. He wasn't going to get a girl pregnant anytime soon, and he wasn't going to get married, or even buy a girl a promise ring.*

JOE'S FATHER INTRODUCED HIM to *Walden* and Thoreau's cabin and his pond. *I find it wholesome to be alone the greater part of the time.* Yeah, that's me. Thoreau loved books and he found joy in streams and forests, and owls and tadpoles. *We need the tonic of wildness. We need to witness our own limits transgressed.* Joe drove his car beyond the borders of Urbana, with no

---

*Reading this, you all might think we were sedated, or that we'd all taken some sort of innocence potion. But the Author, not being one of us, is being a little too respectful in telling our story. Lots of other, bad stuff was happening. Mostly involving hard drinking, schoolyard sadists and guys who didn't care when a girl said no. And of course that confounding race thing that no white people ever talked about. I knew all this, of course. Or I sensed it. So I went into my own little world, which is what this next passage coming up is all about.

destination in mind. To the northwest and the southwest, aimlessly. He watched farmers using tractors to furrow the rectangles and rhombuses of land, like men writing sentences with steel styluses on blank pages of soil. One spring day he borrowed a canoe from one of his neighbors, tied it to the top of his Chevy and drove to a spot just outside town where the upper waters of the Sangamon River flowed.

In the early-morning light, the dirty emerald liquid of the creek reflected a narrow ribbon of sky. Joe launched the canoe, and began to float, under the crowns of the trees and their trunks. He dipped a paddle into the water and gave two good strokes and the canoe moved southward, and Joe entered a space of deep and lingering silence in which the air and trees were still, and even the birds halted their songs. A sunbeam found its way through the trees and struck his bare arms, and he took off his shirt. The first drops of his sweat began a stop-and-go, serpentine drip down his chest, and he felt the primate inside his body coming to life.

THE SANGAMON WAS SINUOUS, steady and perpetual in its flowing, and riding upon it Joe felt connected to the time before electricity and machines. Bits of pollen rose on the air currents, cottony satellites drifting upward while he drifted southwestward, under a railroad trestle, and under a concrete highway bridge, where a passing truck blasted its horn. The river widened and the current slowed and the flat, calm water became a still and perfect plane and he felt alone and whole inside it. When dusk began to paint rust into the sky he paddled to the riverbank and lay down on his back upon the muddy soil. The branches above him were moss-covered and held leaves that were thin and fernlike, and they floated above him with the twisting geometry of constellations. Joe took several deep and satisfied breaths, and heard Thoreau whispering to him:

Consider the trees and the sky, Mr. Sanderson. Those geese flying in formation. The purity of the natural. Understand the truth about yourself. You are meant to float to new places, the undiscovered and the distant. Find a route to follow that is as open and long as this river. Above all, follow the paths that call to you the way the pond and the woods called to me.

Joe returned to his canoe and guided it down to another highway over-crossing, where he left it on the riverbank to retrieve later. He climbed up to the road and hitchhiked a ride back to his car with a passing farmer who revealed to Joe where he was: on State Route 32, more than halfway to Decatur.

"I started by Urbana."

"Urbana? That's forty miles, son."

"It didn't seem that far." In a car, Urbana was less than an hour away. He'd be home to taste his mother's steak for supper.

"That's a long way to go in a canoe."

"Next time," Joe said, "I'll go farther."

4.

Kingston.
Saint Elizabeth Parish, Jamaica

AT THE DINNER TABLE JOE talked about his journey down the Sangamon, and about Thoreau. Living on a river was a goal as worthy as any
you might pursue in a bank or at a university, he said. I can spend my life
traveling the world from one river to the next. The Ohio, the Mississippi, the
Yukon, the Amazon. A few days later Milt announced that they were going
on a family vacation that summer: to Jamaica. "To collect and classify. Ants,
beetles, spiders." In June, they drove south, stopping first in the Ohio River
hamlet of Elizabethtown, Illinois, then headed for Mobile, the heat growing

as they entered cotton country. Finally, the nearby ocean sent a cool breeze and salty fragrance blowing through the Spanish moss, and the perfumed air led them to the Gulf of Mexico, and to Pensacola, Florida, and a beach where the waves were big and churning and foamy, and Joe and Steve swam and sand swirled into their swimsuits and around their private parts.

They reached Miami and the low silhouette of their cruise ship, the S.S. *Evangeline*. Not a huge vessel; the two rooms assigned to them were *not more than 7 x 7*, Virginia wrote in the travel journal she was keeping. Husband and wife slept in bunks, Milt on the upper, Virginia on the lower, with Milt leaning down in the morning to make silly faces at her. It was to be Virginia's first trip outside the United States. On the deck the first night they watched Spanish dancers and enjoyed a champagne toast with the captain, and Virginia looked at the blue-gray chop of the ocean and sensed a gathering storm and felt an echo of Kansas. A whirlpool on the sea, a dust devil on the prairie. They crossed the Tropic of Cancer, and the *Evangeline* entered the Windward Passage near Haiti, and the Caribbean became a bumpy, briny plain covered by a thousand tiny peaks of white stone. Their plates slipped off the table at dinner before the waiters were able to get the railings up. Everyone except Joe got seasick.

As they approached Jamaica the sea calmed and the clouds parted, and the bluish-black silhouette of the island grew before them until it resembled a continent all its own. The Caribbean sun began to bake and burn, and Joe saw his mother squinting and frowning on the ship's deck, like an Illinois ant under a hot lamp. Dr. Lewis, a naturalist at the Institute of Science, greeted the Sandersons at the dock in Kingston and drove them into the green and flowery city, which was crowded with animals and automobiles. Virginia felt her seasickness returning. *Everyone driving on the wrong side of the road*, she wrote later in her travel journal. *A madhouse. Honking, yelling. Goats and burros getting out of the way.* Everyone in this big island metropolis was black: A simple fact, but startling and exhilarating for Joe. The traffic policeman in the starched-white uniform and pith helmet and cream-colored gloves; the vendors in wide-brimmed straw hats; the snappy students pedaling bicycles. They talked to white people in English, but spoke to each other in an ancient, rounded-off form of the language Joe did not entirely understand. For the first time, the varied nature of the human race and the nations of the world became truly clear to him. The colorful photographs in encyclopedia entries (*Jamaica: British Possession, Pop. 1,400,000*) and *National Geographic* articles ("Jamaica: Hub of the Caribbean . . . Haunt of Buccaneers") were now real places. Each spot on the globe was a separate dimension, with its own rules of speech, its own way of walking.

In Urbana "white" was a rarely used label whose true meaning was "not black." An obvious misnomer, given the reds and browns mixed into the Caucasian palette. Here, however, amid the blue-black faces and the russet-skinned, Joe felt his Europeanness, the genetic rope that tied him to snowy valleys where men carved furrows into the icy ground. The Sandersons reached their hotel, the Melody Guest House, and the black city disappeared behind the walls and front gate of their compound. They entered a capsule of whiteness, where the hotel guests sat in wicker chairs, under fans, drinking tea in private gardens. This was what a colony was, shut in, away from the natives. After a few days Joe set off with Steve to explore the island. They jumped on a bus to Montego Bay, and as two white boys they became the targets of startled stares and also a loud comment spoken in patois, which was followed by peals of laughter, including the high-pitched clarinet notes of a woman's hee-hee-hee! Kingston bade them farewell from behind curtains of wandering, wild poinsettias, and their bus followed an asphalt highway into a rural greenscape where palm fronds burst skyward like fireworks, and primeval trees bore fruit the size of footballs. The driver stopped at several spots along the road where no structures could be seen, only fields and footpaths, and people got on and off the bus at these nowhere places.

The bus thinned out and Joe took notice of a young passenger in a collared shirt. They soon fell into conversation. Claude was his name and he soon knew Joe and Steve's story, such as it was: Professor's kids, bug hunting on the island. Illinois. Flat. Boring. First trip to Jamaica.

"What about you?" Joe asked.

"I too have a university affiliation," Claude said. "I study history at the University of the West Indies. The mean, bloody and hidden history of this beautiful island," Claude said, and Joe tried to imagine what that might be, though Claude did not elaborate.

At the next stop the bus driver turned off the engine and without explanation he stepped out and walked up the hills toward a collection of huts.

"Maybe he's got a secret love up there," Claude said with a laugh.

"Yeah, a hidden history," Joe said. Claude and the Sanderson brothers got out to stretch their legs and walked a few yards down the road to a path that led to another hut, where a woman and two boys were sitting.

"Good country people here," Claude said, and he shouted out a greeting as he approached them with Joe and Steve in tow. The two boys were lean and smart-eyed. Claude introduced his new "American friends" and said he wanted them to see the real Jamaica, and then he said other things in patois that Joe did not understand. The older of the two boys disappeared behind their home and returned with a piece of sugarcane and a long knife. Silently, the boy held up the cane and showed it to Joe and Steve, and without a word he took the blade and began to strip the stalk of its weathered and dry skin, and then to whittle at the white, wet flesh underneath.

The boys spoke to Joe and Steve slowly, in single words, as if Joe and Steve were children and the boys had something to teach them, some basic thing they wanted them to understand. *Eat*, the younger boy gestured, with his fingers and his mouth. And when the older boy bit the stalk and broke off a piece, the younger boy said, "Look! Look how him bite. Have it." And the younger boy bit off a chunk of the stalk, and took it from his mouth to show Joe and Steve how to suck the juice from it. He gave the cane to Joe and gestured for him to have a bite too, and Joe did.

"That's sweet," Joe said.

"Buccra tas'e cane an' he say it sweet, but him no know how hard you work for it," Claude said, remembering a poem he'd once read. The woman joined him in a soft, bittersweet laugh.

The boy cut another piece of cane for Joe, and gestured at the nearby June plum tree and the dogs, and spoke faster and deeper in his own language, so that Joe understood very little and finally nothing at all. Being down here in this verdant place amid the sugary plants and the amorous locals, Joe believed he was somehow closer to touching the essence of the world, the unfathomable fullness of the Earth, of its people and all its living things. He felt a sudden, strange, inexplicable sense of belonging.

"I see the driver coming back from his love shack," Steve said. "Guess he's done."

As they returned to the bus, Joe turned to Claude. "Good country people."

"Good people. My people. It's like this: 'We are darkness shining in the brightness. Which the brightness can't comprehend.' One of our poets said that. Or some poet of the world."

WHILE STEVE AND JOE EXPLORED THE ISLAND, Milt conducted his fieldwork with Dr. Lewis, driving out into the countryside to collect millipedes, cayenne ticks, turtle ants and Valentine ants with protruding, heart-shaped abdomens. When Virginia joined her husband on these journeys she saw the soil was a deep red and rich, more fertile than the loamiest patch of the Great Plains. As fertile as sin, like the soil that gave the apples that Eve plucked and gave to Adam.

Milt took Joe and Steve on one final collecting expedition in Dr. Lewis's Chevy, to the Blue Mountains, driving along the edges of river gorges, and they stopped by glades and creek bends where men fished and held their catches on strings. They camped for the night near the top of a canyon, and the next morning they continued their ascent on narrow foot trails, with

Dr. Lewis filling the time by talking to Milt and his sons about Jamaican politics. Dr. Lewis said he was concerned about a new movement called the Rastafarians, led by men who grew their hair long, lived in mountain camps and smoked marijuana. They reached a ridge that offered a view of the vast, open Caribbean and Dr. Lewis pointed to the horizon. "See that shadow? That's Cuba." They were looking at the faint outline of the Sierra Maestra, a mountain range. A rebel army was camped up there, Dr. Lewis explained, fighting a war against a dictator.

Back in Kingston, at the Melody Guest House, Joe met a British adventurer who had spent a year traveling solo around the world—on buses, bicycles, boats and trains. He had an envelope filled with clippings of newspaper stories that were written about him as he passed through. An idea popped into Joe's head: He could be like this Brit and wander around the world and have the locals write about him. Maybe he would start by visiting those black rebels in the hills, the Rastafarians. Or maybe those Cuban guerrillas. He didn't know how and when he would do this, since his mother and father wanted him to go to college. But in Jamaica the idea grabbed Joe, and it never let him go.

The Sandersons returned home separately. The boys and Virginia traveled by air, via Chicago. Milt stayed in Jamaica longer, and drove back from Miami, where he spotted a front-page headline in the *Miami Herald*: "Palace Aid Kills Guatemala President." Castillo Armas, the military ruler installed by the United States, had been shot by one of his bodyguards. A new dictator was swiftly appointed. Not long afterward, a group of disaffected army officers with leftist sympathies rose up against the dictatorship—they were unsuccessful, but from their ranks the first Marxist guerrilla army in Central America was born. The news of the revolt in Guatemala later appeared on page nine of the *Courier*, buried beneath stories of nonfatal traffic accidents, the activities of the 4-H Club, and an advertisement for Purex, "the gentle laundry bleach."

5.

Chicago. Mexico City

CHICAGO ROSE OVER THE TAMED RIVER at its center, with soaring glass and steel constructions whose purpose was to eat the sky. With the Caribbean still fresh and alive and sea-breezy and sand-filled in his memory, Joe found that Chicago's concrete and its vertical ambition felt cruel and otherworldly. The last traces of the mellow island vibe inside his brain were obliterated by the sight of men marching this way and that way, obediently following the straight lines drawn by T-square-toting architects, creators of parallel lines and ninety-degree angles ad nauseam. Chicago's office stiffs wore pressed wool and mirrory leather shoes, and the sheeny black-and-starchy-white armor of insurance companies and finance firms. They took rigid strides, their shoes beating evenly and quickly on the sidewalk. Metronome men. Chicago was monochromatic and perpendicular, a grid stretching across conquered prairies, while Jamaica was color and curves, dead ends and winding byways. Jamaica was improvised and free, and Joe missed it even more as another series of straight lines took him out of the city, on the railroads that followed flat farmland into the heart of downstate Illinois.

His late-summer job in Urbana was at the Crystal Lake pool, before the sun-reddening swimmers and waders. He wore red shorts with a white Red Cross patch. Lifeguard. In a chair over a rectangle of cloudy water evaporating into a chlorine mist. His mission was to protect the swimming youth of Champaign-Urbana, but they were protected in so many other ways. I can see this now. By their American citizenship. By the black door of the vault at Champaign County Bank and Trust, and by the ledgers his mother kept there, added sums and simple interest accruing on behalf of Illinois families who learned to save during long-ago times of hunger, war and drought. This was what it meant to be worldly. I travel and I know a fuller truth. In the water, the boys and girls wore new rubber sandals, new swimsuits. Only a few kids were wearing cutoff jeans, or treading water in their underwear, like that boy over there; he looks like he just got here from Kentucky. Three Negro kids were dressed in new Sears-Roebuck summer wear. Joe pushed back the sunglasses over his nose. His job? To jump into this pool and open the epiglottis of a drowning victim, an act of Sanderson heroism, should the need arise.

After they'd returned from Jamaica, Joe's mother had asked him to stand against the doorframe to be measured, and he understood this as a kind of confirmation of their American good fortune. Beef-fed boys, stretching and stretching. "No, Mom," he told her. "I stopped growing already." He was a respectable five foot eleven, and at the pool he felt the eyes of females drawn to him. Girls fourteen, eighteen, working on their Coppertone tans; they took in his hairy and breaststroke-buffed torso, and looked away. But the girl who caught his eye did not stare at him. She was sitting in a chair far beyond the splashing at the pool's edge, reading. When his shift was over, he walked over to her. Up close, she was not especially striking. A brunette with a rounded nose and round cheeks.

"That's a big book you're reading," he said.

"*The Naked and the Dead*," she said.

"Is it any good?"

"It's very male," she said with a sparkle in her eye.

"Male? What does that mean? Are there only men in it?"

"Well, for starters, yes. But it's more than that. It's sort of like Hemingway without the romance. And it's very bloody. It's about a war."

"War *is* bloody."

"Sadly."

"I'm a bit of a pacifist myself," Joe said. "Ever since I read Thoreau."

"I love *Walden*."

Her name was Karen Thomas. She and Joe began to talk about Thoreau, and with each observation she made about the writer and his times, about the Mexican War and the Massachusetts countryside, he was more entranced. They promised to meet again, and did so, and they took long walks through Urbana in those last days of summer, underneath maple trees that pulsed with the electric rattles and whistles of cicadas. And during the school year, in the afternoons, when Steinbeck occupied their discussions and the maples burst into sunset colors. The first snow of December fell, with flakes following paths down between naked elms, and they strolled holding hands and talking about Emily Dickinson. In the spring when those elms gave leaves, and the scent of first hay drifted from the fields outside town, she told him about a French writer, Albert Camus, whose small volume *The Stranger* he read at her insistence.

KAREN THOMAS was the first of many intelligent, strong and rebellious women Joe Sanderson fell in love with, pined for and admired during his eventful life. Most were avid readers, like him. Some were armed with automatic rifles and construction hammers, and others with a deep understanding of Asian history, European literature and other essential elements of human knowledge.

JOE SAT WITH KAREN in the front seat of his Chevy on a country road; at the drive-in, where the movie on the screen never mattered; and by a patch of woods on the edge of town. His intentions were always pure, most pure with Karen above all. Or rather, he was lustfully chaste. On a day of Indian summer, in the fall of 1959, when they had finished talking for an hour about the future of mankind and their favorite ice cream flavors, Karen gave him one last, slow, full-lipped kiss, and then she did something she had never done before. She brought the tips of her fingers to his cheeks and stroked them slowly and softly, and then she stopped, and simply held his face with her hands, as if she were trying to pass a thought to him through the whorls and loops of her fingerprints. Karen looked into his eyes, and at his forehead, his gelled hair, his sideburns. She was reading him as if he were a text. As if she saw a scroll of paper behind his eyes, an inky waterfall of cursive letters telling the story of Joe. Karen saw him as he truly was, all that was imperfect, admirable, odd and noble, and Joe understood that this knowledge drew her to him and made her want to stay there, holding him. She kissed him once more, and finally she lowered her eyelids and rested her forehead against his, and he closed his eyes too. In this state of shared darkness and silence Joe was at peace. And then the quiet between them, and the way she seemed to know him frightened Joe, because it felt like an end instead of a beginning.

"Is something wrong, Joe?"

IT WAS THEIR SENIOR YEAR, and Joe and Karen and most of the members of the class of 1960 would soon be living in the future their parents were always talking about. Some of them were already on the cusp of greatness, like Roger Ebert, who'd been elected senior class president and who'd told Joe he was thinking of going to Harvard. In January, Joe stepped out the front steps of Urbana High to find his old neighbor standing atop the *Lincoln the Lawyer* statue in the park across the street. The officers of the senior class were having their portrait taken for the school yearbook, and three of them were up there on the pedestal with the bronze Lincoln. Joe walked up behind the photographer and waved and made a silly face, and then flipped them the bird, which caused President Ebert and all the officers to laugh. At that moment, the photographer tripped the shutter.

Joe and his friend Jim Adams were not athletes, or brainiacs or members of the school's Sagamore honor society. Nor were they delinquents or beatniks. Jim wanted to fly crop dusters: he thought of this as a romantic life filled with aerial roller-coaster drops over fields of soy and corn, followed by a landing at the Champaign airport and dinner at home every night. Joe was going to college, to the University of Florida, where he imagined he would be closer to the tropical entrails of the earth. He could hitchhike across Florida to Miami, and sail to the islands of the Caribbean on freighters.

But first, Joe dreamed up one last, great high school prank. He convinced Jim to help him cover the campus with painted *Playboy* rabbits; the famous stylized bunny with the bow tie, one of his ears in a jaunty tilt. But why not something grander. All of Urbana. Champaign too. A big, citywide gesture. Like the French Resistance in an old film, they would paint their symbol on walls across the city—and disappear into the night. "We're going to need a lot of paint," he told Jim.*

They ended up at the unlocked lot behind the Champaign Public Works Department. Joe found a single five-gallon paint container labeled TRAFFIC YELLOW. Joe and Jim lifted the barrel into the trunk of Joe's Chevy, placing it next to their brushes and the stencils they'd fashioned from cardboard. First they drove to the Georgian revival mansion where the president of the University of Illinois lived, and stenciled a rabbit on the asphalt of his U-shaped driveway. The symbol of smoking-jacket-wearing lotharios and naked centerfolds. Masturbators of the world, unite! Another four on Florida Avenue, which was empty of automobiles because it was three in the morning and it was Urbana. They painted more rabbits in front of the U of I's slumbering sororities and the fraternity houses with their feckless "brothers," none of whom had enough character to be up late on a bender. Next, a solitary rabbit on the door of the faux pioneer cabin in the Illini Grove, and then Joe looked at the nearby water tower, perhaps ten stories up, and gave Jim a big grin.

"No," Jim said. "That's too high."

"It'll be a cinch."

They drove to the base of the tower and found a waiting ladder, unlocked and inviting. Joe dipped two brushes in paint and tied them to his belt using Jim's shoelaces, along with a stencil, so that his hands would be free for climbing. He moved up the zinc rungs with a quick bounding. To Jim, from below, Joe resembled a lumberjack with the frenetic legs of a squirrel. The higher Joe got the smaller he became, and Jim remembered the boy Joe he first met in grade school, climbing a jungle gym, lifting himself up into a tree branch. If Joe's mother had been there, she would have remembered the purposeful

---

*Jim Adams told the Author this story. The Author sees it, I think, as my first act of rebellion. In a city that had no graffiti whatsoever (imagine that), we were going to shock everyone with a symbol of the secret force no one ever talked about in our polite Midwestern town. Sex.

strides of the five-year-old she saw marching across her father's land in Kansas, following the one-hundred-yard line of a plow. He reached the platform at the base of the big tank, waved to Jim and quickly painted two bunnies. When he finished he grabbed hold of the railing, and took in the lights of predawn Urbana and the university, the bottled radiance of ten thousand ant-size fires burning inside glass. This is the way a writer sees a city. I am the omniscient narrator of a novel. All-seeing, perched above the flight paths of the bumblebees and the crows. Down there, in that village, my parents and Steve asleep, Karen tucked inside layers of cotton clothing and sheets. He saw the arched metal roof of the Stock Pavilion; a cow there, university owned, with a copper-lined porthole in its stomach so that veterinary students and kindergartners could study its digesting innards. The Natural History Building, with its many gables and pitched roofs: he had gone there once with Jim to see the cadavers stored in its top floor, stiff hobos sealed in steel boxes. His butterflies and snakes stored in cabinets; and the edge of the city swallowed by the black, unilluminated fields that surrounded it. His whole Champaign-Urbana universe was visible from this one fixed point, a settlement that was a small stain on the surface of the globe.

I'll be ready to leave here soon.

"Joe! Let's go!"

The next morning, Urbana awoke to a bunny explosion. No one could say who the vandals were. *The News-Gazette* wrote a small item about it—"Mystery Rabbits Cover City"—and quoted the head of the Department of Public Works lamenting *these miscreants and their very poor sense of humor.* In the days that followed, nearly all the immoral bunnies were scrubbed off or painted over, and the city forgot the Great Playboy Bunny Caper, and what Joe remembered most vividly about the days that followed was the way Karen held his hand and looked at the yellow flecks attached to his skin and scratched at them with her fingernails. She said nothing, which was odd and slightly distressing, the way the unspoken secret floated between them.

That summer he traveled to Mexico City with his parents. Since he had just turned eighteen, Virginia and Milt had agreed that he could return home alone without them, traveling back from that Spanish-speaking country on his own.

EVERYONE IN MEXICO CITY bragged about the new skyscraper, a phallic construction of blue glass called La Torre Latinoamericana; it rose incongruously above the old white marble box of the Palace of Fine Arts and the bronze egg of its dome. El Distrito Federal, as the city was also known, was filled with stone churches and cotton candy and cobblestone, and ladies in handwoven wool and cat's-eye sunglasses. It had wide avenues where buses ran drawing current from hanging wires. Joe walked with his parents on the vast, black stone plaza of the Zócalo, and after five days Milt and Virginia said goodbye at the hotel, and his mother gave him a long, serious look and told him to be safe. Joe was alone.*

Ten minutes later the skies opened in a torrential downpour and Joe watched from the window of his room as vendors ran laughing in the park called the Alameda Central. They vainly sought shelter in the narrow marble arches of the monument to Benito Juárez, while fat raindrops and then pellets of hail bounced off the old president's marble head. The storm stopped in an instant, and Joe went out into the Alameda with hailstones crunching under his shoes and watched as two boys gathered the icy pebbles into rocky, black snowballs and threw them at each other.

Two days later, as he strolled by the Palace of Fine Arts he was approached by a thin young man of about his own age, in gray slacks and sunglasses. With gestures, because the young man did not speak English

---

*My high school graduation present was an entire country and me in it all by my lonesome. Any surprise I ended up addicted to the road later? First road-bumming lesson: Feed myself and stay out of trouble. Second: Take in the sights, and make friends quickly.

and Joe didn't speak much Spanish, he asked Joe to take his picture before the white building, and Joe obliged. The young man said, "Gracias. Soy de Guatemala. Es la primera vez que viajo fuera de mi país," and Joe nodded and smiled, even though he understood only that the young man was thankful, and that he was from Guatemala, and nothing else.

"De nada," Joe said. "Yo soy americano. De Illinois." The skinny young Guatemalan nodded, and they shook hands. These words and gestures constituted Joe's first independent conversation in Spanish, and they left him grinning, and eager to practice more. He saw another young man on the Alameda carrying a thick book, and they began talking in the Spanish phrases Joe could muster, and the little English the young man spoke. Mi casa, Illinois. Estados Unidos. Tu casa, Mexico. My name Francisco. Yo soy estudiante. Me study, yes. You? Sí. Francisco was carrying a geometry textbook, and Joe had a Spanish-English dictionary, and they exchanged these books and perused them, and then they walked toward the Zócalo.

One thousand years of human history was buried under their feet and arranged in stone before their eyes. "Palacio Nacional," Francisco said, pointing at one building. "Catedral," pointing at another. "Bandera," pointing at the flagpole in its center. The cathedral had been built four centuries ago by Aztec workers with stones from the pyramids the Spanish ordered demolished, and under the building foundations there were still-buried images of beaked and plumed deities, waiting for archaeologists to uncover them. To Joe the ancientness was plain to see on the surface of the plaza, in the Indian faces of the vendors and their wares, which included odd candies that were made of jellied fruits, and wooden toy buses. They walked through the cloud of smoke and ash created by a taco vendor's charcoal stove, and stepped into the path of another vendor, who offered postcards for sale, black-and-white images depicting corpses of men and horses covering the Zócalo after some historic battle or massacre, and others of Pancho Villa and Emiliano Zapata grinning as they sat in the president's chair at the National Palace. Francisco led them back to the Alameda Central, where an itinerant and semi-mad preacher was proselytizing. The preacher stared at Joe and stopped his rambling sermon midsentence at the sight of Joe's blue eyes, which reminded him of the Spanish priests of the Holy Inquisition, burning heretics alive at that very spot, hundreds of years ago. The preacher began to scream, "¡Los quemaron! ¡Vivos!" Next, Joe and Francisco walked down a street where they saw a hammer and sickle painted in dripping red on a stone wall, at the spot where the famous communist leader Julio Antonio Mella had been assassinated many years earlier. To Joe the hammer and sickle were like images from a horror movie. *Commies, in Mexico, I didn't know. Wait till Steve hears this.* A block later, after Joe looked up *lunch* in his dictionary, they entered an otherwise nondescript restaurant called the Café La Habana. Fidel Castro, then an exiled revolutionary, had planned his invasion of Cuba in this café just a few years earlier, sipping espresso at a table by the window with his brother Raúl and an Argentine doctor named Ernesto Guevara. Castro was now the new ruler of Cuba. Francisco overheard a waitress discussing Castro with a customer, but didn't bother to translate for Joe as they ate their tortas.

When Joe and Francisco parted company, Joe promised to show him the sights of Urbana should he ever visit the University of Illinois. "I guess it's not as interesting as Mexico City," Joe said in English. "But it's got its charms." He looked up the word that explained what that place looked like: *plano*; n. flat.

On his last full day in Mexico City, Joe took a twilight walk through the city, beginning in the Alameda across the street from his hotel. He sat on a cast-iron bench in the park, at the spot where the pyres of the Inquisition had burned, sending screams and ashes climbing toward the hail-filled clouds above, and wrote a letter home to his family. *Really everything has gone along fine, though the first couple of days alone were a little lonely . . . Hey Pop, you'll be proud of your old son because Saturday I talked very intelligently in my broken Spanish with a Mexican boy for about an hour and a half.* He described the drunken revelry of the American tourists in his hotel—*hell raising, pardon me, Granny*—and the inevitable arrival of the police who took away *a Harvard man* in handcuffs, and other events that he summarized with the words *Much fun!* Finally, he signed off with the signature *José.*

The next morning, he headed northward.

JOE TOOK A GEAR-GRINDING third-class bus, traveling with people who were carrying baskets and burlap sacks. After the bus left Mexico City it entered a bright and blue-skied savanna, and men boarded the bus wearing straw hats, and the women wore big, unadorned dresses that looked rugged and timeworn. The passengers got on and off at villages where all the streets and roads that led from the highway were unpaved, and where the churches and the walls were made of adobe brick, or at crossroads where there was little else besides yellow grass and lonely elm and oak trees. Each time the bus stopped, the air filled with the scent of cooked corn, burning charcoal and overripe fruit.

When the bus reached San Luis Potosí, Joe took a room in a cheap hotel, and the next day he changed direction and headed east, for the Atlantic coast, and then took another third-class bus up into mountains that were lush and forested. He lost track of where he was, and where he was going, and finally he stopped in a village where there were stalls that catered to tourists, and he learned that there was a waterfall nearby.*

Joe followed a path down the hillside that led to the waterfall, and a boy trailed after him, and ran ahead, and looked back, as if he were showing Joe the way. They reached a pool of bluish-green water, and the spray curtain of the waterfall. The boy pointed at these natural wonders and held out his palm. Joe gave the boy a coin and the boy set off running with it. Vendors

---

*Next bumming rule: Don't be afraid to get a little lost.

approached him, holding whistles and flutes for him to look at, and said "bonito," which he knew meant pretty.

A girl stared at him. She was about fifteen years old, he guessed. Long-limbed and smooth-skinned, with a mischievous and curious air.

"Hola," Joe said to her. She took two steps to leave, then turned on her heels and walked toward him.

"Las otras cataratas son más lindas," she said.

"No entiendo," Joe answered.

"Venga. Conmigo."

She gestured for him to follow her. And since she was womanly and beautiful he did so. She led him up a path, and he understood that this was something very bold for a girl from a Mexican village to do, as it would have been for a girl from Urbana. "Where are we going?" When he slowed down, she took his hand in hers, and they walked through a dense forest and reached a waterfall that filled a limestone bowl with unnaturally blue water and a dreamy mist. The girl let go of his hand, and made a sweeping gesture, as if she had gifted him this paradise in miniature.

"Bonito," Joe said, because he could think of no other Spanish word to say.

Her name was Juana, and she wanted Joe to see the water here because it was the same color as his eyes.

Joe heard giggles coming from the trees. Juana ran toward the laughter, and from the forest six heads of children popped up, boys and girls, and those boys and girls started running away, and the girl trailed after them, and Joe understood that these boys and girls had been following them, and that it had all been a game. The girl had taken his hand on a dare.

She turned and shouted: "¡Sólo quería enseñárselo! ¡El agua es el mismo color que sus ojos!"

"¡No hablo español!" Joe shouted back. The girl took a few long, light and springy strides, and she was gone, and Joe realized he would never see her again and never understand what she had said. Afterward, when he sat down to write this episode into his journal, he felt strangely powerless, deprived of the essential information at the end of the story. He was certain there was some deeper message in these last words of hers, something he badly needed to know.

No one in the world knows I exist.

Something has to change.

—Emmanuel Carrère, *Limonov*

♊
=

The Part About the World: Pax Americana

6.

Gainesville, Florida.
Hanover, Indiana

ON THE DAY HE LEFT FOR COLLEGE, Joe was seven inches taller than his mother. He carried a hard-shell suitcase into the Champaign train station, and she followed behind him, into the station portico, alongside Milt. When they reached the platform, she gave Joe a motherly once-over and an unshowy smile of approval. "Well, this is it now," she said. "Off to be a student."

Virginia Colman had reached the end of the boyhoods in her life.

"Let me get a picture of you two," Milt said.

She stood next to Joe, and Milt snapped their picture. Joe in leisure wear on a hot August day; khaki pants, a shirt with broad crimson stripes. Virginia in a summer dress, carrying a purse. Milt had given him cash and Virginia had washed his clothes one last time, and she had hovered nearby as he packed in his room, a few books on the bed that he would take too, wrapped up in brown paper and twine. I carried you under the hard shell of my belly and pushed you from my too-small womb, big-shouldered baby, slippery and sloppy out into the world. Spoons of applesauce in Arkansas, spelling lessons and games of checkers with nickels and pennies on the checkered tablecloth. She had watched the Urbana barber plop him up into a booster seat in his big black leather chair and tame the blond bangs reaching for his brow. Now he shaved and folded his oxfords and his socks into neat rectangles in his Samsonite suitcase.

My boy. Last little boy. Tall and manly voiced, but still my boy.

On the platform, twenty minutes before it was scheduled to arrive, Joe looked in the distance for the train. Or maybe he was scanning the nearby Champaign streets for that Karen girl.

"I'm not passing through Atlanta, no," Joe said to this father. "New Orleans, yes. Mobile too."

Buttery frosting on your face. First wooden toys. Your kindergarten tears. The lonely look in your wounded teenage eyes that October night. Nothing I could do.

"Karen said she might come," Joe said. A few moments later Karen walked up the steps onto the platform, bounding toward him, trailing two of her friends. "Hello, Mr. Sanderson. Mrs. Sanderson." And then she turned and gave Joe a kiss on the cheek.

"I'm going to miss him a lot."

Vicki and Linda, Karen's friends, gave Joe kisses on the cheeks too, and he rolled his eyes like a movie comedian, and then three more girls arrived on the platform, in summer shorts, including Betty Jo, and they all surrounded Joe and gave him kisses on the cheek, and fussed over him, and complimented him on his shirt, and said it was going to be hot and humid in Florida. Karen stood at the edge of the circle and tried to stay in the funny and charming moment, even though this felt momentous, the good-bye of all goodbyes.

My Joe. My boyfriend. My goofy thinker. He is unaware. Boy in the stretchy body. Charismatic. Charmer. Say little, say it funny, say it gently, Joe, and the girls orbit you in their dresses. Charming when he speaks, but mean in his silence. Because the words he never spoke are ending everything between us. A boy like him, a man, allows his silences to do his dirty work for him.

"Whatta you think you'll major in, Joe?" one of the girls asked.

"Don't know. Don't have to decide yet."

Forever Joe? Not forever. Will you remember our kisses? Our Camus? Our Frost? Our Thoreau? Cabin man, rugged man. Neat now but messy later, when Mom isn't looking. Mom hovers and looks and measures you and measures me. I'm just his girlfriend, Mrs. Sanderson, and not even that as soon as the train pulls away. But you will always be his mother.

A whistle sounded and they felt the train's vibrations before it came around the corner. The Illinois Central. Punctual, of course. A minute early, in fact.

"There it is."

"It's time."

His mother placed a hand on his shoulder. Will the mossy heat make you ill? Ill eventually. Ill without me nearby. He'll manage. Will learn to manage.

"See you, Mom. See you, Dad."

"Bye, Joe."

"Bye!"

"See you at Christmas."

His mother spoke her last words softly into his still-young ear: "Write home, son."

The girls gave a chorus of cheery bye-byes as he climbed the steel steps. He turned from the top and took them all in with one rushed scan of their faces, and it didn't feel like a movie, as he'd imagined it would. Karen with moist, meaningful eyes. His father too. His mother standing back behind the girls, as if to allow Joe a last moment of boyhood. Suddenly as stolid as a silo. She doesn't see that I am looking for her. Looking at her.

Soon after Joe was at his seat, moving southward. He did not imagine he would feel this way. As if he'd lost part of himself back there in the city cut into the corn.

On the platform, his mother watched the last steel car disappear around a bend.

He will always need me.

MANY TRAIN HOURS LATER, Joe watched the sunrise over the Gulf of Mexico from his moving window. He began to write a first letter home. After he'd moved into a campus dorm, and looked out the window at the sturdy, mossy willows on the University of Florida campus, he finished it. *It was sad as heck leaving all you people but luckily I've been almost too busy to be lonely here.* He pledged into a fraternity, Lambda Chi Alpha. *The guys are really a swell bunch, very widely varied in interest and background. Millionaires to poor folk—drinkers and goof-offs to serious students—pansies to real tough guys.* They were all white, of course, and among a few an obnoxious and assertive *Southern feeling* (as Joe described it in his letter) expressed itself even before their first sip of vodka. "All those uppity Negroes in Nashville," one of them said. "They wouldn't dare in Gainesville."

The next time Joe wrote home he said his classes were harder than he'd expected. His mother wrote back with the news that Roger Ebert's father, Walter, was seriously ill. Roger had given up on the Ivy League and stayed in Champaign-Urbana to study at the University of Illinois because his father had lung cancer. At mail call, his fraternity brothers made fun of him: "Sanderson! Joe! Another letter from moootheeer!" He wrote back that all was well, even though he'd been forced to drop one of his courses because it was too hard. *I really can feel how much I am missing the fall— cider and doughnuts, moonlight and crisp night air, cabin, football games out of town, and of course crab apples in the orchards.*

At the frat house, he played bongos for his drinking brothers, wore his green swimming trunks while doing his homework and learned to bartend. His grades dipped below a B average. In the presidential campaign that November he supported the somber Nixon over the handsome and pampered Kennedy, and he wore a Nixon-Lodge button on Election Day. His mother wrote to tell of the death of Walter Ebert. *I hope Roger and Annabel get along all right*, he wrote back, *and I know you people are doing everything you can for them.* He went home to snowy Urbana for Christmas and saw Karen, and their meeting was friendly, awkward and passionless. She talked about a boy she had dated, and measured Joe's reaction: half-hurt, distant, distracted.

Back in Florida, in January, all the talk at the university was of Fidel Castro going communist in Cuba, and the uprising the anti-Castro Cubans in Florida were planning. One of the Lambda Chi Alpha brothers announced, "My friend José called and asked if I can lend him a rifle!" There was talk of secret meetings of anti-Castro Cubans on campus, of underclassmen headed to the Tampa training camps of the counterrevolution. *Everything in preparation for a revolution, and believe me I feel right on the doorstep*, Joe wrote home. He raised money for a student college fund for exiled Cubans. But he was getting a C in English.

In the second week of the winter semester he skipped classes to take a bus down to Key West, so that he could see the imminent Cuban counterrevolution unfolding with his own eyes. *Everything here is one big romantic adventure*, he wrote to his mother and father. *Cubans all over town, a jumping-off point for refugees and freedom fighters. Utter tension everywhere to rebel against Castro. You might have read about the three boatloads* *of Cuban refugee fighters landing here in Key West a few days ago. The boats are in the harbor now and the fighters have been sent to Miami.* Two fishing trawlers, an aging yacht. Joe spent three days in Key West, listening to the angry Spanish being spoken on the streets, sneaking into a bar, trying to decipher the many meanings and uses of the oath *¡Coño!* On the beach, he stared at the azure, flat waters of the Straits of Florida, Cuba just ninety miles away. The horizon was filled with puffy mountain ranges of cumulonimbus clouds, and at night their round peaks were illuminated by electric pulses of blue light, and he imagined a rebel army on the water, headed toward the thunder and a war. *I can only be glad that my stay here will let me live, somewhat, this whole situation, and not just see it,* he wrote home.*

Joe headed north on the bus, back to school, traveling over the string of keys, on an asphalt-ribbon of road that floated over the blue leopard spots of a shallow sea.

HE DECIDED THE University of Florida didn't suit him and he began to make plans to transfer to a college closer to home: Hanover, in southern Indiana. *The weather is a ghastly 70–80 out,* he wrote home. *Complete hell for studying.* He traveled outside Gainesville in search of new adventures for his journal and his letters, and he saw the evangelical preacher Billy Graham speak at a football stadium in Jacksonville. Chiseled-faced, suntanned and dressed in tailored wool, the reverend possessed the gift of perfect enunciation, his voice filling the bowl of the arena with one precisely uttered syllable, Bible parable and verse after the other. Joe joined a

*I guess this is what you call foreshadowing. Being a good literary character, I foreshadowed my own future story by seeking out those anti-communist Cuban fighters. If they had invited me on one of their ships to join their army, I would have, in a heartbeat. I was a Republican then too, so the story would have been totally different, and I'd probably be writing this novel myself, from a condo in Miami.

paleontology professor on an expedition, and picked at the fossils of skinks, snakes and shrews protruding from the mossy limestone of a huge, old and eroded sinkhole.

For Mother's Day, he sent a letter home addressed to *Mrs. Mom Sanderson*, and signed it *much love* with the *Playboy* rabbit logo alongside it. When he left for home in June, he knew he wouldn't be coming back to Florida, and after a long train ride he entered Urbana to find the pale yellow shadow of a subversive bunny still visible on the tin shell of the water tower in the center of town. In Urbana he had done the boldest things he could do, and yet he was still an unremarkably average Joe here, and unfamous. A few days later he got sad and stupid drunk with Jim Adams, and ended up firing a rifle randomly into the night woods outside Urbana, crying as he fired at critters that weren't there.

JOE ENTERED SOUTHERN INDIANA, and drove past yellowing cornfields and white wood-frame houses that were square, squat and unassuming. On his first try at finding Hanover College he drove straight through the town (population 1,065) and ended up in more corn on the other side. He joined a new fraternity and surveyed the local landscape for places to explore, beginning with the next town down the road. *Started off the year by drinking a beer or two at a Madison tavern*, he wrote home. *The whole atmosphere the first night, homosexual piano player and all, brings back the wanderlust, so I'll probably head for Kentucky this weekend.* One of his new fraternity brothers bet him he couldn't swim across the nearby Ohio River, so one warm day Joe donned his Florida swimming trunks and swam into the gentle brown-black ripples and easily made it to Kentucky terra firma on the other side. The river held his attention much in those first days. *I sleep from 7:00 p.m. to 2:00 a.m., hit the books till 7:00 a.m., have breakfast and drive to the river for a shot of bourbon to wake me up and have a little talk with the Dawn,* he wrote home. *During this 30–45 minute period, I do the only creative writing I have allowed myself, and it's the minimum that can keep me on an even keel.*

His grades were not terrific, in part because he spent hours working on his novel, *The Broken Fawn,* a series of dreamy, stream-of-consciousness stories about a young man growing up in the Midwest. *Rain stalks him, animals are his witness. The soil exists to hold him upright, the clouds to shelter him from the sun.* When he wasn't writing, Joe followed narrow roads into the wavy topography of the countryside; unlike central Illinois, the farmland here rose and fell like a blanket God had shaken and allowed to remain suspended in the air. His English professor told him about a local writer who was trying to live like Thoreau, but on the Ohio River, and Joe quickly read his book, *Shantyboat,* which described his journeys up and down the waterway. His name was Harlan Hubbard and Joe found him inside his floating ice-box abode, a mile downstream from Hanover. Mr. Hubbard was the first author Joe had ever met. He was a shy and spry man of about sixty who told stories about river currents called "chutes," and about the muscadine and elderberry he'd found on the riverbanks. "How do you write a book?" Mr. Hubbard said, repeating Joe's question. "All I know is I go someplace, see things and scribble down what I see."*

JOE SANDERSON the student remained an incurable procrastinator, driving through Indiana in search of adventure and scribbling down in his journal the odd phrase he heard, the strange sights and anecdotes. The funny things farmers told him. "My dog won't chase no rabbits 'cause I guess he

---

*Of all the advice I ever got about writing, only Harlan Hubbard's truly made sense to me. Go out and live. Drift down a river. Scribble down some notes. For better or worse, that's pretty much the way I worked for the rest of my life.

just knows them too well." He subjected his liver to the elixirs on offer in the bars of northern Kentucky, and sometimes a thin beam of sunlight squeezed into those dark spaces through their leather-covered doors, a crack opening in the crust of a brick and wood-paneled Hades, allowing bats and lushes to enter. He drank Old Taylor and read *From Here to Eternity*. When he absolutely could not postpone studying any longer, he drove to the truck stop on the edge of Hanover and drank coffee and ate fried eggs, and daydreamed stories about the bristly truckers sitting at the counter.

Finally, he fell for a girl: Linda. She was from Chicago and she was black, and like a fish out of water in Hanover. They took a long walk together through the campus and its wintry landscape of fallen leaves, and she told him about her corner of Chicago, and how different it was from the Chicago that Joe said he knew, and afterward he thought of Linda's deep and soft voice and the writers she liked (I must read this Baldwin fellow), and how lonely and determined she seemed. They drove down to the river, and she told him about the place of the Ohio in the history of her people. "That side, slavery, this side freedom," she said, and they watched the water move past them like a vast liquid conveyor belt. Swim, paddle, liberty. Joe reached out and placed his hand over hers, and squeezed her fingers. They took sips of whiskey and kissed and their tongues intermingled, and their hands intertwined, and they both looked down at them. Two colors, we see it in our fingers, the tribes we belong to. Is anyone watching us? On their fourth date Linda presented him with pictures of her Chicago family. A very dapper man in a thin mustache, taken many years ago, his wool suit pressed but too big for him. The same man as a boy, a fuzzy photo, surrounded by five other young men, all dressed in suits and ties, denuded Chicago trees behind him. "Bronzeville," she said. "This is who I am, Joe." What is she telling me? That I cannot be black, I cannot be this noble and proud? However much I try? Is that it? Linda studied Joe and saw the confusion she had expected to see. She gave him a sad smile. Such a cute boy. But it's hard enough to keep up an A average, even without the stress of dating a white guy. She moved her hand away and raised it to touch his shoulder, in a sisterly way, as if to say thank you. Good man, good Joe. Goodbye.

Later, in his frat house, one of the brothers made a point of saying: "You know, if you date a colored girl, you'll have to de-pledge. That's the rules." The mighty rules. Fuck the racist rules. She doesn't want to go out with me anyway.

I'm wondering if I made the right decision about heading for college, Joe wrote home. *I spend the evenings at the truck stop, studying and writing, and though I get my work done, I'm in a world removed from college life. Reading and roaming and writing as much as possible on the weekends. Unless I get squared away, I better consider the service . . . If it were momentary depression, I wouldn't be concerned, but it's been weeks, and bumming on the weekends isn't enough of an outlet.*

He continued to read, but rarely anything related to his studies. Emerson; *Tropic of Cancer*; Huxley; *Advise and Consent*; D. H. Lawrence, *Sons and Lovers*; *Youngblood Hawke*. Books by smart men who thought and screwed and churned out reams of pages and never set out to get good grades. Who is Sanderson? The virgin sophomore. Chaser of the elusive B plus.

The best stories came from oceans and islands. Cuba. Ithaca. Oahu.

Joe decided to suspend his college education and get back to Jamaica. Once he got there, a truly robust novel would start to write itself. He'd sail, fly or swim to the island, and fill pages with wet ink and an orgy of adjectives.

Even before he took his final class and exam in Hanover, Joe began planning for a return trip to the Caribbean.

7.

Terre Haute, Indiana.

Clarksville, Tennessee.

Miami

TO SAVE MONEY ON BUS FARE, he was going to start his trip hitchhiking
from Urbana to Miami. Then he would fly to Jamaica, or take a ship there.
Virginia listened and watched Joe study highway maps at the table, and she
imagined her boy out on the side of a road, his thumb extended. With his
wrestler's lean body and swimmer's pectorals, he was more than capable of
protecting himself at any crossroads where his journey might take him. She
made him a macaroni and cheese dinner, and listened to him and his
brother call out, jokingly, and in unison: "More cheese, Mom!" One solo

journey across the continent and the waves might be enough to get it out of his system, and then he'd come back to school and serious study and work.

On the morning Joe was to leave, the three men in the Sanderson family waited for Virginia to join them at the breakfast table, and when she slid her chair forward, the four of them looked up at one another across the angles of the square table. Here we all are. All grown-up. Four grown-ups. The full fatty aroma of the bacon on his plate invaded Joe's nostrils, and he cut a piece of its striped skin and chewed, and the meat crackled saltily in his mouth. "Mmmm. Mmm. Mom, I'd say this is a great meal to start a trip bumming." Virginia raised the corners of her lips, sphinxlike, and none of the three men at the table could tell what she was thinking, but all three felt she had somehow mastered the moment: Joe was giving up college, against her objections. And he would step out the door carrying his suitcase, without serious argument or protest from her.

Dust hovered over the breakfast table and moved slowly, hypnotically through the shaft of summer morning light streaming through the kitchen window. What was the dust? Flakes of skin from his sunburned forearms, crop soil and washed linen dissolved into particulates, orbiting in air currents. His mother scrubbed, wiped and sprayed, but she could not erase the dust. He walked in dust the way fish swim in water and he was leaving on this trip to escape the dust. The dirt that covered his glasses, his nearsighted eyes peering through it at everything. Flecks from the dead wings of his butterflies and dragonflies. The dirt from the bottom of his kindergarten tennis shoes, and the cellulose escaping from the crumbled paper of his failed fiction in the wastebasket. When he walked out the door, a vortex of dust would follow him.

Joe thought he would wait for his mother to wash the breakfast dishes, but he was eager to get going. While she was still in her apron, drying off the last plate, he stood at the entry to the kitchen with his suitcase and said, "Well, I'm off." His father was already in the living room, reading the morning paper. Steve was fiddling with something in the garage.

"Say hi to Dr. Lewis," Milt said.

His mother turned from the sink and looked at him. What did I do to cause this? The son who wants to drift away. From home, from responsibility, from study. From me. She dried her hands on her apron and said, "Have a good trip, son."

Joe lifted up a hardened leather suitcase with a brass lock and walked out the front door, passing under the maple trees along Mumford Drive.*

His final destination was to the southeast, but he took his first steps away from home to the northwest and the nearest highway. Inside the house, his mother went to the living room window and watched him advance to the end of the block. She saw an undisciplined young man who also looked happy as he took a few final appreciative glances at the neighborhood and its lawns and garages. Happy counted for something.

U.S. HIGHWAY 150 ran down to Kentucky, and it seemed a good place to get going, and Joe stood with his thumb out on the stretch that ran through Urbana, on University Avenue. He waited five minutes before a driver stopped. "I'm going to Indianapolis, that help you?" said the man, who was about thirty and heavily cologned, sweating in summer seersucker, with a silver ring on the pinkie finger of his right hand. "Sure, why not?" The driver guided his Chevrolet Impala off U.S. 150, onto a long curve, the onramp for Interstate 74, a brand-new superhighway that ran wide and unfettered across central Illinois, four lanes of freshly poured concrete vaulting and dipping over otherwise troublesome crossroads. Off to see the Rastafarians, what a way to start. The edges of this byway were sculpted into gentle, unnatural slopes. "When they finish it, we'll be able to drive to Indianapolis in two hours," the driver said. "Never have to stop." The driver floored the accelerator and pushed the Impala past seventy miles per hour, and the road

*And now, at last, the true bumming begins.

signs announced they were speeding through Muncie, but they never actually saw the town; instead, they passed through an abstraction called Muncie. The Impala hit eighty and at this speed the familiar farmland and the prairie began to shrink. What an unromantic and sterile way to see the world. In less than an hour they were in Danville, and the interstate ended with a series of barriers and traffic cones, and a herd of yellow metal grading machines and bulldozers were parked at the spot where the new, concrete interstate was preparing to obliterate another cornfield.

"I should get off here, 'cause I'm headed south."

Joe stood with two feet on the roadside again, until a big semi clanked and air-braked to a stop. The trucker at the wheel said but three or four words to Joe as they rumbled southward. He had smoky teeth and skin, and the tragic yellow eyes of an imprisoned tiger, and he took Joe into Terre Haute, Indiana, and dropped him off in the town center, where Joe found a diner and ordered a cup of midday coffee.

"Is there a good place around here to hitch a ride and head south?" Joe asked the waitress.

"Ain't no better place than right outside the door, right here," the waitress said. "You're at the corner of Seventh and Wabash. It's the 'Crossroads of America.'"

Joe looked outside the diner's window and saw an unremarkable intersection with squat brick office buildings. "Wabash Avenue is the old National Highway," the waitress explained. "It'll take you to San Francisco. Or New York. And Seventh Avenue is U.S. Highway 41. Runs from Canada to Miami." Joe stepped outside with his suitcase, into the middle-of-the-day light of a midsize city halfway between the northern and southern borders of a Midwestern state in the middle of North America, and the middleness of the place was overwhelming. I need to get out of the middle, to the south, to the edge of the continent, where ocean waves are waiting for me. The buildings were middle-size and the people too. A midsize sedan stopped before him and he looked inside and saw a middle-aged man and

Joe said thanks and took a seat, and this new driver proceeded at the speed limit southward, toward Kentucky, and as night fell the headlights illuminated the hypnotic pulse of white highway lines, until Joe finally said to the man, "You can drop me off at this motel coming up here," because he could see a sign of curlicue neon letters announcing VACANCY.

When the first morning light filtered through the curtain of his room, he got up and walked back toward the highway. He saw a man in a white shirt and black tie loading up a car in the parking lot.

"Early riser," the man said to Joe. "Me too. The Lord's work begins with the light, as far as I'm concerned."

"Couldn't agree with you more," Joe said. "Genesis."

"A man who reads the Bible! Now that's a good start to my day. Where you headed, son?"

"Florida. Miami."

"I can get you as far as Clarksville if you need a ride."

His new driver was a man of about forty, a pastor who led a flock of Baptists in a church on the outskirts of Clarksville, Tennessee. Joe told him he was headed for Jamaica.

"Is that a Christian country?"

"Well, it's part of the United Kingdom."

"Always try and surround yourself with good Christian people, Joe."

They drove south toward white clouds clustered like a vast bouquet of bleached flowers on the horizon, and the pastor took shortcuts onto skinny farm roads that curved and wound their way along gullies and into shallow valleys framed by hills topped with mushroomy oaks. The pastor said he considered the "unviolated land" of Kentucky and Tennessee to be a fairly accurate representation of what paradise itself must look like. "Cleansed of sin, we'd be in heaven itself, Joe. Right here in Kentucky."

"It's beautiful country," Joe said. "But to be honest, I'm not religious. And I'm not sure there is a heaven."

"I knew there was a reason why I had to pick you up," the pastor said, and of course he launched into his finding-Jesus story. It began with the U.S. Army in Europe, where the pastor-to-be had helped liberate the concentration camp in Dachau, and had fired his gun only once in combat. For the most part, his World War II had been a campaign of licentiousness. He'd fornicated his way across France, Germany and Austria, "because I was a good-looking young man, spit-and-polish, never a hair out of place, even on the march, and horny as hell." He attracted European women the way other men in his unit attracted body lice. As a result of all that screwing, he'd picked up a disease, but even that didn't stop him, until finally he'd ended up with a Bavarian farm girl whose father shot him in the shoulder with a 12-gauge shotgun.

"Son, do you really want to be picking shotgun pellets out of your shoulder for the rest of your life? I mean, that's a metaphor."

"I understand."

The minister made his Jesus arguments and filled the passing miles with a rambling talk about his past "sex addiction," the northern lights (which he'd seen from the deck of a troopship), Holstein cattle and the caloric properties of German beer; and about Mary Magdalene and the relative effectiveness of various gonorrhea treatments. All these things served to illustrate that the path to eternal grace was just sitting there for the asking if Joe wanted it.

"I see it," Joe said, with a faux sincerity that nearly produced an actual welling of tears. "I see the Lord's plan for me."

When Joe got out of the car the minister gave him a manly squeeze of the shoulders and also a Bible. A King James filled with a fireworks of red-font letters said to be the words spoken by the Lord himself. Joe held the volume with him while he stood on the pebbly driveway of a gas station in Clarksville, his thumb extended again. A station wagon pulled up and a woman with untamed raven bangs rolled open her window and asked, "Where you headed, stranger?" The back of her station wagon was filled with six kids.

"Whatcha standing on the side of the road for, mister?" one of the kids asked as Joe opened the door and stepped inside.

"Where are you headed with that suitcase?" asked another.

"Are you selling Bibles?"

"Are you running away from home?"

When he reached Nashville, Joe bought a postcard that showed the limestone columns of the Tennessee capitol building and wrote home. *Down in the boondocks of Tennessee. Traveling slow, but have met some real interesting people. Told a Holy Roller preacher he converted me. Told a carload of kids my mother wanted me to be a minister so I ran away from home. They asked if I carried a gun or knife and I said, "No. I'll throw my Bible at any troublemakers."*

Between Nashville and Atlanta he met five different drivers, including one man with a neatly trimmed gray mustache who looked into Joe's eyes, and at his mannish musculature with the strange longing of unrequited love. And a burly salesman from Chicago who said he carried a gun. "People tell me, 'Aren't you afraid of picking up hitchhikers,'" said the man, who smelled of perspiration and pastrami sandwiches. "And I say, 'No, not a whit.' And you want to know why not a whit?"

"Why?"

" 'Cause I'm packing. Smith and Wesson are my bodyguards. Right in the glove compartment right there. Take a look."

Joe opened the glove compartment and saw a black revolver that was scratched and ancient. Like an artifact from a Chicago crime museum.

Three hundred miles later, the Chicago man dropped Joe off at the long pier in Jacksonville, and Joe walked with his suitcase onto the nearby white sands and felt the road still moving underneath him. *I sure have covered a lot of ground.* He sat on the sand and watched the sky and the sea begin to darken, and saw heavenly bodies begin to rise up out of the water; a constellation shaped like a dolphin and a fiery Saturn. Across this ocean, the Rastafarians awaited him. *Maybe this is the end to the first chapter of my book. From Champaign County to the Atlantic Ocean. I did it. I'm here.* He remembered the faces of the children in the station wagon, their innocence and their hunger for wondrous things. One day, boys and girls, you can be like me, and bum across America. He celebrated by lighting a cigarette whose tip crackled orange and warm against the night sky.

Out at Miami Airport! he wrote two days later, in his next letter home. *I can't believe all that hitchhiking's over with. Altogether it took 24 rides. The variety of people was unbelievable. To mention a few—the Holy Roller preacher, the gunman, 2 homosexuals, a Cuban boy and a 65-year-old "lady killer" and very eccentric man who said Christianity didn't amount to the square root of a damn! This last guy was the greatest. He picked me up at Jacksonville Beach and I chauffeured his '62 Chevy for the next 250 miles. We hit it off great. Talked about theology, sex, politics, philosophy, business, the past, the present, every darn thing you could think of. He bought me a Howard Johnson's lunch and rescheduled his whole route to get me here.*

IN MIAMI, Joe took the cheapest flight to Jamaica he could find, which turned out to be on an old DC-3; the plane puttered into the air with a luxurious shimmy of vibrations that the passengers felt primarily in their pelvises. When Joe went to the bathroom, somewhere over the Straits of Florida, he lifted the toilet seat and saw the Caribbean speeding by below. He watched his yellow water obliterated into mist, drifting down toward the marlins and the waves below. He returned to his seat, and to his book, Hemingway's *The Old Man and the Sea*.

Sitting one row ahead of Joe, a woman turned to rest her head against her seat, and she caught the movement of Joe's eyes as he read. The back-and-forth of his pupils, their jump from one line to the next, the inverse action of the novelist's typewriter. *He always thought of the sea as la mar which is what people call her in Spanish when they love her.* The woman passenger had a daughter of eleven and she saw a child in Joe's alert cerulean eyes, and in the waves of bemusement and puzzlement that moved across his sun-reddened face as he read.

8.

Maroon Town, Jamaica.

Kingstown, Saint Vincent.

Imbaimadai, British Guiana

UP, UP ON THE CURLING BACK ROADS of Saint Elizabeth Parish. Island
vistas, the hill upon which I am standing, more hills in the distance, destination somewhere in the green folds of the landscapes. I'm probably the only
hitchhiking white man on the entire island. His novel was up here, someplace, if he could ever find these people. You're looking for the Rastas?
Why? Everybody know the Rastas. Directions in patois, Jamaican English.
"Follow me now," which means listen to me. "Whe ya gah to do is . . ." The
friendly instructions of the locals, but do they really know where it is, or are

they just being polite? "Little bit down front way." The arms of a man ges-
turing, the index finger of a girl pointing. "You go back so." Joe was making
circles in the country roads and footpaths. "See the man dare. Ask im."

Before Joe could see it, the Rastafarian camp announced its presence
as a vibration. Then as a steady, man-made pulse. Whack-whack. Pause.
Whack-whacka-whacka. Pause. Whacka-whack. Joe turned around the last
bend, and up a rise, and he saw his shadow moving along the red, rutted
surface of the path. His silhouette, long and lanky; the bulb of his head.
The walking form of an idealistic American bum, as if on a film screen, the
cover of a book. The camp came into view, shelters made of wood. Slapped
together. A round pillar that once held up a porch roof in Kingston, an old
light pole. Around the edge of a wall of plywood and tin, he saw the source
of the music: two men chopping wood. They were facing away from each
other, but they chopped, subconsciously, in the same rhythm.

The first woodcutter stopped and turned to look at Joe; he saw a young
white man of about twenty, thin, dressed in khaki pants and a sweat-stained
collared shirt. Holding a suitcase. Disheveled, earnest. A lost tourist, perhaps, even though no tourists came this way. Joe had arrived among the
Rastafarians two decades before the movement became a fad among the
college kids of the United States and Europe. No one then dreamed of
white reggae bands, or blond-haired guys growing dreadlocks.

The second woodchopper noticed the growth of beard on Joe's face,
and intuited a raffish quality to the stranger; he surmised that Joe was a
white man who wanted to become a Rasta, even though he'd never met a
white man who had expressed this desire. Joe had been hitchhiking across
the island for two weeks, living among the poor in and around Maroon
Town, in homes without electricity, learning to use slop jars and wash
pans, eating ackee, salt fish, curried goat, playing "Jesus Loves Me" on borrowed guitars, attending a Pocomania gathering, and writing home to tell
Mom what he'd seen: *The drums, the hysteria, the dancing!* He was a mess.

"What you want here, man? What's your business?"

"I'm just bumming from town to town."

Joe saw words painted onto the planks of one of the shelters.

INFORMERS BEWARE.

"I'm not an informer."

"No, you are not," the first woodcutter said. "You don't know anything about us. You have no information. No information, no informer!" The second woodcutter laughed.

"I'm a college student from Illinois. Just traveling around. Name's Joe."

The woodcutters sized him up and decided he posed no threat. He needed water, he was lost and soon they would get him on his way. The first introduced himself as James, and reached over to a nearby bucket and scooped out water with a tin ladle and handed it to Joe.

"You share our water," James said. "Now you can share our company, Mr. Bum." The second woodcutter, Cyril, stretched out his arm to offer Joe a seat on a bench. Both men were several years older than Joe: James had long dreadlocks that bounced on his head like a fountain of black icicles; Cyril's were shorter, and tucked into a cap. They sat down next to Joe, who told them he had hitchhiked across the United States and Jamaica to meet the famous Rastafarians.

"To see us? That's crazy. What for? You're wearing all that road on your face and your clothes."

A woman stepped forward and presented Joe with a bar of yellow soap and a bucket of water. The men laughed as Joe rose to his feet and scrubbed his face and hair, working the suds into his beard. "Take that shirt off," the woman said. "Me wash it." He poured the last of the water over his head and worked the soap into his chest hairs, which curled, causing James to chuckle and say, "That's it, that's righteous clean." As clean as a white man on a billboard. Smoke Lucky Strikes. In Technicolor. In Stereo. With Added Flavor. Give us a Bayer Aspirin and take our headache away.

Joe sat down and quickly recounted his travels across the United States and Jamaica, concluding with, "And then I walked here."

"Here," James said. "With us. Why are we here? You might ask us that question. It is a good one." James explained how his mind had been awakened on the streets of Kingston, listening to the speech-sermons of a Rasta leader who recited Psalms to people hungry to believe in paradise. An escape from Babylon. He told Joe about a king in Ethiopia, whose rise was foreordained in the Bible, and how the Jamaican police tried to break up their gatherings. Bloodied officers, bloodied Rastas. Other camps had been raided by the police, and brothers and sisters had been thrown into jail. For the crime of believing that the black men and women of Jamaica were God's chosen people. "The Rasta men, they rise up, and we rise up with them."

James and Cyril returned to their woodcutting work. "It's going to be cold tonight." Joe offered to help, and took an ax, and began to expertly chop, turning a log sideways and splitting it. He saw the woman who had brought him water, now carrying another bucket, and he offered to help her too, and she said he was a sweet boy. A child stared at him, and Joe showed him his pocketknife, which contained a small magnifying glass and together they studied a line of passing ants. The men in the camp watched Joe do these things. They were expecting to be raided by the police again at any time; the police might not be as vicious if they saw this white man here. The woman returned. "Come inside, eat," she said, and she laid out a mat for him on the dirt floor. After Joe ate he looked at the mat and felt very tired. "Me just lie down for a sec," Joe said, and he fell asleep at six in the evening, with his head resting upon his folded hands.*

The woman put a blanket over Joe and she studied him, as one studies a flower or a ladybug one encounters in a garden. Stubble growth of man-child beard, cheek hairs sparse and downy. A citizen of the most powerful country on Earth, the United States of America. He has never carried a crop over his shoulder, or suffered a day without a meal. The woman stepped outside and

---

*Bumming Commandment One: If someone offers you a free place to sleep, take it with a smile. Don't sneer or make a face, even if the accommodations ain't exactly ideal.

gestured to the woodcutters to come inside and look at the stranger sleeping. They saw the Joe his mother saw when she peeked into his room on Sunday mornings. Pursed lips fluttering, a child suckling at the buttermilk in the air. James felt that the Creator was showing him a truth: human vulnerability was universal, and brotherhood the natural way of the world. Cyril noticed the young man's leather suitcase, and the wallet peeking out from his pocket. Cash. Comfort. If we were the criminals the British think we are, he wouldn't have a thing left. Sleep, white man, sleep safely here.

The camp dwellers left Joe to his light snoring, and in the darkness of a dream he traveled to a winding strip of asphalt amid meadows and rolling hills. The black road began to move beneath his feet, and then he rose over the road and began to turn and tumble inside a sunlit cloud of dust. While still dreaming he blinked hard, trying to wake himself up, and the Jamaican room around him came into focus for an instant, and it felt more like a dream than his dream, and then he slipped back into sleep and found himself sitting at his kitchen table in Urbana. His mother stood before him, expressionless. She placed a plate on the table for him with two pieces of freshly buttered toast, and his desire to bite into the toast caused him to wake up.

His eyes opened to the unilluminated room of the shack. Nighttime. A smoky purgatory. Straw mat under his cheek, scratchy. He remembered the woman and the meal, and the camp outside. He was bumming. In Jamaica. With the Rastafarians. A candle burned in the shack, and a moth flew past the flame and singed its wings. Joe got up and stepped outside, and found Cyril and James gathered by a fire. He sat down with them and started to light a cigarette.

"No tobacco in the camp, Mr. Joe Bum."

"That's fuckery."

"Fuckery?"

"Oppression."

They invited him instead to try the wisdom weed. Cultivated in the nearby hills, they said. It grew between mango and breadfruit trees, seeds secretly tucked into the earth and nurtured to life by Rastafarian hands. They placed a pinch of what looked like a dried flower bud in the bowl of a pipe made from a gourd. Water floated inside the contraption. "Chalice pipe," James said, and he held a flame for Joe. "Hold it in your lungs, Joe Bum. Don't puff it out quickly, like you do with that evil tobacco." Joe's lungs burned with unfamiliar inner heat. Against the law. Here, home, everywhere illegal. Really far from the Urbana city limits now. He held the smoke in for about five seconds. His exhale was followed by a violent cough.

"You'll get used to it," Cyril said. By the fourth puff Joe decided he liked the tension in his chest muscles from the act of inhaling, but he felt no different, and an hour passed uneventfully, with James telling the story of his hair, which was a twenty-year epic involving his grandmother's scissors and assorted barbers in a place called Rose Town, and then finally his enlightenment by the movement, and the growth of his beard and his locks. "The creation is alive in our hair," he said. "We want our hair to be living amongst us. Because we have locks, you know who we are."

Joe looked at James and saw the flickering yellow flame of the fire ferociously alive in the swirling brown lava of his irises, and in the creamy liquid of the sclera. He could feel the core of the log in the fire expanding, and when it crackled each pop was like a note made by an ancient musical instrument, and Joe began to hear more distant and delicate sounds coming from all around him. A creek ran somewhere nearby, bell-tinkling and whispering a song of rest and seduction. Didn't hear that before. On the other side of the camp, someone played a guitar. He could hear the springy resonance in the strings and the hollow body, each note a plea of wire and wood.

After a while, his acoustic powers faded, and about that same time Cyril retrieved the pipe again, and circled it around their group, which had grown to six men. The camp dwellers asked Joe about this new American president with the wavy hair, Kennedy. "Irish," Joe said. "He wants to go to the moon." They looked up at the white scythe blade of the waxing moon.

JOE SPENT FOUR MORE DAYS with the Rastafarians, chopping wood and hauling water, and helping Cyril erect a small shack to house another family. He met a Jamaican communist and told him he wanted to write a novel about the Rastafarians, but was surprised and confused when the communist objected: "No, you can't do that. We'll write our own books, thank you." The communist was a bit of a kook. He said the American CIA was active on the island, and Joe thought that was the craziest thing he'd ever heard. That night a new family arrived at the camp, and there were many greetings, and later the playing of barrel-shaped akete drums, and some of the men danced in a slow motion, rhythmic swaying. A kind of moving prayer. Joe stood up and clapped, and an older man studied him. "It's nice to see you interested in knowing truth and right," the man said when the music stopped. His locks and beard had wandering gray strands. "Give thanks that you are here. You have a heart of joy. It's the goodness of your heart that brings you to this place."

The next day, Joe left, with the members of the camp giving him a series of handshakes and pats on the back. The Rastas had asked him if he could help out with the food, and he had discovered he was out of money—they were kind enough to give him a few coins so he could mail a letter home.

Two weeks later, the Jamaican police raided the camp. They knocked down every structure, and cleared out every man, woman and child, and pulled every marijuana plant they could find out of the ground.

HAVE BEEN AT A RASTAFARI camp the last few days and was it ever an experience, Joe wrote home from Montego Bay. *A night of drums . . . and believe me, not for tourists. Under the influence of ganja, the drummers went on for literally hours without letting up. They had a special chant, usually along the lines of: "The white man surprise me forefather, and still he suppress me now.*" And then he got to the main, urgent point of his missive: *I'm in a kind of a pinch right now. I'm completely out of money, and in debt for a few pounds.* He'd gotten credit from a local innkeeper. *Need money like hell, so as not to be tied down here in Montego. A pound a night with a big breakfast is darn good but I shouldn't be spending even that, and besides the wanderlust is digging in deep. One of my new Rastafarian friends lent me the 6d for the stamp. So I need $$. The cashier's check you sent last time was fine.* Joe thought of his mother reading his note, his plea for emergency money, and he felt like he was ten years old—and definitely not like the author of a book. *I love mango juice running down my chin, but I can still smell the cherry crunch and ham*, he wrote. *Sure miss you folks.*

VIRGINIA READ THE LETTER TO MILT, who merely looked up from the cherry crunch she had prepared for dessert. "I sent him the money, of course," she said. She was seething, but said nothing more. Their disagreement over Joe filled the wordless space between them. Milt would not intervene and use his influence over Joe to get him back in college. A few days later, Virginia contacted a lawyer she knew from her work at the bank, and when Milt came home she told him, "I'm going to file for divorce." Milt nodded and said he would move out to the cabin they owned in the Mahomet woods, and after he had packed up his things, she made him a cup of coffee and they sat together in their Mumford Drive living room for the last time. Twenty-six years of marriage. In their thoughts they both returned to Lawrence, Kansas. University summer school, 1933. Tall Milt, studying bugs after defying his father. Petite and pretty Virginia, with the wavy hairstyle of a starlet in the moving pictures. Green gingham dress for school, $2.98 from a Chicago catalog. Walking together one icy morning on her family's farm, they saw three haloed suns on the horizon. "You see, Milt. Sometimes we have three suns instead of just one. That's why our wheat grows so tall." Parhelions. Sun dogs. Milt told her he had played with bugs as a kid. He'd captured a green June beetle, *Cotinis nitida*, on an Oklahoma farm, and tied a string to one of its legs, and watched it deploy its diaphanous wings and fly, and in this way the insect became a slave-kite and a toy. The heart of the attraction: our desire to be more. One day you're a boy, the next you're a man, married. Wedding night. How life begins. The bump in her gingham dress when they went to tell her mother and father.

IN JAMAICA, Joe remained unaware of the domestic contretemps his bumming had produced. He lived for two or three nights more as a pale pauper, taken in by country families, waiting for money from home. Finally he approached the inn at Montego Bay, stumbling down the town streets exhausted at ten in the morning. A policeman appeared before him. *I arrived in Montego only to be interrogated for 6 hours at the police station*, he wrote in a letter home afterward. *I found out later that someone had warned the people here that the police were watching me, but I came into town unaware. I stumbled into town sockless and dirty from head to toe, and must have looked like the wrath of God (at least I felt like it). I was taken in, searched and questioned about the Rastafaris, ganja, Communism, etc. It was all kind of amusing. They couldn't understand why I was mixing with every element on the island and living so untypically. They said if I didn't start living like most foreigners I would be deported. I replied that my life was mine and I would keep it that way, so they could jolly well deport me and I didn't give a damn.**

AFTER THE POLICE LET HIM GO, and after finally receiving the money his mother had sent him, Joe traveled to the beach resort of Ocho Rios. He cleaned himself up and got a room in the same hotel that was home to James

---

*My first time under arrest! And definitely not the last. The Author, I take it, is happy to see me locked up, with the taint of crime hovering over me. Give the hero an edge, let his beard grow a bit, make him a bit of a rascal. Yeah, I get it. Plus, this actually happened.

Jones, the author of *From Here to Eternity* and probably the most famous American expatriate living in Jamaica. Joe found the mustachioed writer and his protruding ears sipping cocktails poolside, in a cloud of pomade and whiskey, and spoke to him just long enough for Jones to offer the essence of his advice on book writing: "Go out and associate yourself with the hardest, most foulmouthed people you can find, Joe. Failing that, seek out the people who are having the most sex."

Two nights later, in Kingston, Joe lost his virginity—at precisely the same time Jamaica was becoming an independent country.*

JOE BEGAN TO FREQUENT various bars in a rough corner of Kingston known as Back O'Wall, and had several adventures: one night, he saw a police officer get shot, and got him into the car that took him to a hospital, and the next day he refereed between two warring parties at a car accident. And then he got a job as a bartender at a brothel in the center of the city.

THE NEW PAUL JONES

FOR YOUR ENJOYMENT

WITH GIRLS AND MUSIC OF YOUR CHOICE

CHINESE, INDIAN & COLORED

COURTEOUS SERVICE, CHOICE LIQUEURS, REAL FUN!

S. WONG, PROP.†

Miss Wong paid him a few pounds per week, plus the tips he earned at the bar, and gave him a room to stay in, and made him part of the female

---

*The Author and I are going to spare you the details. I told my dad the deed happened on a boat in Jamaica. Or it may have been with a "lady of the evening." What I will say was that it was not a fun time. I felt awful afterward. Which is the opposite of what you're supposed to feel. Which is love, right?

†The Author found this card stashed in the Sanderson family archives.

family of the New Paul Jones, where the girls kissed him, and pinched his butt, and teased him the way older sisters might. His room was on the second floor at the end of a corridor, past the last two rooms where the "girls" worked. Joe was the friendly white American face at the bar, greeting the ingénue boys who hailed from chaste towns filled with soda fountains and good girls; and the hardened, cargo-ship sea dogs, who fingered the knives they carried in their pockets. "You're a real American, not a limey?" "What are you doing here with these blackbirds?"* Two U.S. Navy destroyers pulled into port, disgorging their lascivious mariners, and he served them beer and whiskey, while the girls got iced tea from an old rum bottle. He watched the working girls guide men by the hand up the wooden stairs for a bit of "sugar bowl." When the bar emptied out at about four in the morning, Joe would go up to his room and listen as moans, whispers and the chirping of bed springs passed through the walls. The long, low larynx note of a man finding release, the cough of the woman beneath the man. He was inside the machinery of a coital factory, the floorboards squeaking from frantic missionary position thrusting. Buttock slaps and counterslaps followed by female laughter. Chuckles and gagging, murmurs and apologies.

During the day, in his room, he used a stack of beer cases for a writing table. *I am absorbed into the flaking paint of bamboo, blue eye shadow and bar counter, becoming as much a fixture as the douche bowl . . . My beard grows longer, turning reddish against my pallid skin . . . I am barely able to resist the attempts of my newfound sister-mothers to shave it off completely . . .* When the police started prowling nearby, Joe remembered his brief detention at the station in Montego Bay and kept moving. He was living like an outlaw, "mixing with every element," and he was excited and afraid, but felt protected, somehow. Joe was alone and free, and could go anywhere and do anything—as long as his funds held out. Everything was cheaper in the

*The Author actually swiped these lines of dialogue, and some other details, from one of my novels. The man has few scruples.

countryside, so he moved in with a fishing family in Negril, the Connells. *Am watered and fed for 30 shillings a week*, he wrote in his next letter home. The Connells went out on the ocean on a baby-blue wood skiff, fishing with big nets they untangled and fixed at sunset on the sandy shore, a short beach walk from their home, which was made of smooth plank wood painted yellow and red. The Connells noticed that Joe was a strong swimmer and told him he should buy a spear gun. Slithering and bare-chested, he swam twenty feet down to the bottom, two minutes holding his breath, eye-to-eye with pincer-toothed barracudas and lobsters with gunslinger claws.

Jamaica was the world, a kind of anti-Illinois with one adventure after another waiting, and Joe didn't want to leave it, even if the cops were after him. Next, he worked on *The Rosalie*, a salvage boat. *To sit behind the wheel, in the deckhouse of a 110-foot ship with a clipboard of engine instructions, the wind decombing hair and beard, is the goddamnedest romantic dream a young man could live.* His final gig earned him a few pounds at an archaeological dig outside Kingston, where he unearthed a glass bottle from the seventeenth century. *Dad: Finding Phyllophaga grubs at the Arawak site. Mom: Send some turkey potpie.* His money was going to run out again, and he figured he could ask his mother for a loan and a mailed bank check just once more, before going back home. He wrote and asked her to send a cashier's check to Trinidad, and he bought a cheap passage on a ship to get there, via the Leeward and Windward Islands.

The bow of the *Federal Maple* cut into the foamy prospect of the open ocean, where hammerhead sharks prowled carnivorously, while gulls on the hunt circled in the skies above. The first island, Saint Kitts, rose from the horizon like many mounds of green sand gently sculpted by a blissful child-giant. Montserrat he saw at night, for a few hours, and found its capital, Plymouth, *a hilly little village with streets to wander, and rum to drink.* He slept and woke up as the ship pulled into Antigua, *an island of low rounded hills like moss-backed porpoises, one after another.* His next letter arrived home with a stamp for another territory Virginia had never heard of: Saint Vincent. She admired the frugality Joe described, the good Midwestern squeezing of the dollar. *Nine islands, nine countries, nine cultures— approximately $5 an island.* Baby flying fish bounced across the waves like skipping stones. On shore, a stone boathouse awaited him, the reptilian limbs of barnacled pier pilings. He set foot on Saint Lucia, an island with massive stone arrowheads poking into the sky, and Barbados, where he entered the Animal Flower Cave and saw its swaying anemones.

When the *Federal Maple* pulled away from Kingstown, Saint Vincent, Joe watched the island trees below him bow in the wind. Farewell to another nation, another lived day. Is there a smart, beautiful woman around? Perhaps she'd like to talk to me. I'm a man of the world now. I ask the big questions about life and my times. Why do men use machetes to work the land in one country, and diesel-fed combines in another? Why do farmers carry the fruit of the farm on their heads here, and store it in steel cylinders back home? I'll write a novel to teach the world what I have been taught by the world.

BY THE TIME THE *Federal Maple* reached Grenada, in the dark, Joe was out of cash and hungry enough to hallucinate. He heard the loud murmuring of an unseen multitude coming from the dock at Saint George's. When the dawn light heated up the sky, the faces below him came into focus. "Migrants," said a deckhand. "Going back to Trinidad. No more work here." In a letter home, Joe described what he saw: *Impoverished Trinidadians herded aboard like cattle in Kansas City, carrying with them string-tied cardboard boxes, battered suitcases, clean but ragged clothes, crutches and bandages and solemn, wide-eyed children. They sleep on benches, boxes, the deck, the floor, a baby on top of a mother, a girl in the lap of a stranger, a man on the garbage can.* The moving mass of the world, its familial love, its poverty, the mother's half-awake squeeze of her son, the boy asleep with his mouth open to the sky, to catch the first ocean raindrops. Joe went two days without eating, and began to feel desperate and small, until one of the crew members finally gifted him a piece of chicken. The final hours to Trinidad the ship sailed through rain, and the ocean and sky were the same color, but then a rip appeared in the shroud above him, an eye-shaped hole that filled with an eerie whitish-blue light and the sliver of a crescent moon.

In Port of Spain, Joe traveled directly to the brand-new U.S. Embassy. There were two letters from his mother, but not the expected bank draft. He talked his way into the office of an embassy mucky-muck named Humphrey to see if the United States of America could spot a weary traveler fifty bucks. *No Funds Humphrey loaned me $2 out of his own pocket*, Joe wrote home in the letter he mailed later. He used this money to send a telegram to Urbana: *Need funds. Please wire immediately. Love. Joe. Stop.* That night he slept in a Salvation Army mission, and the following morning he went to the embassy to check the mail, and discovered a letter with $150, and a wire for $150 more.

Dear Mom and Dad and Steve: Ah, but didn't the eagle shit! Excuse me momma, I'm being over-exuberant. Got the moneyed letter this a.m. and you people will never know how glad I was. For the past two nights, I walked the streets staring into restaurants and the pastry shops. I am now fed and bloated.

In Trinidad, Joe heard stories about the diamonds to be found in the jungle rivers of South America. In British Guiana, a fortune awaited. He figured he'd find a few precious stones and pay back his mom all the money she'd lent him.

Joe's next letter home arrived two weeks later with four five-cent postage stamps from Georgetown. *Hallelujah*, he began. *I done come through the rye!*

THE VAST, UNCONQUERED JUNGLE of an entire continent crept into Georgetown and swallowed a bit of it every day, forcing the locals to fight back at the intruding treescape with machetes, bulldozers and electric saws. Cloud animals migrated in from the rain forest and tinkled streams of water on the town, turning its streets into muddy lakes. The locals were Amerindian, West Indian, African and Chinese. Living in seemingly peaceful cohabitation, Joe thought, until he read the local newspapers, which described a low-level war being fought between the races and their political parties. Just a week earlier, *terrorists* (interesting word) had set off a bomb that destroyed the new library at the U.S. Consulate. He sought out a Brit named McNichol, who ran an operation that dredged up gold and diamonds from the gravelly bottom of the Mazaruni River, and soon Joe joined him on a flight out into the bush on a Cessna, puttering above the last roads, footpaths and huts of Georgetown, and then over a leafy ocean filled with voracious egrets and parrots and rivers of toothy fish. They landed an hour later on a grassy strip cut into a peninsula of land where two rivers met.

The settlement of Imbaimadai consisted of a dozen shacks raised up over the ground on stilts, and it greeted Joe with the pink light of a late afternoon in Eden, and with the oval faces of children running across the runway to greet them, their features in half shadow. People the color of clay, blackest bangs and brownest eyes. The original inhabitants of this place: the Arakuna and the Akawaio. Joe joined a crew that operated a machine that sucked up gravel from the bottom of a river, working with local men of mixed African and Amerindian ancestry who wrestled with hoses as thick as anacondas, spending their day covered with mud, wearing shirts half-eaten by river bile. "You clean the land, you chop in the bush," they explained to him. "You get mineral in the box, you wash it down." He drank cassava juice and heard of sacred trees in the jungle, and folktales featuring tapirs and a tribe called the Sky People.

At the end of most days, Joe held a sprinkle of gold specks in his palm, or a diamond not much bigger than a grain of sand, and he joined his fellow crew members in making camp with hammocks and tarpaulins strung between trees. He ate "bakes" for breakfast, which he described in a letter home as *a cross between dumplings, bread and pancakes*. A classic bum meal. Now I'm a jungle drifter, that rarest of vagabond species. They traveled upriver and reached a waterfall of roiling white mist four stories tall, and Joe made dives into the pool at the waterfall's base, and at night he listened to the raindrops on the tarpaulin above him and wrote home. When he returned to Imbaimadai he gave the letter to the store owner for the next Royal Mail pickup.

VIRGINIA OPENED THE LETTER and read it, and she wondered who her son was becoming, out there in the wilds of South America. A writer? A treasure hunter, a hobo? In Urbana, it was a time of changes. She sat down at the kitchen table before three lined sheets, to write a letter that Joe read ten days later, when he came out of the bush and picked up his mail at the Imbaimadai airstrip. She did not mention her impending divorce but, instead, the happier story of Steve's sudden marriage. Joe's brother and his new bride, Maggie, were moving into their own Urbana home. *I'm damn happy for the both of you,* Joe wrote back. *Maybe the little ones will call me Uncle Diamond and pull at my 4 carat beard?* He asked for a picture of their family castle. *Some of us are doomed to live under tarps and sleep in smoky hammocks all the rest of our days.* And to his mother: *Beautiful description of the wedding, Momma. Thomas Wolfe couldn't have done any better.* Two days later her birthday arrived while he was on a tributary of the Mazaruni, hunting with McNichol; they shot a bush deer, a tiny animal with delicate forelegs and the big, meaty haunches of a donkey. The British treasure hunter dragged it back to their canoe, and on the way Joe noticed an orchid growing inside the root system of a Mora tree, a jungle colossus as tall as an Urbana office building. The flower was ivory with thin lavender lines at the base of its petals.

Late Happy Birthday to you, Momma! Joe wrote the next day. *I had an orchid for you, but before the canoe reached Imbaimadai, one goddamn 40 lbs. bush deer chewed through plastic to bolt one flower! Short of vivisection, I could do nothing. I'm tempted to whack off a small deer tail to send in the flower's place. Bush deers—bah! Mothers—hurrah!*

Mothers. Mother Earth. Mother lode. McNichol said he expected to find a mother lode soon. When that happened McNichol said he'd extract what he could before the masses of prospectors got wind of it and descended on the site. He'd then invest his capital in equipment to sell to those prospectors, who would dig and dig, with the desperate and focused purpose of burrowing animals, hundreds of them carving a canyon into the flat savanna with their shovels, their palms and their fingernails. "I'll get rich off the hole itself, from all that digging and digging." Joe looked into McNichol's eyes, which were the green of the jungle and the river, and saw how this fantastic vision brought him joy. This Brit would destroy the jungle and every living thing in it and dig a wet hole down into hell doing so. What kind of novel would that make? Not a happy one.

Thank God I've cleaned most of the scum of my greed out of my system, Joe wrote home a few days later from Georgetown. He was at the airport in the capital of British Guiana, checking in for the first leg of the long flight home, when he heard that President Kennedy had been shot in Dallas. The next day, in Chicago, he saw mourning people sleepwalking through a bright fall morning of stunned quiet, holding newspapers showing the departed president alive and grinning in the Texas sun. On the train to Champaign-Urbana he was transported into the warm box of color that was an Illinois autumn. The cornfields had dried into yellow papier-mâché stalks that caught the rays of angled sun, and the tops of the trees were the red of dried blood and the prairie grasses bronzed, and Joe felt every plant possessed a tragic incandescence, as if a celestial alchemist had tipped his wand over the landscape and conjured a final glowing tribute to the fallen president.

In Urbana each Old Glory was at half-mast, and in the days that followed Joe stood beneath them and studied their flapping nylon stripes; he noticed the skins of the flagpoles were often flaking and rusted. He felt the urge to climb each pole with a paintbrush in hand, and he wondered if he could make a bit of money and pay for his future travels that way.

9.

Decatur, Illinois.
Fort Leonard Wood, Missouri

VIRGINIA OPENED THE DOOR of her Mumford Drive home and in its frame she saw a cask-aged version of her son. Veneered skin and a sparse spray of reddish-blond hairs over his cheeks, swelling at his chin to a russet foam. For a moment, she found this sudden outbreak of ruggedness charming. My son, "road bum." Look at his face and see the journey. Home safe. Then Joe and the beard showed up at the Champaign County Bank and Trust to cash a check he'd earned painting flagpoles. His facial hair prompted a silent, startled look from the tellers and from Virginia's bank manager. They were living in the Golden Age of Aftershave and the only men who wore beards were merchant seamen, mountain hermits and the grizzled authors who wrote about them. She asked him to shave it off.

Joe was whiskerless as he began to write his first Jamaica novel, *The Shroud Has No Pockets*. He typed sixty pages on his Underwood, but never finished it.*

JOE STARTED ANOTHER NOVEL, *The Prince of Castaways*, a story set in the Jamaican fishing village of Savanna-la-Mar. He enrolled at the University of Illinois, mostly so that he could stay out of the army, but he spent too much time writing in his father's old cabin to keep his grades up. Each morning, in the hours just before dawn, he typed to the earnest tweeting of sparrows and mockingbirds, a Kool poised on his lips his only companion. A match, the spark, a two-second flame, ashes sprinkled on his writing table. Three months later he approached an ending. By Joseph Sanderson. By Joe Sanderson. My words, mine, now and for eternity between the bound cloth covers. After three months he had a stack of pages, and smoked one last Kool to celebrate. He went to the public library and in a directory of publishers found the address for Grove Press.†

THE MAINTENANCE SUPERVISOR at the elementary school in Champaign listened to Joe's offer to bring the flagpole up to patriotic standards, then told him how to do it: "You gotta climb the thing. You do it steeplejack

---

*It ended up in a box in my dad's house, after he moved to Arizona. A dead manuscript in a box is the saddest thing a writer can know. Almost as sad as being trapped inside the footnotes of the novel you were never able to write, looking over at the flurry of words hacked out by the Author as he steals your story.

†Great publishing house. Still is. Jack Kerouac and Henry Miller wrote for them. Naturally I thought they would publish the bold and brilliant young writer that was me.

style. I got the ropes." Joe pulled himself up like a caterpillar, hands and knees squeezing the steel. A can of paint dangled from a rope tied to his waist. He wrapped another rope around the pole and slid upward, climbing two stories above the elementary school campus, looking over the schoolhouse into the yard where boys and girls stopped playing and turned their heads up to stare at him. Hey, that man. What's he doing? Is he an acrobat? Spider-Man? Is he gonna fly or spin or jump?

Spray-paint gold on the ball at the top. Splash of white on the pole, brush your way down.*

HE DROVE AROUND Champaign-Urbana and found three other flagpoles to paint. And then out of town, into other Illinois cities. In Decatur a newspaper photographer spotted him up in the air and made Joe the subject of a photo-essay. Famous again. With his earnings he bought a rickety old Ford truck and drove it to more painting work in Indiana, Iowa, Minnesota and Missouri, sleeping in the back alongside his ropes, brushes and paint. After the last of these sky-climbing missions he came home to Mumford Drive and discovered the Selective Service was after him. The United States was at peace, but the draft from the last war was still in place, and the military was demanding he do his duty. He signed up for the Army National Guard, hoping to complete his military service before he hit the road again. Two weeks later he was on a bus headed for Fort Leonard Wood, Missouri, and basic training.

*From here on out, all of my bumming is gonna be self-financed. Más o menos. Just like Thoreau, who worked a few weeks of manual labor each year and spent the rest being, well, Thoreau. Paid for with flagpole money. No more gifts from Ma and Pa. (Though sometimes a loan, which I always paid back.) I'll be a grown-up road bum, and not just a spoiled college-professor kid skimming off the fat of the family savings account. The Author approves, I think. And so do you.

THEY SHAVED OFF HIS HAIR, dropping a pool of blond strands around the chair, where they democratically comingled with the sheared Cs of black Afros and the rusty-red raccoon quills of Irish pompadours. He lined up for inspection in his freshly issued fatigues, along with a cross section of middle America: the muscled and the flabby, the crooked-toothed masses and the orthodontiaed minority. An eyeglasses-wearing Texan on his left, and a Dakotan with a stony Mount Rushmore brow on his right. Like a dog newly assigned to an owner obsessed with obedience, Private Sanderson was told to sit here, stand there, lie down, rise up, eat, shower. Shave, Private Sanderson. We'll frighten the enemy with our baby-faced, razor-nicked soldiers, our beardless formations.

The physical challenge of basic training was easy. Crawl, climb, march. Run through curtains of Missouri mosquitoes, out into the Ozarks, where they bivouacked and Joe laughed as his fellow recruits whined about sleeping on air mattresses. I slept on benches and floors in Jamaica. Later, he stood on guard duty with his M14 at the entrance to a base, waiting and dying in the dark, hours ticking away, uselessly. Finally, the shooting range. Disassemble your weapon, check the sights, steady position, control your breathing. *Dear Mom and Dad. The son of New Paul Jones applied his gutter academics to shoot highest in the company today on rifle range.* Later, he qualified as an Expert. In his specialist training as a medic he performed passionate resuscitation on a pliant rubber dummy, bandaged and splinted unwounded fellow soldiers, took pulses and blood pressures and practiced tourniquets.*

He was assigned to the base hospital and most days did nothing but read novels.

---

*Like all the shooting I did as a kid, my soldier training and medic work is going to come in handy later. You'll see. The Author will get to all that. Eventually. I hope.

Went AWOL for two hours and they wouldn't do a damn thing! I cursed and moaned and demanded my rights to a rebel's prestige and they nearly threw me out of the Orderly Room. What's America coming to? Soon he was "short" and finally a civilian again on the bus back home to Illinois, planning his next trip. Southward, in the general direction of the equator and the Orinoco, to spread a bit of Joe Sanderson love and peace into new territories. A year after Joe left the army, President Johnson sent the first troops to Vietnam. And Joe's mother met the second great love of her life: a geologist named Calhoun Smith, a friend of Milt's who worked at the U of I. They were married, quietly, at the county courthouse. Neither of her sons was invited.

ALONE AT HOME, showering, Joe caught a glimpse of his naked body in the bathroom mirror. Pecs. Abs. Adonis? *I'm a specimen all right. Toned from basic training and from road bumming. This explains the stares I get at the pool.* He put on his glasses and peered at his unshaven mug in full focus. For the first time in his life he was not put off by the sight of himself. *Look out, ladies, here comes Narcissus!* The women who met him found him to be handsome, full of himself, distracted, lonely, and well-read; unlike most Illinois men-boys from educated families, he seemed unfocused and undirected. He told them he was writing novels; most did not believe him. Maybe they sensed his own doubts about his abilities. Grove Press sent him his novel back in the same box he'd sent it in, but with a note on company stationery. *Regrets, not for us. Worthy material. Difficult market. Thank you so much for thinking of us.* His first rejection letter, and he could tell every word was malarkey. So he called the Grove offices to see if he could get any more feedback. After a few minutes on hold, they tracked down a "reader" who sounded young and well-bred. "I thought it was really impenetrable. Nice setting. But I just didn't get what was going on with your characters. All they do is make speeches. But thanks for calling. You're the first writer who's ever called me. I never get to talk to anyone."

UNDETERRED, JOE PLUNGED deeper into another novel, *Caledonia*, making use of his experiences in the diamond fields. Joe had never taken a single writing class, or opened that basic guide for American writing, William Strunk's *The Elements of Style*. He wrote aggressively robust sentences, favored the passive voice, mixed up his metaphors and filled *Caledonia* with long descriptive passages and few other willful characters besides the one modeled on himself.*

After ninety-four pages he did not have a discernible plot. He got bored and gave up. The experience of being on the road was more fun than writing about it. He had to get back on the road. But where to? How about everywhere? A bumming trip around the world. Down through Mexico and Central America to South America, then east across the Atlantic into Africa and Asia. Maybe a ship from Tokyo to San Francisco on the way home. He went to Chicago and obtained a visa from the Japanese consulate, and he gathered his belongings and prepared to set off from Urbana during the final days of summer.

---

*Is this really necessary?

10.

Tampico, Mexico. British Honduras.
Guatemala City. The Panama Canal.
Lima, Peru. Santiago, Chile.
The Strait of Magellan

A RIDE IS ALL I ASK; good company and bumming tales are what I have to offer. Thanks, buddy. Thank you, sir. Missouri? Sure. Tulsa? That'll do just fine. He joined the denim brotherhood of drivers and bums at gas stations and highway turnoffs. Slow road climb to the ridgeline and back down. Unsettled skies of early summer, driver's eyes on the blackening horizon, scanning for lightning bolts and funnel clouds. Prairie grasses, never plowed, home to rattlers and assorted other varmints. Joe

Sanderson, great-grandson of wagonmen who traveled on rutted roads through these grasses, now following the sunset, sort of. Erect corn and swaying mustardy wheat catching the wind, car radios transmitting teenage anthems. *I see a line of cars and they're all painted black.* Reverb, sitars and steel guitars. His first wired money would be waiting for him at the U.S. Embassy in Panama, down in the umbilical cord of North America. After that he'd hotfoot it all the way to Tierra del Fuego. *Dear Mom and Calhoun,* he wrote from Mexico. *Forty-four hours later, $8 and six car rides and a Mexican bus, and I'm in Tampico. Not bad, eh? I mean, for the educated bum, that is.*

Drank beer with a Detroit boy clear to Tulsa, Oklahoma; gallons of beer with 3 Lawrence, Kansas, fellows who own a tavern there; short rides with a University of Missouri student, a Vietnam vet and a Negro driving a stationery company van; then a last ride, clear to Brownsville with a 50 yr. old man and a bottle of Scotch. Claimed his second wife was top Houston businesswoman, claimed also he'd been worth $1½ million in better days, lost everything, and hated the federal income tax with a passion, far more than he hated integration of the races. Huh?

Mexico slowly brought Spanish to his tongue. Huevos tibios: hard-boiled eggs. ¿Con salsa? ¿Con salsita? It doesn't mean little salsa, but more like, *With salsa, dear?* A language full of little endearments like that. At the bus station he had a passable conversation with a Chinese Mexican guy named Félix Chuang.

"Estoy viajando a Panamá," Joe said. "Después a Sudamérica. A Tierra del Fuego."

"Un viaje réquete largo," Félix said, and Joe loved the sound of that word. Re-que-te, which through a kind of linguistic osmosis he understood to mean "heck of," as in "That's a heck of a long trip."

"El sol quema," Joe said, pointing to his peeling arms. Réquete quema. ¿Cuántas horas a Mérida? By the time I get to Chile, I'll be speaking like a native, seducing the señoritas with my fluent Castilian. ¡Qué bonito su pelo! With your looks, Sanderson, and Spanish on the tip of your tongue, the sky is the limit.*

He sat next to Félix on a third-class bus following the Atlantic Coast of Mexico, rolling into Veracruz and into the oil fields and the Olmec country to the south. The bus stopped in a town with the unpronounceable name of Coatzacoalcos. Looking out the window, he saw a street half-flooded from a recent rainstorm, and a row of cement storefronts, and a woman standing before a cart stacked with fried cakes wrapped in paper, a boy sitting next to her on the curb. The woman looked twenty and forty at the same time, and had the elegant thinness that is born of perpetual motion and labor, although at this moment she was standing perfectly still, while at her feet her son was gathering pieces of discarded paper and folding them into boats and launching them across the black puddle before him. The boy had a fleet floating on the water, and his mother looked down just as a car drove by and made a wave in the puddle; the boats rose and fell, and the boy squeal-laughed at the miniature maritime scene he'd created.

An entire novel was unfolding in the frame of his window. I know what that boy is thinking: When is Mom gonna be done working? The mother looks down and turns up her lips. An entire novel that I'll never know or write. The bus set off and Joe saw shoebox storefronts with hand-painted signs, and more faces, and he thought of all the interlinked stories in this street and city. He felt like a man walking into a forest where the stories were like spiderwebs strung between the trees: invisible filaments of narrative were sticking to him, but he could never hold them and know the full beauty of their structure, of their spider-spun art. The bus rolled into the countryside, into a landscape of yucca plants and swamps. More Mexico,

---

*Sí, aprendí español. Bastante bien. Réquete bien. Like a native, eventually. Just ask my Salvadoran friends, those cipotes who are all grown up now, grandfathers even. They remember.

más Mexico, más, más, más mysterious Mexico. México misterioso: the Indians, the Spaniards, the Chinese, oil derricks and walls covered with the oxymorons of government graffiti. *Long Live the Institutional Revolutionary Party!*

"No comprendo México," Joe said to Félix.

Félix laughed and said, "Rulfo," and he opened his suitcase and reached inside and produced a thin book. *El llano en llamas.* By a writer named Juan Rulfo, and Joe understood that Félix thought this book explained Mexico. Joe opened it, and of course the whole thing was in Spanish. With his dictionary Joe managed to understand the first sentence.

I am sitting next to the sewer, waiting for the frogs to come out.

Over the course of the next hour on the bus, Joe and his dictionary and his embryonic Spanish brain decoded a few more sentences, and Joe gathered that the narrator of the story was a boy who had been sent by his godmother to kill the frogs because their croaking was keeping her awake at night. Intriguing.

Joe returned the book when they reached Cozumel and his new friend got off the bus. "Gracias, Félix." Joe was proud of himself for talking to Félix and reading a paragraph of his book. Really starting to get good at the whole Spanish thing. A short while later he reached a territory where his Spanish was useless, because the people there spoke the Queen's English.

WELCOME TO BRITISH HONDURAS

British soldiers in long, loose-fitting khaki pants patrolled the streets with fixed bayonets and the slow, deliberate, feline strides of men expecting to be ambushed. In Belize City, Joe breathed the wet, smoky air that follows a tropical riot. Here and there, a looted building, the remnants of a half-hearted barricade of sticks and barrels. *The British soldiers are a pasty-faced bunch of kids, and they look scared to death,* Joe wrote home. He boarded a puttering old boat southward and arrived in the Guatemalan city of Puerto Barrios; here too he found troops on a war footing. A few days earlier a band of Marxist guerrillas had infiltrated the town and painted the graffito *Patria o Muerte* on the walls. Fatherland or Death, though Joe misunderstood it to read Patria *de* Muerte, Fatherland *of* Death, and he inserted this phrase in his next letter. Here I am, in the Fatherland of Death, and doesn't that sound horror-movie scary. These were the same rebels who had taken up arms after the banana war that worried Milt all those years ago, but they were a small, hidden force, and Joe knew nothing about them. He traveled in a steam train southward and uphill, blasting a white mist into the groves of banana trees. At toy-size wooden train stations, old men in straw hats watched his train roll past. By the time he reached the capital, night had fallen.

The next morning, Joe emerged from a hotel near the main plaza of Guatemala City, stepping out into "the Land of Eternal Spring," as the locals called it. The sky was, in fact, the richest and deepest blue he'd ever seen, as if Guatemala were the source from which all the blueness of the world's skies was born. Mayan Indians walked about the city, many wearing sandals and ornate patterns of hornet-green and sunflower-yellow threads woven into their clothes, walking past the limeade stone of the National Palace, speaking in the odd constant clusters of their indigenous languages. He saw a black graffito that screamed, once again, *Patria o Muerte*, but the newspapers mentioned that all was calm since the army had lifted the state of siege a week earlier. *I missed the major part of the riots in British Honduras by two days,* Joe wrote home. *Just like I missed the real action of ten thousand Mexican students rioting in '58, the Festival rumble in Trinidad, and the Jamaican militia called out against the Rastas. Oh well, I guess I can't be at all the revolutions.* An idea took root in Joe's bumming brain: Maybe one day he'd wander into "action," events so dramatic and violent, that the publishable plot of a novel would present itself to him. Effortlessly. With Joe in a starring role, of course. A war, a revolution, an uprising, a coup. Something.

HE ENTERED A COUNTRY called El Salvador. Named after Jesus, the nation was, appropriately enough, at war with no one. In the town of Sonsonate he sat on a bench in the town square, and was surrounded by the courtship rituals of the town's youth. Lean this way, look that way. Boys with their fingers in their belts, girls with ice cream cones, group giggles, one boy's bold march across the concrete square toward one girl. Puppy love. They are here, in the center of their Salvadoran everything, and I'm just a visitor. I would march across the square for . . . ? For Karen Thomas, if anyone.

He got a ride into a valley where the hillsides were covered with cornstalks and the trees speckled with vermilion coffee beans, and was deposited at a crossroads littered with piles of burning trash; a vortex of vultures circled overhead, gliding through the climbing pillars of sweet, sticky smoke. The vultures and their greasy wings transmitted a dark meaning he could not decipher. Avian augurs, summoned by unseen witches. A brand-new Chevrolet Impala passed, and the driver slowed down and stared at Joe. In El Salvador, the rich inhabited a smug bubble of comfort floating inside a universe of poverty, and the driver was perplexed by a blond man's presence outside this bubble, standing next to a pile of smoldering garbage, no less. So he circled back and invited Joe to a bar in town; as they drank rum, he warned Joe how dangerous the roads of El Salvador were at night. *Was all for continuing, but people in the town said that not only was the city itself unsafe, but the Pan-American Highway especially*, Joe wrote home. *Bandits, etc.* The idea of being robbed didn't faze Joe much: he was carrying a .22-caliber revolver in his backpack, a Smith and Wesson, having crossed four borders without a single customs inspector asking to see the contents of his U.S. Army–issue rucksack. He crossed four more with his gun undetected, and reached Panama.

The vessels passing through the Panama Canal seemed to offer the possibility of a cheap ride across one ocean or the other. Cruise ships and tankers floated past him in the canal's bathtubs, following paths across the meridians of the world. None offered free passage, so he bought a ticket on a freighter headed to Colombia, and he arrived in the port city of Cartagena, and explored its old center, and saw sunflower-and-royal-blue colonial buildings and colonnades and ferns growing in the balconies. Parrots squawked inside the homes as he passed, the way dogs barked in Urbana neighborhoods when he strolled through. "¡Cua, cua, cua!" a parrot yelled. "¡Carajo!" He hitchhiked toward Bogotá, upward into thinner air, marveling at the serenity of Colombia and its serpentine highways. But the Colombians who rushed past Joe on the Pan-American Highway, where he stood with a raised thumb, saw a vision of a disturbing future. The rush of passing traffic lifted the loose strands of the gringo's unbarbered blond hair, the frayed bottoms of his blue jeans. Here come the American hippies we've been hearing about, ready to share their addictions and excesses. Free love: unfettered, degenerate, and syphilitic.

When he reached the equator a square sign announced with simplicity and understatement: LINEA EQUINOCCIAL, LAT. 0° 0. *Made friends with a beautiful little "Brigitte Bardot" singer (radio, TV, nightclubs) and her "friend," a professional wrestler ("El Incognito," wears a hood like an executioner's!)*, Joe wrote from Guayaquil, Ecuador. *The singer cuts wonderful hair and makes a good cup of coffee and her friend is going to see if he can get me a few bouts with other mat-rats. Huh? What say? I see the headline: "Young Novelist Wrestles His Way Around World." From the looks of the local fighters I'll need brass knuckles and a pogo stick to win, however.**

The singer and the wrestler told him to stay and drink in more of Ecuador, but he felt the pull of the south, and he moved quickly to depart for

---

*Ah, that time. The bumming beauty of it all and the freedom to be a screwup, a happy wanderer, a failed novelist. As another gringo writer and onetime fuckup put it: "That world! These days it's all been erased and they've rolled it up like a scroll and put it away somewhere."

his next country, only to discover after some consultations with the locals that he had failed to obtain the proper visa before walking across the border from Colombia. *Entered Ecuador illegally (so I found out today)*, he wrote home. *But I met a fellow at a travel agency who promised to fix things up . . . He's likewise going to write me the phony plane ticket I need to walk into Peru.* These were the machinations to which good bums had to resort, because the laws of the world were not written for Illinois hitchhikers to drift across borders willy-nilly. He told his mother to write to him care of the United States Embassy in Santiago, Chile.

IN URBANA, Joe's letter arrived in the mailbox on a Friday afternoon, for his mother to find when she got home from work. Another country. Ecuador, with a spacecraft hovering in the stamp over said country. She didn't want to open it immediately. *Will I ever lose this sense of worry?* She lingered at the door; the air was summer heavy. Mist clouds floated over the city, and an air conditioner hummed somewhere. Ecuador, he's reached South America. Virginia stepped inside, retrieved her letter opener and removed Joe's written pages. *Dear Mom and Calhoun*, he says. Nice he mentions Calhoun. He's fine, eating well. Another pretty woman, a Brigitte Bardot this time. Another one! Like moths to light with him now. Where does he get this from? Not from his father. No Romeos in Kansas or Oklahoma. None. They call it charm. He could charm the pants, no the skirt . . . This is a skill, a quality. He means no harm, he means to care, but they don't know, these girls. Wants me to remind Steve to send five hundred dollars to Santiago.

The words *entered . . . illegally* caused Virginia passing concern, though it seemed like the sort of problem her son routinely talked his way out of. If he kept moving he would stay out of trouble; it was the idea that he would join up with assorted agitators and prostitutes again that worried her the most. The following afternoon, a Saturday, she and Calhoun had the widow Annabel Ebert over for lunch. Calhoun cooked a meal for them on the grill. Annabel said her son, Roger, was in Chicago, starting a new job at the *Sun-Times* for the newspaper's Sunday magazine. Roger had written some book reviews for the *Daily News*, and Annabel clipped them from the newspaper with pride. From success to success. Roger is a professional writer, my Joe wants to be a writer. Roger has the discipline to finish things and see them through, and he was wise enough, in Virginia's estimation, to conquer small things first, starting with a story for his high school newspaper; unlike her son, who took on the biggest thing you could think of all at once, a novel, and had failed. Predictably. Again and again.

"I'm so excited for Roger, living in Chicago," Virginia said.

"I miss him. You're so lucky Steve is here."

"I am. And Joe: well, he's being Joe," Virginia said.

"Where is he now?"

Virginia explained that Joe was headed to the tip of South America. He'd been to about twenty countries so far, by Virginia's count.

"He has a visa to go to Japan," Virginia said. "He says he's going to go all the way around the world."

"Wow, that's something," Annabel said. "That's really something."

That night, Virginia took the letters from the shoebox where she kept them and looked at their stamps, the names of countries, the symbols of their currencies, their smudgy postmarks. Really something. She ordered them by the dates Joe had sent them. The first one from Tampico. The second one from Guatemala City. She numbered them. A week later, when the next one came, from Lima, Peru, she wrote a five in a circle on the envelope.

JOE'S BUS FOLLOWED sand dunes and the Pacific Coast for the final stretch into Lima. In the space between his eyes there was a compass, pointing south, as if he were a migrating bird obeying instinct. South was the only reason for his existence. Entering Lima, he saw wealthy white Limeños cruising in sexy Fords and Chevrolets, and the faces of the Inca carrying shovels and pushing carts, and he felt the anger and resentments between these opposing versions of Peruvian reality. In the center of Lima, he saw a stone-paved plaza, lemon-colored colonial buildings, a bronze conquistador, his equine mount. And in the rocky mountains that surrounded the city, he saw the concrete-and-brick Machu Picchus where the poor lived, and he sensed displacement, the retreat of rural villagers to an improvised city, as if fleeing a war, burning homes in the Andes. But there is no war, only the daily routine of work and family. Lima was endless, or rather, its boundaries were porous and undefined, and each time Joe traveled beyond its fringes to desert beaches and plains, the city came back to life again, as if Lima were a living thing sending out spores to conquer new patches of sandy soil. Finally, he escaped the metropolis, and hitchhiked toward Lake Titicaca, and when he reached its waters he found them surrounded by a rim of hills that were a bleached and powdery brown, white mountain peaks beaming majestically on the far horizon.

The buses here were cheap and he took another one into Bolivia. Road dust and shrublands and reed grasses the color of urine. Altiplano. High plain. Altitude, twelve thousand feet. He'd traveled from the center of North America to the center of South America, and now he entered a high-altitude dream where farm people lived in mud homes with mud-walled corrals to keep in sheep, goats and llamas, actual llamas, mystical creatures, long-necked and flapping their tongues. Women in woven shawls and long skirts and with thick calves, men with wool vests, children in their wake, scratching at the soil with sticks, making circles and ovals and squares. Their Altiplano faces began to melt in the darkness and the bus window now reflected Joe's ungroomed mustache. Twenty-four years old. Prescription spectacles. The bus stopped at a crossroads with a lone light pole, an oasis of light in the desert dark, overlooking a cluster of travelers, a shack. The bus driver got off to stretch his legs, and Joe followed after him, stepping into the pool of light and a crackled road tarmac. Two dozen sets of eyes fell upon him.

The Aymara men and women who saw him were disturbed by the unexpected appearance of a European man in the middle of the night in the middle of the Altiplano, and by the way his pale skin and egg-blue eyes gleamed in the gray light. He was an alabaster apparition, an omen, and for several of the bus passengers he triggered memories of recent encounters with bad luck, the demons that haunted their lives on the shrublands and in the hilly city of La Paz. A rain-swollen river, a house-swallowing whirlwind, a traffic accident, a rampaging goat. The white ghost insists on traveling with us, among us, and hurry, hurry, bus, and get us to the city so that we can be free of him and his evil portent.*

SUPPOSEDLY, I'M WRITING A NOVEL. But what is an adventure written on paper compared to the four-dimensional, full-color experience of a journey on the road with the rising sun, two snowcapped volcanoes and llamas bolting across the tracks? Again, the strange animals, small-headed; they turned to look at Joe as he passed. Being a writer isn't just what you live, the places you see, the adventures that unfold before your eyes; it's the old soul you become, the road-bum knowledge that seeps into your brain with each kilometer. He could begin to see the central fact, the lesson of the road. The big world is tied together by asphalt, sea lanes and footpaths, and everywhere you go humans are puttering away for more or less the same reasons. For family. Toil, till, harvest, over Peruvian potato patches and Illinois

---

*I didn't know a novel could do this either: just become the people on the road, one after the other. It's a cool trick, I guess. Omniscience. The writer as God. I was never that full of myself. Certainly not at the age you're reading about now. I was the happiest I'd ever been, going where the road took me. Do people still do that? Just go? Without bothering to buy a car, or getting travel insurance, or making reservations, or checking what the weather is like where you're headed?

corn. The train entered Chile and his exhausted eyes glimpsed the Pacific, blue and infinite, waiting for him with seashells and mermaids and sand to heat his tired toes. Ocean thoughts lulled him to sleep, and when he woke up he was in Arica. At the edge of Arica he stood on the asphalt of the Pan-American Highway again, and stuck out his thumb. A mint-green Buick slowed down and stopped, and a harried woman in a blue evening dress stepped out and opened the door, and took the back seat, while the driver, a man with a cigarette drooping from his lips, gestured for Joe to take the front. "Voy a Santiago," Joe said.

"¿Santiago? ¡Son mil quinientos kilómetros!" Yes, Joe's next destination was fifteen hundred kilometers away, nine hundred miles, and he couldn't wait to reach it. Letters from home were waiting for him at the United States Embassy in Chile's capital, along with a check, hopefully. Joe hopped into the Buick, but before he could say "Gracias," the driver and his female passenger began to argue; or, rather, they resumed the argument they were likely engaged in when they stopped to pick up Joe. "¡Tú!" the man yelled, and the woman replied, "¡No, tú!" and the woman reached forward, and removed the driver's panama hat, and struck him with it, yelling, "¡Mentiroso!" until the car stopped. The woman got out, and as the driver turned the car around to head back to Arica, Joe said he would get out too; he found himself standing on the southbound side of the road hitchhiking, while the woman did the same on the other side. A northbound car appeared and took the woman away, leaving Joe alone in an otherworldly landscape of dunes and gray cliffs, baking under the resurgent sun, expecting a spacecraft from Earth to land at any moment. Just as he was contemplating walking back to town, a Jeep with three nattily dressed men pulled up and stopped.

"Where are you going?" one of them asked in English.

"Santiago."

"We are too!"

They were all wearing sunglasses and grinning, and they smelled of alcohol, and they engaged Joe in a bilingual conversation. They were three whitish-blond Chilean brothers, headed back to Santiago after a road trip to Peru: *towheaded boys that looked like Aussies*, he would later write in a letter home. As the Jeep drove deeper into the desert, the two passenger brothers fell asleep in the open-air vehicle, hypnotized by the straight road and the empty desert; it was like a drive across Kansas, but with no thing living anywhere, except maybe the bacteria clinging to the beads of fog blowing in from the ocean. "Atacama!" the driver shouted. Not a single bug on the windshield, no roadkill on the asphalt. Nothing. A universe of umber sand, dead mountains. No towns or gas stations. Amusements only for the devotees of rocks. The Chilean passengers resumed their drunken carousing once they woke up, drinking red wine straight from a bottle. The driver took a swig too, and sped up, and when he did so the Jeep yawed, like an airplane being buffeted by crosswinds, the pickled torsos of his passengers swaying in unison. Bad suspension; my brother would sort it out in an hour.

For three days he traveled with the Chileans, stopping for roadside naps and meals. When they entered cities and towns and other settlements, they caught the stares of workingman Chile; of women tending to big pots on the roadside, and men in overalls, carrying wrenches and tools. When Joe and the three brothers entered the proletarian suburbs of Santiago, they found a city filled by the smoke of winter fires, and a haze that turned the massive Andes into a stained patch of sky on the horizon, the mere suggestion of a mountain range. And they saw graffiti that hinted at the coming class war: red stars, men carrying hammers and raised-fist symbols painted on brick walls, a rebellion of the black-haired against the blond and the fair, the chiseled Indians against the tall police and their polished black boots. Battles to be fought in the brick-lined alleys, in the warrens of shacks by the river, at night, by flashlight, with fire and stones.

Hitchhiked 1,500 kilometers with a wild bunch that somehow kept the Jeep aimed toward Santiago, Joe wrote home, when he finally reached the apartment where the Chilean brothers lived, on an entire floor of a building overlooking the national military academy. *Traffic accident in the desert (smashed windshield) which cut up two of the Chileans—I came out un-scathed. White wine to sterilize the wounds and my red handkerchiefs for bandages and we blasted away, drinking the balance of the wine. Drove steady except for breakfast by the sea and sidewalk steaks while a carpenter built us a new windshield. More wine the next day, enough that we kid-napped a penguin at a restaurant 200 kilometers from Santiago. Stayed overnight with the Chileans (Scottish mother, Swiss father), realizing the next day they weren't just rich, but really repulsively rich. Got a good night's sleep (1st horizontal sleep in 4 days) and some damn good meals the next day, then ducked invitations to stay on longer.*

No more brie, thank you. I just couldn't. The bacon was excellent. Just like home! He slipped away to the U.S. Embassy, where a small stack of envelopes was waiting for him, including some forwarded by the embassy in Panama. Steve had sent the precious funds, his flagpole money. Writing from Arizona, his father said a fellow scientist had named a new species of riffle beetle in Milt's honor. *Xenelmis sandersoni.* His mother said it was a hundred degrees in Urbana. Joe wrote back: *Any chance of mailing some August dust and sweat in exchange for a little Chilean snow?*

He left Santiago, headed through crop fields and dormant vineyards, splurging with his flagpole-painting money on the relative comfort of a second-class bus. After many hours the land became darker and evergreen, and a stormy winter wind blew through the pine forests and the eucalyptus tree farms. He reached the port city of Puerto Montt. *Leaving for Tierra del Fuego tomorrow a.m. by boat—a weeklong trip*, he wrote home on August 30. *People here tell me I "might" get treated to my first iceberg. Sounds out-landish, I know, but I guess I will be roaming fairly near Antarctica.* His passenger ship sailed past an island where spirits were said to live in the trees, and around many others that were uninhabited but for seals and pen-guins, and he saw no icebergs but much snow falling on the waves, and on a gray and gloomy morning his ship docked at the pier in Punta Arenas. He found the cheapest lodgings in town and wrote home.

And so, a week later, here I are—The End of the World! Cold? Jesus Gawd! What looks like ice crystals drop out of the sky even when it's cloudless, and talk about digging under the blankets at night—you betcha! He described the journey from Puerto Montt thusly: *Quiet sailing. Rode third class, including meals, for $9.30, spending nearly all my time in the 1st-class lounge and bar (of course), drinking, swapping lies with the captain, beating everyone at chess, and in general enjoying the Mississippi River boat atmosphere at a pauper's rate.*

Hit town last night and got into a place called El Scorpion Nocturno—$1.80/day with meals. Of course, there were a few suspicious looking ladies wandering about, but I smiled innocently like a choir boy, bewildered that the thermometer has so little sway over virtue.

He tried to see if he could do a one-day bumming trip south out of Punta Arenas, on Chile National Highway Number 9. Several drivers passed him and his outstretched thumb and gave him perplexed looks as he stood on the edge of town. Finally a taxi driver stopped and asked. "¿A dónde va?"

"To the next town," Joe said in Spanish.

"There is nothing," the taxi driver said. "This is the last town, the last place in Chile where people live."

"Where does this road go then?"

"To the fort."

"A fort?"

"A national monument. But no one goes there now, joven."

"¿Por qué?"

"Because it is very, very cold. But I will take you."

They drove away from the town's asphalt streets, and into an unpopulated, windblown and foggy pampa-scape, where there were no trees but many bushes, clinging to the soil against the winds that blew in from the

South Pole. Joe explained his mission, his travels overland and by ship from the United States, and on all the roads of South America.

"This is the end of your trip!" the driver said. "There is no more road after this."

The narrow road turned to gravel, and after thirty minutes they reached a sign that read FUERTE BULNES and the road became a loop and circled back on itself, and Joe realized this was, in fact, the end, the last stop in the chain of highways connected to Cartagena, on the northern shores of the continent. The bottom of the bottom. It was an old fort built by colonists who no longer lived here, and now a tourist attraction that no one visited in the winter. He saw a fence made of sticks, a palisades and a Chilean flag, its red and white stripes snapping south in the wind, in the direction of uninhabited, inhospitable islands and Antarctica across the ocean.

Climbing the slope on which the fort resided, he saw the soapy blue current of the famous straits sought out by European mariners. Calm ocean water, sheltered from bigger, meaner seas. Magellan and his crew navigated through this channel, their Portuguese sails catching the wind, steel helmets rusting in the misty air, the captain and his sailors thinking: Is this the way, have we found it? Asia and spices and riches! Magellan's eyes upon the way forward, to Japan and then Africa and home to Lisbon. And now my eyes on this same body of water, lonesome waves. From Urbana to here. If Mom and Dad could see me. Now I know what the explorers knew: how big the globe is. My world is roads, oceans, rivers, bays, deserts, jungles, bridges, gas stations, crossroads, signs, swamps, dust and ice. Big, but finite.

There was only one thing a bum could do when he'd reached the end of the world: turn back and bum northward and eastward to the next place.

11.

Buenos Aires. Lisbon. Paris. Tangier.
Tripoli. Damascus. Jerusalem.
Baghdad. Kuwait. New Delhi.
Kathmandu. Kabul. Teheran.
Istanbul. London

AND NOW THE GREAT EXOTIC EXPANSE, the empty empire of sheep.
Patagonia. So many sheep, as if in a dream. Endless ovine munching on
tufts of tawny grass. Joe's eyes fixed on the woolly animals, fighting off
slumber as he listened to the throaty exhortations of the truck in which he
was riding; deeper into Argentina's own version of nowhere, following
three other trucks, in a caravan headed all the way to Buenos Aires. Two
thousand five hundred kilometers on one ride, a new Sanderson record.
The trucks plowed into a gray sweep of shrouded sky and light rain and wet

pebbly ground. They had set off from the Argentine town of Río Gallegos, where a small plane had deposited Joe from the island of Tierra del Fuego. With nightfall the caravan became a swarm of amber and red lights floating over the moonlit flatlands, until the first truck flashed its lights, and the next truck and the one after, and finally all three trucks began to drift to the side of the road. "Señor Joe, vamos a parar—para la cena," the driver said, and Joe understood everything. Which was fortunate, given how hungry he was. Dinner, thank God. But where, without a town or a shack in sight?

Joe stepped off the truck and followed his driver, and he watched as the lead driver in the caravan set loose a long-haired dog that sprinted into the night toward the faint, puffy forms of a cluster of sheep. Amid cheers and cackles from the truckers, he heard the paw thuds of the dog's aggressive running, its bark circling the sheep, and soon three of the drivers had wrestled two ewes to the ground. They produced knives, and the black blood of the murdered sheep flowed into the sandy soil. Joe helped the men drag the carcasses back to the roadside, where another trucker had produced firewood and a set of steel bars and began to assemble a spit to roast the animals.

Quite a breed these truckers, Joe wrote home later. *We rustled two sheep. Barbecued them after midnight. Can't say I regret the crime though. 'Twas very good meat.*

The odd raindrop exploded into steam as it struck the fire. Heavy, darkest meat, might not sit too well. The lights of another truck appeared on the horizon and the truckers slowed their chewing. The vehicle stopped and a driver stepped out, and the truckers embraced him. ¡Viejo, boludo! He was followed by a skinny young man with unkempt brown hair and the thin physique and disoriented air of a child. A Frenchman, it turned out. Patrice was bumming his way around the world and he fell into conversation with Joe. Me, hitchhiking. Moi, aussi. Patrice had set off from the French city of Lens, to Istanbul, across North Africa to Morocco, then turned south, traversing Africa from the Atlas Mountains to Table Rock at the Cape of Good Hope. "The Sahara, the Sahel, le Congo, toute l'Afrique."

He had taken a cargo ship from Cape Town to Brazil, and now he was here, in Patagonia, headed for Tierra del Fuego, and then San Francisco, California.

The drivers and their bumming passengers retired to their trucks for a few hours of sleep. Before dawn the truckers awoke and started their engines and while those machines were warming up, Joe and Patrice stepped out and shook hands and wished each other good luck and *bonne chance* and they were on their way again, their bumming journeys dripping imaginary lines of ink into the roads behind them.

IN BUENOS AIRES, Joe got his mail from home, and a check, and began a roundabout journey across and along the muddy Río de la Plata and its tributaries. He entered Uruguay, and Brazil, riding in trucks, buses and assorted Fords and Peugeots, and made his way to Iguazu Falls and Paraguay, where a long-billed toucan buzzed over his head at the border post. *Steak and eggs several times a day, 50¢ a plate!* he wrote home from Asunción. *Yes, they're still taking reservations to South America and I'll expect you folks soon.* He returned to Buenos Aires and its stone buildings filling each block to geometric perfection, and the teams of waiters at the cafés, dressed in white and black. Joe's clothes were unlaundered, his hair reached his shirt collar, and his appearance provoked derisive stares and contempt from all the cosmopolitan Argentines around him. Two months earlier there had been a military coup, and the country's new rulers had banned miniskirts and decreed that long hair on men was henceforth illegal, and the police had taken scissors to clip the hair of the radicals at the University of Buenos Aires.*

Joe stood before the freighters at the Buenos Aires docks, looking for a

---

*I was still carrying my .22-caliber revolver. Silly me. If the Argentine police had caught me, it wouldn't have been fun. But I lived in a kind of innocent haze then. People smiled when they saw me coming. We American boys were the tanned princes of the world. People didn't hate us then. As much.

ship to take a sandy-haired hobo to another continent. But no freighter would have him. *Was dealt a bad set of cards for ships to Europe so I've had to swallow my River Rat pride and walk the gangplank for a tourist ship,* he wrote home. The R.M.S. *Arlanza,* of the Royal Mail Line. *For gawd's sake, don't let the word get around or I'll be slaughtered on the flyleaf of my 1st novel.*

Freshly showered, his clothes laundered and patched up, he fell in with a group of Brits and Britain-bound passengers. *Student bums, a couple of years younger than I, and a Hungarian refugee headed to England. We spend hours among each other taking in the sun. A real ship of fools.* He became close with a young woman named Helen, who he described in a letter home as *the inevitable British girl returning to U.K. after a "smashing" lecture tour of Argentina.* Helen of the rosy hue, with a feminine form befitting her name. Hellenesque. Hellene. As if imagined by the sculptor. She saw in Joe a rugged Americanness she associated with westerns. *A Fistful of Dollars. For a Few Dollars More.* And she was not surprised when, a few days later, she woke up after another amorous night with Joe in his third-class berth, and squeezed past his naked body and peeked into his rucksack and saw a .22-caliber revolver, a black instrument of death. My American pistolero. What crimes have you committed? What enemies do you fear?

The ship reached Rio, a city shrouded in fog, hiding the famous concrete Christ statue he wanted to see as they pulled into port. Joe left Helen for the day and hiked up into the districts he had been told to avoid, the favelas, and he followed winding, improvised concrete stairs poured over the jungle, and found an unexpected integration of the races, an African and European neighborliness on hillside paths perched above the beaches. Big vistas of round rocky promontories, and boys and girls flying kites. Several days later, upon reaching the European mainland, he wrote home. *Just docked at Lisbon, pulling out for Vigo, Spain, this p.m. Ship stopped several hours in the Canary Islands two days ago, but we were still a little way out to sea from Africa—didn't see any of Hemingway's lions roaming the moonlit beaches. Them quid-chewing camels, yes, but nothing else but the tourists on this ship taking "British sunbaths" (lying in the sun on beach chairs, wrapped up in blankets, preferably after tea).*

JOE'S THIRTEENTH LETTER, postmarked on October 17 from Lisbon, arrived at his mother's Urbana home on Halloween. Virginia wrote the unlucky number in a circle. Not superstitious. Fourteen will be here soon enough. This one from Europe. Never been myself. Would have wanted to go. Paris, London. Clean cities. Not enough bugs there to interest my former husband. She put the letter in the shoebox with its twelve predecessors and felt the growing chill and when dusk came she looked through the window every few minutes until the first trick-or-treaters arrived. Pirates, ghosts, store-bought Caspers and Batmen, homemade sheiks and mummies, crunching through the sidewalk carpets of brown leaves. My sons dressed as cowboys and demons back in the day. Steve probably divorced soon. Like me. Life's surprises. Look ahead. How many more numbers and circles on this trip before Joe comes back?

AT THE DOCKS IN LISBON, Joe watched a small woman with black hair join the line of passengers, and kept his eyes on her until she turned up and glanced at him. She gave him a perplexed squint of her big dark eyes.* A waif in a mint-green sundress, unmistakably Portuguese, and he immedi-

---

*What happens next is that I meet one of the great loves of my life. The Author spoke to this woman, and this frightens me. She's the one who told him about me carrying a gun, and she'll keep showing up for the rest of the book. What did she tell him? That I was sweet and handsome, of course. A dreamer like her, a kindred spirit. That's what he's whispering into my ear right now, to reassure me, because like all good book characters, I worry what My Author will do to me. She said she was still in love with me, fifty years later. So I guess that means I wasn't a total jerk, right?

ately associated her with the romance of Lisbon's narrow streets and vertical spaces. Later that night, he appeared at the door to her second-class berth. "We're having a party, you should come and join us." Mafalda was her name and she was twenty years old. She was going to London to work as a photographer's assistant, running away from her family; she was related to the counts and dukes of the fading Portuguese nobility, and had been engaged at eighteen to a socially connected man many years her senior, but she had dumped him for a vagabond life. After she related this biography to him, Joe studied her and saw a character in a nineteenth-century European novel, a person conjured by an author's imagination to represent some essential idea of the age in which they lived. Freedom. Impulsiveness. Vulnerability. Her English was fluent and she could also speak French and read Latin. Joe told her about his newest literary discovery: the French writer Jean Genet. *Our Lady of the Flowers.* And then Joe's British girlfriend found him, introduced herself to Mafalda and pulled Joe away. My man, mine. Not yours. Go find your own American.

The next afternoon Joe showed up at Mafalda's cabin door and she invited him in and they sat next to each other on her bunk. "What about your girlfriend?" "We broke up." The door was closed. Their lips met and they stepped out into the bright sun of the deck, the expanse of the Atlantic before them. He told her that he was a writer, and that the pursuit of his craft had taken him to rivers filled with diamonds in South America, and Caribbean islands with long-haired black rebels. Mafalda sensed they were both outcasts, and she squeezed his hands as if to feel the words that were inside them. She was only twenty and she still believed that magical things might happen to her in life, and she wondered if Joe Sanderson might be the first; in the luminous crown of his blond hair, and in the warmth of his demeanor, she thought she saw the nourishing future for which she longed. That night, in the dining room, Helen glared at Mafalda from across the dining room, but all the other young passengers in Joe's circle continued their conversations. Something about their geographic location (on a ship, between continents) and the historical moment (they were all in their twenties, living in the Space Age, on the cusp of the Age of Free Love), added giddiness to their repartee. They discussed existentialism, feminism and the death throes of colonialism; the late Lumumba, the martyred champion of African independence, and the pan-Arab leader of Egypt, Nasser. You must read this, that and the other, they said, and especially Simone de Beauvoir. They conversed amid dancing tobacco smoke and aphrodisiac sea-foam, and when they retired as couples to their boxy cabins they ceased their intellectual conversing and became slaves to their urges and undressed each other, contorting their bodies and hitting their elbows and ankles and skulls on the steel walls, until they were bruised, soothed and sex-sated.

In his cabin box, with Mafalda asleep next to him, Joe had an epiphany: He didn't want to be a novelist because he wanted the fame of being a writer. Necessarily. What he really wanted was a life as interesting as a novel. Like this: being afloat on the ocean next to a winsome Portuguese artist. A life where he didn't feel lonely and small, like a C student or a dropout. On this ship he was a hero. A movie star, a Romeo, a genius. As long as he kept moving, he'd be a hero over and over again. Mafalda stayed with Joe for the rest of their time at sea. They reached Southampton and Joe returned to the ship while she took a train to London. He was continuing on to Antwerp and Amsterdam. But before he left Europe he would circle back to London and see her, he said. "Don't worry, my little tramp." She did not entirely believe him as she watched him walk back toward the ship.

THE *ARLANZA* pulled into the port of Rotterdam. *Pounding the rails since dawn, so don't take my inarticulation seriously (as Grove Press did—dirty bastards). I get into Paris tonight, but still have my nose pointed toward North Africa. Europe, with all of its industrial force and precision, is a little claustrophobic after the aimless Latin American frenzy. Anxious*

to have sand in my shoes and sun in my eyes. Nothing here but smog and
chrysanthemums!

Paris was cold, overcast and filled with fashionable and beautiful women who were allergic to American bums. He felt lonely there, haunted by the ghost of Hemingway and the sight of other solitary people at the cafés, sitting at tables and scribbling into journals as he did. At the Pantheon, he said hello to Victor Hugo, and imagined the great author whispering epic stories from French history to the spiders in his crypt. He headed back to England and found Mafalda in the London flat she'd given as an address, sleeping on the floor of the living room (the flat belonged to a photographer friend) and they made quiet love there at night while the photographer slept in the next room, but Joe woke him up with his laughter. "Your laugh is beautiful," Mafalda whispered. "You're like a little boy with your laugh." They took long walks through the nippy autumn streets. After the second night, she woke up and found Joe was sleeping with a string tied to his big toe, and she followed the string into his bag, and saw it was tied to a gun. She thought of the black revolver later, when he asked her to come with him on his trip.

"It'll be a blast. Western Russia is a possibility. North Africa for sure."

"No, I can't." She said her job would start soon, but the truth was she felt a sense of foreboding. He made decisions quickly, rashly, and changed his mind from one moment to the next. As with Helen on the ship. First her, then me, who next?

JOE REACHED GIBRALTAR and Africa was a charcoal scratch on the canvas of the Mediterranean, and finally it became a town of white buildings sharpening into focus through Joe's spectacles as his ship floated toward it. Morocco. *Africa. Tangier,* he wrote home. *There's Coca-Cola in the casbah, yes, but much of the atmosphere seems not to have changed for centuries. Hooded robes, fezes, veils, opium dens, shop windows full of knives and guns and jeweled everything.* Tangier was filled with European road bums. As if someone had made a casting call to every university town between Manchester and Munich. Send us your philosophers and your dropouts and your junkie apprentices. And your painting students and your gay men and your bold women, yearning to wear Moroccan cotton and be free. *Tangier has more Beats than the Union building, if you can imagine that,* Joe wrote home.

At the insistence of the local drug peddlers, he partook of a taste of hashish. An entire valley of Jamaican ganja in a pebble of green, and a deeper understanding of the word *hallucination.* The crystals in the beach sand became a million blinding suns, and he was repulsed by the deafening sound of a seagull torturing a worm. He tried opium, and the flame and his inhaling breath produced a pleasantly pungent cloud of flower-smoke, and in a minute he was inside a dream of bliss, and he closed his eyes and saw the spring meadows of a perfect, unsullied land, and he felt all the joy and warmth of human existence would always be his. The next day he smoked it again, and a third day, and then he sold his .22 to buy more, until he realized that he would soon go broke chasing opium smoke, and he stopped and slept and vomited and suddenly he wanted to buy his .22 back and shoot someone.

AT ABOUT THIS SAME TIME, his mother was working at her desk at the bank when a young undergraduate walked past on the way to see a teller. Virginia thought he looked a bit like Joe; tall, clean-shaven, lanky strides. And then he turned to look at her, and she saw his pupils were dilated; he was a human with blue owl eyes, otherworldly, and in that instant she realized how far Joe was from her supervision, alone, on the other side of the world. For the rest of the day, she imagined her son in various drugged states. Vulnerable, not fully himself, suddenly a boy again. Like a kindergartner at a carnival, unaware of dangers, unaware of the possibility that a stranger might take him by the arm, and guide him away.

TWO DAYS LATER a detoxed Joe had tea at the Gran Café de Paris and wrote letters home, and a young man of about eighteen approached his table. He asked Joe, in English, "Are you a writer, mister?"

"Yes."

The young man had wiry hair and a whispery voice and introduced himself as Abdelqader and asked if Joe had met a Mr. Bowles, the most famous of the many foreign writers living in Tangier. "No," Joe said. Abdelqader said he was friends with Monsieur Bowles, who was in Paris at the moment. Monsieur Bowles had introduced Abdelqader to many other American writers who passed through Tangier, including a Mr. Truman Capote and a Mr. Williams Tennessee. Monsieur Bowles was helping a Moroccan writer with his memoir, Abdelqader continued. His name was Mohamed Choukri. Abdelqader and Monsieur Choukri were both Riffian Berber people who came from the mountains and Monsieur Choukri's book told the story of the drought there, and how Monsieur Choukri became a pickpocket and landed in jail, where he learned to read and write for the first time when he was twenty years old.

Abdelqader took the cloth bag he carried over his shoulder and showed Joe pages from a notebook filled with Arabic writing—his own book manuscript. Joe told Abdelqader about his travels, and when they parted Abdelqader watched as Joe walked down the street. A tabby cat followed after the American writer, and then a yellow dog, and after Joe disappeared into the medina, Abdelqader saw a hawk flying high above the street, and Abdelqader wondered if the animals were djinni sprits protecting the American Joe.

In his room in the medina that night, Joe listened to the call to prayer, sung at sundown by a voice at a mosque somewhere. The Arabic words were beyond his comprehension though the pious meaning could be felt in the intonations of the voice, the lilting vowels. Allah. No God but God. Mohammed is the messenger of God. Allah, one of the many names of God.

HE TOOK A TRAIN to Marrakesh and found swinging London women there, dressed in bright, short dresses, and German men in seersucker suits. Just off the Air France flight, sporting the latest fashions for an excursion to Africa. And the local people in loose-fitting kaftans and tightly wrapped *shesh* turbans and big, wide straw hats. Donkeys trotting in short strides and women selling grains from burlap bags as big as barrels. Magicians and child acrobats. Fiats and Citroëns parked in the plaza, and horse herds, and drooling camels, and men leading Barbary apes tied to strings. Boys selling water from leather bags, wearing tin drinking receptacles on their bodies. *Fantastic place, Marrakesh*, Joe wrote home, from a café adjacent to the mosque and its square-sided minaret. *Sitting on a rooftop terrace above the main plaza where a 19th-century Coney Island is in perpetual session. The Berber peasants have come down from the mountains to witness big city life, to see what all the stories were about. You name it, Marrakesh has got it. It's the most spectacular gathering of human beings I've ever seen.*

AFTER BUMMING HIS WAY BACK to the Moroccan coast, Joe wrote to Mafalda for the first time. *The road was long and hard between you and here*, the letter began. *The mountains, the crumbling cities, the ragged people— everything was so desolate and deadly I didn't care what happened to me. Walking across the desert picking up crystals, sang ballads to the sun, watched the evening haze leave the mountain peaks. Don't laugh but it looked like Heaven. Rode trucks, motorcycles, buses, cars, burros. Smoked hash with the Arabs, ate roast chicken and toasted almonds, drank mint tea, watched camels pulling wooden plows, black goats climbing thorny trees, saw child beggars blinded by cataracts.* He mentioned nothing about returning to London and told her to write him care of the embassy in Cairo.

THE LIBYAN DESERT was dunes and hollows, and stone-covered plains, and then a steady wind that lifted up curtains of sand, followed by sheets of rain. Fat drops on the windshield, and a current flowing over the highway, ankle-deep. *So, one bitch of a desert sandstorm and several thousand miles later—Cairo! Can't remember where I mailed my last letter. Tunisia? Anyway, thereabouts. Hitchhiked through both Algeria and Tunisia and was just cleaning my toenails for the long run across Libya when I latched onto an impossible lift to Cairo. Met an old Swedish man at the Libyan Embassy in Tunis who was driving through in a VW van. Had picked up a Limey roadbum in Morocco (17 yrs. old, someone slipped him a mickey in Tangiers. Lost nearly all his $). On our second day, we picked up an Argentine student. Slept in the van, ate sardines and got pretty grimy after 2,400 miles.* There was a letter waiting from Mafalda in Cairo, and he penned a reply from his next stop. *Beautiful letters, my dear little tramp. Steals that wonderful laughter you claim I possess. Egyptian sun is burning and I'm half-naked on a rooftop just across the Nile from the Valley of the Kings. My pleasantly insane life moves on by the thousands of miles. So absurd, yes, but more absurd to stay home like everyone else.*

In Alexandria, Joe failed to find a ship that would take him to Beirut, and hopped on a flight to Damascus, a city of women veiled in black, and women in makeup and hair-sprayed bobs, and poor old men in gray suits pushing carts, and young Syrian dandys in polished leather shoes and girls in white stockings. He hitchhiked across Syria toward Jordan and

Jerusalem, and got a room in the Old City, which in those days was still part of Jordan. *Brother Jesus got here on a donkey*, he wrote home, *while I managed a maroon '66 Dodge 440—how about that!* When he dropped off his letter at the post office, Joe thought of home, and the snow that was likely falling there, and how long it would take for his letter to reach his family. He took a few steps to the window where telegrams could be sent, and paid for a short message home.

ON CHRISTMAS EVE in Urbana, a motorcycle puttered to a stop before Virginia Colman's home, and a uniformed man walked up to the door. Western Union.

=MUCH LOVE TO EVERYONE AT HOME MERRY CHRISTMAS
FROM JERUSALEM=
=JOE=

At Christmas dinner, Virginia read Joe's letters from North Africa out loud at the table, censoring the few cuss words and the mention of drugs, so as not to scandalize Joe's grandmother. For the first time, Virginia had put up an aluminum Christmas tree. Calhoun's idea. Much neater, put it away and reuse it every year.

WHEN JOE STUCK OUT HIS TONGUE to seal an envelope addressed to his mother, he could feel the words he wanted to speak but couldn't put in a letter. Yeah, I should be in college, Mom, but I'm not. The world is my classroom, and one day I'll write a book, and that will be my degree. Instead, as always, he described the dramatic events of the road. He'd seen the Jordanian army guarding the holy sites in Bethlehem and the Old City, and stood by the entrance to the Mandelbaum Gate, a passageway through the no-man's-land between Israel and Jordan. *On Friday, Israel opened up the barbed wire to 6,000 Christian Arabs. I was there to watch them cross into Jordan. Wasn't cheerful.* He took a bus to Beirut on New Year's Eve and found a city without a care in the world, the Riviera of the Middle East. A little taste of Paris with souks and high-rise hotels and flashing walls of neon hawking Coca-Cola in Arabic. In the first hours of 1967 Beirut became a screaming, joyful party of Christians and Arabs and Druze, and Sunni and Shi'ite, and Armenians. Gunshots fired into the air, here, there, everywhere, a celebratory discharge of revolvers. *Complete insanity*, Joe wrote home.*

JOE WAS NEARLY HALFWAY around the world from Illinois, and he was bumming now with homeward momentum. He hitchhiked from Beirut to Damascus to Baghdad, where the day revealed a dusty metropolis of wide avenues and cafés that were filled with backgammon players and tea drinkers. He ate a delicious salted fish, watched boys roll up their pants to run into the Tigris, and stood before a mosque of inlaid green and blue stones that was so beautiful he wanted to go inside and fall on his knees and pray. Night came and Baghdad turned quiet and he turned in. *Nothing there but a slow muddy river and Babylon*, he wrote home. He hitchhiked across southern Iraq the next day, standing once at the edge of a sunflower field, listening to an air force of bees until a grizzled Iraqi in a pickup truck stopped and gestured for him to climb in the back, and in this way Joe made it across more sunflower and onion fields, through

---

*The Author is in a hurry. I want him to slow down and smell those Damascus flowers again. I suppose you all are in a hurry too, and anxious to get to the "good" parts, the war we've promised you. But let me just say this: take a moment to appreciate the world as it was. Because just about everywhere I went on this bumming trip, war will follow in my footsteps; even in that café in Morocco I visited, where some jerk planted a bomb to kill the tourists. And Beirut, and Syria. Well, y'all know the story.

marshlands, and eventually to a desert filled with broken-down cars and lifeless khaki sand, and finally a sad border town with a few gray buildings resembling bunkers, and two cigarette-smoking soldiers of the Iraqi army, leaning against a rusty armored car, looking southward, blowing smoke toward Kuwait.

The Japanese visa in his passport gave Joe a sense of purpose; by his own calculations he was more than halfway around the world now, and he'd skirt the Indian Ocean on his way back to the western hemisphere. In Kuwait City, where fleets of German and British luxury vehicles roamed the streets, he headed to the beach, and saw huge tankers just offshore, headed for America; and then, on the sand itself, a grounded ship. A black freighter with a white superstructure and clouded windows, listing diagonally like a drunk struggling to stand upright. Joe walked up to the vessel and was greeted by an American with long blond surfer hair and a saintly smile who was standing on the stern, leaning over the railing.

"American? Yes? Cool. Welcome, brother! Welcome to Noah's Ark!"

The ship was occupied by a score of American and European devotees of the Meher Baba, a spiritualist from India, and their ranks included *a sandals-wearing, very decent, lamblike beatnik* who had been *a confirmed drug addict for 8 years until Brother Baba let him in on the love bit. Beatnik is currently bumming around the world (with German wife) to spread the good news and get other road bums off drugs.* Among the reformed addicts there was *a California bum and his broad, a friend from Boston and a black dog.* They went off into the city every day to beg for money from the Kuwaitis. Some of the Noah's Ark crew were going to India too, so he hitched a ride with them—in another VW van, listening over and over again to the same ten Beatles songs crooning from the small speaker of a cassette player. In Basra, Iraq. *I once had a girl, or should I say, she once had me.* In Shirāz, Iran, driving past olive trees and a gorgeous eighteenth-century castle. *I once had a girl, or should I say, she once had me.*

In Zāhedān, Iran, near the Pakistani border, Joe wrote home, describing the beat-up van and the Noah's Ark crew. *Beautiful, beautiful people. Have been pounding the road hard with them—flat tires, engine trouble, lost dog, etc.—the whole way across the Great Salt Desert, but anxious to get to India so it doesn't matter.* His next cash infusion from home was waiting in New Delhi, and he said goodbye to them at the steps to the U.S. Embassy there, and they kissed him and wished him well.

IN NEW DELHI, Joe was overwhelmed by the great metropolis and its hand-pushed ambition, the frenzy of its people hauling and lifting their way into modernity. *Forgive my unhurriedness, my mellow meandering ways.* Joe felt inconsequential in New Delhi, and also on the train to Bombay and back. He headed for what he hoped would be the relative tranquility of Nepal, on a bus, passing beasts of burden shaking hips as they hauled carts, through the plains of Uttar Pradesh, over long bridges crossing wide rivers and their riverine beaches and frolicking bathers. On the second day, his bus slithered uphill on a curvy highway into green mountains, and finally it reached a city of pigeons and men with painted faces. Kathmandu. *The city is loaded with pagodas + temples + shrines + holy places of all sorts,* he wrote home. *One mountaintop temple outside of town looks like the Land of Oz. Not surprising, since this is Shangri-La country. But I suppose Shangri-La is just another name for wherever you aren't, the greener pasture. And for me right now, Shangri-La is cherry pie and a bowl of tuna and noodles.* Having already reached the figurative bottom of the world on this trip (Tierra del Fuego), Joe decided he should try for the figurative top, and he headed for a mountain town said to be within sight of Everest, and reached a hostel in a valley filled with the smell of onions.

JOE WAS BACK IN KATHMANDU, sitting alone and doing some late-morning patching of his jeans with a needle and thread at his hostel, when he looked through the open doorway and saw a young woman with a burlap bag walking past on the street outside. She peeked in to Joe's hostel and he waved at her, and she waved back, and disappeared. Joe dropped his sewing and walked out and found her applying something with tape to a pole down the block. A small strip of paper. He approached her and she smiled at him while he read.

When the forests have been destroyed their darkness remains.

And then a second.

The nights disappear like bruises but nothing is healed.

"Poetry?"

"Yes, I clipped a bunch from magazines back home," the woman said. "And I'm leaving them scattered around like this. All over Asia, I guess."

Rebecca Olmsted was as tall as Joe, with thick, curly hair she pulled back and tied up over her head in a blond ice cream swirl. She showed him the clipped lines of poems she carried in her bag, along with a pair of scissors and several rolls of Scotch tape. "I could use some tape," Joe said. One of his two pairs of eyeglasses had broken in India, and so they returned together to his hostel to fix them. She was a graduate student on hiatus from the history department at the University of Wisconsin, and she had set off from Madison with her boyfriend. They made it to Australia and Thailand, but said dude had ditched her in East Pakistan. "He left me! On the road! Alone! Asshole!" But she kept going, and only now, in the presence of friendly Joe ("You're such a good listener, thank you"), did she realize how tired she was. "You can bum with me if you want," Joe said, and that night they fell asleep holding hands. Two mutually exhausted Midwesterners, like a farm couple, spent after the harvest. Sleep. After crossing oceans and continents—her to the west, me to the east—we meet on the opposite side of the world. Rebecca became his new bumming purpose: getting her home, protecting her.

They agreed to travel westward together, toward Europe, which was Rebecca's original destination. They bused back into India, to the valley of Kashmir, and to Srinagar, where they slept in a houseboat hotel on a lake: The Golden Hopes, a bungalow palace of bright, aromatic wood tied to the shore amid reeds and lily pads. At night, Joe slept platonically next to Rebecca and awoke around midnight to the sound of water lapping against the boat and Rebecca crying in her sleep. They headed for the resorts of the Western Himalayas, and a mountain trek. *Rode horseback six miles and walked the rest*, he wrote in his next letter home. *Picked up skis from Indian snow soldiers. Incredibly beautiful countryside—roof-high snow, tunnels to the doors, blue sky and hot sun.* They went through the last of Joe's Delhi money, and began spending Rebecca's cash, with Joe promising to pay her back. In his next letter home Joe asked Steve to send him more money to the U.S. Embassy in Damascus—an advance, since he'd spent the last of his flagpole savings.

The long road to Damascus began by crossing between the two armies at the India-Pakistan border, walking past barbed-wire fences and sandbags and machine-gun posts. Then they hitchhiked quickly through Pakistan, through Islamabad and Peshawar toward Afghanistan. "With a girl, you never have to wait more than one truck to get a ride," Joe observed.

"I'd never hitchhike alone," Rebecca said. "Not even here. Even though, I have to say, this place seems pretty safe. The Pashtuns are pretty cool people. Peaceful, I guess." They were passing through a corner of the globe ruled by feudal lords, and from inside the cab of a truck carrying propane tanks they saw Pashtun boys wearing embroidered cylinders on their heads and long robes, and girls in brightly colored scarves with raven bangs showing. The landscape turned scrubby and rocky, and they took a bus that climbed into the Khyber Pass, and Rebecca gave Joe a brief history of the place, yelling loudly to be heard over the engine. "The Aryans in 1600 BC! Alexander the Great in 300 BC! The British Army in 1842!" The bus climbed as the driver shifted gears, again and again, around one hairpin turn and another, and Joe looked out the windshield and saw two hawks high above the pass, mimicking the turning road in their graceful downward glides.

WELCOME TO AFGHANISTAN read the sign at the little border post at the top of the pass. The customs agents served them green tea. In the market in Kabul Joe bought two old flintlock pistols for five dollars each. Kabul was clean and spare, a city freshly swept each day by thousands of brooms made from wide fans of straw. In the dark of a Kabul hotel room, under a spinning fan, Joe felt the beauty of this bumming journey and their youth, and he looked over at Rebecca meaningfully, and she crossed over from her bed to his. The next morning they hitchhiked onward into the Afghan country-side, through valleys of delicate green grasses, and past shallow streams and ranges of dry mountains, and the altitude and the pelvic-memory of making love to Rebecca lulled Joe into a long, midday sleep. When he awoke, he saw their driver had stopped before a collection of mud-walled compounds; a veiled woman exited and reentered an opening in one of these walls, and Joe realized an entire community lived inside; he sensed that if he followed her, he'd be married off to a girl inside, and find an epic and ancient Afghan story to write, but he would never be let out to share it. At sundown they reached the final stretch of road near the Persian border, past the town of Herāt, and their driver pulled his Ford over to the side of the road suddenly; they stepped out and heard distant gunfire. Rebecca crouched instinctively, and the driver motioned for them to get back inside, and they turned around and drove back to Herāt. In town there was much speaking in Pashto and Tajik, and the distant gunshots grew in frequency and became a fusillade. Some sort of battle. Who was fighting? No one could explain, until Joe finally found an English speaker at the local police station who said, "It's the tribes." No further explanation was forthcoming. The firing stopped and the police officer at the desk gave a loud yawn, and that night Joe and Rebecca slept on the floor of the police station, until the same officer woke them up at dawn with a big grin and said, "Yes, yes. Go, go. You go. Okay, okay." He shuffled them out of the station like a farmer chasing chickens out of their pen. As it happened, their next ride was with a truck carrying chickens; it dropped them off at the town of Islam Kala, where Joe stopped at the local post office, purchased an "aerogramme" and penned a letter home. *Slight skirmish in the last village. Ended up sleeping in the cop shop. Still not sure what crap was involved, but interesting nonetheless.*

They moved quickly through Iran, and arrived at the modern metropolis of Teheran. Inside the maze of the city's Grand Bazaar, a young man in a tie accosted them. "You! American? How are you? Greetings and welcomings to Persia!" He was a filmmaker, he said, the Persian assistant director in an Israeli production filming in Teheran. "This is the Hollywood of the Middle East." After a brief back-and-forth in which they discussed Joe and Rebecca's travels, the director offered them a part in the next movie he was working on.

"Who do we play?"

"An American couple visiting Persia."

In his next letter home Joe described his momentary flirtation with Middle Eastern stardom. *They were finishing an Israeli flick and prepared to start on the next one. After showing us around the local sets, the cutting room, laying a dinner on us, they made their offer. Said all of our expenses would be paid before the shooting started. Sounded nice, we told ourselves. But we declined. You didn't need a movie star anyway, huh? More from Damascus.*

Postmarked from Teheran, the letter arrived in Urbana some ten days later. Virginia marked it twenty-eight. The next letter, number twenty-nine, was dated May 11, and described his arrival with his new female friend (another one?) into Jordan. *Rebecca and I showed up at the American Embassy dirty and tired, up most of the night (two hours' sleep at a Jordanian cop* *shop) having hitchhiked from the Persian border. She wearing blue jeans and denim jacket and leather sandals and a red hankie over hair (looking like an itinerant apple picker), me likewise passing for some brand of bindlestiff.* Before that, they had passed quickly through Baghdad and the Iraqi town of Ramadi, where Rebecca had decided to give away most of what she was carrying, because her bumming would soon be over. And in this lighter state they reached Syria, and then Jordan and prepared to cross into Israel.*

THE MANDELBAUM GATE leading into Israel was not a gate, but rather a roadway many hundreds of yards long, running through the no-man's-land between the armistice lines fixed a generation earlier after the 1948 Arab-Israeli war. A Jordanian soldier with a machine gun hanging over his shoulder checked their papers, studying Joe's clean-shaven passport portrait as if it would speak back to him and comment on the unshaven twin about to leave the Kingdom of Jordan. The soldier returned the passport to Joe and stretched out his arm westward. Go forth, young Americans, into the Territory Whose Name I Cannot Speak. Joe and Rebecca entered a cobblestone road, and Joe felt the heel on his left shoe going loose. I'm not going to make it home with these. They passed empty lots of white, rocky soil, and the remains of a villa bombed in the last war, and streets where weeds were colonizing the pavement. They were in the

---

*Do you envy me? Resent me? I wouldn't blame you. I can't quite believe it myself. An average Joe, wandering around the future sites of various regional apocalypses without a care in the world. Making new girlfriends here and there. My letters are carefree, but I didn't have blinders on, I swear. These messages home were to my mom, remember, and like a good boy I didn't want her to worry. Secretly, I was scared shitless. Scared someone would drop a mickey into our drinks and kidnap Rebecca and do horrible things to her. Scared that I'd wind up in some Middle Eastern jail. Scared that Rebecca might fall in love with me, or worse—that I'd fall for her. Always a little scared. But that's something a good Midwestern boy would never tell his mom, and make her worry, maybe for nothing.

purgatory between two states defending different ideas of man's relationship to God. Inside a metaphor filled with rubble and litter. A rusting ruin of a bicycle. Soldiers in blue berets appeared on the roadway, and a blue United Nations flag, and finally the cement cones of tank traps. Then, an Israeli flag.

After inspecting Joe's documents, an Israeli soldier riffled through Joe's rucksack and discovered the flintlock pistols Joe had purchased in Afghanistan and confiscated them. The ancient firearms suggested Joe was headed to a duel somewhere, and the soldier presented them to a sergeant with gray hair, perfect American English and the even temperament of a school principal. "Sir, this is very, very serious. Why are you bringing weapons into our country?"

"I was traveling among the Arabs," Joe said. "With an American woman." The sergeant asked him where he was from, and Joe said, "Urbana, Illinois." The sergeant gave a knowing nod. "You look like Paul Newman," the sergeant said. "But not like the Paul Newman in *The Hustler.* More like that flick where he plays Billy the Kid." In the letter he wrote that night, Joe described the incredibly high prices in Israel, the friendliness of the locals they met (*nothing but, "Shalom, shalom"*), and the rumblings of war. "Six Syrian planes shot down two weeks earlier in the north." He and Rebecca visited a memorial to the Holocaust, and a beach where Rebecca found a utility pole to tape the last lines of poetry she was carrying. *The light was full of salt . . . and the air was heavy with crying for where the wave had come from.* They belatedly celebrated Joe's twenty-fifth birthday with a glass of wine and took a ship to Cyprus, and from there a plane to Athens, and finally a last jaunt to Istanbul, where his next letter home began: *Don't panic, but I'm in the hospital for the next few days. Whatever could be wrong with a person's head—I've got it. Believe throwing it away is the best solution.* But he was well enough, at least, to comment on the march toward war in the Middle East. *Glad I had a chance to get through all the countries involved before things got really hashed up.*

HIS LETTER FROM ISTANBUL was his thirty-first and last letter home on this trip, dated May 27; when Virginia received it in Urbana, she wrote the number in a circle on the envelope. By then, on June 6, the Israelis had destroyed the entire Egyptian Air Force. There was fighting in Jerusalem, and Israeli paratroopers had crossed the no-man's-land and entered the Old City, and the Jordanian army had abandoned its posts on the Mandelbaum Gate, never to return. Joe told people afterward that he and Rebecca were the last Americans to pass through the Mandelbaum Gate before it was dismantled. He thought there was a good chance that was actually true.

IN ISTANBUL, Rebecca slept in the hospital alongside Joe until the doctors said he was well enough to leave. They parted ways, Rebecca going home to Chicago via plane, from Istanbul via Dublin and New York. At the airport, they said their goodbyes. Rebecca gave him a final kiss on the cheek. Joe's last words were, "I'll pay you back, I promise," which left her hurt and angry, though Joe only realized this once he'd walked away. Three days later, in London, Joe blew it again, with Mafalda. He had not written to her since he was in Egypt five months earlier. When the door to her flat opened, his ocean lover froze and her eyes opened wide. She embraced him the way a child squeezes a teddy bear. "My God, you're so thin. Have you been sick?"

Joe and Mafalda walked through Crouch End and the springtime light. Sunday shuttered shops and the promise of warmer and longer days to come. They held hands and held each other on the living room floor of the flat where she was staying, and she told him what had happened to her, after Joe had left London all those months ago . . .

Whoa, hold on a second there, partner. Stop. No sir, I will not allow this.
And I demand you lift me from the footnotes so I can say so. The Author,

being a Ruthless Fucking Bastard, is about to reveal something that happened between me and Mafalda. Involving a certain unforeseen biological event, and a woman doctor in Lisbon. In the name of privacy, libel law, and common decency, stop! Let's just say she told the Author this unforeseen biological event made her feel closer to me, and then very angry with me too. This is the sort of thing that happens to men and women over and over again, all over the world. It's my story, mine, and hers, and I'd like to keep it that way.

. . . JOE LISTENED, and cried with Mafalda, and after his tears were dry he announced he had to leave. "I thought you'd stay," Mafalda said. "A week or two at least."

"I owe people money. I have to get back up on the flagpole and earn some cash."*

Mafalda heard herself saying, "I'll take you to the train station," and walked next to him and rode the Underground with him, stunned. When they were about to say goodbye, he said, "Hey, I almost forgot. I brought you back a present. From India." He handed her a cardboard box that was the length of her palm. She took it without saying thank you, and accepted a last passionate kiss from him, and watched as Joe walked away and boarded the train. Rugged, unfeeling. A lesson for her about the mind of the American male. Her next lover would be British, but a man fated to a tragic end. She made her way back to the Underground and rode back toward her flat. When she reached Highgate Station, she stood up to get off and left the box on her seat. A woman sitting on the opposite aisle called out to her.

"You forgot your box."

---

*Where I come from, owing people money is about the worst thing you can do. A lot worse than being rude, or slipping away from someone who wants to hug and hold and kiss you.

"I don't want it." She walked onto the platform and heard the Underground's doors closing behind her.

AFTER TWO DAYS on rails and in the air and on rails again, Joe arrived at Champaign, Illinois. He hitched a ride from the train station home, holding out his thumb on University Avenue, figuring it would be faster than the bus. A guy driving a Coca-Cola truck picked him up.

"Where you headed?"

"Home. Here. Urbana, close by. Just down the street."

As Joe lifted up his rucksack into the cab, the trucker asked, "Long trip?"

"Yeah."

"So, where you been?"

"Everywhere."

12.

Lafayette, Louisiana. Los Angeles.
Oakland, California. Hokkaido, Japan.
Seoul. Saigon, Republic of Vietnam

POLECAT. FELINE. Scaling high places using my four limbs and paws. Nine lives. Brush, brush, brush. The principal looking up at me. He likes my work. Not as dangerous as it looks, no. One day not long ago a hippie climbed this flagpole, dragged down Old Glory, and then raised it again—upside down. Treasonous, the principal said. But the hippie did call attention to the rusting pole, its unpatriotic oxidation. Don't worry, sir, this here polecat has come to the rescue. Joe liked the quiet. After the Sahara and the Himalayas, and the Strait of Magellan and the Khyber Pass—a summer in

Illinois and Indiana, the breezes and long drives through the corn growing crazy tall. Again. In the streets of the cities and towns he visited: sunshine and a sudden craze for Japanese gadgets. His country and its charming customs more in focus than ever. The 4-H fair and the Turtle Days Festival. Girls in braces and sequined leotards, twirling batons. At his mother's house, he watched television commercials for instant oatmeal. Cooks in one minute. Calhoun opened the paper to stock tables and weather reports. In the United States of America, we have a deep faith in the things we can count, track and measure. Soil acidity, rates of return, gasoline prices. Predictable seasonal trends and objectively verifiable truths. Forty-six inches of average annual rain, the principal said. That's why it needs painting. Brush, brush, brush.

The Midwestern skies brought one day after another of superb painting weather and Joe bought a mattress and tossed it in the back of his truck ("Old Yeller" he called it) along with ladders, ropes and cans of paint. In an Indianapolis department store, he stopped before a display of color televisions one evening and watched snippets of the tropical drama unfolding on NBC and CBS. Troops with untucked shirts and extra ammo followed paths into the jungle. Vietnam. He imagined the caw-caw of unseen birds, and was struck by how informal the soldiers looked: like road bums, but with machine guns over their shoulders. Running their fingers through baskets of rice and flattening the knee-high grass, suddenly, with their wounded bodies. Riding canvas slings to waiting helicopters.

Fall came and the U of I students returned to town in a cavalcade of automobiles and station wagons stuffed with their belongings. They shuffled about the city with their unbuttoned shirts and pillow-heads of hair. The well-groomed Beat was extinct, and America was loosening up, becoming dreamier. One afternoon Joe walked onto campus and saw a group of undergrads sitting in a circle on the quad lawn, holding hands, eyes closed, as if in group prayer. The huge Illinois sky flickered above them. A cloud screen drifted across the sun, and its shadow raced across the wide lawn, like a pool of ink spilling across the grass, or like a specter in a horror film, or like a metaphor for a disease or an alien invasion.

Joe's first published novel was still waiting for him out on the road someplace. "Action" was the missing ingredient. When he sent Rebecca a letter with the money he owed her, she wrote back to ask if he'd be interested in hitting the road again. *You never did finish your trip around the world. Because of me.* Joe proposed East Asia to her, and Vietnam, and to his surprise the future Professor Olmsted agreed. He imagined writing a playboy-bum-visits-the-Vietnam-War novel, and shared this idea with Jim Adams, who told him it was the dumbest thing he'd ever heard, and dangerous too. Joe's friends in Urbana were unanimous in this opinion, which made him more determined to go. In early February 1968, with central Illinois still winter gray, he said goodbye to his mother again. His plan was to drive Old Yeller to Louisiana and Texas and paint flagpoles and earn more money and slowly make his way westward toward California, where he'd meet Rebecca in San Francisco for the trip to the Far East. He parked his truck in the driveway of the new home his mother and Calhoun had moved into, on Slayback Road, and had a farewell breakfast with them.

"Great oatmeal, Mom. This sure ain't instant," he said.

"No, it isn't," she said. "Make sure you write home, son. We really enjoy your letters. Granny especially."

STARTING IN THE TOWN OF MONROE, Joe worked his way through Louisiana, and by late February, he was in Lafayette. *Worked the whole day of Mardi Gras.* From his flagpole perch, he listened to the trumpets and vomiting of the celebrants below. *Jesus, can these Cajuns drink. Let 'em stagger home on their own.* In Lake Charles, he caught the attention of local law enforcement. "Son, we had a little robbery over at the school where you were working." Joe was a young, long-haired carpetbagger sleeping in his truck, so of course he fell under suspicion. "Come into the station at two p.m., if you could," an officer told him. It happened again on the other side of the state border, in Orange, Texas. *A local grocery store got robbed and I'm to report again tomorrow to see if the owner can identify me. Something happens in town, so they raid the gypsy camp.*

The Texas schools were too poor to pay him much, so he headed into New Mexico and got work here and there. He blew out a muffler climbing through Arizona, and when he entered California his truck sounded like *a Kentucky moonshine runner. Real class.* In the southernmost reaches of the Golden State, near the Mexican border, he made $395. *Not bad pay for getting a suntan (sorry) and a beautiful view of the Pacific.* Joe followed the freeways toward Los Angeles, and on a smoggy night he reached that city, turning off on Sunset Boulevard while listening to the voice of the president of the United States on the transistor radio on his seat: with the Vietnam War going poorly, Lyndon Johnson was announcing he would not run for reelection. *Evening newspapers hit the Hollywood streets at 11:00 p.m. with hardly an eyelash flutter from the drag queens,* Joe wrote home. *Nary a weepy tear spilled for LBJ.* Feather boas and Stingrays, carnal transactions on the street corners and outside the nightclubs. The Whisky a Go Go. Is that Peter Fonda? The actor? It is! Surrounded by a cool tribe of men in polka-dot silk shirts and striped pants, and women in long corduroy jackets and high leather boots taking sultry drags from their Virginia Slims and king-size Kools, blowing unfriendly smoke at the Illinois polecat when he deigns to say "Howdy!"

After getting hassled by the LAPD for sleeping in his truck, he tore up his climbing ropes and left Los Angeles, driving north on the Pacific Coast Highway, toward the famous cliffs of Big Sur, and the big bay and the cities beyond.

HE PICKED UP REBECCA at Oakland Airport and they met up with her friends, a racially integrated group of Berkeley graduate students and activists, including a Black Panther supporter named Oscar who was an under-grad at San Francisco State. Oscar was secretly carrying a gun tucked into the pocket of his jacket. Joe could sense the weight of it bouncing, unseen, mayhem waiting in a metal mass the size of a fist. They traveled to an anti-war demonstration at the Alameda County Courthouse, which included the burning of draft cards and the polite retreat of the mostly white protest-ers when the police arrived. The next day, Joe was less than impressed by the youth carnival to be found in San Francisco, the public pot-smoking in Golden Gate Park, hitchhikers everywhere, teenage parents carrying in-fants with unwiped faces. This was the bumming lifestyle taken to a farci-cal, trendy and static extreme.

Sold my truck on Hippy Lane (Haight-Ashbury). $235.00 cash, Joe wrote home. *Know I could have made more from the interest shown, but didn't feel like hanging out on the street any longer. Most everybody there was hustling something. Shades of Tangier. "Opium? Hash? Speed? Acid?" And there I am half asleep in the sunshine, curled up on the hood, with Rebecca holding up the keys and whispering on the sidewalk: "Truck? Truck? Truck?"*

Joe was sitting on the curb next to Rebecca, counting his money for the third time, when they heard a gasp coming from the nearby liquor store. A young white woman of about twenty came out, tears welling in her eyes.

"Someone shot Martin Luther King!"

The news spread along the Haight sidewalks, and very soon many ra-dios were tuned, as if in chorus, to the same San Francisco station. The great prophet of Negro liberation was wounded, and soon afterward he was dead, and that night the radios of the city filled with descriptions of burn-ing cities, and the recorded speeches of the fallen leader, Southern talk-singing his way to the peroration, and Joe felt his country and its people slipping further into malevolence and unreason.

Three days later all was placid and plastic at the San Francisco airport. Joe was traveling alone: Rebecca said she'd meet him in Hawaii a few days later. Her Black Panther friends had gone into hiding, after other Panthers had ambushed the Oakland police. Rebecca wanted to stay to see how it all played out. After *two months of dirt and death* on the American road, as he wrote home later, Joe stood alone among the carefree and cash-rich American vacationers at the United Airlines terminal, listening to them talk about Hawaiian luaus. He entered the great aluminum tube of a Boeing 720, and was sedated and luxurified by stewardesses with soft, efficient hands who gave him headphones to plug into the sound system, and a steaming teriyaki steak meal.

JOE SPENT TWO DAYS alone in Hawaii. Rebecca arrived, and they boarded a flight to Japan together. *Arrived in Tokyo last Saturday night,* he wrote home. *Walked the town until way past midnight, Japanese goose pimples over Hawaiian sunburn. Cherry blossom spring right now. Cold at night, but hot in the daytime. The Baby and I slept in a subway station until dawn.*

Joe proposed they hitchhike to the northern tip of Japan; from there, they'd be able to catch a glimpse of the Soviet Union. Sure, Rebecca said. He likes faraway and remote places. Why is that? If he could, he'd hitchhike to the North Pole and bum a ride with a pack of polar bears over the top back down through Canada. To be alone in the big emptiness, that's his thing. Well, not alone entirely. With me. Calls me "Baby." I'll take that. Only problem: I'm never alone with him. Hotels too expensive. Sleeping in rooms with people he's charmed with his road tales and American-hobo optimism. Maybe we can sneak into the forest somewhere in Hokkaido, just me and him alone with the famous snow monkeys staring at us. A sex show for the primates. And then back south again, hitchhiking all the way across Japan for Kobe and Osaka and a ship to Pusan, Korea. I want to tell him this is sort of crazy, but it's kind of beautiful and exciting too, this geography quest, this curiosity, his hunger for the next country, the next encounter, the next family to invite us for warm soup and noodles and a mat to sleep on. Everyone says they are pleased to have us as honored guests. We are young and beautiful and boundless. Free of hang-ups and rigid think-ing. Joe will write a lovely book about us. They returned to Tokyo just long enough for tall, striking, blond Rebecca to catch the eye of a wandering casting director and earn a part in a Japanese television show. *Serial about gold smugglers,* Joe wrote home. *Filmed her in a nightclub dancing in ten-nis shoes, exactly one foot taller than her Japanese partner. Made $10. I had to settle on potato chips and making time with the lead actress.*

On the ship as it left Ōsaka, between drags and puffs of cigarette smoke floating over Ōsaka Bay, Joe outlined his plans for their Korean jaunt.

"I think we can get close to the action. There's a war going on there. In the DMZ."

"The what? I thought the Korean War had ended."

"The demilitarized zone. It's a low-level-type thing."

"Is it dangerous?"

"No, Baby. The polecat would never place you in danger. We're just going to take in the ambience. The warlike ambience. The movement of the troops, the steely expressions of the soldiers."*

IN HIS LETTERS, Joe did not tell his mother he was headed into a war zone. And when Virginia received his missives, she thought about how content Joe sounded, writing from an exotic corner of the globe where they spoke in the languages depicted on the stamps. Ideograms, indecipherable to her.

---

*What was I doing? Seeking out war like this? I take it young folks these days aren't quite as daring. They've seen too much real-life death and gunfire on television. We were innocent that way; on TV we were watching moms bake apple pie and serving it on checkered tablecloths. When our movie heroes died, it was in black-and-white. Death wasn't gory and stark and in color. And yeah, I'll admit it: looking for war on the road seemed like a game to me. But very soon I'm going to get my first education in true violence. It wasn't in Korea; though Korea was crazy enough, as you'll soon see.

Gone so long, home so briefly. She was growing into his absence and the sound of the world without his voice in it. The Joe-free routines, work hours and home with Calhoun, good man, good listener, even-tempered and attentive. Her second husband never complained on the daylong drive to Kansas for Colman family gatherings. In Lawrence, her sister and jars of preserves in the basement. See how hard I've been working? I am the keeper of the family legacy, Virginia, and you are the woman who counts things and calls that work. Divorced, remarried, so modern, Virginia. Women's lib. The country changing all around us, even in Lawrence. Bobby Kennedy here, at the University of Kansas, to tell everyone he's running for president, standing on a car, shaking hands in the rain. All the Jayhawk rabble-rousers excited for Kennedy. You going to vote for him? "Not likely," Virginia said. "Nixon's the one. I think this may finally be his year."

JOE AND REBECCA hitchhiked north from Pusan, toward Seoul. Past rice paddies, farmers fighting beasts of burden dragging wooden plows, and then a crossroads and a town of shacks beaten down by the rain. A woman in a soaked pink dress with sleeves, carrying water, drops falling from the sky into her bucket. *First impression of Korea—most of them U.S. recovery dollars must have found their way into Swiss banks. Not too prosperous, this country. Orphanages, leprosariums, and various other institutes for war-gimpy survivors. Hitchhiked into Seoul with Jeeps and Army trucks. U.S. soldiers damn friendly to us, but arrogant toward village locals. What happened to good old GI Joe passing out candy to the kids? No more.* In Seoul, Joe and Rebecca dodged trams and stood beneath the old, fragile and tinder-dry wood of the city's medieval gates, then headed north, into an unhealed, cratered landscape that was thicker with soldiers in ponchos and their weaponry.

Joe told the GIs they met on the road that Rebecca was an actress. With her hair down, and brushed out, she looked like one. "She's famous in the Far East and the Middle East."

"So why is she hitchhiking? With you?"

"She's incognito. Researching her next part. A drama about the Korean War. She plays a woman who's fallen in love with a soldier who goes missing."

Being in the back of an army truck got them past three different checkpoints, through brushy stretches of watershed, until they crossed a river and entered a denuded land, with half-empty villages and watchtowers and barbed wire. Great walls of sandbags. One of the soldiers said North Korean artillery shells fell randomly here, now and then. They were still many kilometers from Panmunjom when they reached one last checkpoint, and everyone jumped off, startling the military policeman who found two grinning tourists among the GIs.

"Who the hell are you people? Hitchhikers? How the hell did you get this far? Don't you realize this is a fucking war zone!"*

Joe wrote an amused letter home. *We seem to have been the 1st unauthorized civilians to have made it through for months. Never thought I'd baffle the U.S. military. Great satisfaction. But they took us under their wing and gave us first-class treatment.*

Joe and Rebecca spent two days among the GIs, young men who were very far from home. Rebecca became a one-woman USO show, all the men suddenly shy, bashful boys in her presence. "You're the first round-eyed girl we've seen in thirteen weeks!" Okay, that's enough ogling, back to patrol, back to your post, to your normal sense of dislocation. As if plucked from Poughkeepsie and dropped into a war film without lines to read. "And the biggest drag is that nobody knows that this baloney is going on," one of the soldiers, a Californian, told Joe. "Back home all they know is Vietnam, Vietnam, Vietnam. Vietnam gets all the TV coverage. The Korean War is supposed to be over, right? This will never be over."

---

*I can hear your voices. And the Author can too. With what right, you ask yourselves, does he do this . . . stuff? Was nothing sacred to this blue-eyed man as he wandered the globe? This is the beginning of the people around me thinking I was a little unhinged: that I was trying to destroy myself. I wasn't.

Must have chatted with a hundred soldiers up there, officers right on down, Joe wrote home, after they were safely back in Seoul. *Division doctor has the shakes, gets drunk, listens to Beethoven; gaudy prostitutes in every nearby village, like busted flowers scattered through the dust; the Major wears a cowboy .38 on his hip; a Gunga Din for every barracks; and each night every man not on duty drinking his brains out.* Around them, cordite, acrid ammonia, the wafting aromas of warfare. *Choppers sweeping the countryside for enemy infiltrators. Every once in a while, Allied artillery shells whistled overhead.*

Joe and Rebecca listened to one last American projectile, its brass head cutting through the wet air as it climbed northward, and listened for the distant, distant pop of the blast. Remember that sound, Sanderson. An explosion in another world. North Korea. They bid adieu to the GIs and headed back to Japan.

FROM THE PORT in Ōsaka, Joe and Rebecca traveled to Hiroshima, a city of memorials, rebuilt and spick-and-span, although there were still "A-bomb slums" along the Ota River built of wood salvaged from the fires. Here, my people dropped an exploding sun on the pedestrians and the bicyclists beginning a summer day. Today, flowers and parks. Uniformed children marching through a museum. *We stayed overnight in Peace Park, sleeping on benches beside the last nuclear relic, a bombed-out building set aside as a reminder. Ironic to read the latest news from Vietnam in the morning papers.* Onward to Okinawa, bumming the highways and riding ships. From there, a plane to Taiwan, where they learned Bobby Kennedy had been assassinated.

In Hong Kong they found the British colony was a city in turmoil, filled with the tangy taste of teargas. Thousands of pro-Peking students had been rioting against British rule, running down the narrow streets, a few clubbed for their bad behavior. "The whole world is going crazy," Rebecca said. "Maybe it is like my friends in Oakland said: 'A revolutionary moment.'" They fell into conversation at a café with a Chinese communist who spoke English with a British accent, and Rebecca listened as Chao and Joe debated "the dictatorship of the proletariat," and "the global uprising of youth" in Paris and Prague, and other topics that interested her less now, because she was growing tired of dogmatists and also of traveling with Joe, who wasn't a dogmatist at all, but certainly an obsessive adventurist. He says he still wants to go to Vietnam. Not me. The bombs floating over my head in Korea, the horny soldiers. That was quite enough for this Wisconsin girl. No more wars, no way.

JOE TOLD REBECCA he was writing a book, or wanted to write a book. But the future Professor Olmsted did not feel there was an author in Joe. What was missing? Gravitas. That severity, that intensity you expect. He was not a tortured artist, and yet he scribbled and scribbled. That night in their Hong Kong hotel room Rebecca took a peek at Joe's notebook while he slept. Does he mention me? Yes, I see a *Baby* here. *The Japanese men can't stop staring at Baby. Baby still the hitchhiking magnet. Baby eats sushi. These fucking GIs can't stop staring at Baby.* Not much more than that. Mostly names of towns and times of day and snippets of stuff people say. This is not writing. These are the notes of a scientific expedition. If he ever really writes anything, I'll just be an extra in his story. In the huge cast of his epic, amid all the facts, another girl, his blond sidekick. I can see it here, in these scribbles, and the way he talks to me. Really, I should be in the middle of the story. I am the book, Joe. We are. Me and you. But no. Instead, with each country he talks to me more about other girls. Karen: a saint, apparently. Mafalda: some connection there I don't have. And the assorted others he's started to mention, some whose names he can't even remember. This is a message he's sending. Go off to your next war alone, Joe. I'm headed somewhere more peaceful. A kingdom ruled by a chubby, happy prince. Cambodia.

JOE'S FIRST VIETNAM SURPRISE: the military-civilian air show at Tan Son Nhat International Airport. He watched through the window of his BOAC jet as big camouflaged C-130s and F-4 fighters taxied down the runway, past white Cathay Pacific and Pan American jets. Joe felt he'd arrived at a summer exhibition of the martial and commercial uses of air technology. Cessnas outfitted for jungle missions, old Mustangs, rejiggered from Dad's war to fight Junior's. Helicopters unloading way over there. Are those wounded men, on stretchers? Pilots with eyes behind shaded glasses, and green trucks loading supplies to a gleaming B-52, its wingspan as wide as a football field. Mom makes me do my taxes and pay Uncle Sam part of my flagpole wages and here my money is! At customs and immigration, a military policeman inspected his round-trip ticket: Joe wouldn't be allowed to stay more than a week. "You don't get many tourists here like me, do you?"

"You'd be surprised. Quite a few."

He squeezed through the terminal crowds and entered Saigon. The previous month had been the bloodiest of the war: 2,100 GIs dead. The Viet Cong had attacked the airport during the Tet holiday, and the memory of this siege was present in the scanning eyes of every person who hurried past the airport. Their anxiety seeped into Joe, and he scampered away to the center of Saigon, where dread gave way to the playfulness of slaloming scooters and revving motorcycles. Neon signs pulsed and flickered on behalf of Coca-Cola and Pabst Blue Ribbon. You'd think there was no war to fight here, no bullets to fear, but only pleasures for the gut, the loins and the eye. Inside the Club New York, Joe found mai tais and miniskirts and Michelob, and bare female legs on the barstools. He had a gin and tonic, and the alcohol and the music and the stony stares of the GIs around him made everything feel sullen, suddenly, as if he were at the bottom of a drain where American sadness collected. A U.S.A. funk pooled around army-issue boots and leather shoes. Joe stepped outside, into the evening ballet of bi-cycle traffic, and only then did he understand that he was not inside an American nightmare, no, but instead in a wide-awake country of nimble people pedaling in their sandals, in loose clothing and plastic white sun-glasses. He stopped on the street to admire a Vietnamese Venus in a form-fitting white ao dai and was nearly hit by a motorcycle, then he dodged a few motorcycles more and found his way to a district on the northern fringes of the city, which was said by a GI at the Club New York to be "close to the action." In his hotel room a ceiling fan turned slowly above his head, a fat fly fighting the spinning blades, growing fat on the same heavy, humid air that filled Joe's lungs. Through the open window, he heard the putter of a scooter, followed by the peal of an old woman's laughter.

I'm in Vietnam.

JOE TRAVELED THROUGH THE CITY and got past assorted checkpoints simply by being a wavy-haired, blond and tan American with a pack slung purposefully over his shoulder. To a nervous American GI: "I'm a doctor. Come to help out the villagers." To a South Vietnamese corporal: "I'm an American military adviser. Civilian, yes." Horizontal hand waves told him to proceed. My blue eyes the key to any door here. Into the weekly press briefing too, the "five o'clock follies," where he listened to the droning rec-itations of an Army major. "These revisions bring the total enemy combat deaths, confirmed, for the month of May to twelve thousand five hundred forty-three, which is a twenty-nine-point-eight percent increase . . ." The newspaper scribes and television reporters in the room sank into their folding chairs and felt their oxford shirts clinging to their chests, and they wrote down the robust numbers with unconvinced fingers and filtered out of the room, leaving Joe as the only one to walk up to the major with a follow-up question.

Before Joe could speak, the major asked: "You headed out with the 1st Cav tomorrow? Last time I didn't have any takers."

"Yeah."

"Report here," the major said, handing Joe a slip of paper. "Oh-five-hundred."

"Yes, sir," Joe said, and the salutation caught the major by surprise.

"Who you with?"

"Associated Press," Joe said. "Just got here."

That night, in his hotel, as Joe prepared to leave, he heard the distant sound of an explosion. He walked down to the lobby and saw the receptionist lean out the door and lean back in again, and then the receptionist caught a glance of Joe and gave him a grinning "Good evening." Joe climbed up to the roof and there, above the city, a distant battle came into ear focus. Gunfire and mortars, whistling rockets and their percussive fall into streets and rice paddies. Now and then a distant flash of light reflected by the clouds. *VC pressed Saigon hard all week*, he wrote home many days later. *One of the rockets fired the night of the 16th landed only a couple blocks away. Goddamn noisy, like dropping a grenade inside a VW.*

Joe did not sleep that night, and caught a cab at 4:00 a.m. for the airfield, where he was greeted by sleepy MPs and told to wait, which he did, for three hours, until a grunt GI and a lieutenant guided him to a Huey, and soon they were climbing up and out of Saigon, over the cement-and-tin quilt of the built-up city, and then over rice paddies, and everyone inside the craft besides Joe spent their time staring absentmindedly at the sack of mail the chopper was carrying. Inside there were letters from Biloxi, Miss.; Camarillo, Calif.; Bend, Ore.; Fond du Lac, Wisc.; and many other places. Telling summer stories from back home, of the death of dogs and the birth of foals, of bad weather and car repairs, with the occasional erotic suggestion or motherly word of worry. The helicopter began to descend, and Joe's eyes scanned the morning jungle, until they landed in a windsplash of elephant grass, and Joe followed a GI in jumping off, and he took in the ravaged ecology of charred and sheared trees that surrounded them. How many butterflies, birds, rodents and snakes had perished in the clearing of this land. "Welcome to Strongpoint Bravo," said the captain who greeted them. "Sanderson, Associated Press," Joe lied, and he listened and nodded as the major explained the mission. They were eight kilometers from Cambodia, the major said, right on top of what had been an infiltration route, an off-ramp for the Ho Chi Minh Trail, and two hundred twenty-nine enemy soldiers had been killed here, and one antiaircraft gun captured and so forth and so on. Joe opened up his notebook to write, because it seemed the major expected a reporter would write things. *Mud*, Joe scribbled. *Mud. Much mud. Mud. Muddy. More mud. Mud everywhere. Mud.* He saw one soiled soldier cleaning a dirty M60, and others wearing bandoliers of linked rounds, and their arms and faces were splattered with mud, and some were shirtless and had their torsos painted with mud. They were surrounded by empty boxes and crates, and crushed cans. This sure ain't Fort Leonard Wood.

"You're a reporter?" one of the grunts asked.

"Yeah."

"You see the NVA gun yet?"

"No."

They walked over to an antiaircraft gun on the edge of the cleared land, and the soldier ran his hand appreciatively along the long muzzle of the Soviet-made weapon, and Joe sat in the gunner's chair. Charlie's seat. Looking up from there at the circling American choppers. Not long afterward Joe was rising back up into the sky in the Huey as the soldiers gathered around their letters, squatting to read them in the same way Vietnamese peasants squatted, and looking down at them Joe felt as if he were peering into a jungle library. The strongpoint disappeared, and Joe's heart raced in time with the beat of the helicopter's engine, because he was thinking of that enemy antiaircraft gun, and he imagined others hidden in the jungle, with living VC to fire them. I could die up here, now. And wouldn't that be a stupid end to my story?

BACK IN SAIGON, he took a taxi to the Cholon district, where battles had been fought during the Tet Offensive, and where it was said the Viet Cong still prowled nearby. He found a community of displaced people living in hastily built structures, including Chinese Vietnamese families who had lost their homes in the U.S. bombing that chased out the communists. They were urban refugees who lived amid jumbled ruins of corrugated tin, charcoaled beams and singed palm trees, and their eyes fell upon Joe. This new, tall American removed his shirt and tied it around his waist, which wasn't unusual, although everything else about him was. Joe carried no weapon or clipboard or camera, and he wore no uniform; he was not a soldier, doctor or technician. Nor was he an aid worker accompanied by a truck filled with poor-quality rice in bags stamped with the American flag, the kind of rice you would only feed to an animal. Instead, Joe was a lone American stranger, wandering with no discernible purpose, a grinning voyeur following in the footsteps of the armies that persecuted them: the stealthy Vietnamese nationalists who appeared suddenly in alleyways; the GIs of the 7th United States Infantry Regiment and their escorts of flying gunships; the scrambling squads of South Vietnamese soldiers, looking for people to shoot and things to steal; and the crazed Army of the Republic of Vietnam captain who wore a yellow scarf around his neck and waved a pointing stick as he screamed orders. The sight of the shirtless Joe Sanderson brought forth memories of lost souls, lost loves and ruptured bloodlines. The sudden, unexplainable dead of Cholon: the grandfather; the conscripted son, kissing his mother's hands goodbye; the daughter, asleep in her bed. Phuong. Duc. Khiem. The Chinese characters for their names.

The survivors of Cholon would remember the sight of Joe Sanderson when they moved, some years later, to places like Monterey Park, California, and Bosque Farms, New Mexico, where their lives became one with American madness for the rest of their days. By then, their war memories of men like Joe had become memoirs and poems their children wrote. *mùi Mỹ . . . that American scent / of mosquito repellent / and unbathed skin.*

Spent a lot of time in Cholon with refugees bombed out during Tet by Americans' helicopter gunships, Joe wrote home later. *Not very pretty. But they didn't seem to mind my presence. Not once did I catch any sniping.**

On the northern fringes of the metropolis, Joe got close to an actual battle. Enemy fighters emerged from their hiding places at the end of a sunny morning; he did not see these warriors, but rather heard the distinctive firing of their AKs. He ran toward the sound, like a madman, until he was forced to seek cover in an abandoned foxhole. A bullet struck a mound of dirt ten yards from his crouching skull, and suddenly he wished he'd never left Urbana and never become a road bum. But he stayed, because each bullet fired in his direction carried a sense of meaningfulness. My country and my people set this fiasco in motion. *Sweet land of liberty, / Of thee I sing.* When the shooting stopped, he followed curious civilians to the spot where the victorious soldiers of the South Vietnamese army were rounding up their VC prisoners, kicking and slapping them into a line. He saw the POWs marched out to an army base, close enough for Joe to reach out and touch their bruised arms and bloodied cheeks. Fourteen, fifteen years old. A boys' army. This is the fierce, feared Viet Cong? Surprise, surprise, our mortal enemy is really just skinny kids with big brown eyes.

Joe wrote his first missive home the next day on the narrow rectangle of a torn envelope, which he then slipped inside another envelope, with Vietnamese 20-dong and 1-dong stamps attached, and a newspaper clipping

---

*"Not once did I catch any sniping." Not my best moment. But the Author doesn't care. The whole sympathetic-protagonist thing has gone out the window. Lucky me.

inside. *Quite a war. Got used to dead VC and being shot at, but I can't quite adjust to what you see in the pictures, VC prisoners. They'd been worked over all night long by helicopter gunships. Most were wounded. I'm resting against the cemetery wall on the far right.* His mother held the newspaper clipping between her fingers, and saw a grainy image of helmeted South Vietnamese soldiers (so very small and slight, these people, our allies) walking alongside even slighter prisoners, in shorts. And there, on the right, her son seated on the top of a low fence: his back and bushy hair, so clearly him. Joe had drawn a little blue check mark next to himself, to remove any doubt.

The letter continued: *Just after the area cleared, a firefight broke out. SVN marine got shot. By noon, 70 VC had called it quits, the largest surrender of the war (if you can call the defeat of children surrender).*

The second letter arrived eleven days later, in the folded spaces of an aerogramme Joe mailed when he was safely in Bangkok. He began by telling them he'd already been to Cambodia. *Was quiet and peaceful the 10 days I was there. Didn't mind. Came into Phnom Penh pretty exhausted. Nothing but war action for 7 days and nights in Vietnam.* But he would have stayed if his visa hadn't expired. Vietnam had been a *bullshitter's holiday* of assumed identities, he wrote. Doctor, military adviser, reporter, without credentials but always believed. *If the Yankees weren't so gullible, we wouldn't have entered the war in the first place.* And then he returned to the firefight he had witnessed and its aftermath. *The Gia Dinh battle got rough. Rifle and machine-gun fire came in from the VC position every few minutes, but no one seemed concerned. Bodies of dead VC, shot-up prisoners, the laughter of victorious soldiers, looting the dead in the rice paddies. Spent several hours along govt. bunkers while they displayed their war trophies, read letters from the Hanoi girlfriends of the dead, gave me N. Vietnamese money, showed me the bodies. Disgusting is about the only appropriate word I can think of. Sniper fire in short bursts as I moved between the ARVN and Govt. Marine positions. Too embarrassed to run for a bunker while no one else was around. The firing stopped and I walked on. Soldiers couldn't have*

cared less I was out there. I went where I wanted to. Casual war, Vietnam.
Some VC prisoners were brought in just as I arrived at the ARVN position. I
counted 60. Later, I saw an American adviser who admitted there had been
a few "mistakes" during the Gia Dinh surrender. Told me what I already
knew. I'd seen the "mistakes" lying in the rice paddies. No need to go into it.
Just disgusting, that's all. All but one VC were between the ages of 14 and 20.
None wore shoes. Strange thing is that eventually the VC will probably win
the war.

VIRGINIA READ HER SON'S second letter while standing before her mail-box in Urbana. When she'd finished, she wanted to scream at him. Running from bunker to bunker, dodging sniper fire? His life is the most precious thing he owns. For what purpose, to what end? Foolishness, at play, like a boy, amid gunfire. As if he were in the Mahomet woods. She felt a sense of shame at his antics. And then she read his letter again, and thought of the word he used: *disgusting.* The war was disgusting, and so were the actions of the South Vietnamese soldiers, our allies. My son is outraged. He is angered by the word used by the American adviser: *mistakes.* What does that mean? She stepped inside her living room and showed Calhoun the letter.

"Mistakes," she told her husband. "He says something about mistakes. What does he mean?"

Calhoun read the relevant passages a few times, and looked up at Virginia with a grim expression. "He's saying they shot those prisoners. He's saying these enemy soldiers, who were teenagers, mostly, surrendered to the South Vietnamese army—and then they were killed by the South Vietnamese army."

Virginia knew her son and had no doubt he'd seen something evil. "I'm worried about him," she told Calhoun. "Of course you are," he answered.

A war, in a country so far away, different rules, different people. Not like here, not like any other war. Calhoun says we shouldn't be fighting in the jungle. No way to win. Nixon will sort it all out when he's president. Yes, Nixon. Rectitude, Republican, he will do the right things. Good man. The corpses in Joe's letter stayed with her as she stepped outside into her Urbana backyard. My son among the murdered prisoners. Maybe I should hang some clothes on the line. Hate the sound of the dryer, the machine heat. The wind and the sun are so much better. Pure. But unsettled summer skies. Sunshine, and then gray. The towels might not dry. Is the jungle like this? Vietnam. Hands raised, white flags. Surrender. My son, with thoughts of the dead in his brain. He will lose sleep, he will be unrested, out of sorts. August in Illinois. Wind, clouds, but no rain. Roiling summer skies, dry leaves caught up in a swirl of wind. Crackle of spinning leaves. But it will not rain. Clouds heavy with water, passing overhead. No rain today, or yesterday. So unnatural, so strange.

13.

Vientiane, Laos. Bali, Indonesia.
Djibouti, Afars and Issas.
Addis Ababa. Kigali, Rwanda.
Stanleyville, Congo. Johannesburg.
Lagos. Uyo, Biafra

H E DID NOT SEE THE PLANES THEMSELVES, but instead the ice crystals shed by their engines in the stratosphere. As the residents of Vientiane gathered on the riverfront to watch the sunset over the milky Mekong, they saw the white contrails dissolve into mist. Nearby, a girl performed riverside somersaults for her younger brother. Pleasant little town, the capital of Laos. Here and there, a hint of officialdom, a ministry of this or that, and old French-colonial villas and signs in French, and roofs of steeply pitched tin and tile, and homes on stilts. In the sky, American B-52s made big sweeping turns over the Plain of Jars, dropping finned steel from their fuse-lages. The ground quaked and the jungle burned deeper in Laos, but no one here could feel or smell it. Instead Joe saw silent, orange-robed monks and then heard the scratch and slap of their sandals on dirt and asphalt. He took a final short walk through the dusk to open land where water buffalos pulled plows that cut into the wet soil.

Yankee bombers moving back and forth overhead from runs into Viet-nam and the Ho Chi Minh Trail, he wrote home to his mother. *Why, for God's sake, why? Looking up from the ground were bare-breasted women, kids with malaria, workers making 50c per day. Senator Sanderson isn't at all pleased with the whereabouts of foreign-aid tax money. It's likely that the cost of bombing Laos during any one week would double the standard of liv-ing of every inhabitant for a full year.*

Rebecca rejoined him in Laos. At night, she rubbed his neck and wrapped her arm around him, and began to feel there was something deeply wrong with him. He talked to her about seeing the bodies of Viet-namese child soldiers. Twisted corpses, trying to climb into trenches, or out of them. Corpses frozen in mid-crawl in the roadway. And then a bit later he talked about more wars waiting along the very long path across the globe he wanted to take. A civil war in Yemen, a war in the Congo, in Nige-ria. Did he want to see more corpses, hear more shells flying over his blond head? He was twenty-six, addicted to spectacle and a vagabond life, and committed to a craft he was not trying to truly master. They were the same age, and yet she felt twenty years older than him. She moved south with him, into Thailand, and they took siestas on the sand next to the sapphire Andaman Sea, and in a rented cabin they made love with decreasing pas-sion. In Singapore, they visited a district where local men donned paisley minidresses and knee-high boots; then they sailed on the South China Sea and over the equator into Indonesia. *Up with the roosters this morning for a trip into the mountains,* Joe wrote home from Bali. *Damn relaxing after Djakarta. Tranquil island. Hard to connect what we see to the hell the Bali-*

nese went through during the slaughter of the communists in '65. They visited a water-filled caldera of a huge volcano, and lakeside villages where the schools were closed, because all the teachers had been killed three years earlier. Then they hiked up a trail past wild poinsettias and flocks of hungry children, climbing to the top of a volcano, and in her thoughts Rebecca practiced the lovely goodbye she would speak when they were back down at sea level, preparing to return to Djakarta. "I'll never forget you, Joe Sanderson."*

IN BOMBAY, Joe paid fifty-eight dollars for passage on a ship across the Indian Ocean to Djibouti via Yemen. After two days of rough sailing the rocky hills and promontories of the Arabian Peninsula emerged from the sun-drenched horizon, followed by the white buildings of Aden. If Rebecca had been there, she might have quoted the relevant passages from Marco Polo and his *Book of the Marvels of the World*, which described the vigorous trade through this very port: the eastward flow of Arabian horses to India, the westward shipments of peppercorn, cinnamon and sandalwood. Yemen had been torn up by a war of independence against the British, and a civil war that had ended a few months earlier. *Hopped a bus into the countryside, getting into a few villages no whites had visited since Independence. Hell must be a desert just like Yemen. The Queen of Sheba, I'm quite certain, had air-conditioning in her palace. Cruel boiling sun, hot wind that drives the*

---

*It's hard to see my life played out like this: the silly boy I was, the thoughts of the people who loved me. Imagine yourself, watching the slideshow of your life, listening to your exes weigh in on you. Would you still like yourself afterward? Does the Author still like me? Do you? Like me or not, the Author is sticking with me, trying to squeeze in every country, war and massacre, despite the voice of His Editor and His Agent, who are gently suggesting he trim the shit out of it. I guess the Author is just as mesmerized by the spectacle as I was. The finned bombs, the graves of the teachers. Like me, the Author is sleepwalking through the battlefields, past the corpses, as if they'd all been arranged for him to see.

*nomads crazy, blowing sand, little water, much of it salty. Buildings shelled
and riddled with machine-gun bullets, barbed wire, bunkers, fresh graves.
I'll write again from Africa. I can't believe it's autumn in America. Go out
and step on a brown leaf for me.*

Back on board his ship, he sailed to Djibouti, where he landed amid
old wooden dhows; one of the first things he did was to buy stamps for his
collector brother, issued in the odd name of a territory no one in Illinois
had ever heard of: Des Afars et des Issas. *Africa!* Joe wrote home. *Finally
here after seven days on the sea. Mighty weary too. So I'm here, now what?*
Five days later, from Addis Ababa, he wrote: *Hail Rastafari! Jamaica to
Ethiopia. Now how's that for carving a wide circle into the globe. So much to
see. Young studs boarding the trains with spears, native girls with maybe 50
small braids of hair, nomads carrying huge knives and homemade guns (like
the Khyber Pass folk). Rode night trucks to a savanna, stopped off at a village
(sleeping on feed bags in back of a truck beneath a full moon), moving out at
dawn. Animals everywhere! Herds of antelope, tiny deer the size of a jackrab-
bit on stretched out legs, bands of foxes, wild boar, huge flocks of guinea par-
tridge, and onyx, a large animal the size of a pony with 2-foot-long horns.* He
was zoologically overwhelmed. From a canoe and wild geese on the Sangamon, to hyenas stalking the train tracks in the Horn of Africa. He caught
a long ride in another truck, driving along roads paved and unpaved, and
entertained the driver with stories.

"I started like this: in a truck. Driving, working. Painting flagpoles."

His visa to enter Kenya required that he purchase a plane ticket into
the country, so he boarded a jetliner in Addis Ababa and flew over the
savanna he had just bummed across, now covered by tessellated rolls of
clouds, and landed in Nairobi. He hitchhiked out of town toward Mount
Kenya, and found shelter at a Sikh temple. *Beautiful sunset but the mountain was clouded over, unfortunately.* The next day he discovered he
wouldn't be able to enter the Mount Kenya national park bumming—a five-
dollar fee was required, and he'd have to visit with his own car or a guide.

Undeterred, he returned to the park the next day and passed himself off to the man in charge as an Illinois entomologist specializing in Lepidoptera. *Conned my way into a 2-hour run with the warden. Really great. More giraffe, mother ostrich sitting on a mound of eggs, hartebeest, gazelle, impala, bushbuck, warthog, and the real prize—5 cheetah, the mother with 4 young. Warden said every day she had to make a "kill" to feed the little bastards. Would knock off a gazelle at 70 mph. Almost sad, the beauty of the hours I've spent with animals here in Africa, remembering the repulsive tragedy of Viet Nam. At least nature kills with a reasonable amount of fairness.*

THIS LETTER, which Joe mailed from Tanzania on October 28, was his twenty-ninth since leaving home to paint flagpoles and drive to California and travel to Asia. By the time it arrived in Urbana it was the middle of November, Richard Nixon was the president-elect. Virginia was preparing for the Thanksgiving holidays, when Steve and Maggie would be over and her mother would visit from Kansas. On Thanksgiving Day, the pink bird cooked in her temperature-controlled Westinghouse oven, her mother sat on the couch, hands folded, content to let Virginia do the work for once. Mother, born in the age of kerosene and calico and hay, granddaughter of the first woman to graduate from the University of Kansas. Sassy once, writing in notebooks and on chalkboards with the long, delicate fingers that tremble now when she lifts her plate.

"Where's Joe now?" she asked.

"Funny you should ask, I just got a letter from him. Let me read it to you."

And so, with the meal over, and Steve cleaning out the cranberry-sauce dish with a teaspoon and licking it, Virginia opened the shoebox where she kept Joe's correspondence. She took out Joe's letter.

"*Climbed Kilimanjaro,*" Virginia began, reading her son's words. "*Took me 4 nights and 5 days, but I made it to the crown, nearly 20,000 feet.*"

At this point, Virginia skipped over the next phrase Joe had written—*It was a bitch*—and instead said, "*It was a real bear.*"

"I bet it was," Joe's grandmother said.

"*Still have a bad sunburn to show for it, lips peeling,*" Virginia read from the letter. "*But it didn't require ropes and spikes, nothing but good lungs and caution and endurance. The last couple months of pipe smoking paid off!*" Joe's grandmother chuckled at the joke. "*Caused a slight stir in the base town of Moshi (Tanzania) because I went alone. Climbers usually have guides and a flock of porters. Had to clear it with the police and sign release papers. Brought my own rations (including a bottle of brandy), rented snow goggles, helmet, fatigue jacket, boots, etc., then just up and hauled . . . ,*" Virginia read, skipping the word that followed: *ass.* "*Incredibly beautiful up yonder. Bitterly cold at night, but I took it all right. Began the final ascent shortly after midnight (the third night) and had nearly reached the top by dawn. It was rough but once I got back down Africa seemed so boring I felt like going back up again.*"

"Well, he sure is an intrepid boy," Joe's grandmother said.

JOE WAS GETTING CLOSER to the Republic of the Congo and its war. His next letter was addressed from Bujumbura, in the neighboring country of Burundi. He described an encounter with some wealthy safari hunters in Kenya who bagged a Thomson's gazelle with very long horns and served him copious glasses of "raw whiskey," and a series of shenanigans involving Christian missions in Uganda, Burundi and Rwanda. In search of free room and board whenever possible, he approached a mission in Kampala, Uganda, and announced he was a "theology student," and tried the ploy again in Burundi. *Damn if it didn't work*, he wrote home. *Gave me food and drank scotch and sodas with the abbes that night. Pulled the same stunt in Kigali (capital of Rwanda) and Jesus Gawd was the good Lord waiting for me there.* He told the rector at the French Catholic school that he was a graduate of the University of Illinois, the University of Florida and Hannover College. *I really laid it on*, he wrote home. *The rector thought me extremely intelligent since I agreed with all of his ideas, what but he gets the notion I'm to give a lecture to the students (St. Andre College). And there I was that p.m., stalking the floor, answering questions, scowling like Wagner, giving them my best. Must have rapped for over an hour.*

His audience was composed of two hundred Rwandan teenagers who were captivated, especially, by his firsthand account of the war in Vietnam, and how the Viet Cong had Saigon under siege. They were just as intrigued when he began to discuss the Rastafarians, and the black civil rights movement in the United States, and his brief encounter with the Black Panthers, and what he remembered Rebecca telling him about the Panthers' confrontations in Oakland with the police, and their belief in the right to carry arms, which was guaranteed by the Second Amendment ("my favorite constitutional amendment, actually"). "What do the black people of America want?" Joe asked rhetorically. "They want what I, as a white man, already have: equality before the law. Pretty simple, I guess." The students peppered him with questions: "Were you frightened in Saigon when you saw the battles, Dr. Sanderson?" "Yes." "Do the Black Panthers have a uniform?" "Yes and no." As a white man talking sympathetically about the concerns of black people, and critically about his own government, Joe was a paradox to them. Some sensed "Professor Sanderson" was exaggerating the incidents he described, but he was a witness to history nonetheless, and his presence spoke to the realness of events that otherwise seemed distant and legend-like. They noted the high-pitched oddness of his American accent too, and the nervous pacing of his thin and slight body, and his well-worn leather shoes, and the way he kept readjusting the thick frames of his glasses. This American character comes to speak to us about the Rastafarians and the hallucinatory effects of marijuana. "Stoned," he says, and the French translator does not understand and Joe explains to him, and finally we all understand. Ha, ha, ha! Americans are not what they seem to be from afar. "Dr. Sanderson" had taught these future leaders of Rwanda a basic lesson about stereotypes. America: a powerful land of perfect white people? No, not at all. Nor is Rwanda the small, simple, peaceful land that white men think they see. Among us, we are Hutu and Tutsi: in truth, it's very complicated. We have our own prejudices and misconceptions. The people of the long necks, and their foes, the people of broad noses. Stereotypes. The owners of cattle versus the tillers of the soil. Truths and untruths. Our exiles and our history, unknown to outsiders, including this American Joe who is shaking hands now and nodding as the rector thanks him for "a most illuminating lecture."

Joe bade the students farewell and spent the evening with the school faculty. *The farce would not end,* he wrote home. *Rector had several teachers and my translator take me out to dinner that night. Real aristocrats, these priests. They taste their soup before adding salt and pepper. And it was Old Home Week when we dropped in at the local cathouse. Hooray for French Catholics! But I jumped back into my shower thongs and got out of town before they could have me holding high Mass.*

THE FRENCH PRIESTS in Rwanda warned Joe against going to the Republic of the Congo and its tribal wars. "The army thinks every white man they see is a mercenary. And the rebels will think you're a spy." He entered the Congo anyway, and after Congolese Army soldiers caught him bumming a ride on a truck from Bukavu, they did, in fact, take him for a mercenary—besides being white, he was wearing a GI money belt. The soldiers hauled him off the truck to a military outpost, where he spent the night wondering if and how they would kill him. But soon he was a free American bum again, and suddenly immune to the eastern Congo war bug: there were no battles to see, just refugees. He heard there were mercenaries operating deeper in the country, and to cross the Congo and reach them he hitched a ride with a group of Christian missionaries who were passing out Bibles and clothes, and then with a Rhodesian businessman. Joe was traveling from Hemingway's Africa and "The Snows of Kilimanjaro" to Conrad's *Heart of Darkness*, to river bends and villages where invisible rebels were still operating in the bush, and where he heard stories of recent wartime atrocities inflicted by machetes and by airplanes. He made for Stanleyville, which had recently been renamed Kisangani, though most people he met still called it Stanleyville. The city had been the site of recent war horrors, and Joe traveled toward it in a Land Rover crossing flat terrain filled with wild palms and wild green everything, razor grass swallowing up the roadways. To the next village and a tollgate made of a plastic bucket and a long plastic pipe. Pay, please. A toll for the boys who clear the grass with their machetes. The road becomes an orange lake and then we must push, push, push the Land Rover to the next place. Urrrgh. *Raggedy-Andy rough going*, he described it in a letter home. And now Stanleyville, once an outpost of western colonizers. On the Congo River, the newest of the many rivers of my journeys. I have seen sampans, barges as long as football fields and now the hand-carved canoes of the fishermen of Stanleyville, floating sculptures they propel with paddles and pushing sticks.

Joe wandered about the onetime Belgian colonial city and stood before an old mosque and mansions of flaking paint and moldy plaster that were being consumed by vines and fungi. He watched the moon set over the Congo, the white orb casting pearly light on the ripples of water. The locals directed him to an old hotel, a plaster edifice pockmarked by bullets, and inside he met the squad of South African contract soldiers he'd been looking for; they were also the last white men living in the town. *Once I hit Stanleyville I shifted from missionaries to mercenaries*, he wrote home. *Some change. Whiskey, prostitutes, loaded machine guns beside the bed, shortwave radios. Staying with one at a shot-up hotel on the Congo River. Radio crackling static as they play cards in their T-shirts or become lost in cheap novels.* The mercenaries were themselves destined to become characters in many pulp novels, though never one written by Joe. They had been hired by the Congo government to fight a band of rebels from the bush called the Simba warriors. Some years earlier, the Simba had invaded Stanleyville and held the white population hostage, but now the mercenaries had nothing to do but entertain Joe with their war stories. *Pictures of naked broads on the wall, a window still busted from a mortar shell, heavy bank accounts, jungle philosophy. Drank with them the last two nights and listened to stories of the Stanleyville massacre.* On the third and final night sharing a room with one of the mercenaries, Joe woke up before dawn and saw moonbeams radiating across the body of the snoring soldier-for-hire and everything in the room: moonlight on his machine gun, his soiled underwear, the centerfold on the wall and her bare, voluptuous torso. Light from the underworld gleaming upon objects from the underworld.

JOE'S LETTER FROM CONGO told his mother and stepfather to continue to write to him in Zambia, because he'd be headed there soon. When she received the letter, number thirty-two on this trip, Virginia imagined her son with crow's-feet around his eyes. Maybe he'll come back to us as an old man. He is as far away as he can get, deep in the deepest jungles. Zambia. At the end of the alphabet too. How much farther can he go? How much more lost from us can he get?

ON THE LUMBERING steam train to Lusaka he met an old, aristocratic white man who said he had known the legendary Albert Schweitzer; he bought Joe a nine-course meal. Joe went to midnight Mass in Rhodesia's capital city, Salisbury, which was lit up for the holidays *with enough electricity to light up the entire Congo*; he also met *the only two hippies in Rhodesia* and spent a night giving them inspiration. Joe traveled from the Lowveld to the Highveld, and the water evaporated from the landscape, and Africa turned scrubby again. He reached Johannesburg and its wide, open and clean streets and its late-model cars, and gawked at the signs posted at telegraph offices, bathrooms and on park benches. EUROPEANS ONLY. SLEGS BLANKES NON-EUROPEAN WOMEN. NIE-BLANKE VROUE. BUS STOP FOR NON-WHITES. Apartheid was an incantation of signs. *The racial laws here are crimes in themselves,* he wrote home. *It would be a great honor to be imprisoned or deported for breaking them. Beneath the glitter and the prosperity, it's an insane asylum.* In the next letter, he was already in Cape Town. *Hitched a ride with a couple of whites clear from Durban. Spent a day with the rock-rock, swing-swing teenie bopper set on the way down, then took off across the hills into some seaside wilderness.* In Cape Town he found no ship to Nigeria had room for him. *Anxious to reach Nigeria and get in on some action. I can't stay down here in the sunshine much longer or I'll get segregated, separated, regulated and agitated,* he wrote in his last letter from Cape Town. *Well, pissed off anyway. Haven't blown up any radio towers, but recent legend has it that a stranger has been glimpsed riding in trucks at midnight shouting words of encouragement to his black brothers above the wind.*

WHEN JOE REACHED LAGOS, Nigeria, the army denied his request for press credentials to enter the war zone. His next stop was the aid agencies. *The Red Cross is desperate for workers to hit the bush and drink gin, contract malaria and get shot at for breakfast,* he wrote home, and a short while later he signed a three-month contract. *"Relief worker" is my title, which is a euphemism for doctor, ambulance driver, beer drinker or whatever the hell else is needed.* After a series of pogroms across Nigeria against the Igbo people, the Igbo had created an independent state in southeastern Nigeria named Biafra; now the Nigerian government was trying to starve the Biafrans to death. Armed with a vaccination gun, Joe traveled with an American doctor in a twin-engine plane, crossing over rebel territory to the city of Port Harcourt, once part of Biafra, but recently retaken by the government. Then in a helicopter to a grass field in Calabar, where he heard stories of a recent bombardment by the Biafran Air Force, such as it was. Small planes dropping *beer bottles of petrol, homemade napalm, plus a few proper bombs.*

THE REFUGEES WATCHED from the grounds of a schoolhouse as Joe and a doctor approached in a white Land Rover with big red crosses painted on both sides and on the roof. Fifteen women and thirty-eight children lying on a cement floor, sitting against the walls. They were from many clans, all mixed together, wearing the printed patterns of their villages, their heads covered in scarves, cotton soaked with days of soil and sweat, because they had been too weak, and too busy moving, to wash. Years later, some will say not being able to wash was nearly as bad as the hunger. The refugees had come from three different towns, along red dirt roads, and they had seen this catastrophe unfold by a river and its sacred groves. Walking past oil bean trees in search of something to eat, past a shrine to the river goddess. In their hunger they had long, vivid dreams in which they spoke to their ancestors while their dying children laughed and played around them. Joe noticed a chalkboard with a lesson. *Study makes me wise. Study makes me strong. Study makes me bold. Study makes me whole.* He saw listless, numbed mothers, holding children. "How are we doing?" the doctor said. "Howdy. Yes, I told y'all I'd be back." Joe checked one child, who seemed half asleep, and the boy's eyes opened wider and the doctor came over and said, "You need a little medicine, little man, right now." The doctor reached into a leather satchel and Joe helped him hold down the boy, who was maybe two or three years old; he wouldn't open his mouth, until the doctor forced it open, and shoved in a pill, and the boy chewed and swallowed and managed to cry a bit. "That's a good boy."

"Okay, Sanderson, let's line up the rest of these kids. Inoculation time." The pfft-clack delivering antibodies. The children on their feet. Pfft-clack. Pfft-clack. Later he would fill his journal with the details. The color of the

mud on their feet, the names of the diseases: kwashiorkor, a kind of malnutrition. The wind rushed through the trees on the riverbank outside and he
stood above a puffy-lipped boy whose belly was the size and shape of a
volleyball. "It was so much worse six months ago," the doctor said.

Three hours later they left for another camp, this one a tent in an
open field. Here the people were hungrier, thinner. "Dang, Joe. We're truly
needed here." Children with spindled arms and hunger-bleached hair;
don't grab them too hard, you might break them. A few of the stronger
women spoke of the absence of manioc and yams and described the deaths
of friends and children. Just before sunset, a Red Cross truck arrived with
sacks of food, and Joe began to cook porridge, and then ladled it out into tin
dishes, and he watched the children and their mothers scoop it into their
mouths.

They traveled deeper into the war zone, within ten miles of the front.
"How many people did we feed today? Sixteen hundred!" Dried codfish,
delivered via helicopter, a salty sustenance with protein to build back muscle. Another village, and the chief insists on tasting the milk and porridge
first, to see if it is acceptable for his people. He says proud men with titles
are buried in the villages they left behind, yam kings, speakers of parables
and proverbs. Such a loss.

Finally, Joe arrived in the city of Uyo, where a Red Cross administra-
tor gave him new orders: take a Land Rover and drive three officials of
the U.S. Agency for International Development to Port Harcourt. *Had
just emerged from the woods when they told me I was needed as chauffeur.*
The Americans weren't just the usual aid-worker minons, but rather mid-
and upper-level diplomats and spooks, and their lodgings were at the best
hotel still open in Port Harcourt. Joe joined them by the pool. *After two
weeks in the bush driving a Red Cross station wagon, now I'm ordering
buckets of ice for Cutty Sark,* Joe wrote home. But the hotel is costing me
£4 per night, bullet holes in the lobby windows for free. This shit-show is
over, the diplomats said, and Joe didn't understand. They spoke in a kind

of code about the alliances and the politics that had led to mass starvation, with the acquiescence of the U.S. and assorted European governments. After he left them, Joe took helicopter and plane rides deeper into the famine country, and night flights into the unconquered territories of free Biafra.

Biafra's last landing strip consisted of rows of light along a stretch of highway. Joe and a German colleague landed in the dark, and at dawn they entered a village where the people were eating frogs and minced rodents. They found a man selling two half teaspoons of lifesaving salt, and they arrived at a camp of two thousand people. Joe placed a hand on the clavicle of a girl of about six and saw how her bones were rising and her skin retreating. Her face was becoming a mask, the angles in her skull revealing themselves, and also the humeri and the metacarpals and the long phalanges of her hands. The inner armature of a child. He watched the weakest children sleep with quick puff-breaths, hearts speeding.* *Getting weird here*, Joe wrote from Uyo two days later. *Went to work Monday still scattered from the night before. Couple of hours later a little two-year-old kid died in my arms. Pneumonia. Bought his ticket right on the floor of the clinic. Before noon the German nurse and I were working over a second. Had to keep slapping the child on the chest to keep his heart clicking.*

The top Red Cross guy in Calabar found Joe one morning at the airfield and told him he wanted Joe to help organize evacuations of the sickest people in the areas closest to the fighting. He teamed Joe up with an American helicopter pilot, a quiet old guy from Sweet Home, Oregon, with sad eyes and a white mustache. *We have to get to the isolated pockets where people are dying,* Joe wrote home. *Two more evacuations. Dismal business. While I was in the bush up near the front, a village chief in another area sent word*

---

*I think the Author isn't quite up to the moment here. To the nightmare. It was all much more horrible than this. But could any writer make you feel the sick real of it all? I certainly couldn't. I never did manage to find the words to capture what happens to your soul when a child dies in your arms. Only a genius could, I guess. Or a psychopath.

to nearby refugees that I would bring the chopper down on a certain date to evacuate children. Gave them a false promise based merely on hope. Found out yesterday the refugees came and left. Four kids died. Got back last night to Calabar to hear that one of the children I brought in last week was also dead. But only a few haven't made it. The rest are beginning to smile. So when they call out to me—"Doctor! Doctor!"—I don't scowl anymore.

When an American doctor asked Joe why he had come to Biafra, Joe answered that he was traveling around the world, gathering experiences to write a novel. "There is no novel here," the doctor answered. "Imagine Hemingway here. What the fuck could he say?" In a tent in one of the camps in the bush, Joe witnessed a stillbirth, the sprawled-open legs of a woman in pain. "Acute peritonitis," the nurse said. They pulled a purple-brown corpse from her body, putrefaction filling the air. The dead fetus fell from Joe's hands into a bucket, and the woman stared at Joe and the bucket as he took her child's corpse away, and the crazed look in her eyes would haunt him in the hours, days and weeks that followed. Outside, children were laughing as they played with scavenger dogs. The villagers introduced him to a boy with a disk of black hair on his head, and a dimpled smile, and said: "His father was killed, his mother died. He has no one." Alone, without someone to make sure he was eating, he would die. Take him, please, doctor. On to the helicopter you go, little man, next to three others, now your brothers and sisters. *We brought in some orphans. So we overloaded the chopper heavily the last run*, Joe wrote home afterward. *Low on fuel, red light flashing, pilot giving me his usual you-dirty-bastard glare but we made it all right.*

After his last helicopter run, Joe made a few more journeys into the bush by Land Rover, from Calabar and back. In the final village before crossing the river back to Calabar, he and the lone American doctor still working in Biafra were stopped by a family. *Folks pleading from huts left in shambles*, he wrote later. *Newborn naked child thrashing about upon a bare wood table. Bleeding navel packed with cow dung. Dying from umbilical tetanus and pneumonia. Seven days old. No more anti-tetanus vaccines left. Ampules cost 11 cents apiece. Baby gasping, writhing, will not suck on his mother's milkless breast.** The baby had a seizure, and then his chest stopped moving, and Joe lifted him up, and breathed into his tiny mouth, and the boy's breath and saliva tasted sour, and then Joe pushed on its chest, until the doctor told him to stop. It fell to Joe to write out a death certificate, on the back of some Red Cross forms used to chart malnutrition, and he handed it to the father, and Joe watched as the mother gazed at her child and closed his eyes, and ran her fingers over the sticky skin of his face and arms. She found a pair of scissors and removed the two buttons from the shirt he was wearing; she would bury the child in the shirt and save the buttons for her other children.

The war wound down, and eventually it ended for Joe, and he was swallowed up by the well-fed metropolis of Lagos, where he wept and drank himself into a stupor for two nights. *What is war? For me, dying children. And I wanted to create art from this.* He looked at the notes he had scribbled and felt a sense of uselessness, and then he thought he might never leave Lagos; he'd die drunk in this hotel room with his memories of that last mother's eyes looking into his. Finally, he took the envelope containing his Red Cross wages and bought a plane ticket home: Nigeria Airlines, from Lagos to Monrovia to Dakar to New York. And then another flight to Chicago, because he was done with bumming for a while, and finally the train to Champaign-Urbana, through the fields of robust and erect spring corn. He saw hamburger joints and supermarkets, and silos filled with corn and soybeans, and cows with udders bursting, and fat steers ready for slaughter. Champaign emerged from this fecund landscape, and Steve was waiting at the station this time, because Joe had called him from Chicago and said he was headed home.

"Well, there he is! Travelin' Joe, in the flesh."

---

*Another passage swiped (and rejiggered) from one of my novels.

They took the short drive to Mom's house, and she was there in the doorway waiting as Steve pulled up.

Virginia thought she must look older to him, especially after all her worry-watching the news and scanning the reports from Nigeria, and before that Vietnam. "Hi, Mom," Joe said as he stepped toward her, and she realized that he was the one who looked older. Exhausted and perhaps sad. Then Joe did something he had never done after coming home from all his other trips—he hugged her for a good long time, his big frame over hers, and she wrapped her arms weakly around him, and patted him on the back. Same boy, healthy and whole and back home.

"Sorry, Mom, it's been a long trip."

"Well, come in and eat. Supper's just about ready."

She went into the kitchen, and Steve and Calhoun looked at Joe as he sat before them, and they remembered his many letters, and Calhoun thought he must carry some deeper understanding of the world from having circled it. Steve dared to think that maybe this would be his little brother's last bumming adventure, because Joe seemed to have wrung all the wandering from his thinner, sun-darkened body. Joe said that he'd been traveling for three days, and had had too much liquor on his various plane rides, and he sat at the table, before his mother's roasted chicken, the whole bird there on a platter, steam rising from its brown skin, the sugary scent of cinnamon and baked apples beginning to drift in from the kitchen. "Tomorrow, I'll make you some macaroni and cheese," Virginia said. "Grab a leg, Joe," Calhoun said. "Go ahead." Drumstick. First bite, Mom looking at me. Abundance. A tiny glass tower filled with salt.

14.

La Paz, Bolivia

JOE RENTED A BACHELOR PAD in central Urbana and began to sort through his hundreds of pages of journal notes from Biafra. He started a novel. His unnamed protagonist in the *The Children's Song* was himself, in the second person. *Soon you were screening these fragile victims of starvation . . .* He typed in the mornings, six days a week, as one group of three astronauts took off for the moon and planted Old Glory in the white Sea of Tranquillity; and after a second crew played hopscotch on the lunar surface, he sent off his manuscript to various New York publishing houses.

By the time the third trip of moonwalkers was on the launchpad—
Apollo 13—he began to hear back from them.

AMONG THE STACKS of unsolicited and unagented manuscripts in the old
and paper-crammed offices of the publishing house on Union Square in
New York, Joe Sanderson's stood out; mostly for the subject matter, as outlined in the cover letter. Here was a Biafra novel, from an American who
had worked with the Red Cross in that country. News of the war was still
fresh in people's memories and a Biafra novel had commercial possibilities.
If the manuscript was half good, the reader might champion it and maybe
make his name doing so. For the two days the reader spent with Joe's book,
he felt very far from the place he was (Manhattan, in late winter, a hint of
spring in the occasional glint of sunshine on the upper stories of a skyscraper), and far from the places he had recently been (Yale, and its serene
brownstone and brick). *Fleeing Calabar around midnight, crossing the
river on a bamboo barge . . . poling down a moonlit shimmering swath toward the far shore . . . returning to the empty schoolhouse with your nurse,
companions collapsing beneath a shattered window pane . . .* Obviously Joe
Sanderson had been there, in Biafra. A mother saving the buttons from the
shirt of her dead child. The ring of truth. Something you can't make up . . .
*for they had other kids to attend to . . . other buttons to sew and snip . . . other
children to someday bury.* The reader put down Joe's manuscript after reading those words and decided to step outside into the New York afternoon,
and as he did so he saw buttons everywhere. Tiny white buttons clasped on
Mr. Straus's wrists as he came in through the door; red ones on the edge of
Miss Miller's wool skirt; and big buttons festooned with anchors on a man's
peacoat outside. The reader lived in a button-rich city, and the novel told
the story of a button-poor country. I read books precisely for moments like
these, thank you, Joseph Sanderson, to see Biafra in my mind's eye while I
take the elevator back up to the office, and again while I'm sitting at my

borrowed desk, looking out the frosty window to understand the world as it truly is.

Too bad most of the writing was so unpolished and unformed. A series of notes, really. Joe Sanderson filled page after page with sentence fragments and one ellipsis after another. Maybe six thousand ellipses in the entire book. This guy Sanderson wears out the period key on his Olivetti. I can see him at the typewriter repair shop: It's not typing periods anymore! And there was the problem of Sanderson's unnamed protagonist and narrator, who was prone to long speeches, such as the one that followed the death of a newborn baby . . . *villagers trailing behind you on the riverbank, hungrily listening to your words . . . revolution . . . revolution . . . telling them to stop being victims . . . refuse the blame for their own misery . . . become defiant . . . get weapons . . . break their link in the chain of death . . .* After that the reader skimmed up to the last of the three hundred sixteen pages, and he put the novel back in its box for the return trip to Urbana, Illinois. What was this Sanderson guy like? Maybe a white American man of about thirty-five, with vertical worry veins on his forehead. Troubled by all the suffering he'd seen in Africa, and also filled with a sense of his own inevitability as an author, unaware that his lecturing of the natives was off-putting, an echo of the White Man's Burden. People could read African writers now, after all, there were many, more published in the U.S. every day, and the reader wondered if there might be an African novel in that pile next to the editor's desk.

TWICE MORE JOE'S book-in-a-box bounced back to him. He went to work raising beams at a Champaign construction site and wondered what he would do next. He had circled the world, gone off and seen wars and the aftermath of wars in Korea, Vietnam, Yemen, Congo and Biafra, and he had watched children die in his arms—and none of it added up to a book anyone would publish. He turned twenty-eight, and left for Durango, Mexico, and tried his hand at gold prospecting, and lived in a cave, and he ended up in drinking parties with a Hollywood crew shooting a movie there.*

WHEN VIRGINIA GOT his letters from Mexico, she read them and told Calhoun her son sounded like he was in a rut, which was a strange thing to say about someone dedicated to "bumming" his way around the world. But he was better off in Mexico than in the United States. Her new job, on the campus of the University of Illinois, gave Virginia a hint of the deep unraveling of order unfolding across America. The students in Champaign-Urbana were ready to revolt over the killings of other students at Kent State, and over Nixon's invasion of Cambodia. She went back to work, balancing accounts for the Department of Geology; the undergraduates in her orbit were invariably friendly and polite, even when they were heading off to the protests. "Just a march for peace, ma'am." Someone bombed the campus ROTC office. Had to be outsiders. People from Chicago. The students declared "days of action," and then a strike, and the classrooms were empty, though the staff came in to work, as always.

She left her office one afternoon and came upon a line of buses near the quad, filled with police officers. Students were gathering nearby. She was carrying a set of memoranda and accounting reports on three sheets of paper, headed for the university administration building. Accounts payable, accounts receivable, qualifying cost, contribution revenue, exchange transactions. The essential bookkeeping that kept everything and everyone going: professors, adjuncts, janitors, toilet paper, the mimeograph machine. She looked at the pages and took her eyes off the path and she

---

*The Author is getting impatient with my aimlessness. He's starting to compress my life, squeezing years into paragraphs. And he's going to shortchange me a half dozen girlfriends or more. Sorry, ladies. All in all, this is brutal. I see now the disadvantage of being a character in a novel. There's no guarantees with these clowns writing your story.

collided with a state police officer who was holding a round stick as long as a sword across his body.

"Oh! Sorry."

"No worries, lady. But you dropped your papers."

A hefty breeze blew the sheets away. She chased after them and felt ridiculous, running in stiff wool, fifty-seven years old. One of the papers stood still and she stepped on it and grabbed it, and she took two more steps and caught the second one, but the third was swept away by another gust and jumped, froglike, off the surface of the grass. And then it skipped and slid between two young men in green uniforms who were wearing round helmets. Soldiers? Oh yes, she'd heard something about the National Guard. "Excuse me, dear," she said, following the disobedient memorandum as it was blown deeper onto the lawn, past the bare legs and sandaled feet of students, and she looked up at these young people to see them glaring at the soldiers and police officers behind her. Beads of sweat on the forehead of that too-pale girl; and a sunburn on that young, thin soldier holding a rifle stiffly before his chest. She moved her eyes back down to the ground, and she saw her memo clinging to a concrete path. It jumped onto a patch of grass and joined a herd of other papers, and the herd began to circle, and rose in the air and spun faster, and finally she grabbed one of the flying sheets, hoping it was hers, but when she looked at it, she did not see accounting terms, or lists of figures, but instead a gray, stylized fist, superimposed with a series of words, running on.

strike to end war strike to support the people's peace
treaty strike to march to westside park strike in solidarity with
the indochinese strike to seize control of your life strike to become more
human strike against increased tuition strike because there is no poetry in
your classes strike because classes are a bore strike for power strike to
smash the corporation strike to make yourself free strike to abolish rotc
strike because they are trying to squeeze the life out of you strike

The rhythm of the words mesmerized her, and she felt the presence of the word *strike* among the students gathered on the grass, inside the heads of the boys with their stubbly beards, in the lungs of the girls in their blue jeans and bell bottoms. *Trying to squeeze the life out of you.* So sad. She forgot about her memo and listened to the two students closest to her speaking.

"I don't think they'll arrest us."

"Of course they will."

"Look, that jarhead over there. He's got a flamethrower."

"What?"

"The tanks on his back. They're filled with gasoline."

"Holy shit! A flamethrower." The word spread through the crowd. A flamethrower. Fuck, a flamethrower. What the fuck? Flamethrower, fuck, fuck, fucking pigs with a flamethrower, man.

Virginia heard the snap of papers moving in the wind and looked downward and her precious memorandum was there, at her feet. Faceup. Fiscal year 1970–1971. Virginia Smith, accountant. She bent down and grabbed it and headed for the administration building and after a few steps a young man and a woman caught her eye. They were on the edge of the crowd of students, kissing. A French kiss. No decorum. Going on and on, their tongues. If your mothers could see you. As if it was going to be the last kiss before the end of the world.

AT THAT MOMENT, Joe was hitchhiking through Colombia, where he headed for a river where it was said a man could pan for gold. He found, instead, many ill and malnourished people. A month later, he took a job with the aid group CARE, and worked to bring food and medicine to the jungle region around the town of Barbacoas, until he was arrested and interrogated by the police and accused of subversive activities. He moved on to Bolivia and La Paz, which had become famous among American and

European bums for its cheap drugs and good, indigenous vibes; unfortunately, there had just been a military coup. *Che books burned and buried, vacationing Peace Corps workers with beards and work-worn clothes jailed and sheared. Cops think the gringos are commies; the people think we're CIA. The growing turmoil has the road bums spinning. And they are here in South America by the thousands,* Joe wrote home. *Squeezed out of Africa and Asia by war and a growing intolerance for us gringos. Down here they're at the end of the road.*

Joe's plan in Bolivia was to organize relief work, someplace. He started planning to open "a hippie hospital" and he wrote home to say he was talking to some German fellows about raising money for it, in the town of Sorata. When the clinic opened it was staffed by an American nurse, a Dutch doctor, and Joe; they offered the locals immunizations, protein supplements, prenatal care, free toothbrushes and yoga lessons. When he returned to La Paz, however, the police arrested him and threw him into a vast open cell in the Ministry of the Interior in La Paz, where 150 political prisoners stood together, inside cement walls the color of corn rot. The walls had scratches that were like hieroglyphs from an ancient civilization, and soon Joe joined the prisoners in staring at the scarred concrete, looking for faces, maps, rivers on the walls and on the ceiling until they fell asleep, sitting up, the saliva on their lips glistening in the light. A yellow light. The lightbulbs hung out of reach, protected by wire cages. Incandescent spirals, slow-burning. They remained on day and night, the prisoners told him, a form of torture. "The light is eating my brain," said a voice among the multitude. "If I open my eyes, I'll lose all my memories." The inmates were teachers, students and union guys, arrested in big sweeps through La Paz and the countryside. Police officers pulled them out of this cell, one at a time, and took them down to a room where other men applied wires to their testicles and their gums and electrocuted them. In another room, they made the prisoners stand on a flooded floor and ran the current into the water, so that the electrons ran up through their bare feet, and they felt the amperes flowing into the roots of their teeth, and into the vitreous gel of their eyes.

The next morning an officer led Joe to an interrogation room and left him there for an hour, alone with a table and a file folder. Joe finally opened the folder and saw his passport; on a whim, he grabbed it and walked out into the corridor, which was empty of guards, then through an office where a secretary glanced up at the blue-eyed inmate and mistook him for an American adviser. She smiled at him as he stepped out into the streets of La Paz. He hailed a taxi and rode directly to the U.S. Consulate, where he waved his passport at the first guard he encountered, and took two more steps and stood on the tiled floor of the U.S. diplomatic mission. On U.S. soil, as it were, a free man.

IN THE DAYS THAT FOLLOWED, Joe remembered the men in "the Lighthouse" every time he saw the fading, powdery orange slow of a La Paz dusk. He wrote a letter to the U.S. Embassy describing his detention and the conditions inside the Ministry of the Interior's prison and the torture of inmates there, along with the poor state of health of one elderly inmate, a Professor Joaquin Morales. Two days later Professor Morales was released. Joe contacted the Red Cross and convinced them to send food packages and blankets to the prisoners, and he helped Professor Morales's daughter post leaflets across La Paz one night calling on Bolivians to support the mothers who were gathering every day to protest the incarceration of their sons and daughters. He visited neighboring socialist Chile, and a fortune-teller told him he'd be famous before he turned forty. Maybe doing good works in Bolivia would be his path to fame, instead of writing books. When he returned to La Paz, he learned the government had closed the universities. Trade unions were outlawed. His mother, meanwhile, wrote to announce the birth of a baby to Steve and his new wife, Carol. Kathy, they named her. The Bolivian security services detained him again. Happy

New Year, Joseph David Sanderson: you are to be deported from Bolivia forthwith.*

Joe was allowed one piece of luggage. He loaded up his notebooks and photographs into the same rucksack he'd carried into Bolivia bumming a year earlier. I turned thirty here, and became fluent in Spanish. *Chocho* means happy, *choclo* means corn. He was being deported on a lovely Andean afternoon of thin air and penetrating sunlight and unexplainable and perplexing events, and Aymara and Quechua faces staring as Joe rode in a car to the airport, chaperoned by a man in a leather jacket who was either a cop or military intelligence. The car climbed out of the city, up to the airport, which was on a vast plain that stretched all the way to Peru, where billions of potatoes rested as seeds waiting to sprout from the soil, and where Aymara ghosts wandered at night. Joe's flight took off, and when the climbing aircraft turned, he looked out his window and saw a city of native people growing past the end of the runway, a sprawl of stubby concrete buildings stretching across the dusty Altiplano.

---

*They told me, "We don't like you. We know you are accepting money from cocaine producers (maybe I was), and we suspect you may be selling cocaine yourself (not true, yet). We know you are using marijuana with our youth and corrupting them (big deal). And we believe yoga is an exotic foreign idea with potentially dangerous uses."

15

Cuzco, Peru. Pensacola, Florida

STEVE SANDERSON OPENED THE DOOR. His little brother had an un-trimmed blond biker mustache and sideburns, and rock-band locks curling up behind his neck. We're both past thirty now. "Well, sir, I've got some-one for you to meet. Come on in," Steve said. "Kathy, come meet your uncle Joe." The baby wore a white beanie against the cold, and was wrapped in a pink blanket with gray dots. "Want to hold her? Yes, of course you do." Joe took the child in his cradled hands. A pair of luminous blue eyes peered back at him. The blue of lake ice when you turn it upside down. Eyes startled, searching. Sanderson blue. Wisps of whitish-blond hair. Little splotches of red on her cheeks and nose from the cold. Steve watched as his brother's face softened with wonder. Suddenly Joe was just one more person in the orbit of loving people around this little baby girl, and Steve believed that wherever Joe traveled, for the rest of his days, his path would lead him back to the place where Kathy lived.

URBANA WAS HOME AGAIN, for a while, but only until he saved enough money to return to South America. Months passed, a year, and finally Joe left for Peru, where he found a Walden and became a Spanish-speaking Thoreau. A ranch near Cuzco hired him as a caretaker and he lived alone in his own little adobe-brick house, with an acre to farm, and the responsibility of paying the farmhands who worked the bulk of the ranch. A stream ran at the bottom of his private acre, and fish swam in it. *Big huge enormous trout that barely fit in the skillet*, he wrote home. *Besides fishing 'n' farming, also building a kitchen, porch, front steps, repairing terrace walls, "corral" for animals, fish pond (also useful to cool my heels and chill my wine). The fields themselves are terraced on 5 levels, separated by Inca walls (probably around 500 years old). Even got peach trees and eucalyptus—growing corn + beans + alfalfa (any hints?). And oh, yeah, the rent is two bucks a month!* Steve forwarded Joe a letter from Mafalda in which she wrote to catch him up on her life: a failed marriage, and two children. Joe described his new digs to her: *The sun rises, the sun sets, the moonlight absolutely blows my mind at night when I sleep out by the fire.*

Another year of his life passed in this way. One day walking into town he picked up a newspaper and saw the Vietnam War had ended with the fall of Saigon. On most days he was asleep by 9:00 p.m., and up at 5:30 a.m., and a week could go by without him speaking to a soul. He read *Man's Fate*, by André Malraux, and kept twenty-three chickens outside in a corral, until a hawk came swooping down and hauled two of them off and he felt obliged to move the survivors inside. On the terraces he planted corn like the Incas did, using a stick. He finished building the stone walls of his kitchen, and while cutting grass on the mountainside to make a thatched roof for it he discovered an Inca tomb. *Dug up the skull—teeth in better shape than mine—and gave it to the village school.* He chopped wood, built fences and grew lettuce, cauliflower, tomatoes, onions and broccoli. *It's a good life, only about a hundred years behind the times.*

Joe might still be living on that farm, with a local señorita taken on as permanent company, but for the labor and social dispute that erupted on the property, and throughout the valley of Cuzco during his second year in Peru. The people who worked for the rancher claimed the right to take his land under a new agrarian reform law—they said the property, including Joe's small rented patch of it, was part of their Incan ancestral lands. Four members of the community, all over fifty and dressed in wool garb, showed up at his spread one afternoon to make their claim. When he wouldn't leave, they began to steal his corn at night, and spread rumors that he had been killed. "I thought you were dead," one of his wide-eyed neighbors told him when they crossed paths on the road to his place. Finally, Joe walked, unarmed, over to the huts of the insurrectionary workers and told them he would leave in two weeks, as soon as he brought in his corn crop. The theft of his corn stopped and the hawks overhead disappeared and no longer threatened his chickens. He brought in a big mound of corn and sold it on the cheap to a Quechua woman at the Cuzco market, and on his last day on the ranch he took all the ancient potsherds he had collected from the property and returned them to the earth.

BACK IN ILLINOIS, Joe took jobs in painting and construction. And he signed up for flying lessons and wrote to Mafalda: *Pepe Pelican takes to the clouds! America doesn't seem like "home" anymore and hasn't for a long time. But of course I'll try hard to be a loyal Yankee and a good little white boy—at least until the next revolution comes along somewhere in Latin America* . . . He took more flying lessons, and soloed. *Wonder of wonders, apparently I can fly a goddamn airplane. Much fun dodging clouds, chasing rainbows, and in general wandering alone through the cities of the gods.* He wrote to Bolivia to tell his old friends he was a licensed pilot, and one suggested he come *back home* to South America and set up a *bush flying service.* Andrew Buford was a small-time cocaine dealer from La Paz, who apparently wasn't so small-time anymore, because he said he could send Joe enough money to buy an airplane. Buford also relayed good political news from Bolivia: President Banzer, the nation's torturer in chief, was being forced to call elections. Democracy was on the horizon. Buford offered to pay Joe enough to get his hippie hospital in Sorata started again.

The adventure did not turn out as planned; among other things, the Bolivian authorities refused to license Joe to fly there. On his return journey to the United States, six months later, he was arrested at the international airport in Miami by United States customs officers for failing to declare the nine thousand dollars in cash in his possession. He spent twelve hours in an airport detention facility, in a well-lit room with a table, seated, answering questions from two customs agents, watching them look through his journal. "You've got really lousy handwriting. What's this *K* here? *K* means kilos. 20 kilos." But he was holding nothing that would allow the agents to charge him with drug trafficking. He explained that all the twenty-, fifty- and one-hundred-dollar bills in his possession were the money left over from his failed attempt to restart a Bolivian hospital, which was partially true. In fact, he'd invested a bit in Buford's smuggling operations, and reaped the profits, and also arranged a sale in La Paz to a friend who had traveled to the United States with one hundred and fifty grams hidden in various parts of her baggage and body. The customs agents confiscated his money and slapped a federal charge on him. Failure to declare. He was released on bond, and he stepped out into the Miami sunlight as an accused felon.

JOE WAS TOLD he'd have to stay in the state of Florida until the matter was resolved. He found a house with cheap rent on the Gulf of Mexico, near Pensacola, and a job as a bartender. *I'm gonna by gawd write me another novel*, he wrote Mafalda. *And this time total comedy, zany, utterly absurd. Should be quite a change from the usual cosmic sadness.* He would capture the Wild West feel of Bolivia's drug boom, with some of his past capers thrown in. And since "Joe Sanderson" had been rejected by every New York publisher he admired, Joe adopted a nom de plume for *The Cocaine Chronicles*: Lance Kilooroy.* Buford became "Captain Sunshine," and his aging hippie La Paz friends became "the mad fucking bastards of the Treefrog Beer and Mountain Climbing Club."

Joe wrote every morning in his new beach home, which he called "the Playhouse." He turned on the color TV and he saw that Iran was splitsville with the Shah, and Nicaragua was divorcing Somoza. The places he'd been bumming were being consumed in flames, overrun by crowds and peppered with gunfire. The South African police murdered a writer named Stephen Biko, and "black consciousness" was the new byword of the angry masses who shuffle-danced and sang as they marched. Vietnam, now a unified communist country, was about to invade its communist neighbor, Cambodia. The pastoral, peaceful Cambodia through which he had bummed was now the site of a horrific genocide, the city people being marched into the countryside.

In the world of Joe's travels, and in the bosom of his family, one time was ending, and another was beginning.

His mother wrote a letter from Kansas to say Grandmother Colman had died.

I sat up nights with her from Sunday night on until she passed Thursday

---

*The Author did not make this name up. I did. Kilo + Kilroy. I thought it was funny.

noon. The last thing she said Tuesday evening was, "I'm lonesome. Don't leave me." Days went by. Marg and I were having tea when we heard a gasp, and she was gone. Joe remembered his grandmother's loose-fitting dresses, the spots on her fingers, and the milky smell of her. Her copy of *Huckle-berry Finn*, cloth cover, sewn spine, sketches of Huck and Jim. Joe playing on the rolling farmland, coming back to the farmhouse and Granny's lunches and dinners. The look of contentment when she saw him reading. Standing on a ridge above Lawrence. "That town was started up by people who hated slavery, Joe. Your own great-grandfather came here because he was an abolitionist."

The next letter Joe received from his mother said she was back in Urbana and had more sad news: Karen Thomas was very ill. Karen's parents were keeping vigil at her bedside in the hospital. Joe began to write to her immediately. *Just got a letter from my Ma with your "night alley" photo from the newspaper. Not bad, lady, not bad. Seems we used to wander through some of those alleys once upon a time, no? Ah, the lovely memories of our teen-age years! But what's this I hear about you being in the hospital?* Early the next day, before he could mail the letter, his mother called. Karen had died from brain cancer. He felt the ordinary morning being swallowed up by the telephone receiver. Skinny and seventeen, fall in Urbana, Karen squeezing my hand.

"Joe, are you there?"

"Yes."

The day after Karen's funeral, which he missed thanks to the charges still pending against him in Florida, he received a call from his attorney in Miami: the feds were dropping the case and returning his money. He used the funds to buy an old Cessna and he became a flying bum, enjoying a se-ries of aerial adventures skipping around the South and Southwest. He vis-ited his retired father in Arizona. Milt had added up his contributions to the world catalog of living things and showed Joe his final tally: number of beetle species named, ninety-eight; number of genera named, ten; number of species named after him by other scientists, forty-six. Joe brought him the first chapters of *The Cocaine Chronicles*. Milt dove into the manuscript and after twenty or so pages, declared: "Son, I think some editing might help here." He didn't want to discourage his son, but the young man was thirty-seven now. "Point taken," Joe answered. "But where in the hell am I going to find an editor?"

After a series of conversations and letters between Arizona, Illinois and Florida, Steve put Joe in touch with a woman, Katherine Reed, who edited long, narrative reports for the University of Illinois. She read his manuscript and told him *The Cocaine Chronicles* was "not a great title, it's too generic," and suggested he change it to *The Silver Triangle*, and she assigned one of her underlings to work on the manuscript. All the while, Joe tended bar in Pensacola, working with the television on, watching the world of his travels flash by during the evening news broadcasts. No one else in that smoky bar had been to Lebanon, seen the Congo River, or the mountain ranges that loom over Teheran. In what had been British Guiana, now Guyana, an American preacher led his followers into a mass suicide and mass murder in the jungle. Generals staged a coup in Afghanistan and a civil war had started in the rocky mountain passes Joe had crossed with Rebecca. Thousands of labor leaders and leftists had been murdered after a right-wing coup in Chile. Rifle and cannon fire were tearing up the apartments and office buildings in Beirut. French troops were fighting rebels in the country that was once called Congo, changed to Zaire. The Shah fled Iran, there was a coup in Grenada and another one in Bolivia, with tanks on the streets, and barricades and striking miners, and a helicopter firing on the people below. And in Nicaragua, a revolution led by a guerrilla army. Thin and slight men and women with baby-brown eyes trying to look menacing as they held M16s and old revolvers and hunting rifles. The Nicaraguan revolution unfolded on the wavy color lines of the television set in the bar, armies of adolescents marching along a highway, and of course he should be there, with them, living it. The rebels were in the capital, Managua, nearly victorious, and Joe was not there. He was stuck waiting for his novel to be edited, and suddenly the Nicaraguan revolution was over, triumphant, with red-and-black Sandinista flags flying in Managua, but now there was El Salvador, and a coup and a popular uprising, and even from thousands of miles away he could see how this fight was going to be bloodier than a dozen Nicaraguas. On the television, he saw a woman shouting into a megaphone. "Se siente, se siente, la línea combatiente." I'm the only one in the bar who understands her. A massacre on the stone steps of a cathedral, soldiers firing at men and women crawling up the steps for cover.

El Salvador. His sedentary writing months on the Florida panhandle had left him flabby, in no shape to hit the road again. So he started lifting weights and jogging along the beach, and he was returning sweaty and shirtless from one of his runs when he saw Mafalda standing on his porch. On a whim, she'd taken the bus down from Ohio, the state to which she'd moved some years before, to work at a university alongside a man who was for a time her husband. She was carrying a change of clothes in a small bag, and a jar of peanut butter that had sustained her during the long ride south.

"My little tramp!" he called out.

They embraced and Mafalda stepped back and took a breath and looked at him. *He's been in the sun too much. I see it around your eyes, in the texture of the skin on your forehead, your cheeks.* But his torso, his arms, were firm, she soon discovered. Tight. She told him about her "gypsy" adventures hitchhiking across America, alone mostly. Inspired by and in tribute to Joe. Los Angeles to Vancouver. Ohio to everywhere. They spent several days together inside the Playhouse, emerging only to take long walks on the sand. At his insistence, she read several chapters of his book. Maybe the time for this kind of writing has passed, she said. "This is so male, so macho. It's not a boy's world anymore." He pouted for an entire afternoon, but then he was his charming self again, and the next day he took her for a ride in his plane. Back at the beach house they saw a huge storm on the ocean horizon. Hurricane Frederic. The next morning the radio was announcing mandatory evacuations, and Joe told Mafalda she should probably head back home.

"What about you?"

"I'll ride it out. Should be interesting."

He drove her to the bus station, and later he felt the last touch of her fingers as they slipped through his when they said goodbye at the door of the bus.

Once the waves had nearly reached the house, I put my manuscript and your jar of peanut butter in a rucksack, ready to evacuate, he wrote to her later. *But no go. The wind died down and the house still stands. Walked outside at dawn. Pensacola beach was absolutely wrecked. And a hangar door at Pensacola airport had squashed my . . . sniff! . . . pretty little plane. Insurance company plans to send me check for $5,900.*

He phoned Katherine Reed, the editor, and she said the work on his novel would take at least three months more. No, Joe Sanderson isn't going to wait here in Florida and miss another revolution. He began planning a trip to El Salvador. The road never failed to disappoint, to uplift, to give him a sense of purpose. Se siente, se siente, la línea combatiente. One era was ending and another one was beginning. In Iran, an angry mob had stormed the United States embassy in Teheran and taken hostages, and a sense of powerlessness and outrage drifted across the United States, until assorted yahoos began to beat up swarthy men in U.S. cities, chanting "Fuck Iran" as they did their vengeful work. The world was bloody and aflame on his television, while pelicans glided over his Playhouse porch, and country music crooned on the radio at the bar. Soon he would travel beyond the reach of these broadcasts, beyond American AM and FM, beyond UHF and VHF, into the true world of the tropics, where men and women, and boys and girls carried revolvers, and peered over the tops of bandannas, their young eyes leading them into battle.

While you read this, I am imperishable,

somehow more alive than I have ever been . . .

—Marilynne Robinson, *Gilead*

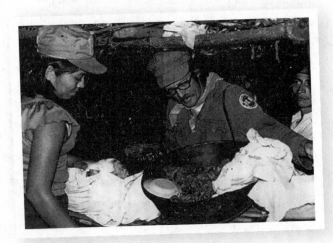

III

The Part
About the War:
Lucas

16.

San Salvador, El Salvador

AFTER TRAINS, AIRPLANES and buses through New Orleans and Mérida, Mexico, Joe arrived in Guatemala City, where a state of siege and curfew kept the streets empty after sundown. He entered El Salvador and walked around a border town a bit, and crossed paths with two National Guard soldiers in smartly tailored uniforms and steel mushroom-top helmets who took long, stiff strides holding rifles with fixed bayonets. Leather shoes, polished to a mirror shine, pressed wool. Joe fell in behind them. These guys would arrest me if they knew the subversive thoughts in my head. He slipped into the town market, out of the sun, into the shade and the many sudden tastes in the cooler air. Wet sawdust, plantains, mangoes, charcoal fires. In the corner, between beams of light streaming through the roof, he saw a woman standing over a steaming tin pot that was as big as his mother's old washbasins. She was fair-skinned, with cheeks reddened from the fire beneath her, which she stoked with pieces of wood, and she stirred the contents of the pot by moving a wooden spoon in one slow oval after another, like some meditation on the eternity of women's labor. He stepped toward her. "Buenas tardes."

"En quince minutos, joven," she said. "Quince minutos más."

"¿Le molesta si espero, señorita?" he asked. Just a couple of days back in Latin America, and its courtesies were already part of his way of being. Not just, *Can I wait*, but rather, *Does it bother you, señorita, if I wait?*

"No," she said with a smile. "No me molesta para nada."

She had not stopped stirring. Atol, they called it. A corn drink. In every glass, a fog of maize particles, kernels stripped from ears grown on hillsides, gathered and ground by this woman's long fingers. She had set-apart eyes and every move she made, every glance she gave him, seemed practiced and deliberate and effortless. He could sense the textures of her story, the village it returned to, the dirt roads. Cornfields, here they're called milpas. The odd things you remember. Her spoon made waves in the syrupy surface of the liquid, and as Joe stood watching her she thought about all the other foreigners who came through this border town, and how none had ever stopped to keep her company like this. Company is good. His eyes. Set into skin browned by the sun, they emitted the piercing blue light of a distant world. "¿De dónde viene?" she asked.

"Estados Unidos," Joe answered. "Illinois. Cerca de Chicago."

She looked down at the liquid in the pot, and she could feel and see the atol thickening, how the waves she was making with her spoon were becoming stiffer, like the ridges she cut into the wet sand at the beach as a girl. She stopped. "Listo," she said, and she took a plastic cup and a ladle and served him, and when he reached into his pocket to pay, she said, "No, gratis," and he smiled back at her, which was like a kind of payment, to see a stranger's handsome face brighten in that way. The first cup of forty, or fifty. And for the rest of the day and week, as she sold her entire batch and the next one she made, and the next one after that, the woman thought that Joe had brought her good luck.

HE ARRIVED AT the shuttered city of San Salvador at night, the storefronts covered in steel and spray-painted leftist slogans. *Juicio a los criminales represores. Apoyo total a la lucha popular.* The next morning he emerged from his hotel to a sunny day. Probably snowing on the plains back home. Here, the evergreen cones of volcanoes on the horizon, looming over a metropolis of everyday Latin American commerce. Vendors in straw hats and baseball caps scurrying down the street. Maybe I'm the only gringo tourist in the entire country. The first night he went to a nightclub with a mirror-ball and many empty tables and no one dancing, and fell in with four burly young Americans with a military bearing and biceps-squeezing shirts: Marines assigned to the U.S. Embassy. Two of the Marines had been in Teheran a year before the takeover. "Iran was hot. But this place is hotter than a two-dollar revolver." The revolution did not seem imminent when Joe walked around town, and after two days he went out to the Pacific coast and met seven Americans who'd come for the waves. *Looking for a revolution and what do I find: a damn surfer colony*, he wrote home. As the surfers performed their hip-swerving dance and tumble on the foamy seawater, a local group of ragamuffin boys and girls sat on the beach and clapped and gestured and hopped on the sand, and for Joe there was something at once satisfying and deeply disappointing in the act of watching the children as they watched the surfers. I came looking for a war but instead I found what I always find: scraggly kids. The young tribe that follows tourists everywhere. He walked up to them and asked, jokingly: "¿Dónde está la revolución?" and they looked at him wide-eyed and fearful and ran away. The next morning he picked up a newspaper and saw a big march was planned in San Salvador for later in the week, so he headed back to the capital.

JOE STEPPED OUT of his San Salvador hotel and a half block away he saw the line of marchers. Thousands of people, suddenly, on streets that had been completely empty the night before. Ordinary working people, and young men and women with the inquisitive eyes of college students, marching behind banners held by many hands, as wide as the avenue. Red and black, white letters, acronyms he is not yet able to decipher. FAPU. LP-28. The raised fists of men dressed in faded polyester blends. MASAS the sign says. *The Masses*, as in the crowds and barricades of Victor Hugo's Paris. A romantic notion of how history is made. Joe sees faces covered in bandannas and understands immediately that they are disguising themselves against the government agents and their cameras. He sees this because he has deeper, road-bum vision now. A woman smiles at him, and he knows it's because he's a gringo "in solidarity" with the cause. In a demonstration, all are equal and all belong. I am a representative of all Americans. A gringo among them, tall and grinning. My body added to the sum of marching bodies. The sum is the point. Never been in a crowd this big. We fill up four, five, six city blocks. There is a metaphor that describes the way we are packed into these streets, plazas and parks. A swelling sea of secondhand shirts and straw and paper hats. A tide of marching limbs in bell-bottomed blue jeans, rising from the street onto the sidewalks. FOR A REVOLUTIONARY GOVERNMENT. More slogans. LA UNIDAD POPULAR ES INVENCIBLE. Here and there a young man with a firearm, clumsily hidden. A little revolver in someone's pocket, an M16 wrapped up in newspaper. Twenty years on the road and finally I land in a revolution.

Joe heard the beat of a snare drum and in the distance some recorded hurdy-gurdy music. He could see the National Palace a few blocks away, its

Greek columns. Someone pointed up at a tall office building. "¡Soldados!" There are soldiers up there. "Keep your discipline, compañeros! Stay calm!" He heard the air-splitting crack of a rifle shot, followed by three more, and then a volley of shots, and he ran for cover and so did all the people around him. A mother running with her son. Joe looked up and could see a soldier aiming downward from the roof of a building, the recoil of his rifle. A kid with a revolver crouched behind a lamppost, the student with the M16 was unwrapping it. "Keep your lines!" a voice on the megaphone says. "¡Calma!" Joe was leaning against the steel grating of a storefront, and the street had emptied except for six or seven young men, a proto–guerrilla army. They resembled a bunch of guys from a neighborhood performing some sort of drill. Performing it poorly. A Mauser, a little automatic pistol, an old hunting rifle, very old. Joe was scared for them because none of them seemed to have fired a gun in anger before. They all started to rush forward, and Joe followed them, and turning a corner he saw a woman lying in the street, facedown, and also a girl nearby, her hands splayed upward as she lay on her back. He ran toward them.

The girl's eyes were fixed in a sleepy squint, and she had the befuddled expression of a child who's already inside the first strange scenes of a dream. She wore a cobalt-blue dress covered with blood from the waist down. Joe became the medic he was in Biafra, and he placed a hand on her throat; she had no pulse. He turned her over and saw a bullet hole in her lower back. A school ID slipping from a pocket in her dress. Thirteen years old. Luz Esmeralda Falcón. He walked over to the woman and saw an entry wound to her neck, and a stream of blood that had flowed into the street and toward a gutter. She also had no pulse, though her expression was more of a grimace, as if she were suffering an unpleasant bowel movement. The last moments of their lives, their final thoughts, written on their faces. As he crouched next to the dead woman and the dead girl, he felt as if someone were standing over him, looking at him, and that he was living inside the head of this other person, a confused and sickened Illinois man with a girl's blood on his fingers; an earnest son, a former Boy Scout and newspaper-delivery kid transported to the sunshine of El Salvador, on a street next to a utility pole, looking up at the crisscrossing wires over a dead woman and child, still and lifeless, looking for the son-of-a-bitch sniper who shot them, while the trickle of blood around them was becoming a coagulating pool, a crimson mirror, until finally a shouting female voice from a megaphone shook him out of his trance.

"¡No tengan miedo, compañeros!" The voice meant to rally the demonstrators, but her words were absurd. *Don't be afraid.* Across the street, he saw a boy of about six huddled against the steel doorway of a shuttered storefront. On the street itself, protesters were carrying the wounded away from the place where the shooting was taking place, and now Joe found himself moving toward the gunfire, in a crouch-walk and then a crouch-sprint. The shooting stopped as he reached the steps of the cathedral. He saw more bodies. Five, lined up. A television news crew pointing a camera at him. Among the five dead he saw two young men with wispy mustaches who looked like brothers; a boy covered them in the black-and-red banners they had been carrying. People were moving away from the plaza, to the north and west, and he followed them for a block, and then there was a sudden fusillade of gunfire behind him, and Joe heard bullets hitting the light posts and felt plaster crumbs strike him on the cheek. He ran one more block to his hotel and banged on the locked door, and a trembling desk clerk let him in.

FIVE DAYS LATER, he was back in the coastal town of La Libertad, amid the sea breezes. The killing in San Salvador seemed far away. When he entered his old hotel, one of the surfers he'd met before spotted him in the lobby and said, "Hey, dude, we saw you on TV."

Joe wrote a letter to his mother. In the aftermath of his recent brush with mortality, he imagined her seeing images of the dead on the six-o'clock news. His mission, as it had been so often, was to amuse her with a good tale, and let her know her son was okay and unharmed, despite having witnessed the public murder of approximately forty-five people.

Your son, the TV star, he began. After so many years since showing my snakes and butterflies on that kids' program I finally made the big time. You've probably been hearing a bit about all the fighting here. Well, it was pretty grim. A massacre on the central plaza. I was there. And according to friends here on the seacoast, I made the evening news. There I was, ambling across a park and in front of a cathedral where a lot of bodies were lying, with both hands and my usual stack of newspapers on top of my head. The National Guard was posted nearby, and sportingly enough they didn't open up on me. There was still a lot of ducking sniper fire before I made it out of there. Real unfriendly. Didn't even allow me time enough to tell 'em I'd been in the National Guard myself! The people on the streets were students, workers, country folk, trying to fight an army with pistols and shotguns and a few machine guns. Lots of them retreated to the university, where they promptly got surrounded by the army. Snuck in the next day to see how folks were doing. Everybody had been fighting all night, pretty tired and hungry, but not too many wounded + dead. Medical students had things pretty well under control so there wasn't much I could do except share cigarettes. Finally the army backed off so everyone could go home.

I'm doing fine but figure I best be getting on my way to Nicaragua, where things have quieted down. Nobody can figure out what I'm doing here. Just like always, they figure I'm a commie or CIA, and that gets old. Hence, time to head on down the line.

He spent a week in revolutionary Nicaragua, where the mood was one of joyful exhaustion, of rebuilding and renewal. The new government had announced an ambitious plan to teach the entire country to read and write, and to cure other ills of the recently ended dictatorial era, and Joe thought he might find a way to stay there and help, perhaps with the anti-malaria program. But his thoughts returned to the bodies on the plaza, the dead girl and the woman, especially, and after two weeks in Managua he got back on the bus and returned to San Salvador. *I'm realizing now*, he wrote home, *that I don't really know the people of these Central American countries well enough.**

JOE RETURNED TO the University of El Salvador, which continued to function as a liberated zone in the heart of the city, and he introduced himself to the people he met, who were huddled in groups in the narrow lawns between the buildings, debating the political situation, or in classrooms emptied of desks, making banners and printing leaflets. His presence elicited curiosity, suspicious looks and the basic question, *What are you doing here?* Or, in the local dialect: *¿Y vos, qué hacés aquí?* I'm just here to show my solidarity, he'd say. He told them the story of his travels, his visits to Vietnam and Africa, and his work in Bolivia, and then more about Vietnam, because of all the things he had to say, this seemed to hold their attention the most.

"You were in Vietnam?" a student named Byron asked him, because he'd heard about Joe from a friend.

Joe described how the United States military, the most powerful fighting force in history, had been surrounded by an army of children in Saigon, and how he'd seen the city shelled by this rebel army. Byron was so enthralled with Joe's account, imagining how the Salvadoran revolution might become as powerful a force as Vietnam's, that he began to tell his friends:

---

*In the name of "art," the Author is neglecting to explain some pretty basic facts: Namely, why the Salvadoran people were up in arms. Back then—and maybe even now, for all I know—"Fourteen Families" owned the country. We're talking comic book evil, and "let them eat cake" privilege. And when the smart and the brave rose up, they were kidnapped and never seen again. That's why all those kids in the march were carrying guns. For self-defense.

There is a Vietnam veteran, an American soldier, here among us, on the campus.

In his jeans and T-shirt, and with his now-bushy hair, and with his gonzo demeanor and a pack of smokes at the ready to share with anyone, Joe was the picture of a disaffected North American GI. As if he'd stepped out of the jungles they'd seen on the television news, or from those American peace protests that featured ex-soldiers in loose-fitting, carefree army fatigues, with cigarettes dangling from their lips. As word spread on the university grounds that the tall, blond man roaming about the campus had fought in Vietnam, the stories about him grew more elaborate. The gringo had been forced to shoot at the peasants over there, in the rice fields. He's wracked with guilt. That's why he's come here. He wants to fight with us.

To others, Joe was an object of suspicion. As veterans of labor strikes and marches and the takeovers of government buildings, they had seen friends and comrades shot in the street, or kidnapped in public and murdered. They were members of mobilization committees and rural cooperatives deemed subversive by the forces of order, and they were used to being monitored and surveilled, and when they met Joe they were not convinced he could be trusted, even if he was a repentant soldier of the American empire. Joe was becoming a fixture at the daily events of the revolution, at the rallies and the occupation of the Panamanian Embassy, at the impromptu barricades in the popular barrios, at the press conferences across San Salvador. A hippie mascot to their revolution. His ubiquitousness and his fluency in Spanish, with its odd Illinois-Peruvian-Bolivian mongrel accent, caused them to worry. It was one thing to encounter an American on the sidelines at the rallies—but quite another when that American understood everything they were saying and could mimic their speech. Joe had quickly learned that *cuilios* was local slang for police or soldiers, and that *cipote* meant child, and he peppered his sentences with the syllable *va*, which was a vocalized pause equivalent to *you know* in English. Joe had pierced the linguistic shield that protected them from gringo power, and when he said, in fluent Spanish, "I want to help you, I can help the revolution," it fed their paranoia.

After meeting Joe at a university rally, a leader in one of the many "popular fronts" in San Salvador assigned a woman from the organization's ranks to talk to Joe and find out if he was a spy. Her movement name was "Mariposa," a common nom de guerre among the proto-rebels, and later Joe would meet another "Mariposa," and so he would remember this one as "the First Butterfly." Mariposa was twenty-five years old, the recipient of an interrupted university education in sociology, and the daughter of an attorney who had been assassinated for the crime of representing a Catholic peasant group. She was raccoon-eyed from too many sleepless nights, and carried with her a copy of a novel by the Salvadoran writer Manlio Argueta that was considered subversive propaganda by the authorities, and she was also among the growing number of women in San Salvador who were familiar with the workings of an M16. She knew the zigzagging paths that led out of the urban sprawl, past shacks clinging to dry riverbeds, and up into the mountains, to the camps where a rebel army was being formed amid the birdsong and the rural compost heaps.

Mariposa found Joe on the University of El Salvador campus and invited him to lunch, and they proceeded to a nearby Chinese restaurant. After an hour of chow mein, conversation and gentle questioning, Mariposa arrived at an understanding of who Joe Sanderson was. He was moderately educated and had spent most of his adult life traveling, allowing himself the luxury of visiting war zones and impoverished communities around the world. Joe was not a Vietnam veteran, though he had been in the United States Army, as a medic. He was genuinely sympathetic to the Salvadoran people, and especially to the plight of its children, and he had worked to bring health care to the poor in Nigeria, Ecuador and Bolivia. He was also a "novelist" who had never published a book. In the end Mariposa felt a sympathy for Joe she had not expected when first meeting him. He was a man who worked hard to retain his boyish belief in a world without borders, where he could go wherever he pleased, living unencumbered by responsibilities, even as one nation-state after another fell apart in his footsteps. I can only dream of living the way he does, floating from country to country. Imagine that. Just drifting across the Caribbean and South America on trains and ships. India, elephants, Nepal, snowcapped peaks. I did not know this species of human existed in the world, men who wander and wander until they turn old, and don't stop. He was tall, sandy-blond, and handsome, and also vulnerable and lonely.

"I'd like to help, however I can," he said.

"Veremos," she answered. We'll see. But then she added, "I think it would probably be better for you if you went home." Joe did not know, and never knew, that his life hung in the balance in that conversation with First Butterfly. If she had reported back to the front's leaders that Joe was unequivocally an American agent, he would have been lured to a remote corner of San Salvador and murdered. His death would have been viewed as one more mystery with a patina of political conspiracy, his body dumped at a trash-strewn crossroads or highway. An American corpse, added to the aggregate of Salvadoran corpses and to the oppressive swirl of randomness and cruelty that was tormenting the country's five million residents.

Instead, Mariposa reported back to the front's leaders that Joe Sanderson was definitely *not* an American agent, but simply a well-meaning gringo vagabond, an eccentric. Joe continued to float around the university and the city, but in the wake of his conversation with First Butterfly he realized how conspicuous he was, because she was able to list some of the many places the "militantes" of her movement had spotted him. Probably he was already in many photographs taken by the Salvadoran intelligence services too. He tried to be more careful in what he wrote home to his mother, and he started telling her he was *taking Spanish classes* at the university, and he referred to the activists there as *schoolteachers*. He read four or five newspapers a day and used what he learned in their pages to find his way to the street battles that inevitably took place whenever the popular organizations (of which he counted at least thirty) declared a mobilization or a general strike. Joe watched students burn tires and schoolteachers throw stones, and more masked young men exchanging shots with soldiers, and sometimes he wondered if there were a point to his voyeurism: what he was seeing was still too complex and chaotic to fit in a novel, and who would he be in said book besides the gringo wandering from one life-and-death event to the next. The only other Americans who crossed his path were the photojournalists, but their cameras had the odd effect, he noticed, of keeping them from being fully immersed in the events they were documenting. Joe believed he was the only American with unencumbered eyes upon the drama, the one pure representative of more than two hundred million people in the most powerful country on earth.

His visa was set to expire again, so he made his way out of the country, for a brief visit to Mérida, where he picked up money Steve had forwarded to him. He was in that Mexican city when he read in the newspaper that Monsignor Óscar Romero, the Archbishop of San Salvador, had been assassinated while conducting Mass. On the day Joe left Mérida to return to San Salvador, he read about the massacre at the archbishop's funeral, and more about the archbishop's activities during his final days, including his exhortations to the troops of the Salvadoran Army and National Guard not to fire on civilians. "No soldier is obliged to obey a law contrary to the law of God." From Mexico, free to speak his mind, Joe wrote to Calhoun and his mother: *The massacre at the archbishop's funeral sounds worse than the one I saw on Jan. 22. Concerned about my friends in San Salvador, but won't know how they made out until my return next weekend. And it's gonna get worse. At least several hundred people are murdered every week.*

When he returned to El Salvador, he wrote home and once again used the silly, perfunctory code that disguised his activities. *So it's back to the books for me, at least for a couple more months. All's well, feels good to be back here, and the family (schoolteachers) send their regards.* He fell in with a group of activists who allowed him to paint banners; then they appointed him a lookout and decoy when they performed actions in a working-class section of El Salvador called Mejicanos, a neighborhood of narrow streets covered with webs of utility wires. If the police arrived while the militants were painting slogans on the walls, or building a barricade, Joe could simply walk up to the officers and pretend to be a lost gringo, and slow down the forces of order long enough for the militants to get away. They called themselves "compas," which was short for compañeros, which was a less-Marxist Latin American synonym for "comrades." The compas were accounting students, high schoolers, middle schoolers, and part-time street vendors, and sometimes they would bring him along in a car, and have him be a passenger while they delivered ammunition or pamphlets, so that the driver could say, *This gringo tourist hired me to take him to the beach*, and Joe could wave at the officer or soldier and say, *Hola!*

You'd love my schoolteachers, Joe wrote home. *Hardworking, fun-loving and full of jokes, and sometimes a bit on the noisy side. Living here and getting fat and working my tail off kind of reminds me of being on the farm! Even got folks pestering me about smoking. And I don't dare partake of a beer in their presence.* He watched them make homemade bombs from milk bottles, and gave some basic instructions on the use and cleaning of their old revolvers. When he wasn't helping out the compañeros, he attended more press conferences. On the stage of the university's law school auditorium he saw members of various popular organizations, and the Minister of Education, proclaim themselves a government-in-waiting calling itself the Democratic Revolutionary Front. (Several weeks later, nearly all of the members of this alternate government were rounded up by the army and murdered.) At this same press conference Joe met a woman who said she was writing for *The Nation*: she was from Champaign-Urbana, the niece of a professor at the Agriculture Department. On May Day, he joined up with her in the center of San Salvador for the traditional workers' march, which was sparsely attended, given the recent public massacres. The next day, looking through his newspapers, he saw a photograph of a line of protesters stand-ing near the central market: on the far right, walking toward the photogra-pher, was a tall, thin figure with bushy, light hair, the only person looking directly at the camera. Himself, the wandering son of Urbana, bum extraor-dinaire, unpublished novelist, and now a getaway driver to teenage rebels. He clipped it out and sent it home. *Thought y'all might get a kick out of this May Day news photo,* he wrote. *That's me with the shades, white T-shirt and pants. At least 90% of the folks you see are armed, semisecretly, with pistols, shotguns (saw-offs), light machine guns, and homemade grenades. Many are wearing masks to prevent identification.*

He moved in with a family of Evangelical Christians who lived in a working-class neighborhood of San Salvador. The rent was very cheap, and had the advantage of being in an area sympathetic to the revolution. *Fighting broke out in the streets behind my house yesterday around 5:45 a.m. when a squadron of neighborhood lads erected barricades across the intersec-tions. But pistols aren't much good against machine guns and tanks, so once Nat. Guard arrived they shot it out briefly and withdrew,* Joe wrote home. *Of course, I didn't dare go into the streets. Spent most of the day studying al-gebra, writing letters to my old high school teachers, and practicing tap dancing (please tell Calhoun to stop snorting!). Anyway, if you want to know what a military invasion is like, it's similar to preparing for a hurricane or tornado. You figure on no power, communications or outside food and water for a few days. Get together candles + flashlights + medicine, and be ready to evacuate if bombing and strafing start.*

VIRGINIA HAD RECENTLY RETIRED, and Joe's letters from El Salvador en-tered the flow of her retiree life, days that revolved around time spent with Calhoun and her granddaughter, Kathy, and visits with Annabel Ebert and other friends. Once a week, she watched Annabel's son, Roger, on her new color TV, talking about movies. Breakfast at the Union with Steve, the occasional wedding. She made strawberry shortcakes and pork roasts. Reading her younger son's missives, and his descriptions of massacres, murders and battles caused her moments of unsettledness; she studied the clipping he had sent, and briefly examined it with the magnifying glass Calhoun used to study his atlas. In the tiny pixels she imagined she saw a smirk. Self-satisfied. Here I am again, in the middle of trouble. Very funny, son. Finally she set his letter down and numbered it and put it in a shoebox. The very large number of letters in these boxes was reassuring, because they were a reminder that Joe had been to many dangerous places and always survived to return home. She numbered the letters when she opened them, and then she numbered her replies. Here goes number fifteen.

Have a happy birthday and all of us will be thinking about you on your day, she wrote. He was going to turn thirty-eight. The string of years that went back to Fayetteville and that bassinet. A time when he was small enough for me to carry. I can remember, will always remember. Candles on the cake, pin the tail on the donkey. *We are planning on depositing twenty-five dollars in your Urbana Home Loan account as a present. You should buy swim shorts with it.* Here we live the rhythms of the seasons and of our granddaughter's childhood. *Kathy makes up and folds down her own bed when she stays here.* At night we watch the television news, wondering if we might catch a glimpse of you in El Salvador. In his next letter home, Joe joked about being out and about with his friends *the algebra and Spanish teachers*, at the scene of a barricade, and being *wounded* while running away from the National Guard: he had jumped over said barricade and tripped, scraping his knee, thus meriting a *Purple Heart*.

Now that you have been awarded a Purple Heart, she wrote back, *we hope that you receive the proper treatment. And will you please stop studying so hard. I can't remember that you were that great at algebra and you must drive your Spanish teachers crazy.* All I can do is joke with him. Nothing else. Virginia waded through three newspapers every day and clipped out stories about El Salvador to send to him once a month. She watched the television news and saw corpses in El Salvador and flaming vehicles. Our new peanut-farmer president says he'll stop sending money to El Salvador, but he can't fix that country, just like he can't fix this one. *I am making two of Kathy's sweaters larger for her,* she wrote to Joe. On a typewriter now, keeping a carbon. *I knitted them so I know just what to do. Grandpa Calhoun measured her on her place on the wall and she has grown at least 3 inches in the last 6 months.*

JOE HAD NOT YET RECEIVED his mother's birthday letter before he got around to writing and sending his next one. *A grim and gloomy day,* he began. *A kid I worked with at the university got shot and killed by the military during the last strike. Friends were burying him right on university grounds beside other graves.* Joe did not know Manuel as well as he knew other comrades in the Liga Popular. Manuel was the memory of a face at the edge of the gatherings. Feeding ink into the mimeograph machine in the league's office in a university classroom. One conversation with him about a Creedence Clearwater Revival song, of all things. "What is he saying, Joe?" "Earthquakes and lightning. Terremotos y relámpagos." They buried him after a eulogy delivered by a comrade whose tears flowed down from amber eyes into the red bandanna covering his face, after digging a grave in a patch of lawn near the Department of Odontology. In the days that followed Joe watched as future dentists walked to their classrooms passing Manuel's resting place, and he listened to Manuel's friends tell stories of his commitment to the cause and his love for the Rolling Stones and the way his hand trembled when he first held and fired a revolver. In moments of quiet Joe sensed that their memories of Manuel were taking corporeal form in the skin and muscle around their temples and behind their eyes. Death was transforming their cause into a journey toward the afterlife. Manuel was canonized in their remembrances of him, and a few compas wrote about him in the private journals they kept, in notebooks with printed covers depicting cartoons of horses and daisies, and they penned poems to him peppered with the joyful salutation ¡Compañero!

A few days later Joe was at the university again, too early for there to be much going on, and he said hello to the few members of the Liga he encountered; they were in the office reading newspapers and typing up letters, and he left to see if he might meet up with that woman who wrote for *The Nation*. Two blocks from the university he saw a small armored personnel carrier, and thought little of it. Later that day, he was inside a store in the center of San Salvador when he heard a breathless radio report describing how National Guard tanks and troops were sweeping through the university, exchanging gunfire with the students and activists. The siege that followed lasted three days; Joe saw pictures in the newspapers of corpses of young people lying on the campus passageways, and when it was over the government announced that the University of El Salvador would be closed indefinitely. He felt compelled to write home again. *Just a quick footnote to let y'all know I'm fine, in "peachy" shape in case you got the news about the military invading the university. Matter of fact took place about 15 minutes after I left. Don't know how my friends made out, but it was rough.* Thirty students were killed, the newspaper said. A crew of Dutch filmmakers was on the campus when it all started, and they captured the soldiers maneuvering between the Chemistry and Pharmacy Buildings and the School of Economic Sciences; and also dramatic, hand-held shots of some of Joe's "schoolteacher" friends running down the corridors, urging calm, and then one student running with bloodstains spreading across his shirt, falling to the ground and screaming out, "Lord, help me. Take pity on me, Lord." Within months these images were being screened in Amsterdam and Copenhagen and Stockholm, and in American universities, where they were seen by audiences of sympathetic faculty members and their students, who were shocked by the full-color images of the young man's chest wounds, and by the sounds of his moans as he slowly died, on camera.

THE CAMPUS REMAINED occupied by soldiers in the days and weeks that followed. *Still haven't gotten back to my Spanish classes at the university,* Joe wrote home. *Military might just figure on staying until the weeds grow tall.* He returned to the streets for the next general strike, setting out from his San Salvador room on a torrid August day of blinding sun. In Mejicanos, he came upon a pair of toaster-shaped armored vehicles headed east, and he followed them, and soon heard the sound of distant gunfire, an exchange of automatic weapons that was more concentrated than anything he'd heard since coming to El Salvador. The firing became sporadic, but Joe kept up his forward march, for a kilometer, and then two, toward the scene of the battle. He removed his shirt and tied it over his head, and the people running away from the battle did double takes when they saw a bare-chested gringo walking in the opposite direction. Joe saw an armored personnel carrier retreating westward from the battle, followed by a military ambulance. Then he crossed two blocks that were eerily empty and arrived in the neighborhood of Cuscatancingo, at the Y junction of two streets—just in time to see a squad of rebels withdrawing to the east. They were gangly and young and their faces were covered, and they were wearing khaki pants and blue jeans, and T-shirts honoring a Texas football team and Coca-Cola, and they were carrying M16s, and they had enough training to engage in an orderly withdrawal, one man covering for another as they filtered down side streets and between buildings. In three minutes they were gone, and the residents of Cuscatancingo emerged from taking shelter in their homes and gathered in the street, and they sensed they were standing in a limbo between warring armies, and they felt the hot humid air around them shifting and rustling through the trees. They listened as four house sparrows jumped on the utility wires and began to cheep and chatter loudly, and the sound was soothing to them, and to some it seemed divine, or surreal, as if they were at the mercy of a great, demented storyteller who had transformed Cuscatancingo into his stage, and who could fill it with explosions or singing birds to fit his narrative whims. A group of pamphleteers appeared, passing out slips of mimeographed paper, and Joe joined the other people in the silent crowd in reading that the day's actions were meant to pressure the government to lift the state of siege, reopen the university and release political prisoners, and to make other demands to which the dictatorship would never concede. One of the women passing out the pamphlets broke the quiet by giving a speech explaining how the people could not be crushed, and she continued speaking until a man of about twenty appeared behind her, a rebel fighter with a revolver on his waist; he placed his hand on her shoulder, and she stopped midsentence, and the man began to speak to the crowd.

"We have a wounded compañero. He needs first aid. Does anyone here know first aid?"

"Yo sí sé," Joe said, and all eyes turned to the speaker of these three awkwardly phrased Spanish words, and to his unshirted torso and the long hair that flowed from underneath the shirt tied to his head.

"You? Who are you?"

"A gringo. A writer," Joe said in Spanish. "I was a medic in the army."

The rebel fighter went by the nom de guerre Fito. He had small, mousy eyes and had grown up in the neighboring community of Ciudad Delgado, and he had known these same streets with the alert eyes of a child, and now he knew them with the analytical eyes of an underground political organizer. He was well acquainted with the community's characters and lunatics, but the bare-chested Joe was a stranger, an apparition. Fito made a quick assessment of Joe and the danger of trusting him, and he said, "Vení," and Joe obeyed and followed after him, and they slipped into the same zigzagging pathways the rebels had followed in their retreat.

"He's wounded in the leg," Fito said.

"Is he conscious?" Joe asked.

"Yes. He is. He was when I left him fifteen minutes ago." He gave Joe a small canvas bag, a first-aid kit.

They walked into a warren of shacks, pathways that were like alleyways but only as wide as Joe's outstretched arms; and then into the brush of a steep ravine, downward, turning their feet sideways to keep from falling, and all the while Joe tried to remember what he could from his medic training, all those years ago in Missouri. *Kid I was then, dumb army games. Bullet wound, what's the protocol? Pressure, elevate, cover the wounded man to prevent shock. Something like that.* Deeper into the brush. *You can die from a leg wound if it hits an artery.* The city disappeared and they were in a green place, and Joe could see a grayish stream cutting through a chalky canyon, and Joe wondered how they could be in this untamed place because he had studied the geography of greater San Salvador and he knew they were still well within the boundaries of the metropolis. He heard a distant siren, and another, and a truck horn, and he felt the city above him, invisible, and he realized he was in an open green oasis that somehow existed in the middle of San Salvador, unseen to the city dwellers above. A place that captured the detritus from the city above, the wastewater, the discarded papers and the lost toys, the runaways and the fugitives.

"Ya mero," Fito said, and he turned to see if Joe was keeping up, and of course Joe was right behind him because he'd spent much of his life walking up and down wild and unknown places, for as long as he could remember. *Daniel Boone was a man, / Yes, a big man! / With an eye like an eagle / And as tall as a mountain was he!*

"¡Miguel!" the fighter called out. "Aquí estoy."

"¡Fito!" a voice called back. "¡Aquí, aquí, aquí!"

Fito pulled back branches and waded into them, and Joe followed, and finally Fito grabbed one last branch and they saw the wounded fighter, a teenager with bright brown eyes and thin hairs growing on his cheeks and chin, and bloody smears on his forehead.

"Gracias a Dios," the wounded man said.

"Te vamos a arreglar bien," Joe said, and the wounded man squinted up at him in confusion, not because he didn't understand what Joe said, but rather because he was perplexed by Joe's strange Spanish promise to "fix him" and by Joe's bare and sweaty chest hairs and the shirt on his head, and his angelic blond mane, and he thought that maybe the appearance of this fair-skinned foreigner meant he was in a dreamspace, near death.

"I'm going to die here, I'm going to die!" the wounded man yelled out. "¡Madre mía, no quiero morir!"

Joe knelt down and pulled back the wounded man's hand from his thigh, and examined the wound, from which blood was still flowing. This guy might go into shock any moment now. Joe took the wounded man's hand and squeezed it, and he gently forced the man to lie down, saying, "Acostate," in perfect Central American Spanish, and the wounded man obeyed. Joe opened the first-aid kit and found bandages and a bottle of expired hydrogen peroxide, and he began to slowly clean the man's wound, which was covered with mud and coagulated blood, working with soothing strokes, like a mother wiping off a baby, Fito would think later. Joe studied the wound again, which was actually two holes through the thigh, each the size of a thumbprint, a line of bloody tears slowly seeping out from each one. Through and through. Must have just missed the femoral artery. Otherwise, he'd be dead already. Lucky bastard. Apply pressure for the moment.

"Puchís, hombre, no es nada," Joe said, while he was squeezing and holding the wounded man. "Relajate." This command and Joe's squeezing, and his lighthearted repetition of "no es nada," caused the wounded man to obey and relax and finally Joe took the bandages and some gauze from the kit and very thoroughly and methodically dressed and wrapped the wounds, and brought a sense of order and care to this moment in the ravine, and this further calmed the wounded man and the fighter Fito too, who had been worried that Miguel would bleed out. "We're going to cover you because you might feel a little cold and we want you to be comfortable," Joe said, and he removed the shirt from his head, and placed it over the wounded man, whose nervous, rapid breathing began to slow into a regular rhythm. "He needs to rest a bit, and then you can move him," Joe said to the fighter. "But he'll be fine."

"Gracias," Fito said, and he told Joe they would leave Miguel for the moment, and that other compañeros would come to carry him to a place of safety, and he spoke to Miguel and said goodbye, and Joe shook the wounded man's hand, and he heard Miguel whisper, "Gracias, brother," and the sound of the English word *brother* caused Joe to raise his eyebrows and laugh, and he walked away, following the fighter Fito on a march upward, out of the ravine.

Halfway up, Fito stopped and turned to Joe and asked, "What do you want?" By this question he really meant: Is there something I can give you, in thanks? And: Why are you here?

"I want to help," Joe said. "I want to be a part of the revolution."

Fito turned and continued his march upward. This is very intriguing. This norteamericano speaks directly. They reached the place where the pamphleteer had addressed the gathering, which was deserted now except for two boys of about six who were playing a game that involved jumping over the two-foot-high street barricade of boards and bricks that was left over from the battle fought earlier in the day. Fito remembered the deliberate and patient way Joe had dressed Manuel's wound. When you're in a movement long enough you realize that each day is an improvisation. You build a revolution with what you have, what falls to you. The many different talents people have. The street urchin's ability to spy the police officer around the corner; the savvy peasant who can find the trail through the brush or the pool of drinking water; the bookworm with the sudden courage of a lion. The stranger with deep compassion; the older man who can dress a wound and march up and down a ravine and not get winded.

Fito told Joe to meet him in two days at a restaurant near the center of

San Salvador called ComaRápido. EatFast. "If I'm not there at twelve, then come back the next day."

"Está bien," Joe said.

"Don't tell me your name. I don't want to know it. Pick another name that I can call you."

Joe thought quickly of an appellation that had been bouncing around in his head. Lucas. As in Lucas McCain, "the Rifleman" of the TV show of the same name. A kind man who was also handy with a firearm. A fair, good man. An American. And a marksman.

"Lucas," Joe said.

"Lucas," Fito repeated, and he grinned back at Joe. "That's a good name."

I am Lucas. Mi nombre es Lucas.

17.

Mejicanos

THE CLOCK MOVED PAST TWELVE and Joe paid for and ate two pupusas, garnishing them with cabbage slaw, as per the local custom. At 12:26 p.m., the guerrilla fighter named Fito entered through the door in a freshly laundered polo shirt, looking like an office stiff eager to get a burger. Fito walked toward the booth where Joe was sitting and said, "Seguime," and Joe followed him to a table in the back where the restaurant was emptier. After a minute or so of sitting and listening to the sounds of the restaurant, Fito began to speak. "If you want to work with us, you need to know how we operate." By "we" he meant the Ejército Revolucionario del Pueblo, or ERP. They were not a "front," or a "movement," or a "league," like the many other organizations Joe had seen operating in San Salvador, but rather an "army." The People's Revolutionary Army, with all the discipline that name implied. I'm going to have to come up with another code word in the letters to Mom and Calhoun. I can't call them "schoolteachers." I'll call them "scientists."

"You haven't been organized before?" Fito asked, by which he meant had Joe ever been a member of any other revolutionary fronts or movements.

"No."

"Well, when you operate underground, the way we do here in the city, you have a very disciplined structure," Fito continued. In other words, Lucas wouldn't be able to drift freely around San Salvador the way Joe had been doing, because after a day of conversations with his comrades, and questions placed to a member of another organization, Fito had learned that Lucas was known as the gringo who floated around the city, and who had helped here and there with the groups based at the now-closed university. "I need to know if you'll accept this kind of discipline."

"Yes."

Fito told Lucas that his next contact with the organization would be tomorrow at a San Salvador bus terminal. He would be guided to a safe house where he would likely have to stay for some time; Joe nodded and said he understood. His only problem was his Salvadoran visa, which expired in one month. Would he need to have a valid visa if he went underground? Joe removed his passport from his pants pocket and placed it on the table, and Fito picked it up and opened the pages, and for the first time he glanced at Lucas's real name—Joseph—and he chuckled as he looked at the ridiculous number of stamps inside it, most of them from South American countries. Peru in red. Chile in blue. A big stamp from Brazil: Visto. República Argentina. Bolivia. He saw the manic, improvised life of a free man wandering across borders, chasing a personal ambition.

"Let me think about your visa problem," Fito said. "For now a cama-rada will meet you at the bus station tomorrow." Fito stood up and left Lu-cas at the table, and Joe wondered if he had become a member of the Ejército Revolucionario del Pueblo in the conversation that had just unfolded, or if more tests and questions awaited him.

"HOLA, LUCAS." His contact was a young man of about twenty-two with a long, avian neck, and a wry, knowing smile. As if he had heard a funny joke about Joe. Follow me, at a distance, the young man said. His name was Mauricio and at a very young age he'd been a pickpocket and a petty thief, and once he'd escaped from a prison for boys in the aftermath of an earth-quake that had somehow, mysteriously and mythically, unlocked two prison doors. Today he was valued for his ability to sniff out the presence of police officers, soldiers and informers, and was thus the perfect man for this job of escorting Joe through the city to the safe house without being followed. They entered an industrial district, near San Salvador's largest cemetery, and Mauricio opened a metal door and Joe stepped into a shady space, and when his eyes adjusted to the weak light Joe saw he was in a room filled with refrigerators. Tall and short contraptions, and long ones for storing a side of beef, and boxes with wheels for carrying ice cream. They walked through this hoard of steel, aluminum and tin, and reached another metal door that led to a room that was just big enough for Joe to stretch out his arms, and here there was a bed, which was just long enough for Joe to lie down flat, and Joe threw down his duffel bag. He met the shop owner, whose name was Leopoldo. Rest, Leopoldo said. After a goodbye from Mauricio, Joe stretched out on the bed, which was covered with dusty wool blankets that scratched his arms and tickled his nose, and he opened the book he was carrying, *Darkness at Noon*.

When Joe shifted onto his stomach after a chapter of reading, he looked down and saw a bloodstain on the cement floor, and then, underneath the bed itself, fragments of a bandage. The same bandage he'd wrapped around the wounded man in the ravine.

IN HIS FIRST TWO DAYS of self-confinement, Joe spoke a handful of sentences with the repairman Leopoldo, who provided him with two uninspired but hearty meals each day, and he read *Darkness at Noon* three times. He wandered into the refrigeration workshop often and noted that there were no doors keeping him locked inside, and that he could leave anytime, though of course he would be giving up a chance to join the movement. So he stayed inside, obediently, and didn't ask the laconic Leopoldo any of the questions he would have liked to ask, and finally on his third day in the room he heard a knock on the steel door of his tiny bedroom and opened it to see Fito.

Fito began to speak casually, as if he and Joe were old friends, and Fito had just stopped by to say hello. "This room, Lucas. It reminds me of the one in my grandparents' house. I slept on a bed like this one. Too small. But that room had a big dresser in it. Too big. It barely fit. And the room smelled of mothballs. On a farm."

"My grandparents were farmers too. I went there every summer. To Kansas."

"Kansas?" For Fito, the name possessed magical qualities.

"Yes. With horses and cows and wheat." Joe was proud of himself for remembering the word for wheat: *trigo.*

"Corn," Fito said. "On my grandparents' farm."

"You learn a lot when you live on a farm."

"Sí. My father grew up on that piece of land. He never went to school, and neither did my mother, but . . ." A car passed slowly on the usually quiet street outside, and the shuffling of its poorly adjusted valves caused Fito to stop midsentence, and Fito studied the metallic sound, which was like two knives scraping together, and the menacing noise carried the possibility of his own personal apocalypse, of his death and the fall of the safe house, and the murder of Leopoldo and this good gringo. But then the car was gone and Fito resumed, midsentence, ". . . they learned to read and write and taught me and my brother, even before we started school. When we came to the city, they sent us to good schools. My brother and I both read Baldor's *Algebra*, back to front. Learning was important to my parents."

Fito turned quiet. They heard Leopoldo in the workshop, taking something apart, and tossing a tool to the cement floor.

"So are you sure you want to do this, Lucas?"

"Yes."

"Why?"

Joe talked about El Salvador and said he had seen similar inequality and injustice in his travels around the world. Nigeria, the children he'd cared for, and those who had died in his arms; the murdered prisoners of Vietnam. He talked about having a sense of personal responsibility, because he was a Yankee who had been raised in comfort while his government sent troops and weapons around the globe, and this last statement of his was the most "political," Fito thought. Lucas never mentioned "class struggle" or "dialectical materialism" or any of the other ideas that Fito had studied when he joined the movement. Fito had come to understand that there was a scientific underpinning to the Salvador revolution. In the inevitable march of time each comrade was like an electron in the molecules that would produce a new epoch of human history. But to Lucas the Salvadoran revolution was more like a painting or a prayer. An armed act of beauty against evil. When Fito reported back to his superiors in the ERP, he summarized Lucas's motives thusly: he was not joining them for "ideological" reasons as much as he was for "metaphysical" ones.

"What he believes in is a universal idea of justice. He comes to collaborate with us. Because he doesn't agree with the policies of his country. He's a writer, a poet."

A week later, Mauricio the ex-pickpocket returned. He guided Lucas to an empty soccer stadium and dirt running track and told Lucas that he should run, to get in shape. Joe did so, and his smoker's lungs began to betray him after two laps, but he kept on going. Thirty-eight, thirty-eight, I'm thirty-eight. One foot after another and here's the kid Mauricio handing me some water, gracias, and run some more, and the kid is squinting up at the sun. No shit, it's hot. It's fucking hot. Five laps. From the dark room with refrigerators, out here into the burning hell of Central America. Fuck. Seven laps and now I'm sorta just shuffling along.

When Joe had run nine laps, two small boys climbed up into the stands and clapped every time Joe passed, and when Joe had reached twelve laps the group had grown to four boys and Mauricio motioned to Lucas that they should leave, and they made their way circuitously through the city back toward the safe house.

Many days passed this way, with Joe guided out to various locations to run and exercise, and to the post office to check for his mail, because they allowed him to write letters from home and to receive them.

My new home is absolutely splendid! Joe wrote to his mother and Calhoun. He could not tell anything approaching the truth of his current situation, so he spun an elaborate fantasy. *Could spit into the nearby river on a windy day. House built on a bluff four blocks from the beach. Made out of wood, walk-around balcony on two sides, with a hammock, of course. Has a funky swimming pool, and fat + useless ducks, butterflies + lizards + flowers. Real tranquil.* Well, the tranquil part was true. *Believe I'll do a bit of gardening while I'm here. Either that, or purchase a case of gin and a Holy Bible. Guess I'll be on ice about a month, which is fine with me. Got plenty of poems to scribble and seashells to pick up. Plus lots of half-naked village maidens washing clothes in the river!* Mauricio mailed the letter, and ten days later when Joe returned to the post office with Mauricio, he received an answer from his mother.

Your research on jungle hammocks, native girls and gin sound very interesting to Calhoun. One of these days, I'll ship him down there, she wrote. As always, she kept Joe abreast of the news from Urbana and Kansas. Her sister Marg had joined the Daughters of the American Revolution, and then Virginia did too, and she'd discovered that Joe's great-great-great-great-grandfather Thomas Richardson had fought in the Revolutionary War; in the very first battles, in fact, "the Lexington Alarm." Steve had obtained his pilot's license, and purchased an airplane. *Steve and his family are flying to Peoria this weekend. They will stay at a Holiday Inn and relax by the pool. Did I write before that Kathy swam 4,000 feet without stopping? We think she is quite a swimmer for an 8-year-old. Marg writes from the farm that they are having a very bad drought. Calhoun has recovered from his hernia operation and Blue Cross has paid for all but $90 of the $450 surgery bill. It sure is sad listening to reports of health-care bills. We are very lucky. Many retirees are going to die in debt.* She closed with her usual admonitions. *Take care, write when you can, don't drink too much gin, and all that sort of stuff. We will just sit here waiting for your next letter.*

After another visit to the post office with Mauricio, Joe stepped inside the workshop and found Fito sitting on top of a meat locker, waiting.

"We thought about your visa problem, Lucas," he said. "We have an idea. We want you to bring some things for us from the United States. From New Orleans. Can you do this?"

"Yes," Joe said, and Fito motioned to Mauricio, who stepped nearer to them, and together the two guerrillas gave Joe some basic pointers on how an undercover operative of Revolutionary Army of the People should conduct himself in the field. Neither Fito nor Mauricio had ever been to the United States, but they assumed it had police agents and spies who monitored "suspicious" people. They gave Lucas a mailing address and phone number to use should he need to send an urgent message to El Salvador, and they told him how he should address this telephone contact, and how he should carry himself in crowded and public places, always keeping his eye on the front door. Joe might have found it all amusing, but he did not, because Fito and Maurico spoke with the severity of men who'd seen comrades die due to a lack of such discipline. They told him what it sounded like when someone tapped your phone, and how to check and see if someone was following you. They spoke for an hour and they made Joe repeat and recite all the instructions they gave him, and finally Fito stood up and said, "Buen viaje," bon voyage.

As Joe left El Salvador, he thought about the people who lived there, and the events he had seen, the killing and the wounded and the tanks and the soldiers and the dead, and the graves on the now-closed campus of the university. When he boarded a Pan American flight in Guatemala City and stepped onto a 747, he felt like Alice in Wonderland, and he consciously tried to avoid the seductions of the alternate reality taking shape around him. I am alien to all this. To the champagne the people around me are drinking, to the seductive wool wrapped around the torso of the stewardess.*

WHEN JOE ARRIVED IN CHICAGO, he remained on guard against the lure of savory hot dogs and the fat floating on the pepperoni pizza. The sanitized spaces of North America, the smell of cleaning solvents. Was there someone watching me get on the plane in Phoenix, off the plane at O'Hare? He made note of the police officers on the Chicago L. Finally, he boarded an Amtrak train, smooth sailing and of course I am scot-free, unfollowed and unseen. The train worked its way free of the industrial lots, the rail yards, the trash heaps on the edge of the city, and Joe slipped into a reverie of reflection, and he saw all the life events that had brought him to this moment,

---

*I landed in L.A., and then I went to Arizona. Told my dad all about the revolution in El Salvador, but not my part in it. I was paranoid. Incredibly paranoid. I didn't want to tell him anything that would get him in trouble. But I did describe the massacres and the dead. He bought a bottle of wine for us to share, but I talked so much, we never got around to opening it.

and he felt a sense of purpose he had not felt in many, many years. As if he had been following some foreordained path. He was not a mere vagabond. All his travels had prepared him for this. His time in the army, even. The train passed through fading farm towns where station wagons and pickup trucks waited at the railroad crossings, and finally the train approached the Champaign station, and he saw the green and orange skyline of the city's trees, the light refracting through the dust and the autumn-ing leaves, trying to seduce him into the trances of his boyhood. Sleeping in on Saturdays, maple syrup, and melted butter. Joe stepped off, and onto the platform. He felt the ghost of Karen, suddenly, unexpectedly. The day he left for college, eighteen years old.

Joe walked into the station and he heard Fito's voice whispering to him: Careful, Lucas. He found a pay phone and called home.

"Hi, Mom, guess who?"

18.

Urbana, Illinois

JOE TOLD HIS FAMILY he would stay for two weeks, and then go back to El Salvador. Think of this as my holiday visit, he said. "It's Christmas in September," he told his mom on the phone from the train station. That first night he collapsed on a rollaway bed inside the small "study" his brother Steve had added to his new home in Savoy, just outside Champaign, a room that was twice the size of the space in which Lucas had slept for a month in San Salvador. In the morning, Joe opened his eyes fully to the dry fall daylight, and to the rows of accounting binders his big brother kept here, and his ears filled with the sound of Steve in the kitchen making breakfast before going off to work, because it was a weekday. He heard his niece, Kathy, in the living room. "Can I say hi to Uncle Joe again?"

"I think he's asleep."

"Awake!" Joe yelled.

"Go say hi then. But hurry, because we have to get you to school, young lady."

Joe went alone that evening to have dinner with his mother and Calhoun, and it occurred to him that he had never sat down for a meal at his mom's home with a secret as big as the one he carried now. *I am Lucas.* Virginia caught the amused upturn of the corner of his lips at the dining room table. *Teenage Joe, inside the body of a man of thirty-eight.* And then he turned older and looked preoccupied. *The things he describes in his letters, the stories I clip from the newspaper. Bodies left to rot in the trash dumps. Battles in the capital city. We won't speak of any of that now.*

"We're surprised you came back to us, Joe, what with those naked village maidens you were living with," Calhoun said.

"The maidens are nice," Joe said. "But this pork roast is sexier."

Calhoun expounded on their new residence, the Clark-Lindsey retirement "village." Trimmed lawns and park views, and the vans that delivered dinners to some of its residents, and Joe half listened as Calhoun continued with his survey of the benefits of retirement living, and Virginia looked across the table and saw Joe's distant look, and she felt the effort of an especially difficult concealment. *When they get to a certain age, you can't force them to answer your questions anymore. When was that? When they're eight or nine. Eleven.*

In the living room after dinner, she presented Joe with her latest batch of clippings from the *Tribune* and *The News-Gazette,* the dramatic events in El Salvador as recounted by correspondents for the Associated Press and United Press International, all gathered in a file folder. He opened it and said, "Thank you, Mother," and looked at the rectangles of newsprint, and began to read, and he perused the action shots of National Guardsmen and bandanna-faced protesters and the portrait of a priest who had been assassinated, and a thumbnail map showing the location of a village where sixteen people had been killed.

"It's awful there, Mom," he said, suddenly. Joe thought of an image he'd seen back in El Salvador, a photograph in the local tabloids, more horrible than any of these clippings. The corpse of a woman whose killers carved the initials of a death squad into her chest. The letters *E* and *M*, the lines cut by a pocketknife, he guessed. Something he could never describe to his mother.

"So why are you going back, son?" Virginia asked, and to both of them the question seemed especially bold and direct.

"Because I'm needed there."

"Virginia, you forgot to serve your dessert," Calhoun interrupted. "Joe, she made this wonderful cherry crunch. In your honor."

Virginia turned to look back at the table and the kitchen. "Oh. How could I forget?"

Joe closed the file folder as his mother stood up and returned to the kitchen. They never discussed El Salvador again.

JOE BEGAN HIS NEXT DAY with a visit to the office of his brother, Steve, in the Department of Agricultural Economics at the University of Illinois, Steve's new fiefdom, where he managed a troop of staffers, distributing dollars and requesting appropriate documentation from professors and maintenance men. Joe saw an attractive young secretary in a print dress of crazy autumn colors, but he did not flirt with her, but instead was mesmerized by a device on her desk; a humming computer terminal, its glowing amber letters reflected in her hazel eyes. She typed onto a keyboard and lifted up a telephone receiver, and brought the receiver to rest atop a metal box that was the size of a large book, and she pressed several more keys on her keyboard, and the box began to squawk and squeal. The box was talking into the receiver, connecting the computer to the telephone line, and Joe felt childlike and guileless before this new invention.

"It's called a modem," she explained. "We use it to connect to the network."

"The network?"

"It's a circle of computers, all connected to one another. We use it to send our reports to the central administration. And they send reports to us and to Springfield."

The box continued its squawk-squeal, and a living string of amber letters materialized on the screen, moving left to right like a tiny locomotive, and Joe looked at the phone line, and realized it was carrying information, and for the rest of the day he was disturbed by the idea that data was traveling on wires back and forth across the university and across the state and country. Obviously, this new technology could be used by "el estado," the State, the powers that be; by the FBI and the CIA and the Department of Defense, to control and monitor, and he remembered Fito's lessons about security, and the letter Fito had given him to mail. A missive with a San Francisco address, which he had deposited into a mailbox in Los Angeles. Sealed. A rebel communication that would be carried to its final destination by waddling American mail carriers in quaint gas vehicles. On the way back to El Salvador he was supposed to pick up an envelope in New Orleans, and carry it on his person back to San Salvador, but the enemy had satellites and now "modems" to carry information, to listen and to spy and transmit. His paranoia was heightened when he went to drink coffee with Steve and his brother explained how the university was beginning a new initiative to fully computerize administrative records, and how Mom was lucky and smart to have retired when she did.

Later that day Joe had lunch with Jim Adams inside the old offices of the long-defunct newspaper Joe had once delivered, *The Courier*; it had just become a restaurant, of all things.

"So what's going on in El Salvador, brother," Jim asked. "Is it as bad as it looks?"

"Worse, much worse."

Joe quickly changed the subject. Jim Adams was a helicopter pilot now, in addition to being a fireman, and they talked about flying, and how Steve was becoming a real ace of the air too, and while Jim explained the ins and outs of helicopter piloting Joe remembered what it was like to be in the air, all-seeing, above speeding automobiles and farmers in their fields, and he thought of all the eyes in the sky, the ears and the data on the telephone lines, and at that moment a white man in a white shirt with a breast-pocket pen holder appeared at the restaurant door. He looked at Joe directly and purposefully, and took a seat across the room. A man of about Joe's age, with a thin mustache.

"Something wrong, brother?" Jim asked.

"I wonder if I'm being followed," Joe said.

"What?"

"I think I'm being monitored. Last night, when Steve's phone rang, I answered it. I heard a click. It's what you hear when they're tapping your phone."

"That's crazy. Nobody wants to tap your phone, Joe."

"Sure they would. The CIA, the FBI. Fuck, I don't know, all sorts of people."

"Because you were in El Salvador?"

"Something like that, yes."

Jim looked at his old friend and remembered the assorted drunken excesses of their youth, and Joe's lonely ramblings when he returned from long trips. A human being can't keep traveling forever; now it's finally caught up with him. Maybe he's done too many drugs. Stuff we can't get here in Champaign-Urbana. Or maybe it's drugs he's dealing, maybe he's bringing this crazy powerful stuff here.

"You mixed up in something, Joe? The cops looking for you? The mob?"

"The mob!?" Joe shouted, and everyone sitting at the adjacent tables turned to look at him, and he snort-laughed and his sudden amusement infected Jim. The waitress brought the two laughing Urbana townies their hamburgers, and the suspicious man at the table was joined by a woman, and she squeezed his hand.

ON HIS THIRD DAY HOME, he finally got around to opening the box that was waiting for him in the mail at Steve's house. His manuscript, returned from the editing service, a box filled with flawless pages typed in a small and delicate font. He began to read his novel, or rather, a regurgitated and reprocessed version of what had been his novel. All his ellipses and repetitions had been shorn away, his run-on sentences tamed, as if by an especially finicky and meticulous barber. *We have edited* The Silver Triangle, began the letter from Katherine's underling. *We kept the original chapter 1—a bit more subdued now and with two long passages about Sunshine deleted. (Cabron is the main character) . . . Will it sell? We don't know. It could.**

THE WEEKEND ARRIVED and Joe dedicated it to his niece Kathy. He took her to Crystal Lake park and told her to listen to the throbbing buzz of the cicadas. "It's a love song. The cicadas are telling each other, 'I love you!'"

---

*Excuse my French, but I fucking hated it. *The Silver Triangle* was like a dog whose nuts had been cut off. And don't just take my word for it; the Author agrees. My version was better. So there.

He led her into the big brick building that housed the university's natural history museum, and showed her the skeletons of ancient sea monsters, and the stuffed and still seabirds, and a hairy bison in a big glass box. They drove beyond the city limits to a harvest fair with hog pens and poultry, cotton candy and arcade games. He looked at Kathy enjoying it all, her summer-lightened blond hair and cheeks reddened to the color of apples, and he felt his eyes filling with the mournfulness of a man gazing at a tangerine prairie afternoon for the last time. Beyond his niece, the flat plain, a silo jutting up on the horizon two miles away. As if all that talk of the round earth were a lie.

Illinois. What does home mean? Is it always with you, do its people and its landscape live inside your brain forever? He studied Kathy and the other girls and boys at the harvest fair, through the Illinois dust that was covering his glasses, again, and he remembered peering through those same concave lenses at other boys and girls at that first big street rally in El Salvador. The dead girl, a corpse in a blue dress, in a city surrounded by volcanos, an un-prairie. And now Kathy was tugging him toward a carousel of live ponies, and he helped the attendant by lifting her up onto the animal and she rode behind a pair of sad equine eyes, and she smiled at him and waved and said, "Goodbye, Uncle Joe," as she rode away and, "Hi, Uncle Joe," as she came back. On the drive back home, Joe stopped when he noticed a dark line of clouds on the horizon. "Looks like a storm coming," he said, and from the side of the road they watched distant lines of lightning striking the ground, and heard the delayed rumble of thunder, and for many years afterward when Kathy thought about her uncle she would remember sitting there, in the car, next to him, tasting the stormy air and looking at jagged white roots of electric light on the horizon.

THE NIGHT BEFORE Joe left for Central America he sat down in Steve's living room and the two brothers drank Hamm's beers and talked about cars and other inconsequential things, and the mood was light until Steve brought up El Salvador, and asked if Joe knew how long he'd be gone this time, because usually on his trips Joe had a plan for when he might come back.

"No," Joe said. "It might be hard to reach me. I might not be writing as often. I'll put a code in my letters that means A-okay. It'll be 1200." This was a transponder code pilots used when they were flying in uncontrolled airspace, out of radio contact and using eyesight to find their way. "If I write *1200* at the top of my letter, you'll know I'm flying in clear skies, so to speak. Tell Mom that too. Okay?"

"Agreed."

Obviously Joe was hiding a lot about the dangers he was going to face. Why else would he put transponder codes in his letters? Steve imagined a near future with Joe incommunicado. Empty mailboxes and silent telephones. And I'll be the one here, talking to Mom every day, trying to convince her that you're okay. Questions I could ask, but not my place. What are you truly up to? All sorts of possibilities suggested themselves, most of them involving illicit acts. Steve's only recourse was big-brother benevolence. "You know, Joe, if you want to settle down in Urbana, get your own place—well, I could set you up. I could help you get established. You want a job at the newspaper, I could help you with that. That guy over there owes me some favors. Or at the bookstore. If they don't have a job open, I can ask them to create one for you. If you wanted to open an ice cream stand, I could get you a bank loan from this guy I know."

"Thank you, Steve. But I'm not interested. Appreciate it, though. Truly." Joe looked at the table and the empty cans. "How about one more beer before we call it a night?"

Steve returned from the refrigerator with two frosty cans and the sense that he had done right by his brother, even if Joe had turned down his help. "Really nice spread here," Joe said, looking around. "I'm proud of you, big brother. You've gone and made a man of yourself."

That night, Joe went to bed in Steve's study but had trouble sleeping. He listened to the university's FM radio station, which played songs that were long and obscure, and like messages from another world. "London Calling." Samplings of garage-band Americana. No FM radio like this in San Salvador. Free form, a bit of this, a bit of that. Ska sped up into rock and roll. At 1:30 a.m., when Joe vowed to turn off the radio and go to sleep he heard the youthful-voiced DJ say, "Well, it's time for last call. And tonight we have something special for you, Champaign-Urbana, in honor of all the good vibes brought to us by, well, by the brothers of this here group. Funkadelic. A gift from the music gods. Good night, Champaign-Urbana."

Suddenly the transistor radio on his brother's studio desk was filled with the wailing and the wah-wah of an electric guitar. Two guitars: one keeping a rhythm, with six notes repeated at the pace of a prayer; the other playing a free-form solo, a wordless language describing a lifetime of ecstasies and mourning. Joe could hear the scratches on the record, and he imagined the needle and the turntable at the college radio station, and the guitar player's fingers working the fret. Rapid-fire notes and slow vibrato. Funk. Psychedelic. Oscillations and feedback and the soul of a wounded but resilient people. Electromagnetic waves from African America. This is what I'm going to miss when I leave the United States of America. *I have tasted the maggots in the mind of the universe*, a voice sang. The buzzy speech of the Stratocaster track went on for ten minutes, and the radio was silent for five seconds, until the DJ said a single word: "Funkadelic."

The next morning Joe packed his few belongings into a half-empty duffel bag and carried it into Steve's living room. Kathy had gone off to school, and Joe joined Steve in the front of his Chevrolet, and they drove to pick up Mom and Calhoun; when Joe got back into the car he sat in the rear seat next to his mother.

As they approached the train station Joe said, "You don't have to park. If it's okay with you all, I'll go in by myself. Just drop me off in front." At other times, they had all stood together on the station platform. This time he wanted to be alone.

"Bye, Steve," Joe said from the back seat. "Bye, Calhoun. Mother."

"Well, son, don't forget to write," his mother said. "And don't forget these." A plastic container filled with cookies she had made the night before. So much more to say. Thoughts and advice. Unspoken. They reached across the back seat to hug each other, and Virginia placed a hand on her baby boy's shoulder, and he opened the door and stepped out of the car a man of the world, looking weary behind his weak, forced smile, carrying burdens in his squeezed brow. He turned to look at them one more time and raised his hand in a half wave; the station doors settled behind him, and he was gone. Back into the envelope and the mailbox. She wondered how many months or years would pass before she saw him again.

Virginia returned home, and for the next few days she lingered over the leftovers in the refrigerator. The pork roast dinner she had made for him. The extra, unused cookie dough. Such a gift, to be able to cook for your son.

19.

Usulután, El Salvador

IN NEW ORLEANS, Joe performed his revolutionary mission in ten minutes at a post office, picking up an envelope that had been mailed to him there, care of "General Delivery." A legal-size envelope, rather thick, sealed with too much glue. On his short bus trip to the airport the salty gulf air awakened memories of his younger selves, and he felt a twinge in his lower body. When he reached the airport and checked in he had two hours to kill admiring the bare legs of the woman tending the airport bar. High skirt, hallelujah, God bless America and the sexual revolution. A good time was had by all. He began to write a letter home.

Now I've eaten so many durn cookies in the past 19 hours that I'm about to crumble. I must be the first guy who ever marched off to the Latin American wars loaded down with homemade cookies. Weeeeee! Well, it was a wonderful 2 weeks in the States. Sorry I was so inarticulate when we said goodbye, but I know you'll understand. Forgot to tell you that my friends in El Salvador told me to be sure to say hello to y'all. I know they'll be pleased (and surprised) to munch on a few cookies and brownies. As for me, that last Sunday nite supper ought to hold me for at least six months.

Joe boarded a flight direct to Mexico City, and thence to San Salvador, and when he landed in that wartime capital the next morning he took a taxi, spotting National Guardsmen in force at several points near the airport. A state of martial readiness, as in Saigon, and a sense something awful could happen at any moment. In the center of the city he found a working public phone and called his contact and was told, "The entrance to the cemetery. We'll be there in thirty minutes." Forty-five minutes later Mauricio drove up to the cemetery gate in a dusty navy-blue Datsun. "Flor will be your new contact," Mauricio told him, after he got in the car. "Lucky you." He asked if Joe had the envelope, and Joe said yes and pulled it from his rucksack; Mauricio held it for a second and enjoyed the revolutionary mystery of its six ounces of weight and the American stamps and the United States address written on it, and smiled at it as if the power of the organized masses were somehow concentrated inside.

Mauricio took Joe back to the refrigerator safe house, and Joe continued the long letter home he had started writing in New Orleans. He listed his location as *San Salvador, Library*, though the letter itself described a bucolic river setting and village maidens, a contradiction his mother and Calhoun did not fail to notice when they received the letter eight days later.

Woke up this a.m. to the sound of the river and the buzzing of mosquitoes! After jogging the tide line, it was off to town this a.m. to count noses. So far, no one's turned up. Almost noon and hopefully "Flower" will pick me up here at the "library" for "luncheon date" soon.

The next morning, just after dawn, he heard a knock on his door, and before he could say "Adelante," the door opened and he saw a short, fit woman with powerfully thick eyebrows, and brown-freckled cheeks and a round-tipped nose, and two black braids framing her face. "¿Lucas?" she asked.

"Sí," Joe said.

"Vení," she ordered, and Joe got up and stepped out of his room and into the refrigerator workshop. A group of five young men were coming in through the front door. More recruits from the college campuses and the reformatories, it seemed. Like good young troublemakers they brought a long wooden box into the dark space. They pried it open with a screwdriver and studied the contents: two M16s, a German G3, one automatic pistol and five .38-caliber revolvers. "It's what they could give us," Flor said. She was in charge and chose a weapon first: the automatic pistol, which she inspected, ejecting its cartridge expertly. After the rifles were claimed Joe was left with a .38 revolver.

After some quick and rudimentary weapons instruction from Flor and another compa—"Don't point it at me, pendejo!"—Flor announced the plan. They were going to ambush a local National Guard post that was perpetually understaffed (with but two soldiers), and liberate the weapons stored there. An hour later Lucas was on the other side of town, standing watch on a wide avenue, while Flor and the rest of the unit hit the post a block away. Joe heard a single shot, and a few moments later his new comrades were running toward him, carrying armfuls of freshly purloined M16s; they loaded them into a vehicle, driven by a compa who quickly sped away. At that moment, Joe saw a National Guard Jeep rolling toward them about three blocks away; he fired his revolver into the air, in the pre-arranged warning shot. Well, that feels pretty silly—and pretty useless. The Jeep slowed but was still advancing, so Joe/Lucas lowered his .38 and calmly aimed in the general direction of the Jeep. He fired one shot, though he was too far away to hit anything. He fired a second, and the two soldiers inside stumbled out and crawled away.

Lucas began to walk backward, to join the other compas, and he heard one of them yell "¡Puta!" A National Guard truck had pulled up a half block behind the Jeep, and five soldiers were jumping out, and the young compa alongside him opened up with his M16, thank God, a sideways rain of covering fire. Joe fired a third shot and in this fashion Lucas and the compa protected the retreat of the remaining members of the unit, who dispersed into alleyways and later hid their weapons and walked across town, back to the safe house separately. Two hours later Joe knocked on the metal door of the safe house with the prearranged signal, and the door opened and he stepped inside. Flor beamed and he saw dimples under her freckled cheeks for the first time, and she said, "Todo un éxito." It took Joe's nervous and exhausted bilingual brain two seconds to remember that *éxito* meant success.

Joe wrote a blasé letter home that said he was safe and bored in El Salvador. The only hint of the firefight was in the two words he gave as his location: *Dodge City.*

HIS REBEL FRIENDS, Joe soon discovered, employed the same method to plan their revolution that he used to write his novels: make it up as you go along. And so, just days after his first taste of true "action" (at last!), they told him he needed to get out of San Salvador immediately. He'd been seen on the street, a conspicuous gringo, firing a revolver no less. They sent him to the port city of La Libertad, the last tourist spot left in El

Salvador, a place where it was still normal to see a wandering North American.

JOE WALKED THE FINAL BLOCK toward the address the compas had given him, and he saw another American walking toward him. A woman of about his age, with wind-catching bangs of unkempt blond hair and a cross dangling from her neck. She gave him a knowing and somewhat goofy smile that seemed of the Midwest. They walked past each other without saying a word, and he found the address, a very common-looking house with bars over the windows, and he knocked on the door, and stepped inside, not knowing that he was going to spend three very boring months there, doing little more than listening to the radio and writing letters home, and talking to the elderly man who ran the house, and the man's grandson, and going out to the nearby beach to take long and pointless walks along the sand.

JOE'S MOTHER HAD GIVEN him a letter from Mafalda during his brief stay in Illinois; it described a strange, free "gypsy" life, in which she inhabited a tent outside the city where her children lived with their father. Now he wrote back to her, beginning with nonsensical descriptions of village maidens, along with mentioning the *7,000 dead this year* in El Salvador. He said he was in the company of new friends. *Who knows what they're up to? I don't ask, I don't get involved*, he wrote. *Why shit, honey, I'd live in a whorehouse, search for diamonds, or smuggle cocaine, anything, before I'd become a goddam revolutionary.*

Reading in Ohio sometime later, Mafalda wasn't impressed. His letters were empty of true emotion, or feelings expressed for her. Joe Sanderson was at play in the world, in different countries, but always in the same place in relation to her: a voice inside an envelope. Once upon a time we were kindred spirts. You taught me to love the wandering free woman inside me. But now? This relationship isn't going anywhere.

She did not write to him again.*

EVERY DAY THE OWNER'S eleven-year-old grandson Werner arrived with food for Joe, and for a dog who lived in the spacious two-story house. Joe was free to wander the city, but given his semi-clandestine status, he did not seek out friendships, or hang out at bars, and he lamented the fact that he did not feel like writing a novel because this would be the perfect place to do it. He was inside a book plot now and had no idea what might happen next. At varying intervals he traveled to the post office in San Salvador to pick up his mail, which often included a thick envelope from his mother with U.S. newspaper clippings about El Salvador; sometimes they had been opened, clumsily, by a police officer or mail spy. He returned to La Libertad and waited for Werner's daily visit, which came every afternoon at about three. Werner had coloring and features that suggested Morocco, and Joe began to try to engage him in conversation, which was difficult because the boy was clearly afraid of him, and Joe sensed Werner knew he was a guerrilla fighter in hiding.

"Do you know why I'm here?" Joe asked the boy one day.

"No."

"Well, I'm circling the world. I stopped here because I've seen so much I needed to rest. This is the calmest place I could find. Do you know how many countries I've been to?"

"No."

"About seventy. I think. Maybe eighty."

---

*One day, a writer will be brave enough to tackle Mafalda's story. She's a novel unto herself, her own epic of bumming and loving and loss and beauty. The Author shortchanged her. He had his hands full with me, I guess. With the knuckleheaded me.

Werner narrowed his Arab eyes, as if he thought Joe might be taking him for a fool. On his walk through town the next day Joe found a stationery store that also sold textbooks and school supplies, and he purchased a small folding map of the world and brought it back and when he saw Werner he opened it up.

"I've been almost everywhere on this map," Joe said. "Pick a spot, and I'll tell you about it."

Werner brought his finger down on the largest country on the map, a huge splotch of red.

"That's Siberia," Joe said. "I've never been there. Try again." The boy brought his finger down in the southern hemisphere, and Joe cried out, "Africa!"

Joe began to tell his stories of Africa. He did not describe the wars he had seen on that continent, but rather, the animals, the children and the mountains and rivers. He spoke of shepherds guiding goats across the steppes of Kenya, and of seeing ibises with their horns as long as scepters, and children playing at rolling hoops along the red-dirt roads with sticks. Werner pointed to other places, and Joe described boys diving for fish in Jamaica, and the way he saw two dogs circle and capture a sheep on the Patagonian pampa, and how there were hills looming over the ocean in Brazil where barefoot boys flew kites. Joe's stories contained ocean waves and dogs and more children and their games, and they felt familiar to Werner, as if Joe had whispered them into his ears many times before. Joe shared more during each visit, and Werner eventually decided he too would one day travel to other lands beyond La Libertad and El Salvador. This idea stayed with him for many years after his brief friendship with Lucas ended, as Werner grew into young manhood. Eventually Werner came to see that he needed to leave El Salvador to have a better life, and he remembered Lucas's stories when he took his first, long, dangerous journey, along rivers and in rail cars, through Guatemala and Mexico, and along the wide highways of the United States, through many different ecologies—deserts and cotton fields and orange- and rust-colored Appalachia. Finally, Werner reached Washington, D.C., with its white marble monuments and vast lawns and vistas. By then, the war in El Salvador was far in the past, and Werner could only wonder about the fate of the man he knew as Lucas, whom he had last seen the December before his twelfth birthday. Werner started a family in the American state of Maryland, and he began to forget the stories he had heard in the house in La Libertad. And then one summer his oldest, college-student daughter took a summer trip to Europe, and she sent him postcards from Prague and Warsaw, and she called him from Moscow in the middle of a Maryland night on WhatsApp, and he could see her on his telephone, standing in front of the Kremlin, the sun glinting off the onion-topped towers behind her, and at that moment Werner felt a strange doubleness: that he was once again a boy listening to Lucas tell stories of faraway places, and that he was a middle-aged man whose daughter was telling him about her journey to "el este más este." And not for the first time Werner felt grateful for having met that American whose final fate he had never learned. What happened to the man he knew as Lucas was a mystery, unlike the fate of the two other Americans he had met in La Libertad during his boyhood and wartime years, Sister Dorothy and Jean Donovan, the religious workers who lived down the street.

JOE SAW SISTER DOROTHY twice more during his walks through La Libertad, but had never spoken to her, and he never met Jean Donovan. They were on the periphery of his quiet, underground existence. *Nobody home but me and my mutt,* he wrote to his mother. *An ugly grumpy boxer who belongs to the owners. Needs braces on his lower teeth, and he ain't too smart.* One morning, a military operation unfolded in the hills above the city, and the next day Joe recounted the events in a letter. *A bunch of local kids went up into the hills with slingshots to shoot at flights of migratory birds. This is a yearly custom. Some crazy peasant reported the hills were full of guerrillas.*

The military lobbed a couple of grenades, and scared the hell out of their own troops, who panicked and called in reinforcements. Hence the planes and tanks that followed. Nobody got hurt, but one little fat boy (11 or 12 years old) got captured with his bag of rocks and was marched away crying by a column of soldiers. Jesus, you'd think by now I could do a little better at picking my revolutions! At home in the United States, Ronald Reagan defeated Jimmy Carter in the presidential election. Joe wrote to his Republican mother to express his opinion. *Well, it'll be goodbye to Jimmy the Hypocrite. But Reagan as President? Woe-is-us. A Hollywood stuntman for president?*

A month after the election, Sister Dorothy Kazel and Jean Donovan headed out in a white van from the same La Libertad street where Joe lived. They went to the airport in San Salvador to pick up two Maryknoll sisters who were returning from a conference in Nicaragua. On the trip back, somewhere near the airport, the four women were abducted by Salvadoran Army troops dressed in civilian clothes, and later raped and murdered, their bodies dumped in a countryside locale where the troops ordered some peasants to bury them. Within hours word had gotten out, and a dozen journalists and the United States ambassador were at the site, watching as the bodies were exhumed and pulled up with ropes from a shallow grave. *Well, as you know by now from the news media, we had another real bad week,* Joe wrote home. *Two of the murdered nuns were gals who lived down the street from me. The padre from La Libertad, our town, flew back to the States with the bodies. As you might know, all U.S. military and economic aid to El Salvador was immediately cut off.*

The women had been planning to continue their ministry of hymns and Bible verses and parables in El Salvador, teaching the locals that Jesus was a prophet of social justice who believed hunger was a sin perpetrated by the rich upon the poor. The photographs in the San Salvador tabloids showed their bodies, still dressed in long, modest skirts and high-buttoned blouses, being dragged like dead livestock from the hole in which they'd been deposited. Joe tossed his newspapers on the kitchen table and opened a beer and daydreamed about the nuns and their final hours. National Guard officers giving the orders, more than likely. Dispatch the four American outsiders, squash the uterine menace of their Christian practice. Grunts carrying out the orders with their fists, their erections and their semen, on a roadside near the airport. Many other victims, in police stations and army barracks where the national flag flies, with its brave blue stripes and the masons' triangle on the coat of arms. Sister Dorothy, I saw her here. Her final moments playing out in the headlights and carbon monoxide cloud of her hijacked vehicle, at the mercy of men who maim and penetrate.

A few days later, Joe traveled to San Salvador to pick up his mail and meet briefly in a park with one of the comrades, who said they were planning a "big action," for January, before the new United States president came to power and could restore military aid to the country. He told Lucas to report to his San Salvador contact in two days. *Afraid I can't go into much detail, but, as they say, the situation is "deteriorating rapidly,"* Joe wrote home. *I'll keep checking with my math professors for the usual weather reports.*

LUCAS AND HIS FELLOW rebel grunts waited listlessly an entire morning, in a safe house in a middle-class neighborhood with sunshine streaming between the daisies in the curtains. Finally, a mustachioed comandante arrived. But instead of orders, he began with a speech about "contradictions" and "social forces," reading from notes he'd written in pencil on a piece of graph paper; he puffed at a cigarette and blew the smoke away from his face. There are fifteen of us here in this living room, the comandante said, and maybe ten thousand more in other safe houses and in camps outside the city and in the provinces. When our barricades go up and we take this barracks, and that one, a spontaneous upswell of the masses will follow, overwhelming the enemy, and the enemy's battalions will dissolve, and the junta will head for the airport and fly off to Miami or Buenos Aires. That's the idea: a final offensive. The comandante explained these things and licked the bottom of the black brush on his upper lip. He had the whiff of some kind of official revolutionary training. A year of instruction in explosives and guerrilla tactics and spycraft in Havana, maybe. Joe had heard stories.

For the final offensive, Lucas graduated from a revolver to a hunting rifle. Pretty much everyone else had an automatic weapon. M16s, AKs, a Galil. His unit was to be one of several operating in Mejicanos. The hour of the offensive was being brought up by a day. In fact, it had already started in Morazán, in the northeastern part of the country, and in Chalatenango to the north. Rebel radio stations were broadcasting from the mountains: "At five this afternoon, at points all across the country, the General Command of the revolutionary forces launched their final offensive against the criminal regime. Compañeros! The hour of national liberation has arrived. We call on the people to raise barricades and provide water to the people's fighters. We call on the people to establish local authorities to replace the corrupt officials. The insurrectionary moment has arrived . . ."

Lucas's unit arrived in Mejicanos by car and truck, speeding through intersections as they drove toward their first target: a local police station. When they arrived, neighborhood kids were already inside, and one or two rebels entered, and Joe watched as the kids ran out with typewriters and batons and revolvers and telephones, and many more rebel fighters joined them and fanned out across Mejicanos, in their jeans and untucked plaid shirts and old soccer jerseys. Joe saw a rebel fighter of about eighteen, who he later learned was named Yanira, wearing an olive-drab shirt captured or stolen from the Salvadoran Army, and a blue bandanna tied around her neck, and a brown cap, and ammunition carriers on her belt. The neighborhood people gawked, because her face was round and striking, and because they had never seen a woman holding an automatic rifle before. Another woman, a comandante, appeared with a bullhorn and pointed its coned speaker up in the air after climbing the hood of a car. Tita was her name, and she couldn't be more than twenty-five, Joe thought, although she had the deep voice of a matron or a mother superior. More people came from the surrounding streets. Now they were a crowd, standing in liberated territory, staring at Comandante Tita and her wide shoulders, with an M16 set over one of those shoulders, and Joe felt as if he were inside a movie where a flying saucer descends from the heavens with beams of multicolored lights, and an alien emerges bathed in an ethereal glow, and the stunned populace gazes up at the space creature in wonder. Comandante Tita announced they were going to move slowly toward their next objective, the San Carlos army base, and whoever wanted to join could. A dozen men and boys stepped forward and took assorted rifles and handguns from a selection arranged, swap-meet style, on a blanket on the ground. Two neighborhood kids with identical mouse eyes, brothers, picked up revolvers and fell in behind Lucas. He began to hear shots fired in the distance; other units had begun the attack on the San Carlos base. Joe and the men and women around him marched with the pace of cautious felines, and within ten minutes they had reached the base, which was surrounded by white walls and a wrought-iron front gate.

An uneven barrage of single shots popped from the rebels' a-little-of-this-and-a-little-of-that arsenal; from puny pistols and M16s and a beautiful new Belgian FAL, and Joe felt exhilarated, even though the attack felt more symbolic than real, since none of his comrades were actually advancing into the base. This is no way to defeat an enemy in a fixed and fortified position. What's the plan? Finally, an order: Lucas, move back, be the retaguardia, watch for any enemy reinforcements, and within fifteen minutes a toaster-shaped armored personnel carrier was rolling toward Lucas's position, and there was nothing to do but to slowly pull back, and the two brothers who had been following Lucas dropped their revolvers and ran down an alley and disappeared. Joe and his comrades moved away from the army base in hurried crouches, like Groucho in a Marx Brothers flick, until they found a roadway that was not under fire.

His unit began a general retreat northward, on streets that rose into more affluent sections of the metropolis, where families lived behind walls, in compounds tended by platoons of maids and gardeners. Word came down the line: We are headed to a new objective. Nearby. The compa directly in front of Lucas introduced himself. His nom de guerre was Fideos, and Joe thought that was an interesting moniker with which to go into battle.

"Do you like noodles?" Joe asked Noodles, who smiled and said, "Of course." Joe and Noodles followed the line of soldiers along wide and empty streets, and finally into the open spaces of a kind of villa with big lawns and white buildings. "Qué lindo esta quinta," Fideos said. "I never thought I'd be inside one." A bullet whistled over their heads, and Lucas and Fideos dropped to the ground seeking cover. The rebels were being ambushed by a sniper. A soldier. No, a security guard Joe could see in the distance, firing a weapon from the roof of a small building. The sniper slipped away and Joe heard a scream-wail behind him. Yanira had been shot. "¡Ayúdenme! ¡Ayúdenme! ¡Ayúdenme!"

She'd been shot in the chest, and before Joe could step forward to offer first aid, another compañero was doing so, a medic Joe called Doc Holliday in the notes he wrote later, because he was carrying two revolvers in gunslinger belt holsters. Immediately, and without any prurient hesitations, Doc Holliday removed Yanira's blouse and scissored off her bra and treated her wound. Blood oozing from her torso, just below the ribs, and Doc Holliday held her hand and soon two other compas had fashioned a stretcher from some blankets taken from the residence, which Joe now learned belonged to José Antonio Morales Ehrlich, one of the heads of the four-headed civilian-military junta ruling El Salvador. From his obsessive newspaper reading Joe knew that Morales Ehrlich had married into one of the biggest landowning families in the country, and that his two adult sons had been in the guerrilla army. "¡No está! ¡No está!" Morales Ehrlich was not in the house. As Joe processed this information, the shooting started again: a group of police officers were attacking from another roof, and the compas returned fire and one of the cops fell and the others disappeared, and Joe followed some anguished voices out into the driveway of the compound and found two compas crouching over a comrade.

The wounded fighter was a woman of about nineteen, with the big eyes of an Egyptian pharaoh and mestizo skin imbued with the red sheen of coffee beans still on the tree. Joe stepped back and watched Doc Holliday try to treat her, but it was no use. She'd been struck in the neck and was dying very quickly, blood rushing up from her mouth and onto her chin. Twenty minutes later Joe took a small, hand-size notebook out of his back pocket to describe what he'd seen. *Dead in the driveway wearing khaki pants, soft khaki shirt, black T-shirt, no shoes, relig. string charm around neck (black) + badly painted pink nails. Expression was mixture of serious-ness and serenity. Noodles was shaken when he saw.* Noodles and the dead girl had been part of an ERP unit that had been based in the mountains outside San Salvador; maybe he was in love with her, or maybe they were like brother and sister, because now Noodles began to weep and say, "María, María, no." Joe watched Noodles cry and finally he placed an arm on the fighter's shoulders, and gave him the kind of manly squeeze he'd rarely given any male, and Joe said the first thing that came to mind: It's okay to weep. "Llorá, hombre, llorá, porque es muy triste perder una amiga así." The sound of Lucas's English-accented Salvadoran Spanish settled Noodles down, and the two men crouched together on the lawn of the man-sion where one woman fighter had been wounded, and another killed. More rebels arrived, and they milled about the lawns of the quinta, looking at its white-washed buildings and its octagon-shaped windows with stained glass depicting pale cherubs playing trumpets. Two compas returned from the main house with shovels and started digging a hole in the lawn between the guesthouse and the swimming pool to bury the girl fighter. The dirt under the grass was soft and the compas were quickly done, and they low-ered the rebel girl into her grave. Joe caught one last glimpse of her finger-nails, and realized he was wrong: they were not "poorly painted," but rather scratched off. In battle, perhaps, while firing her M16. Maybe one day they'll invent a nail polish to withstand the rigors of combat. Stupid thought. My crazy brain. Dirt covering her face now, her eyes, forever buried, how fucking horrible. Jesus, a dead girl soldier, will someone tell her parents? Suddenly two domesticated geese came waddling through the lawn, pets of the family that lived here. One of the rebel fighters, a short peasant man, very calmly reached down and grabbed one bird and snapped its neck, and caught and killed the second one too. He put them in a sack and draped it over his shoulder.

THE QUINTA WAS FILLING with comrades from various units of the Ejército Revolucionario del Pueblo, and from the Fuerzas Populares de Liberación and from the Partido Comunista de El Salvador, this last group being, despite its name, the most conservative group in the rebel alliance. Lucas saw people he recognized from the university when he was still named Joe, and they walked over and put an arm around him and said, "Qué bueno verlo," while the burial detail finished its work.

A bit later, Joe overheard other rebel fighters give an update on the general situation: in the city below, the army had retaken Mejicanos up to the market, but not the bus terminal. Joe could see helicopters circling over that part of the city, but in others the helicopters had been driven off by rebel fire. Joe wandered over by where the chiefs were gathered, debating what they should do next. As he approached, the comandante with the thick mustache looked at him and said to the other chiefs, "Let's send Lucas too. He's the perfect scout." And then to Joe, "Lucas, vení, te necesitamos."

Lucas was to slip back down into Mejicanos and give an appraisal of the enemy's strength, and any pockets of resistance. He surrendered his weapon and he took off his shirt and tied it over his head. Back to my demented-hippie routine. Back into bullshitter mode. Joseph Sanderson. I am just a lost gringo, señor. They told me there were pretty women in this country but now I see there is a war. I am very frightened. Or, as we say in my country, "freaked out." Can you point the way back to the Marriott for me, please?

Joe walked down into the empty city. There were no troops. Not a soul on the street, like Champaign-Urbana on a Sunday evening. Everyone inside their homes behind locked doors. A curfew's been declared. At one corner, he saw a boy and a girl sitting in their doorway, making brass mountains from the shell casings they'd found. Shuttered businesses. He walked into the heart of Mejicanos and did not see a single soldier or police officer, and he marched briskly back up to the quinta and found a reduced group of rebels, including the chief who had sent him to do reconnaissance. "It's quiet down there," Joe said. "No army, nothing."

"Yes, we know."

"Are we going to attack again?"

"No. We're pulling out."

Lucas and about fifteen rebels made their way out of the city into the hills, walking on footpaths into a rural darkness, following the sounds of feet breaking branches and plopping in the mud, until they began to see the first lemon radiance of dawn on the eastern horizon, and they heard a smattering of voices, mostly male, and they entered a clearing in the mountain brush, and Joe saw the shadows and heard the voices of about sixty men and women. Lucas and his comrades joined these rebels in sitting down on a patch of dirt to rest, and when the sun rose fully there was no reveille, no call to battle stations or orders of any kind, but rather more sitting around while the chiefs waited for information and debated what to do next. Joe took out his small notebook. *Whole show was an unnecessary rout. And yet with zone quiet all p.m., no return was mounted. Sat around eating oranges, tortillas, smoking cigs, talking. Some FAL and M16 training but nothing very disciplined and poor guard mounted. Gotta do better than this to give folks a reason to come out and join the insurrection.* Word spread in the camp of what had happened in the rest of the country: In the east, in Morazán, an attack on the barracks in the regional capital had fizzled out, and the compas in Chalatenango were on the retreat. The final offensive had been defeated.

Lucas was ordered to slip back into the city. Unarmed and alone, again. Not for reconnaissance this time, but rather to return to the refrigeration workshop and hide out and await orders. Two days later, he walked to the post office and sent his father and his mother and stepfather letters, each topped with the code *1200*, and in these letters he did not attempt to describe, in any way, the battles he had witnessed, the gunfire and the dead. He simply wanted to communicate the fact that he was safe. However, in the letter to his father he included the fourteen pages of notes he'd scribbled during the offensive. *Just a few things I'd like you to take care of for a while, Dad. Field notes from a revolution.* Joe expected his father would find his writing in these notes to be largely indecipherable, and he hoped Milt would not try too hard to read them.

In Arizona, Milt studied the pages with the patience of the veteran entomologist he was: with a magnifying glass he was able to make out *Yanira shot* and Joe's description of the rebel girl's corpse, but not much else. There were many words in Spanish, but he knew of no Spanish speaker he could trust to help him translate something so sensitive—the notes appeared to be evidence of his son's involvement with a rebel army fighting a government allied with the United States. Milt was worried by a few entries that were scribbled in tortured loops and lines, as if Joe had been sitting in the dark, or under fire when he wrote them. On other pages Joe's scrawl resembled Milt's own old-man's knot-writing. Milt wondered what *Cuart. San Carlos* meant, and who *M.E.* was but he finally gave up and filed the notes away, as Joe had asked him to.

MILT TRIED TO BE especially thoughtful and precise when writing back. Now that he was retired he had taken to typing his missives to his son, without knowing that his ex-wife Virginia was doing the same thing. Both of Joe's parents wrote long letters describing their daily lives in northern Arizona and in Champaign-Urbana, and during the next two months Joe spent living underground his letters from home were his chief source of entertainment.

I still get tinges of loneliness now and then, which last for only a few minutes, Milt wrote. *My gimmick for overcoming the feeling is to get in the pickup and take off to where there are people. I've discovered that all they need to do is talk, not necessarily to have any substance. I exchange comments over purchasing a doughnut with the man walking the dog, the coffee lady on the track in Buffalo Park. This morning I decided to walk down the road here and the former mechanic at Kmart recognized me and stopped to talk. It seems to work.*

His mother wrote: *We ate at a reserved table at the Village dinner last night and Kathy said she felt like a "queen in the dining room." Of course that will get her more invitations from Grandma and Grandpa. She will be here all day Monday and Tuesday and start school again on Wednesday. In the meantime, she's gotten out all her second-grade workbooks . . . Your old friend Jane stopped by and brought us an apple pie last weekend when she heard our neighbor Mr. Love had died.* Jane was one of his former girl-friends, a woman he met at an Urbana construction site. *I am returning her pan with a raspberry yogurt cream pie in it for dessert this afternoon when we have lunch with her.*

Joe read and reread these letters, and in the long silence in the safe house he had time to think about the person he was, Joe David Sanderson, son of Virginia and Milt, and how he possessed qualities inherited and learned from both. The silent observer that was his father, scientifically inclined, the thinker who relishes his solitude. His mother, among people, at the service of those around her. He remembered driving through the empty farm roads of central Illinois, and all the highways and footpaths and rail lines and air routes that led him to El Salvador, and not for the first time he felt he was the only man in the world who truly understood the love and the hurt in both places; in the prosperous north and the hungry south. He imagined his mother here, in El Salvador, baking a raspberry yogurt pie, and imagined taking Noodles to see the wonders of the Illinois State Fair. Cotton candy and faces covered with pink sugar, and the sawdust-covered floors of the Ag pavilions, and giant Illinois swine, corn-fed.

Joe's mind wandered and wandered.

The cinder-block walls of this room, San Salvador outside. Alone, in a bed, remembering the eyes and the waists of his lovers. The drive-in, a boat in the Kingston Marina, the cabin, Jane, the hotels, the houseboat. It still works. Sleep. The dirt tossed on the rebel girl's eyes, a scene from a horror flick, buried under a lawn. Dirt in my eyes too, one day, maybe. What bullets do to the flesh of boys and girls playing at war. Take me up into the hills and I'll be an Indian and you'll be the cowboy, and I'll climb up into a tree and ambush you with an AR-15. Run away, run away. Follow the broad-shouldered woman leading a neighborhood into combat. I followed her like a boy. I've always been a boy. A boy up to this moment. A boy to the women who loved me. That's why Jane slapped me in Chiapas: she saw the letter I was writing Mafalda. What an idiot I was. Now I can see.

Rebel messengers arrived to deliver news that was mixed and contradictory. Fito said Lucas might ship out with a guerrilla column in the east next week. *Afraid our postal service is going to get even more raggedy in the near future before it gets better, but so it goes,* Joe wrote home. *Everybody battening down the hatches in these parts, the usual tropical storm imminent . . . One thing I need to say: despite the deterioration of local scene, do not contact embassy. If I stub my toe, friends will contact y'all . . .* A week passed and he wrote again. *Just a quick note to let you know I'll soon be on my way as scheduled, math books under my arm, ready to explore the fascinating world of Einstein. If only my old high-school teachers could see me now! Unsure which direction I'll be heading, so be patient. Lots of possibilities have opened up for post-graduate work and I'm not sure which to take up: between my math studies and a little lepidoptery work in the boondocks I'll be very occupied.* After he sent the letter he was told he'd have to wait again.

Word came that he would be needed for an intelligence-gathering operation. Lucas would do anything. He was prepared to walk through fusillades of machine-gun fire to escape this room.

THEY SENT HIM to the other side of the country. To the city of Usulafter. His job was to scope out the main military base in town, for a future attack, and to get a general sense of the weaponry the army had at its disposal there. They figured a U.S. vet like Lucas would know what he was looking at.

JOE WALKED AROUND THE BASE, taking notes on two sheets of ruled paper ripped from a notebook, making a sketched map of the strongpoints at the edge of the base, lists of armored vehicles, maps of 90-mm-cannon emplacements. When he was done, he walked to a restaurant and met his two guerrilla contacts, Rigoberto and Pablo. They had just ordered a couple of steaks when suddenly an army sergeant in a metal helmet burst through the door, followed by two other soldiers, each of them taking three or four long strides into the restaurant, toward Joe's table; the first grabbed Joe by the neck as he sat, flinging him to the ground wrestling style.

"¡Hijueputa! ¡Documentos¡ ¡Enséñame tus documentos, hijueputa!"

Joe said in Spanish he couldn't produce his documents with a hand on his neck, and the sergeant grabbed him by the belt and shirt and lifted him up and hustled him outside, knocking over two tables more on the way out. He pushed Joe down onto the half-paved sidewalk outside, handcuffed him and reached into Joe's pockets. As he pulled out Joe's wallet, the two pages of notes slipped out and fell onto the gravelly ground before Joe's eyes. A death sentence as soon as the sergeant read them and realized what they were. He heard the sergeant standing over him tell a private, "Agarrá esa mierda," but before the private could comply and retrieve the sheets a truck drove past, just a few yards away, and Joe's notes were sucked up in the vacuum created by the truck's undercarriage, and the incriminating sheets were lost in a cloud of windblown street trash. The sergeant lifted Joe to his feet, and pushed him into the back of a truck, next to Rigoberto and Pablo, and Joe had time to realize that despite the miraculous escape his notes had made, the three of them would soon be executed anyway. What a way to fucking go. Be a stoic sonofabitch and don't give away anything. This will hit Mom hard. She'll have to tell Kathy. The look on their faces, oh fuck, fuck.

Fifteen minutes later, after some rude questioning of Joe and a few slaps and kicks of Rigoberto and Pablo, the sergeant seemed to accept Joe's explanation of his presence in Usulután. I was just hitchhiking across the Pan-American Highway, trying to get to Honduras, and these two young guys started talking to me. I always like to make friends on the road. Which way is the bus station, I should be on my way.

THE ERP HONCHOS shifted Lucas from safe house to safe house on the outskirts of the cities of Usulután and San Miguel, where he stayed with groups of other city folk preparing to join a rebel column in the mountains. A university student, a nurse, a doctor from Mexico who was slightly younger than Joe. They were cared for by working families loyal to the revolution. Joe had time to write three different letters recounting his recent, brief detention in Usulután. To Steve: *Was sitting in a restaurant with "friends" when shit hit the fan. Machine guns. Cuffed and jugged, then inexplicably freed. Usually these are one-way deep-six trips so I figure everything from here on out is extra, a luxury, on the house! I done used up my nine lives long ago.* To his father: *Luck finally ran out last weekend, then immediately swung back in my favor (getting adept at clinging to the rebounds!). Picked up at gunpoint by the local Tonton Macoutes, cuffed, then inexplicably released (with apologies). However, one glimpse of Satan's red cape was all I needed.*

Joe was more cryptic in his letter to his mother and Calhoun: *I sure hope you folks are taking it as easy as I am. Haven't put in a lick for days. What happened is this: the Welcome Wagon finally got around to paying me a visit (silver bracelets are a special item for strangers these days). However, I'm a busy man—places to go and people to see—so I quickly declined their gracious hospitality . . . and promptly used an old ticket on the Underground Railroad. Well, I must say compared to the old Civil War routine in Kansas and elsewhere this is a really classy setup. Get my a.m. coffee and cigarettes, stuffed with food, daily newspapers, radio/TV, the works! The conductors are top-notch, accommodations at all stops are excellent (sometimes I even get to wash the dishes and swat the kids), so all in all I couldn't be in better hands . . . Shall bring y'all up to date soon as me and my pals get our fill of chasing butterflies in the boondocks.* A week later he wrote a new letter. *Hmmm. This getting pampered like an old dowager has its limits. Getting bored and restless but can't budge until the train's ready to move. Play card games and whatnot with the kids and they beat me every time! Kathy didn't teach me a durn thing.* His next letter to Steve said he was in the eastern third of the country, where *dozens of bridges have been blown out and roads cut,* and where much of the populace had been without power for weeks.

In Illinois, the Sanderson family received these letters and were quietly and privately alarmed. But they placed great value on keeping their composure; there was rarely any weeping, complaining or raised voices in any Sanderson household. They rarely, if ever, panicked about anything. So they did not call one another to agonize over Joe's recent brush with the authorities of a murderous regime, or try to piece together what exactly Joe might be up to in his Latin American war zone. At their next gathering, at Steve's place for dinner, Calhoun was the only one who brought up the subject.

"Your brother, in his last letter to us, he said something about 'the Underground Railroad.'"

"Yes, he told me the same thing," Steve said. "I'm not sure what he means by that."

"And he sounded well when you talked to him on the phone," Virginia said. "What was it, a week ago?"

"Yes. The same. For those five minutes."

Virginia waited, but Steve added nothing more. She read his face and saw a big-brother annoyance with his little brother. Steve and Virginia were powerless to do anything to help Joe other than to send him money when he asked for it, and now he made a point of saying he didn't need money at all. Underground Railroad? Butterflies? Boondocks? Virginia allowed herself to wonder where Joe might be at that precise moment, a Sunday night in Illinois and a Sunday night in El Salvador. Was he being smuggled into a countryside without bridges or electricity? Who exactly were the math professors? If Virginia had been the type to vent her emotions, she would have begun by complaining about the childish tone of Joe's letters. His light-hearted descriptions of violent and deadly encounters. She understood it was his way of telling her not to worry. But she was clipping the newspapers and watching the news every day: no other Republican woman and member of the Daughters of the American Revolution in central Illinois knew as much about El Salvador as she did. This is a very, very serious situation, but he plays the jaunty boy in his letters to me. If they could kill four American churchwomen they could kill anybody. I didn't think I could be as annoyed with him as I am now. But keep him close. Continue clipping news of battles and executions from the newspaper, and send them to El Salvador. Tell him about the spring planting, the news from Kansas. About his niece who never stops asking about him.

THE NEXT LETTER Milt received from Joe began, *I continue to wait for the next train to leave my deserted island*, and Milt was annoyed, because trains don't leave islands. That's a mixed metaphor, son. Joe was more forthcoming in his letters to his father, though he never did explicitly say he was with the guerrillas. Joe was with a family that supported the rebels, as far as Milt could tell by reading between the lines. His companions included a girl of eleven and her mother, who were about to join the revolution too. The girl and her mother recounted stories of burned villages and army patrols and hiding from the bombs of the Salvadoran Air Force, Joe wrote. Joe mused about what he should take on his journey *into the boondocks,* by which Milt understood the mountains, because all guerrilla armies fought in mountains. *Books? Of course. Which ones? I finally came up with a Spanish/English dictionary. And rather than additional books (Spinoza, Blatchley's* Coleoptera, *etc.) I opted for three empty notebooks: a few sparse journal entries mixed with poetry ought to be adequate to maintain sanity, along with being economical weightwise. In all, my "worldlies" have been reduced to ten pounds of non-essentials that I will happily chuck in a pinch! Actually the only crucial items in my possession will be (1) glasses and (2) El Salvadoran butterfly net,* by which he meant his weapon, Milt gathered. *Otherwise, naked as I came, naked I can leave! Oh yes, plus about $40 tucked away someplace.*

After twenty years on the roads of the world, Milt's son had reached an exalted bumming state. He was traveling exceedingly light, with no need for cash, while having the absolutely most glorious adventure an American lover of free peoples could imagine. Had any other American achieved such heights of hitchhiking excellence? No, Joe was the champion. These thoughts brought a smile to Milt's face that stayed there as he walked through Buffalo Park in Flagstaff. He marveled at the fact that his son, who was approaching forty, could be in El Salvador and remember a book as obscure as Blatchley's *Coleoptera,* a 1910 survey of the beetles in the state of Indiana. It was a foundational text of Midwestern entomology and Milt remembered Joe as a boy sitting on the living room floor with Dr. Sanderson's copy, studying the pages filled with species names and drawings of thoraxes and abdominal segments and spiky insect tibias and femurs.

JOE'S NEXT LETTER to Steve said he was setting off on the "Underground Railroad" with his "math professors" in two days. He gave a set of instructions for Steve and his mother for mailing future letters to El Salvador. They were to write to a "Leopoldo" at an address in the capital. If possible they were to address their letters *in longhand, and a variety of longhand. Don't use my name on the envelope address. Stagger mail rather than sending always on the same day of the week,* he wrote. *Sorry for the nonsense, but I don't want to get my friends in trouble.* Joe said he would likely not be able to write as often as the two or three letters a week he'd been sending.

Tell Momma all is well, I'll be home whenever, and plant rhubarb in the spring garden, Joe wrote. *I'll keep in contact the best I can. So it's 1200 until then.*

Eight weeks passed without a letter from him.

20.

La Guacamaya, Morazán

DUSK WAS HIS DAWN. Joe rose from fitful sleep and opened his startled eyes to the warm hours of the dying afternoon. Puta, I wanted to sleep some more. When he joined his fellow rebels to resume the march, he took his first steps with his eyes facing the slanted rays of the setting sun, seeing dragonflies and mosquitoes and spiders in the milky last light of a country evening. The color drained from the coffee fruit and the cornstalks, and the landscape became a shadow painting of tree branches and trunks, and the soft bellies and breasts of the mountains turned black and menacing. Joe felt exhilarated and very young, despite the fact he was older than everyone around him, and as he marched, the tadpole eyebrows and brown pupils and babyish complexions of the rebels' faces disappeared too, and he listened to their shoes and boots flopping on mud and rocks. They marched at night to stay out of sight of the Salvadoran Air Force. Men with machetes up ahead cleared the path. Swish, issh. Clunk, clunk, crack. Even when they were slowed down by thick brush, Joe had trouble keeping up. He followed the warnings passed back from the front of the rebel column: "Look out, there's a rock here." "A tree branch." He stumbled into a hole and twisted his ankle and marched slower still, and the peasants chuckled at him. "Se está quedando atrás el gringo." Yes, I'm falling behind. Not used to walking blind. To a peasant the night path and the day path are the same path. I haven't got my night legs yet.

Their destination was the main rebel base in the northeast. Their column consisted of forty-five eager and underfed and perpetually hungry human beings who were surviving, in part, by eating roots the peasant soldiers dug up. Joe lost another notch on his belt but he still lumbered, big and clumsy next to the young men and women who bounced along the night paths like sparrows. One morning, as they prepared to sleep after a long day's march, his new comandante, an erudite and tall man, told Joe with a sly grin: "You know, they say the optimal age to be a guerrilla is between twenty-five and thirty-five. I am thirty. Exactly the right age. You are not." His nom de guerre was Sebastián and it was an open secret he was in love with one of the members of the column, a young woman named Máxima.

At dawn their nightly march ended with the sight of pink light coloring the slopes of the San Miguel volcano, and its conical beauty reminded Joe of Kilimanjaro and allowed him to forget, momentarily, how hungry he was. When the moon rose over the volcano the following night, Joe saw a possum scurry up into a tree; he asked the comandante permission to shoot it so they could eat it for dinner. Lucas struck the animal in the head with a revolver, a single shot from a distance of five meters, and the rebel soldiers around him *oo*ed and laughed in appreciation of his marksmanship. They returned to the march, and finally they unburdened themselves of the things they had carried during the long night. Joe set down the backpack that held his mostly unfilled notebooks and the rebel fighters around him removed the ammunition packs that were attached to their belts, most of them hand-sewn by their mothers from canvas scraps and nylon fabric. Then, for the first time in his life Joe ate possum, an exceedingly greasy meat that tasted like moist chicken. When they were finished the comandante poked a stick at the bones in the fire. "We'll be entering ranch country soon," he said. "So let's find a cow to steal. A rich person's cow. A bourgeois cow." The sun rose above them, and the men and women of the rebel column rested with possum protein in their stomachs, and dreams of beefsteak in their heads, and they felt sleep welling inside them as the daylight grew brighter around them, and it was hot, even in the shade of the branches. They slept on the ground, on pillows of joined hands, alone with their memories of the march and the events that had brought them here, to this grove of trees with the sound of a river a few paces away. Branches and leaves and insects and pollen on the surface of the water, floating past.

Comandante Sebastián crawled next to Joe, looked across the column of sleeping compas and began to whisper into Lucas's ear—in English. "Lucas, can I tell you something?" His accent suggested New York City. "I need to tell you something." And when Lucas gave him a confused look, Sebastián explained: "I lived in Newark for five years when I was a kid."

"No sabía," Joe said.

"You know that woman you see at the end of the column? The tall one? She's my girlfriend."

"Máxima? No shit."

"Yeah. But she's angry with me now. Because I yelled an order at her. Many orders. But one day soon we'll be alone and together again. I'm telling you this because I have to tell someone. I'm going to write poems to her and win her back."*

Sebastián rolled away and tried to sleep with an arm and then a shirt over his eyes. Lucas knocked out quickly and snored. At the other end of the camp, Máxima snored too, small puffs next to the trumpets of the boys around her. How many kilometers today? Fifteen. Joe fell asleep, and into a sweaty dream with orange noon light glowing behind his eyelids.

THE NEXT NIGHT, marching through open fields, the rebel column stopped on the edge of a cattle pasture, and two guerrillas very quietly approached a cow and rustled it away, despite some sturdy bovine resistance. The rebel column and the purloined animal marched along a river, and Joe saw a wild horse wading in shallow water and his comrades stopped to admire it for the apparition it was, a yellowish-brown animal that glowed in the dawn light as if it were made of gold. Later they camped at the opening to a cave whose walls were covered with small and ancient hand-size paintings. With each night of marching they entered a landscape that was greener, and a light mist fell on them, and Joe was relieved to be cooled off after so many warm nights of sweaty marching and days of sweaty sleep. With more tree cover, they could march during the day. One afternoon they followed a narrow gravel road and entered a "caserío," a collection of homes with cement and adobe walls, and roofs of thatched branches and leaves. The settlement seemed abandoned, until women and girls and boys emerged from the brush around these homes; they had been hiding and now they revealed themselves, a small community of very poor people, dressed in timeworn clothing that hung on them like laundry; they seemed to be a mix of indigenous Mesoamericans and Africans, with wide faces and full lips. Joe shook

---

*The Author isn't being a sentimentalist. The Salvadoran revolution really was like that. All those handsome and pretty young dreamers thrown together in the prime of their lives, facing death. When the bullets weren't flying, it became a real love fest.

hands with a boy whose pants had rectangular patches at the knees and whose shirt was filled with finger-size holes.

The only adult male in the village carried a machete with a curved tip, and Joe learned this was called a corvo. The man shook hands with Sebastián, speaking in a heavy rural accent Joe struggled to understand, and he led them up a short path to a cluster of singed adobe bricks and blackened palm fronds. "The army burned these houses down, Lucas," Sebastián explained. "For collaborating with us." Joe sensed that before the arrival of the army, the people here had lived in a deep and pure isolation. The children played games with rocks and pieces of string and ants, the way his father had in Kansas, and Joe was reminded of images he had seen of the poor during the Great Depression. This settlement had no electricity, and only a mud path connected it to the rest of El Salvador. The caserío existed in a state of timelessness, and this was disconcerting to Joe, because it ran against his notions of history, of the power of modernity to leave at least some trace in every corner of the globe. The army had taken away a young man from the village, Sebastián said, and he had not been seen since, and the soldiers had poisoned the wells and warned that worse would happen if the people did not tell them where the guerrillas were hiding.

The rebel column left the village and headed north, and Joe saw two helicopters prowling ahead of them, and the comandante led them to the top of a small, wooded hill where they could hide and watch the enemy aircraft. Smoke began to rise from an unseen source two or three miles away, carbonous columns billowing upward from the lush forest canopy in pulses, as if produced from the breathing of two giant animals with fire in their entrails. The rebels watched silently and impotently, and Joe looked at the comandante, and saw a fire alight in his pupils, and thoughts of retribution forming inside his New Jersey–educated brain, but orders were orders; they were to avoid contact with the enemy. They continued their march northward, toward the main rebel base; the comandante said they would be there in two or three days.

When they paused their advance to eat, Joe began composing two letters: one to his father in Arizona, another to Mom, Calhoun and Steve in Illinois. *Dear Papa—After twenty-five days in the bush I'm finally down to my last belt hole! Can count the weeks like tree rings. After several decades of learning to live off the land I'm faring well and still a tough old bird at nearly 39.* He referred to the rebels he was with as "butterfly collectors" and described his adventures in the eating of reptiles, roots and marsupials. *Granted, possum goes better with sweet potatoes and gin, but it was tasty all the same.* He told his father how the army was burning the homes of the peasants, but he also described the flora and fauna he had encountered—a *species of rattlesnake, a small boa called mazacuata, and what appears to be a rear-fanged viper called mica. Often incredibly lovely at night when the moon comes up—trees silhouetted along the mountain crests.* The next day he resumed his letter writing by confessing to feeling old and run-down. *Tough old bird or not, I'm suspicious that this just might be my last collecting trip. The knees and lungs just don't function as well as they should. Weighed down with equipment, hungry + fatigued—sometimes reminds me of climbing Kilimanjaro.* He kept up the patently nonsensical fiction that he was on an expedition with "math professors," and also railed against the Reagan administration for continuing to fund the Salvadoran army. He summed up his days of marching with a reflection: *I've come a long way, baby, from those 20-mile Lincoln Trail hikes I used to make in the Scouts with Troop 12.*

Joe put the letters back in his rucksack, down underneath the extra ammunition he carried there, because there was no place where he could send a letter from, of course, no mailbox, no stamps for sale by the roadside in this war zone. At the end of each day's march he wrote a little more. He told his family the spirits of his comrades had lifted because they were entering territory that was, for the most part, "liberated," and he described how groups of children came out to meet his band of "math professors" as they entered each village. The children marched alongside them, a rebel column in miniature, carrying sticks and "mini-machetes," laughing and walking stiff-armed, like soldiers in the movies, following the column through each settlement and then on the paths that led away from them.

Joe and the rebels entered the department of Morazán and in one morning they covered twelve uphill kilometers at a leisurely pace, and they arrived at noon to a series of footpaths in an expansive mountain valley. A squad of guerrillas was there to greet them, a scout party from the main rebel base; their ranks included a boy of about sixteen, and a woman in her late twenties with a rosebud mouth who wore a tight white blouse with an M16 slung over her shoulder and two ammunition belts arranged over the burned-brown skin of her upper chest, and Joe felt weird and weak pangs of arousal. Lucas was tongue-tied in her presence, but he was going to make the effort to talk to her just the same, when suddenly they heard voices yelling from the nearby caserío, followed by the increasingly clear and loud sound of propeller-driven airplanes approaching. The woman fighter stared suddenly into Lucas's blue eyes as if they were responsible for bringing the Salvadoran Air Force upon her, and she turned and ran, sprightly, up the path, and Sebastián found Lucas and yelled at him, "Vos, quedate aquí," and Joe understood that he was to join the civilians in taking cover in the trenches that had been dug nearby. Bombs fell into the forest and exploded, close enough to be felt as a kick-your-ass thud in the soil of Lucas's trench. A P-51 Mustang flew lower over the valley and unleashed several bursts of cannon fire. American army surplus, a World War II relic. Thanks, Rosie the Riveter. Dropping ordnance on huts and cornfields. The air assault and a firefight in the valley below him lasted three and a half hours, and except for his glimpse of the Mustang, it was a largely acoustic event for Joe; his only job was to keep the group of old women and toddlers in the trench next to him calm. The planes disappeared and the shooting died down and he watched army helicopters descend toward a point near the bottom of the valley, and then quickly rise up and disappear to the northeast. That evening, Joe took a few moments to add a summary of the day's events to his letter to his mother and Calhoun.

Got attacked yesterday (not quite everybody loves math professors!). First by airplanes, a bombing and strafing run—then by govt. ground troops. The peasants immediately mobilized and little kids no older than 7 or 8 were running around with small machetes, cords of rope, tiny canteens, etc., etc, to help out the guerrillas. Well, if it's the little guys against the big guys, I'm all for the little guys. Anyway, the govt. troops got their asses kicked. We could see the choppers moving in to evacuate casualties. So as locations go for studying mathematics, we've picked a real ducky spot!

Their march continued into the high country of El Salvador's alps, and they reached a ridge with many layers of mountains visible on the horizon, and Sebastián said the farthest one was in Honduras, and when they began to march again the comandante fell back toward the end of the line and talked to Lucas/Joe, and he explained how the Ejército Revolutionario del Pueblo had been working here in Morazán for a decade, building a network of supporters that included several Catholic priests, and peasants who became key members of the organization. "That's why we're the toughest guerrilla army in El Salvador, Lucas," he said in English. And then he switched to Spanish to say: "We were smart and planted roots here. We didn't have the arrogance to arrive suddenly and surprise the people and expect them to support us." As the rebels approached the next settlement they saw a thin, welcoming column of cooking smoke rising in the air, and when they met the people who lived there they were greeted with tortillas and beans, and warm atol to drink.

Joe was on his third tortilla and his second plastic cup of atol when a new squad of rebels appeared, and then another; many friendly embraces followed. He had arrived at the main rebel base, which was not a single camp, but rather a collection of small camps spread throughout a patch of highland forest and brush. "Bienvenido a La Guacamaya," Sebastián told

Lucas. "Follow me, there's someone I need to introduce you to." They walked through a forest of thin trees until they came upon a copper wire stretched along the branches above their heads, and then an outcrop of rock with a kind of cave beneath it and a table adorned with a red flag and the letters FMLN. A thin man with a thick black beard, and who was as tall as Joe, stepped forward to greet them and shook hands with Sebastián. "Lucas, this is Santiago. The famous Santiago of Radio Venceremos. Santiago, this is Lucas, the gringo you heard about."

Santiago was a Venezuelan radio man who had worked with the Sandinistas in Nicaragua, one of the thousands of foreigners who had traveled to that country to lend support to its victorious revolution. He had then come to El Salvador to place his radio experience at the service of the Salvadoran armed struggle, and now he showed Lucas the main instrument of his work: a Viking Valiant radio transmitter, made by the E. F. Johnson Company of Waseca, Minnesota. Vintage equipment, from the 1950s. Joe's brother, Steve, gadget man that he was, would have loved seeing it. With this small steel contraption, which resembled a bread box with dials and needles affixed to its face, Radio Venceremos was broadcasting to all of El Salvador, an hour or two every day. The enemy had already tried several times to silence the transmitter with ground invasions and aerial bombings. "The war in this region has become, in part, a war over this transmitter," Sebastián explained, and Joe marveled at the ability of such an antiquated instrument of American technology to cause havoc in the strategic calculations being made in San Salvador, and in the U.S. Southern Command in Florida, and at the Pentagon, and the State Department and the White House in Washington, D.C.

After a short discussion about radio frequencies and North American politics, Lucas asked Santiago if there was a way to get a letter to the United States, because he knew his family would be worried about him, not having heard from him for several weeks now. Santiago said he thought there might be. The next day, after consulting with one of the comandantes, Santiago said yes, a courier would be leaving for the south soon and taking several letters, and Joe finished the two letters he had started while on the march.

I'm presently gnawing on a chunk of raw brown sugar and a lovely blue and orange hairstreak seems to have the same idea, he wrote to his father, describing a butterfly that had landed on his dessert. *Have learned that the pattern here is that the army gets their asses kicked by our people, then go on a rampage in the countryside taking it out on the peasants. Such classic stupidity.* He noticed a lizard lifting its head up nearby, and added, *A coffee-colored skink just crawled up to my hideaway, so I'd best pause to say hello. Much love, J.*

To his mother and Calhoun he wrote that he was happy at his new digs, high in "territorio libre." *Plenty of food, pleasant sleeping at night, and among friends, so I'm quite content. Just hope that this crap gets done with in the near future. Got a real terrible hankering for an ice-cold beer. Once the shooting stops, I'll likely be able to return to the U.S. for another visit, but I won't know for sure until later. All's well! Much love, J.*

In the days that followed, the guerrillas based in La Guacamaya and the narrow valley of the Río Sapo launched an attack on the village of Villa El Rosario, and briefly occupied it, holding off an army counterattack, and during this time Joe's two letters home remained in a tin box in the rebel camp, unmailed, until finally there were a few days of calm and one of the local peasants sympathetic to the cause received the order to carry a small stack of letters to a post office distant from rebel territory. The courier walked and took buses for three days and sixty kilometers to the town of Santa Rosa de Lima, in the department of La Unión, where she purchased stamps and deposited the letters in three different mailboxes over the course of two days. These delays and peregrinations meant that Joe's letters, which he had finished writing on April 12, 1981, did not reach the post office at Santa Rosa de Lima until April 27. They were postmarked there, on that day. The one addressed to Virginia and Calhoun arrived at the Clark-Lindsay retirement village in Urbana on May 6.

Virginia was unaware that when Joe addressed his envelope he had done so left-handed, as a security precaution to keep his American-educated handwriting from arousing the suspicion of Salvadoran postal workers or anyone else glancing at the mail. The seemingly childlike writing on the envelope worried her. Who wrote this? And how did they get her address? She found herself trembling as she stood before the mailbox in the village's common area, and finally she gathered herself and opened the envelope, and she was relieved by the familiar sight of her son's cursive. The code *1200* was missing. But it did begin with a relaxed *Howdy all—*

21.

Villa El Rosario

MANGOES HUNG FROM BRANCHES like fleshy teardrops ready to plop onto the leafy soil. In his journal, Joe named the place "Limetree" for its orchard feel, because there were avocado trees too, and zapotes, a tree whose fruit, when opened, was the deep orange of a persimmon. The members of Lucas's rebel column rested and picked these fruits from the trees and ate them at will, and they feasted on big meals of beans and handmade tortillas as thick as the pancakes you'd find at an American truck stop, all prepared by campesina women who were like mothers to the young men and women of the rebel column; these women laughed as they served Lucas and they said things in their rural accents he did not always understand.

The Salvadoran Air Force did not possess enough bombs to hit every hiding place in this corner of Morazán, and the ground approaches to their base were wooded and intercut with steep ravines. A few weeks earlier the Salvadoran Army and its new "rapid-force" battalion, an elite unit trained by United States Army advisers, had attempted to invade La Guacamaya from the north, but the rebel army had humiliated them, capturing soldiers and weapons, as Joe heard many times in war stories told over campfires. "The cuilios were crying on the radio, they were running away. For three weeks they tried to come back at us, but we stopped them at El Mozote. Many cuilios died there."

After a few days Joe felt like his old bumming self again, fitter than ever and ready for his next mission, but no order came, and the days slipped past one after the other, the monotony broken only when another pair of air force planes arrived—small jets, whining as they cut through the air with strange, V-shaped tails. Fouga Magister, French made. A toy, really. I could probably fly that thing. They dropped their bombs and from his foxhole under the mango trees Joe heard explosions and the sound of shrapnel cutting through the trees like hundreds of American garden tools hacking at the branches and leaves all at once. The planes made big turns and jet-squealed away. No one around him was hurt, but the compas said one of the planes had dropped napalm near the spot where the radio station operated, and soon the order came to march down and across the ravine to the Radio Venceremos base.

As they got closer to the transmitter they could smell the forest burning, and they climbed the ridge toward the radio's cave and saw the fitful flames of leaves burning here and there in the treetops. The small fires consumed themselves quickly, and blackened leaves spin-danced to the ground, and the smell of gasoline and burned oil filled the forest. Such a familiar scent. Where, when? Years ago, years and years. Like yesterday.

Urbana. The driveway, Steve working on his MG. Fiddling with the engine and flooding the carburetor with leaded gasoline. The Illinois sky covering them. A cloud-spotted shell with the power to warm him with sunshine and awe him with thunder.

Drops of falling water tapped at the leaves in the trees. Está lloviendo. The radio man Santiago emerged from the overhanging rock that protected the transmitter and noted the napalm fires were out. The rain thickened and Joe remembered the word for downpour in Spanish, *aguacero*, and this useful noun cleaned the gasoline vapor from the air.

The next day Joe marched back to this same spot in the rain, and began his new assignment—as a member of the radio station crew. The order had been given by the top commander in the rebels' mountain redoubt, a leader whose nom de guerre was taken from the name of a Biblical prophet.

AT THE AGE OF TWENTY-EIGHT, Comandante Jonás was the most re-spected field general in the rebel army. He was a big, burly man (by Salva-doran standards) with a copper face, a mustache thick with what looked like black carpet threads, and the confident and self-possessed bearing of a judge. His nom de guerre was Spanish for Jonah, and in Joe's journal he became "the Whale."

Comandante Jonás was one of the original members of the Ejército Revolucionario del Pueblo. He was as well-spoken as the university-educated comrades in the organization, but unlike them he possessed deep reserves of street cunning. His career in popular resistance had begun when he was a ten-year-old passing out leaflets in support of striking teachers alongside his older brother. He was from a poor family that lived on the banks of the riverbeds that surrounded San Salvador, in homes with dirt floors and cardboard walls, and like a small and alert minority of the hardened people who lived in such places, he had come to believe that only a revolution would restore and protect the humanity and the dignity of the people he

loved. By the time he was twenty he'd become a leader of the ERP's underground urban cells, and he may or may not have been among those responsible for the purge that led to the secret execution of Roque Dalton, El
Salvador's most renowned writer.

Roque Dalton wrote sardonic poetry about the Salvadoran oligarchy and injustice, and he had been thrown in jail by the government,
escaped and spent some years in exile in Cuba. But he never lost the air of
happy-go-lucky bohemian, and he soon found himself in conflict with
the hardened and humorless men building the ERP's underground organization. When he suggested that the ERP was too focused on armed struggle, the leadership lured him to a safe house outside San Salvador and
accused him of being a lush, a womanizer and a CIA agent. They may or
may not have held a "secret trial" before they executed him. Although no
one in the ERP now spoke of Dalton openly, his death had become one
of the threads of fear and discipline that held the organization together.
When Joe met Jonás he had wondered but did not dare ask if he had been
one of the leaders present at Dalton's execution. No other leader he met
seemed to intimidate the compas around him as much as Jonás did. His
soldiers believed the comandante was ruthless, a quality that also delivered victories on the battlefield. Now Jonás said that Lucas was to work
with the radio station support crew, and that he was to be kept away from
combat: "He's our only gringo. We have to protect him."

At about the same time, Jonás gave the order to attack and occupy one
of the smaller towns in Morazán, Villa El Rosario.

IN THE EARLY-MORNING darkness Lucas and his unit set off to the southwest, and two hours later they reached a hillside where a town was visible
below their mud-caked feet; a cluster of red-tile roofs centered around the
tall façade of a church. One thousand one hundred souls lived down there.
From his rearguard position Joe heard a flurry of gunfire, and when his unit

received orders to enter the town, thirty minutes later, he walked carefully down to a road, then past a sign that read VILLA EL ROSARIO, and finally down empty streets of cobblestone and dirt, alongside Carlos, the handsome young compa with a narrow face who had been assigned by Jonás to be Lucas's bodyguard.

Women and children stared at the rebels through the windows of whitewashed adobe buildings. It had been two months or more since Joe had been in any truly built-up place. He approached the first little tienda he saw, held up a bill of the local currency and asked, "¿Cigarros?" The girl behind the counter trembled as she handed him a pack of cigarettes. He lit a smoke and strolled through the town. With a camera in his hands and nicotine coursing through his veins, he reached the open lawn of the central plaza and saw the thick stone walls of the Catholic church and the moment felt dreamy, as if he'd been killed and had entered a rebel heaven. Joe saw a group of compas surrounding the two National Guardsmen they had captured, and he stepped forward to take their picture, because that was his job now—official Radio Venceremos photographer. Equipped with a 35-mm camera and an M16 rifle. One of the prisoners was several inches taller than the rebels around him, and the rebels took the shirt off the soldier's back and held it up and riffled through its pockets quickly, and then tossed it to Joe. "See if it fits you, Lucas." Joe removed his pack and tried it on, and yes, it fit very nicely. Just in time too. The blue denim shirt his father had given him ages ago was falling apart, and from that moment forward Lucas wore the olive drab of a National Guardsman, and sometimes he felt more soldierlike than he had before, and at other times he felt like an old man playing at being a soldier.

The relaxed voices of the compas joking, and the sight of their boyish and girlish faces began to bring the people of the village out into the streets. A man who seemed to possess some official authority stepped into the town square and waved. "The mayor," Carlos said. Jonás approached the man and identified himself, and the mayor began to nod furiously in agreement with everything the comandante said. When Lucas tapped his cigarette ashes onto the street, the mayor turned to look at him, his eyes bulging with fear. The mayor believed this smoking, light-skinned German must be the rebels' executioner. He could not stop staring at Lucas, and Joe finally took a few steps toward him, and held out a cigarette, and the mayor reached out and took it, and Joe could see tears in the mayor's eyes as Lucas struck a match and lit the mayor's smoke for him. Jonás gave the mayor a light tap on the back and said, "Don't worry, hombre, nothing will happen to you. Because you are on the side of the revolution today."

A compa reported back to Jonás that the perimeter of the town had been secured, and there were no army troops in sight. Villa El Rosario belonged to the rebels, and Jonás told the mayor, "Let's gather the people here, in front of the church. We're going to address them. Explain things." Four dozen women and children, and the mayor and a handful of other men watched as Lucas's unit found a table and set up the radio equipment before the church. They were going to broadcast live on Radio Venceremos, using a mobile unit to bounce their signal off the transmitter in La Guacamaya, and when everything was ready a compa named Maravilla, who was Venezuelan, like Santiago, took the microphone and began to speak. "People of El Salvador! This is Radio Venceremos! Broadcasting from the liberated town of Villa El Rosario, in the department of Morazán, occupied this morning by forces of the Farabundo Martí National Liberation Front! Now Comandate Jonás will address the people gathered in the town square!"

Comandante Jonás spoke calmly into the microphone. If Joe had been writing down his speech, he would have used plenty of commas and periods, and a few semicolons, but not a single exclamation point. Joe expected the eloquence and idealism of a Che Guevara, or a Danton, but instead Jonás spoke to the people of Villa El Rosario and the radio audience about "one more step in the advance of the revolutionary cause," and sounded a lot like a Marxist schoolteacher. He explained how the rebels had been slowly building up their forces in Morazán, defeating enemy invasions and building networks in the mountains, and the comandante's drone caused Joe's thoughts to drift away, to wondering what they all might be eating that evening. But the flatness of the speech did little to take away from its impact in the rest of El Salvador, as thousands of people listened in their kitchens and bedrooms. During the comandante's pauses they could hear a barking dog, the murmur of a crowd, and some scattered applause. And the call of an owl, or was that some sort of radio interference or modulation that sounded like an owl? The voices and noises that came through the static and the electric warbling on the radio's speakers announced that something new and dramatic was happening. Many saw, in their mind's eye, a crowd of peasants with machetes and a town several times larger than Villa El Rosario's actual population.

Maravilla took the microphone again and began interviewing a few local citizens whose countryside voices carried a mountain lilt. "We've seen the rebels march in and, honestly, they have all behaved very well," a woman said. "They're all very young and respectful." The hourlong broadcast was heard as far away as Nicaragua and Guatemala, but its greatest impact was felt in the colonias of San Salvador, where the revolution had been defeated three months earlier. The cause came back to life again as crackled voices proclaimed victory from Japanese-made radios, the volume turned down low enough to keep the sound of the miniature insurrection from passing through the walls for their neighbors to hear.

NIGHT WAS FALLING in Villa El Rosario and the compas looked for rooms in which to sleep. Carlos said he'd found one, and he was showing Lucas the way there when he saw a woman of about twenty-five with a stethoscope over her neck and a revolver on her belt walking in his direction. She had the confident, slightly haughty mien of the Salvadoran middle class and was not a fighter, but one of the women who worked in the rebels' medical and public health units; the feline smile she gave Carlos suggested they knew each other. Carlos walked past her, took four steps more and stopped. "It's the last house down the street," he told Lucas. "Knock on the door. They'll be expecting you." With that, Carlos abandoned his gringo-protection duties and spun on his heels and walked after the woman. He disappeared for an hour.

The rebel occupation of Villa El Rosario drifted into a second and then a third day, and Carlos kept seeking out his new love interest. Once when Carlos and the rebel nurse were talking in the plaza, Joe approached them, and Carlos gave him the same look Steve had when Joe was cramping his style with a girl in Urbana. All across the town of Villa El Rosario, the defeat and retreat of the army had set loose romantic impulses, and members of the rebel columns and support units and a few of the locals exchanged suggestive glances, and every day at sunset a few couples walked to the fringes of the village. Under a sky colored the cherry and orange of carnival candy, they whispered to each other, and allowed their fingertips to touch and even to intermingle, and they adjusted the weapons on their shoulders, and a few dared to set them down, and to Joe they seemed as young and chaste and sexually frustrated as he was in Illinois twenty years earlier. He wondered if the arrival of darkness would see their inhibitions finally in retreat. Probably not. These young salvadoreños were all pretty prudish and frightened about sex, and when the sun rose the rebel army remained as virginal as it had been at sunset.

Each morning began with a flurry of activity, because Jonás had the compas busy creating a little commune in the village. The mayor, the post-master, the town judge, and the members of the town council had snuck off, so Jonás appointed a new council. He ordered a census, and the rounding up of abandoned livestock, and the establishment of a health clinic, and the publishing of a village newspaper, and the creation of a town garden, and Joe grinned as he pulled weeds and helped plant tomato seeds at said garden, because everyone knew the army would be back eventually, and these tomatoes were more likely to be eaten by an army sergeant than a rebel jefe.

Sure enough, on the fourth day of the occupation of Villa El Rosario, at about the same time that Lucas was discussing with a local resident the problems in raising watermelons, they began to hear gunfire coming from outside the town.

The army was trying to cross the Río Torola and attack the town from the south. But with the recent rains the river had started to rise, and the rebels ambushed the cuilios as they waded in a waist-high current. Two enemy soldiers were killed, their bodies floating away, beginning the slow drift toward the Pacific until army medics retrieved them. In the village, Joe took pictures of the victorious rebel unit returning to town, covered in mud and grinning with a war booty that included a 60-mm mortar and an army radio. Joe had snapped his last shot when Carlos approached him from behind and said, without preamble, "She's angry with me. She's not talking to me now." That night as Lucas set down his piece of plastic sleeping tarp on the dirt floor of a village home, he tried to rest on a spot next to Carlos and was kept awake by the rebel soldier's anguished murmurs. When Joe closed his eyes he could hear the psychic furniture rattling around inside Carlos's brain, and he vowed to sleep somewhere else, alone.

At dusk the next day Joe wandered through the town and found the post office, a building identifiable by its timeworn and fungi-stained official sign; he noticed the door was ajar, and walked in. The post office, it turned out, occupied only the front room of the building, and the rest was a residence, now empty. He stepped into a room with a bed. ¡Gracias a Dios! Tonight I'm going to sleep like an old man. Joe felt happy to be alone, at last, after months of the forced companionship of his rebel existence, after eating, sleeping, farting, yawning and scratching his bug-bitten arms and his itchy crotch alongside the limber boys and girls of the revolution. A room of my own. Finally, a room, a bed, quiet, me all by myself. And what's this? A toilet too! After weeks of defecating in the woods and bushes, the comfort of porcelain, a slow twenty-minute exercise of his bowels while reading a magazine dedicated to Mexican soap opera stars and their entanglements.

Life is good. As the occupation of Villa El Rosario entered its second week, Joe slept in the post office residence, and when he woke up, he took up his old habits in the hour before sunrise and sat at the postmaster's table, underneath a wall of mail sorted in slots. He wrote in his journal, describing the Easter procession he'd seen that day, a hundred or so people marching through the town, carrying a mini Jesus on the cross, the wood-carved prophet casting a perplexed stare at the machine-gun-toting rebels lining his route. Such a pleasure to be alone to write.

"Where were you?" Carlos asked after the first night Lucas spent away. "Gringo loco, you scared the hell out of me."

"I have a deal for you," Lucas said. "You leave me to be alone un poquito here in the town at night, and I won't bother you with your girlfriend."

"But she said she doesn't want to talk to me."

"Try again. She wants you to try again."

That night, in the darkness of the empty post office, Joe passed the shadows of undelivered letters and packages. It's been ages since I've heard from home. I wonder what Mom is up to? Did she get my letters?

OF COURSE VIRGINIA told no one outside the family what Joe's last letter said. How would she explain it? Speaking truthfully, she would have to say: He wrote to tell me he's with math professors in El Salvador, armed with a butterfly net, and he says the army attacked him and his friends. No, it doesn't make any sense. The fanciful statements in his letter were a silly dance around a truth he could not tell her. "Just Joe being Joe," she told Calhoun. "He'll explain it to us when he gets home." Unfortunately, at the same time, she was continuing to clip stories about El Salvador from the newspapers. "Salvador Rebels Said to Gain Territory. Town Not Yet Retaken." What was her son doing, exactly, with the rebels who were clearly the "math professors" of his letters? Probably he was tagging along in the rear. Like a kid on the edge of a playground who doesn't belong to any one of the school cliques that hate each other, but watches them, amused, from a distance. She parried the question when it came up at dinner at the complex. "What's your younger son up to?" "He's in El Salvador, studying the war there." "How do you study a war?" "I suppose you watch, you read, you listen—those are things that Joe has always been good at."

Virginia did not speak about Joe to Steve, other than to ask, after weeks had passed without another letter from him: "Do you know if your father has heard from your brother?" "No, Mom. I don't think so." The agreeable days of Illinois spring soothed her with sunshine and cool breezes. When she returned home with Calhoun to the Clark-Lindsey retirement village from her short, crosstown expeditions, she looked across Race Street and saw a grove of trees. She remembered Joe telling her, during his last visit: "I used to collect butterflies there. In those trees. See, Mom? University Woods." Now she was living next door.

ONE MORNING AFTER BREAKFAST, Joe found Carlos in the town plaza, alongside Comandante Jonás, who was leaning over a map with several other comandantes around him. "There are one thousand five hundred soldiers getting ready to hit us from the south," Carlos whispered. "But not today. Most likely tomorrow. First they are going to bomb us, with artillery. That's what our intelligence agents have discovered." Carlos pointed across the plaza lawn to a spot where said "agents" were gathered—a group of three boys and one girl huddled around three different captured army radios. "Those kids are from the orphan school up in La Guacamaya. They learned to listen to the army's radio messages and decode them."

Rain was falling now in big, lonely globes, and several residents were trying to round up the cows that had been wandering through the streets. The lawn in front of the town hall became a corral, and some children chased chickens into the building itself, and also a pig with hooves blackened by parasites. Joe said out loud, in English: "I guess they'll be dry in there. Guess it's making a good use of city property." He lit a cigarette and saw Santiago nearby, smiling, and wondered if the Venezuelan radio man understood English. No, Santiago was amused by the braided-hair girl of about seven who was chasing a turkey in circles, trying to coax it into the town hall as the rain thickened and became a percussive force that pounded the ground beneath Joe's feet. Lucas and Carlos ran for shelter inside the church, with Santiago running after them, because the radio unit was already inside, preparing for its daily broadcast.

An hour later, with the rain still falling, Santiago began: "This is Radio Venceremos, broadcasting on the twelfth day of the liberation of Villa El Rosario . . ." The radio audience heard thunderclaps, and the patter of rain, which many confused for radio static. Soon after the broadcast ended the army opened up with artillery fire. Distant pulses, like thunder. I am Thor, mortals tremble before me. The gunners on the other side of the river finally found the range and their shells began to land in Villa El Rosario, and the town erupted into a chorus of weeping children and screaming babies.

Out of the church and into the air-raid trench. Joe and his comrades could thank God and the foresight of Comandante Jonás for this hole in the dirt. Being shelled was different from an air attack. You could see a plane attacking you, but an artillery projectile was invisible to the eye until it exploded. The gunner imagines me as a coordinate on the map, and he fires into the air seeing the trajectory as a diagram he projects onto the sky before him. Army lessons, Fort Leonard Wood, what every infantryman must know. The projectile blasts into the air, and falls toward me, whistling downward, minding Newton's laws. A boom in the distance, brass and TNT detonating in the mud. Buuuaaam. Closer. Buuuaaam. Buuuaaam. Boom! The stone and mud architecture of the squat town trembled and murmured. And then an explosion so close Joe was deafened by the sound of cracking tiles and splintering wood, and moments later he felt a wave of heat pass over him, and he whispered to Carlos, "Nos van a vergear," which was a crude Salvadoran expression for being killed and crushed that Joe liked, because it was derived from a slang word for penis. The shelling stopped. As their numb eardrums adjusted to the relative quiet, Lucas turned to Carlos and his eyes said, Do you hear that? Screaming. A girl screaming.

They ran toward the town hall and saw it had taken a direct hit, and they stepped into the smoldering rubble and found a child covered in blood. A girl in braids. The girl with the turkey from before. She was painted with a red-black ooze of blood and entrails, and feathers too: the exploded animal parts of the pigs, chickens and turkeys that had been rounded up into the town hall. Lucas lifted her up and could feel her breathing, and he wiped the bloody feathers from her face and she opened her eyes, but at the sight of Joe's open baby-blues she screamed: Joe's eyes were emitting a piercing light, the cool and cruel glow of a world where girls like her were slaughtered alongside their farm animals. Lucas carried her out of the destroyed building, uttering the sounds American and Salvadoran fathers made to comfort their children. "Shush, shush, está bien, todo bien. Sin miedo, todo bien, shush, shush," and the girl closed her eyes and cried very loudly. Lucas took her out onto the lawn, and when the girl opened her eyes again she saw a dead cow, several neat and bloodless shrapnel cuts in its flanks. Two, three, four dead cows more. She turned quiet. Maybe they're just sleeping, she thought, and the idea comforted her as Lucas carried her away, still saying, "Shush, shush, todo bien."

THE ARMY'S GROUND invasion began the next day, with the sound of distant gunfire to the south; the townspeople returned to their homes and locked their doors and shuttered their windows. Lucas joined the radio unit by the church, and there they saw Comandante Jonás. "Two weeks! We held this town two weeks! And thanks to all of you we told the whole world about it. Every day!" Now they would do what rebel armies did: head for them thar hills, and disappear into the verdant and muddy waves of unconquerable, mountainous Morazán. The months that followed were likely to be free of army invasions too, because it was nearly May and the rainy season would soon begin in earnest, with showers falling six or seven days a week until October. Here, as in other corners of the world, mud and the weather were the best defenses against invading armies.

The holy rain is covering our retreat. Slip-sliding up and down. Swiiip. Feet up in the air, tumble down. "¡Puta!" Mud faces. Taste of mud. No chance the army will catch us, we can barely march ourselves. Two hundred villagers trailing behind us, with pots and pans, afraid the army will kill them all. An old woman with a cane. They made slow progress back toward La Guacamaya, and it was almost dusk as they reached the last river they had to cross. Two weeks earlier, Joe had forded this same waterway when it was a half-dry stream of bare boulders, its current barely deep enough to cool his ankles on a hot day. Now it was a brown torrent filled with waves and whirlpools, and Joe worried as the compas ahead of him waded into it, carrying their M16s and their FALs and mortars high above their heads. Sure enough, the fourth compa in the line lost his footing and fell into the water, and the river carried him away. Ten meters downstream, the river wrangled the compa into a pool of churning brown liquid, and a fluvial riptide pulled him under, and there were urgent calls from both sides of the bank. "¡Se está ahogando! ¡Ayúdenlo!" The compa fought to keep his head up, and went down again with a gasp-gurgle, and Lucas tossed off his pack, and with his boots still on, he became Joe the Lifeguard, a superhero from the Heartland of the United States of America. He jumped into the current and swam toward the drowning man, and was soon close enough to grab him by the collar and lift his head up and out of the water. "I got you," Joe said in English, and he kicked his legs against the water and paddled with his free arm and pulled the guerrilla fighter toward the edge of the river. My boots are still on, but if I could make it across the

Ohio, this little river won't kill me. Joe reached a spot where he could stand, and he gave the compa one more pull and brought him to his feet too. The rescued man took one deep breath of rainy air, and vomited into the river current. Lucas slapped him on the back to get the last of the water out of his lungs. "¿No sabes cómo nadar?" he asked.

"No," the compa answered, he did not know how to swim.

Lucas looked up at the young rebels gathered on the riverbanks, who had been watching. "Do any of you know how to swim?" he asked the rescued man.

"I don't think so."

The rest of the guerrilla column made it cautiously across, grabbing a rope one of the comandantes had ordered strung across the channel. Joe Sanderson, lifeguard, stood on the riverbank nearby with his boots off, ready to jump back into the water to rescue them if need be.

THAT NIGHT, as they warmed their soaked selves around campfires, Lucas found the rebel commander he had seen at the river crossing. His name was Bracamontes, and he was a former peasant, quieter and more unassuming than the other commanders.

"Comandante, can I speak with you?"

"Yes, of course."

"Well, I know you are a comandante, and we have to follow your orders. And I don't mean to tell you how to lead us. But I have to tell you something. A suggestion I have."

"We're all here to learn, Lucas. Any information makes the revolution stronger. What is it?"

"We need to teach these compas to swim."

Two weeks later, during a break in the rain, with the sun out but the local river still high, Lucas marched his first group of students to a still stretch of the Río Sapo where the water was deep enough to dive into, and as wide as your average American backyard swimming pool. He told them to remove their shoes and roll up their pant legs, and Lucas himself took off his purloined National Guardsman's uniform, and the unshirted sight of him provoked giggles among the compas, because few of them had seen such an abundant display of chest hair. *A caveman is going to teach us to swim.* "Primera lección es flotar," Lucas said, and that made sense to his young trainees: first, you float. Lucas took the first compa into the water, a young man with two hairs growing from the center of his chest. Like an Illinois preacher performing a baptism, Lucas forced the compa back-first into the water. "Relax, relajate, tranquilo," Lucas said, and he held the compa on the water, and the young man's hair was a black nimbus in the clear water: to Joe he looked like some teenage mestizo Christ, brown and beatific, a warrior now a child again, in my arms. I let go and he floats. See that, compa? The little fat you have in your skinny body will keep you from drowning. He held all fifteen of his students in the same way, watching the water lap up against their cheeks, their tawny eyes shifting back and forth. Are you going to let me sink? Fear, wonder. I float. And now a woman fighter, wide-faced and chestnut-cheeked and nineteen, and Lucas will not stare as the river water covers her blouse and the form of her torso. Moss particles slithering in the liquid over her neck and along her clavicle, her raven mane of corkscrew curls rising and falling in the water. Stretch out your arms, Ofelia. You next, María. Floating Furies. Now let's learn to paddle, stretch out your body, I'll hold you this first time. His swimming course lasted four days. He and a few other swimmer compas taught one hundred other compas how to swim. That's it, very good, you're swimming now, you'll be safe in the water next time, and listening to his accent, and remembering his rescue of the rebel in the river, many of the compas felt very fortunate to have this gringo teaching them something so essential, so basic to their survival.

"AGRICULTOR" WAS THE expression Comandante Bracamontes used to describe himself to the city folk who were coming to Morazán in greater numbers. A farmer, a tiller of the soil. As the revolution gained momentum in Morazán he was beginning to meet, for the first time, large numbers of foreigners too. A radio operator from Venezuela, a doctor from Mexico. A Colombian journalist. And Lucas, the norteamericano, who carried an air of mystery around him that was greater than all the other foreigners put together. Lucas had a way of looking at you. As if he were sizing you up, as if he knew things you did not know and found them amusing. Bracamontes was therefore not surprised when Lucas asked him, after the swimming lesson, "Comandante, why are you a comandante? What are your qualifications?" No Salvadoran compa had ever dared to ask him such a question.

"Well, I've been with the movement a long time," Bracamontes said. "Before that I was a farmer. So I imagine you could say I don't have educational qualifications."

"I'm just interested in how you become one."

"By fighting. For many years. Since back when all we had was revolvers and machetes and bombs we made from cans. A man came here from the city. He made contacts with the priests here. When I joined there were twenty or thirty of us in these villages. What about you? What makes you think you can be a compa, up here in the mountains fighting with us?"

"I know how to shoot well. I know the M16 very well."

The conversation led, inevitably, to a marksmanship challenge. With several other comandantes and compas watching, Lucas and Bracamontes found their way with their M16s to a guarumo tree on the edge of a clearing. Joe tapped the perfect cylinder of the trunk with the palm of his hand, and then took his pocketknife and carved an *X* at about the height of a man's chest. They walked away from the tree, Lucas secretly counting the paces, and when they were one hundred meters away, Lucas stopped. We'll be lucky to hit it from here, Bracamontes thought, it's too far. "Usted primero, comandante," Lucas said. Bracamontes lifted his M16 and he fired three shots and was very proud of himself when the third glanced off the cylinder of the trunk with an audible swick that left a mark they could both see.

"Muy bien," Lucas said.

Joe lifted up his M16 deliberately and remembered, as he always did when he had a weapon in his hands, his father's instructions back in Illinois. And basic training in Fort Leonard Wood. A memory in your hands and fingers. Control your breathing. Very gentle on the trigger. *Daniel Boone was a man, / Yes, a big man! / With an eye like an eagle* . . . Lucas fired one shot that struck the tree trunk dead center, two inches below his *X*. And then a second that hit inside the *X*'s two raised arms. And a third that struck the *X* dead center.

"¡Puta, Lucas! You win!"

Joe lowered his weapon and said with a grin: "You aren't ready yet to be up here in the mountains, comandante. You just wounded the enemy in the ribs. You have to hit him in the chest."

The gathered compas studied Lucas, and gazed again at the distant, wounded guarumo tree, and they saw the American in a new light. Of course he hit his target. It's because he's a Vietnam veteran, because the gringo army trained him to shoot at communists. It was as if an American comic-book hero, drawn in primary colors and carrying a futuristic weapon, had suddenly emerged from the dots on a printed page. A GI. This is why they rule the world.

"Next time we're on the march, I want you next to me, Lucas."

"Sí, comandante."

"But let me ask you one more question," Bracamontes said. "The most important one I can ask. Why are you here?"

The question carried notes of both curiosity and suspicion. "I'm representing the people of the United States of America," Lucas said, and he suppressed a chuckle at the sound of his voice saying this. He'd been practicing this speech in his head for months. Lucas explained that most people in the United States had no idea what was happening in El Salvador, nor would they be able to pinpoint the country on a map. If the North American people had seen the bombing of the villages, the kidnappings and the killings going on here, they would be lining up to volunteer to come and fight with the compas like he was. "But the average North American has no idea. He's just concerned with getting by every day. With sending his children to school and paying his bills on time." As he spoke, Joe thought of his brother, of Jim, of Jane the construction worker, and Linda sitting on the bank of the Ohio River, and the pictures of her parents in Chicago, and of all the faces of the people who'd carried him on his hitchhiking adventures across the roads of America, squinting as the sun warmed their windshields. Joe tried to explain to the compas his country's work ethic, and the poverty there. South Texas. Louisiana. Mississippi. Having visited many countries of the world, he did not think of the people of the United States as more cruel or selfish than people elsewhere. They believed in individualism, yes, but they were generally generous toward strangers. And they believed in fairness and equality before the law, even if they didn't act on those ideals all the time. "The typical gringo believes in, as we say in English, 'Giving everyone a fair shake.'" After much bumbling in Spanish and English and pantomiming, Lucas found the words to explain what this meant: "The same opportunity to succeed as everyone else." If the average norteamericano came to El Salvador, he would see that the people of El Salvador were not getting "a fair shake." Lucas said he was here in Morazán because the Salvadoran people deserved better, and he said these things in his Spanish idiolect, a mishmash of La Paz, backwoods Colombia, San Salvador and of the squeaky Illinois tenor of his nasal English. After twenty minutes, he was done, and the compas nodded, and many saw the United States in deeper textures. They watched their gringo silently as he lit a cigarette, and a few noticed that his hand was trembling.

THE RADIO VENCEREMOS CREW set up in the ruins of an old hacienda, but once again Joe found a spot to sleep alone, and to think—an abandoned peasant house nearby. He began to write a letter home, still unsure if and when he would be able to mail it.

Just finished my morning pot of coffee and I know for durn sure y'all don't go to half the trouble I do to get a little caffeine in my system, he began, just after putting the date and his location at the top of the letter: *April 28, countryside. First, swipe somebody's sack of coffee beans, spread them in the sun to dry, toast briefly over open fire, bust the shells open with a mortar and pestle, flip remains in the air to let the wind blow away the husks and the chaff, put beans in flat metal pan to toast over fire until dark brown, grind again with mortar and pestle, and you're all set to throw the grains into a pot. And after all that work, you'll want two pots!*

He told his mother and Calhoun that he was eating well, and had put on a little weight. *I'm happy as a clam. My new digs are on the outskirts of a hacienda, in an abandoned peasant's house I call "the Manger" because a bunch of goddamn cows occupy it at night (wreck everything, eat my bananas, crap all over the floor). Have a bamboo table to do my scribbling. Armed peasants passing by on the trail with their cows give me fresh milk every morning. After a dozen days of fighting in this area, the guns have finally fallen silent and everyone is beginning to relax. No doubt about it, the bad guys definitely got their butts kicked.* He stopped and put his pen down, and did not work again on the letter for three days because he was still uncertain how or when he would be able to send it home. Finally, one afternoon, as he sat with the radio people who were about to begin transmitting again, he heard a series of explosions.

"Mortar fire!" Santiago called out. The army was across the ravine, maybe a couple of kilometers away. A half dozen shells fell, like the first one, harmlessly into the brush, hundreds of yards off target. Joe heard gunfire. A ground assault was underway too. Somewhere out there the army was flailing in the mud. More mortar shells whistled overhead. If it was possible to slow the mortar shells down, and study their winged bodies as they fell, would Joe see the muddy handprints of the soldiers on their steel tips? The order came to move out, and they began to march, and the sun gave way to clouds and a light rain, and sprinkles gathered on the peasants' heads and the dripping water drew muddy lines on their faces, as if soil were oozing from their pores, and they all moved along, rebels and refugees, carrying pots and pans tied to their belts, and burlap and cloth and nylon bags, and when they had walked for a day and escaped the army, again, Joe found another quiet place to write and continue his letter home.

At his new location Joe renewed his "nesting instincts." Inside the shelled remains of a schoolhouse, he found a teacher's desk and moved it out under a shade tree. By now, several more compas in the radio crew had noted his desire to be alone, and they discussed among themselves this peculiarity of the gringo Lucas, who also needed his supply of cigarettes, and was willing to beg for them, and his writing supplies, and a few were beginning to resent him for these peculiarities; though petty resentments were common on the radio crew, because rebel life was harsh and most of them were educated people who were not used to sleeping on the ground and eating the same meal every day.

Spoke too soon, Joe wrote home. *Bastards started shelling us and had to move off to a new location. I did, however, remember to carry along my bag of coffee. My scholarly companions are pretty useless when it comes to preparing a cup, but among the hundreds of refugees who departed with us I'm sure to find a scullery maid or two.* They moved twice more, and each time Joe found a new place to write and be alone, following long days of taking photographs, monitoring English-language radio broadcasts, and sometimes even cooking meals for his comrades before the crack of dawn. *The math gurus seem pleased with my work and with me—always the closet masochist, I cheerfully put in 15-hour workdays. First to see the dawn, last to snuff his candle. And I love it, of course! So keep that quart of vanilla ice cream (and chocolate syrup) in the refrigerator and tell that dirty son of a bitch new president to stop dropping bombs on El Salvador so we can get some sleep already,* and he playfully ran thin Xs through *dirty son of a bitch* so that he could pretend at being polite. *Found a friendly pigeon to see this letter on its way. Hope it doesn't take too long to reach y'all. Ignore the postmark. Breakfast time. I'll swap tortillas for pancakes anytime! Love. J.*

Lucas gave the letter to a rebel agent who was headed out of the country, one more small envelope among a dozen different messages and reports for sympathizers and fund-raisers and procurers of armaments. When Joe's letter arrived eleven days later in Urbana, it was with a U.S. postage stamp, and an Oakland, California, postmark, and a return address listing the sender as an "R.M. Roofs" of Mexico City.

EACH TIME THE REBEL TRANSMITTER MOVED, its new location became a hub of activity. One person after another came to tell a story to the radio people, or to get information because the Venceremos crew monitored the BBC and Voice of America and Radio France. Comandante Jonás visited often, and Joe also met a Mexican doctor who had worked in emergency rooms in that country, and a farmer-turned-explosives-expert named Nivo who talked to Lucas at length about his plans to make a small tank from an old tractor—he'd heard Lucas was a smart gringo, and thought he might offer some advice, but instead Lucas peppered him with questions about the manufacture of gunpowder and detonators. Joe also met a former Salvadoran Army officer who had defected to the rebels, and a guerrilla fighter named María, whose true name (Ana Guadalupe Martínez) was known to everyone, because she was the published author of a book, *The Clandestine Prisons of El Salvador*, describing the seven months she'd been tortured and raped by army intelligence. She had the well-spoken and approachable disposition of a young and beloved high school teacher, her voice a calm string analyzing the intervention of the Americans; she wanted to talk to Lucas about the U.S. military advisers who had arrived at the Ilopango airbase to train elite units. With a series of patient questions about the U.S. Army and its training methods, she got a better sense of what these elite units might do. And from her Lucas heard more about the early days of the revolution in Morazán, including the story of a campesino who had escaped from the army and the rural police so often, local legend had it he was capable of transforming himself into a banana tree.

But mostly Joe wrote in his journal, usually in the cool air of the early morning, and it was on one such morning that a woman in crisp olive-drab fatigues who had caught his eye suddenly came up and started speaking to him.

"Lucas. El famoso Lucas."

"I'm famous?"

"You are, here among us. And you will be to everyone when we read your statement."

"What statement?"

"The statement the comandantes say you'll make about the war. It will be my job to translate it into Spanish and then we'll read it on the radio. If you're willing."

Her nom de guerre was Mariposa. She was the second "butterfly" Joe had met in El Salvador, and she possessed large, dark eyes that were like the spots you might see on the wings of certain Lepidoptera species. Unlike most of the other younger women he'd met in the guerrilla army, she was unafraid to speak to him, or to stand in his tall presence; she had grown up with four rambunctious brothers, one of whom was a rebel soldier. When she spoke it was with a crisp, enunciated, radio-announcer's voice. After three long conversations, including a walk through a grove of trees, she had learned all about Lucas and his travels, and about his hometown; the other compañeros in the radio and medical units who saw them on these walks falsely pronounced them a couple. Their conversations were, however, the most intimate Joe had had with any man or woman since becoming Lucas. Among other things, Mariposa coaxed from him a summary of his relationships with women.

"The last one you mentioned," Mariposa said. "What was her name?"

"Mafalda."

"She sounds like the one you were destined to be with."

"She's married now, unfortunately. With children."

"Well, that's convenient for you. Because it seems to me that's exactly what you're looking for: someone who cannot have a commitment to you. You've never stayed in one place for very long for the same reason. You never completely committed yourself either to a woman, or to a cause."

"I suppose you're right."

It was difficult for a Salvadoran man to admit to a woman that she was right, but Lucas did not argue with her or seem otherwise upset. Mariposa liked talking to Lucas because he was older and mellowed, because he had seen everything there was to see outside El Salvador. He could say things that were either silly or profound. Jokes she didn't understand, and the observation that the best thing about traveling around the world was meeting so many children, and answering their questions. Why are you riding this ship? Where is Illinois? Do you miss your mother? When Joe met a child, he was in the presence of the hopeful, inquisitive essence of humanity, and he found this was true everywhere he went, even in the places where children suffered because of war and poverty.

After hearing this, Mariposa took him to see the farm hut with the bombed-out roof that served, now, as a school for about fifty students split into two groups. They visited the younger class. "Eme es para mama, mango, manzana," said the teacher, who had left her old M1 rifle leaning against a wall by the entrance; she stood before twenty boys and girls seated on the floor, and a wooden board that served as a chalkboard now displaying the maternal consonant. "Eme. Mamá. Mango," the children said, and they practiced the four strokes that produced a capital *M*, a sound born from the lips of suckling infants. Mariposa explained that a few of the children had living parents among the fighters, but most were orphans.

The class ended, and Lucas and Mariposa watched as five boys and one girl took to their jobs; they were the "intelligence officers" Joe had seen in Villa El Rosario. The children turned on captured radios and scanned frequencies; hearing no army transmission, they talked to Lucas and Mariposa. They said they knew the different voices of all the army commanders, and they could tell when an officer was hungry, or in a bad mood. When an officer thought the war was going well, and when it was going poorly.

"What do you hear from them now?" Mariposa asked. "In these last days. Since we took Villa El Rosario."

"They're very, very angry," said a boy of about eleven. "They want to kill us all."

Cerro Pando.

Perquín

THE LIEUTENANT COLONEL entered the minds of his men at reveille, and he remained with them until they returned to the barracks and to their stiff cots, to sleep underneath the portraits of Miss December and Miss April they had taped to the walls to help them forget about the lieutenant colonel. He was an order or an observation floating down the chain of command. A tactical insight, a hope, an urge first expressed in his spare sentences, his raised eyebrows, the ridges of his fingerprints resting on a map. His desires became the commands of his captains, his lieutenants and his sergeants, and these were the voices that were heard by the rebels' child-intelligence officers on their captured army radios. The lieutenant colonel was the two gold stars of his insignia on the shoulders of his loose-fitting battle fatigues; and he was the cow, goat and chicken blood his crazier grunts painted on their faces when they went into battle. To the public, the lieutenant colonel was a media celebrity. He was the man photographed grinning with visiting journalists and dignitaries: the joie de vivre of his gap-toothed smile was precisely the opposite of what people expected, given his reputation as the leader of the most ruthless unit in the Salvadoran army. The lieutenant colonel was a series of quotes attributed to him, which he may or may not have said, including: "That radio transmitter is like a scorpion stuck up my ass." He was the nickname the rebels gave him, "trompita de cuche," for the swine snout they saw in his weak-chinned face. To the United States military advisers who met him he was very Salvadoran-looking, that mix of Indian, African and European that was common in the middle of the Central American isthmus. Less European maybe, they observed, above average on the melanin spectrum, certainly. Dress him in jeans, give him a rake and send him to Miami to work as a gardener and no one would know the difference, they said privately, and they chuckled over their beers as they said so. In the field, the lieutenant colonel usually wore a floppy-brimmed hat, and sometimes a bandanna tied over the curly sponge of his hair, an affectation that added to the American-trained-paratrooper myth of Lieutenant Colonel Domingo Monterrosa. In the quiet of his office, he studied topographical maps and aerial photographs, and reports of interrogations of captured men and women, a pensive index finger on his lips. It was raining hardest now, and Morazán was muddy, but then a new weather report landed on the lieutenant colonel's desk. A three-day break in the rain was forecast. He gave the order for the helicopters to start up the following morning, and he watched two of the best platoons of the Atlacatl Battalion set out, bouncing up off the ground at the airbase in the provincial capital San Francisco Gotera, to probe and study the terrain to the south of the guerrilla bases.

JOE STOOD ABOVE the Radio Venceremos typewriter, pounding out Lucas's statement to the American people. In the novel I'll be Lucas too. The characters are all around me: Santiago, who is in love with Marcela, who is in love with Rafael; and this little guy, El Cheje, which means "worker" and "woodpecker." He's a laborer from Mejicanos. Santiago calls him an "hácelotodo." A jack-of-all-trades. He can fix anything. He's here working on the generator, and he's telling me stories about Mejicanos, but Lucas has to focus, because now this typewriter has become an instrument of the revolution. In between Cheje's anecdotes Joe typed one declaratory sentence after another. *I call upon the Congress of the United States . . .* My Road Bum's Manifesto from El Salvador. *Our representatives in Congress have traded the freedom and the safety of the people of El Salvador to serve the interests of a few Salvadoran exiles in Miami.*

Joe typed out and revised and retyped out two double-spaced pages, and showed them to Santiago, who read some English. *I write to my Congress not only as a witness to the suffering and the agony of the Salvadoran people, but also as a North American citizen and combatant who is working hand in hand with the people, fighting the dictatorship and its North American advisers.* Santiago gave a summary to Comandante Jonás, who gave his approval, and Mariposa read out her Spanish translation of Lucas's statement on the radio. "No entiendo porque nuestros representantes en el congreso . . ." Yeah, that's me, my words—in español. After a good twenty years of trying to publish a novel, it was the first time Joe's writing was reaching the general public. As if the radio signals were the pages of a book, floating down from the sky, falling into backyards and farm fields, and onto the roof of the United States Embassy, transformed into the disembodied voice of a woman.

THE EJÉRCITO REVOLUCIONARIO del Pueblo had a number of women in positions of authority: women who had seen combat, women who had helped bury other women and girls who had died in battles and bombardments. It could be said that the war was a battle for women's power, and a war to defend women against exploitation and violation, as much as it was a war of national liberation. As the uneventful days of the rainy season dragged on, the women cooks of the ERP grew more frustrated with, and finally complained about the base injustice to which they were being subjected. Why was it, they asked, that all the cooks were compañeras, that no men were getting up at 2:00 a.m. to begin the kitchen work? They said they would go on strike until the gender inequity was addressed. In response, Comandante Jónas ordered that the men in the rebel army would be required to perform kitchen duties, and so it was that Lucas found himself awake in what seemed like the middle of the night, preparing corn masa, sitting over large pots of beans and sweating inside the cooking tent. Of the men in the radio unit who were required to cook, only Lucas and the Venezuelan compa Maravilla did not complain about it. After four days of male cooks, a countercomplaint rose from the ranks: the food stunk. The beans the male compas prepared were undercooked, their tortillas were misshapen globules, oblong spacecraft with raw centers, inedible. ¡Puta! ¿Qué es esta mierda? The strike ended and the women returned to their cooking pots and posts in the predawn darkness and Lucas was suddenly ordered to report to Comandante Jonás. His new assignment would be with la comandancia, the central command of the guerrilla army. No explanation was given.

AFTER THEY'D BEEN marching for an hour, the rain suddenly stopped and Joe watched as Comandante Jonás frowned at the blue patches opening in the gray carpet above his head. Their mission was to study the terrain just past the southern edge of guerrilla territory, near the hill called Cerro Pando. They would be safer under the cover of bad weather, but now the sun was eating up the last of the clouds. The reconnaissance mission was headed toward the junction of two rivers, the Sapo and the Torola. Lucas watched Jonás following the path of a butterfly that flew alongside and ahead of the rebel column for about three seconds; it was metallic blue with black spots, and Jonás stopped and wrinkled his brow at it quizzically, as if he were trying to determine the butterfly's military purpose, its use in a counterattack. The butterfly disappeared, and the comandante saw Lucas looking at him. "The army is going to come through here one day in large numbers, Lucas. We need to study this ground so we can cover a retreat from La Guacamaya. What do you see?"

"It's too open here, comandante. There isn't as much cover."

"Correct," Jonás said.

"But those ridges up there; it will be dangerous for the army if we're up there and we catch them down here," Lucas said. Jonás nodded and ordered the men upward, and they climbed toward the ridge, past thin oak trees and over muddy ground, and Lucas climbed fastest, just to show these young-sters that the old gringo still had some pep in him. In fact, he was feeling stronger and healthier than he had in ages, and when he reached the ridge he turned to look down at the compas scrambling beneath him, and to examine the terrain. He saw a river, brown and swollen. And a column of army sol-diers, some twenty or thirty, meandering through the trees and the brush. They were about two hundred meters from the last member of the rebel reconnaissance squad working his way up the ridge, Comandante Jonás.

Oh shit. Lucas ran back down the ridge, almost falling down thanks to the downward momentum of his M16 and his field pack and his panic. "¡Soldados!" Joe cried out, and several members of the rebel reconnais-sance squad turned, and saw the soldiers, who were scrambling to take cover and draw their weapons and open fire. Lucas reached the coman-dante and said, "There are twenty or so. Down there. About two hundred

meters." Jonás pointed to the higher ground where Lucas had been standing, and he ordered the rebel squad farther upward: "¡Arriba!" and told
them to form a line on the ridge. As they began to climb toward that position, Joe heard several shots to their left, and saw a second group of about
twenty soldiers approaching through the oak trees and the shrubs. Men in
green canvas hats and black berets, army paratroopers, drawing weapons.

Joe took four steps toward the paratroopers and crouched behind two
large boulders. "¡Apartate!" he yelled back at Comandante Jonás. Get out!
Lucas then opened fire on the army soldiers with a one-man fusillade from
his M16, covering the retreat of the comandante and the other squad members straggling up the hill. Full auto. Bah-dah-daht! Sweep across the field
of fire. Bah-dah-daht! Lean forward and use two hands and place your
body weight behind the weapon to keep the barrel from climbing out of
your grasp. Bah-dah-dah-dah-dah-daht! The bastards duck and hide. Bah-
dah-dah-dah-dah-daht! A shining brass comet of expended cartridges shot
out backward onto the ground behind him. Joe ejected the empty magazine, and reached into his pack to load another. The paratroopers were
kissing the ground, cowering behind trees to escape the percussive killing
sound of the bullets Lucas was firing at them. He emptied half of the next
magazine, this one more deliberate and loosely aimed at the patches of enemy olive drab he could see. Comandante Jonás, now safe at the top of the
ridge, looked back; he saw the usually mellow North American, a man who
conveyed a middle-aged restraint in camp and on the march, suddenly
transformed into a beast. "Un gato furioso," as Jonás described it later to
the other comandantes. A crazed cat. After his second fusillade, Joe rose to
his feet and scrambled up toward his comrades, who were now firing down
at both groups of army soldiers in an organized defensive line.

The lieutenant in charge of the army platoon ordered his men to pull
back, because he had deduced that they were facing fifty or one hundred
men, and not ten; his mission was reconnaissance, not to engage rebels who
might wipe them out from a position on higher ground. The rebels slowly

and cautiously pulled back too, northward toward La Guacamaya. An hour later, when it became clear the army was not pursuing them, Jonás put his hand on Joe's shoulder. "Muy bien, Lucas. Muy bien. You allowed us to organize the line."

"How did you learn to do that, Lucas?" one of the compas asked. He was the youngest one, in fact. Seventeen.

"Yo soy army," Lucas said. By which he meant, I am United States Army–trained; the beneficiary of taxpayer-funded lessons in warfare imparted when I was the age you mocosos are now. Aggressiveness and awareness of your surroundings. The uses and misuses of the M16. It's coming back to me now. "Yo soy army." Normandy, the Rough Riders, Gettysburg. Lectures from captains while standing in clouds of cordite. The martial posture beaten into you by drill-sergeant jerks. The practicality of it all. What I know and where I'm from. My ancestor who fell upon the British after Lexington. American knowledge and history placed at the service of the skinny boys and girls of Morazán.

"How did you make it fire so many bullets so quickly?" the teenage compa asked.

"What?"

"Mine only fires one bullet at a time." Joe was stunned that this teenage fighter did not know how to change the rate of fire of his M16.

"Here." Lucas moved a switch. Click, click. "This is full auto. Semi. But don't use it unless it's an emergency. Because you'll just waste bullets."

"Mine is different," another compa said.

"This is a newer M16. The newest one. Where did you get this? One of the weapons we captured recently, right? Do you know what these lines mean?"

"No."

Lucas explained how the rear and front sights worked, and how the rifle's angle of fire could be adjusted with a small wheel to hit targets that were farther away. "Oh, so that's what those numbers are for."

Later, when they made camp for the night, Joe sat next to Comandante

Jonás in the darkness and said, in a low voice: "The M16 is a very useful weapon. A very good weapon. Unfortunately, the compas don't know how to use the M16. You need to train them how to use it." Jonás nodded in agreement, and when they reached La Guacamaya the next day the comandante spread the story of Lucas the Beast, and his very intelligent and courageous decision to make himself a one-man linchpin of fire.

Joe did not feel brave. That night, as he tried to sleep on top of one sheet of plastic, and underneath a second one, he saw boys in green marching toward him, and he saw his own bullets aimed at them, their steel tips and lead cores striking trees and dirt. He saw a Salvadoran man-child falling to the ground, afraid of dying, and for all he knew the dude might be dead. Joe imagined his actions replayed on a movie screen at an Urbana drive-in, his friends and family watching. Like Audie Murphy, the reckless hero of black-and-white movies. Firing at brown-skinned peasant soldiers I see through my eyeglasses. This mess I got myself into. I came here from Urbana. Couldn't let the comandante die or be captured. Save his life, save the lives of the compas. Those army kids, clutching at the dirt with their fingers, trying to dig themselves into the ground. Could have shot a dozen men back there. Unlikely. But even one. Killing isn't in the road-bum manual. How will I explain this to Steve and Mom and Dad? Will I ever tell them? Where are they now? Summer in Urbana. Rain here, rain there. The air over Joe's mountain sleeping place rumbled with thunder. He remembered the prairie lightning with Kathy. Tall girl. All us Sandersons are tall. Prairie stock. How does the Salvadoran army bury their dead? Big green lawns with grave markers, like back home, I guess. Everything makes sense back home. The steady progression of normal days. Kids in school, crops in the ground. Mashed potatoes served in a white porcelain bowl shaped like a boat. A plate of mashed potatoes with gravy. Simple pleasures of living people, far from these mountains where we are trying to kill and maim each other, with bullets and jellied gasoline.

Joe wondered, as the night dragged on, if he'd ever be able to fall asleep.

AFTER LUCAS BECAME the Beast he was assigned to a combat unit. With a comandante called Che, who had a reputation for being one of the toughest fighters in the guerrilla army. Che's column, some two hundred men and women, were going to march southward, out of Morazán; they were going to take the enemy by surprise and hit him in his unprotected gut, some thirty miles south, in and around the city of San Miguel. In the weeks that followed Lucas and his unit entered and occupied and then withdrew from several villages and communities in the department of San Miguel. Whenever they entered a built-up place a compa said to Joe, "Hey, Lucas, we found something for you." A notebook. Pens. He began to compose another letter home over the course of two weeks during which his unit and others operated on the fringes of San Miguel city, blowing up electrical towers and bridges, including the suspension bridge that linked the eastern third of the country to the capital, transforming it into a limp mass of tangled cables. It seemed to Joe that the guerrillas could wander about the country at will.

Apparently we're down out of the mountains for good and could well be on the verge of wrapping this show up, he wrote to his father. *However, the "verge" could still be several months more of fighting. Switched camps 5 times since I last wrote. Military occupied 2 of our old camps, but found nothing but discarded candy wrappers and latrines. Why they should be in hot pursuit of a band of lepidopterists is, of course, beyond me.* He told his father to ignore the reports Joe himself was hearing on Voice of America about the army wiping out rebel bands. *I'm still alive, and thriving, or as Mark Twain once said: News of my recent death was greatly exaggerated.* They'd crossed paths with a couple of European war correspondents, and it seemed possible to Joe that he might be in the newspapers again. *Since I'm the only North American butterfly collector out in the field throughout El Salvador, my photo has been taken numerous times*, he told his father. To his mother, Calhoun and Steve, Joe wrote: *Me and my pals went on a sort of "pie stealing" raid the other night. Came down out of the hills to a local village. Drank my first Coca-Cola with ice (!) plus saw my 1st TV set in many months. Felt like Huckleberry Finn all over again, and at 39. I do miss some of the amenities of civilization (mainly food + cigs + privacy + books).*

Joe wrote his letters alongside a sleeping rebel squad. *I grow weary of it all now and then,* he told his father. *The routine, the frustrations, even weary of the responsibilities. And of the moral obligation I feel to see the whole thing through to the end. Have certainly adopted well to camp life, and companionship. Yet I remain solitary, an individualist, despite the negative connotation that carries to those struggling for a collective society.* He told his mother not to worry about him. *I've been healthy as a hog for months. Not so much as a cold. Did my afternoon splash in a nearby creek, combed out my flourishing bronze beard (who found 2 dozen gray!!! strands?). Word just came that all us math scholars are to whack off our beards, trim our hair, sew on that missing button, tuck in our shirts, and in general prepare ourselves for mingling with civilized folks. So it looks like we're finally bringing this show to a close at long last. Hooray! All's well—1200. Save me a pork chop.*

After the army counterattacked, Joe added another entry to both letters. *The bad guys got mad at us again and 9 truckloads of them showed up at a small village near our last camp this morning,* he wrote to his mother. *But we already had a 2½ hr. jump on them and are presently sitting on a hillside overlooking the valley munching cheese and rolling cigarettes.* He wrote to his father that the peasants had abandoned their farms in the valley, and were fleeing as the army advanced—*Who's going to milk the cows today?*—and said he could hear scattered gunfire coming from the valley. He mentioned the wandering cows to his mother too, and said that he'd picked up a Salvadoran newspaper and seen a photograph of the damage a tornado had caused in Lawrence, Kansas. *No story to go with the picture; hope the family is OK on the farm.*

Joe's final entry in both letters was dated July 6. *All continues going well*, he wrote to his father. And to his mother: *All's still well—1200—hope y'all had a good 4th of July.*

Lucas wrote the addresses on the envelopes left-handed, and "Pedro Gonzalez" on the return address and handed it to a rebel courier. Two weeks later it arrived in Urbana. After she'd read it several times, Virginia placed the envelope in one of the shoeboxes where she'd kept all of Joe's correspondence since he left for college twenty-one years earlier. She was on her fourth box now. Many of the letters were tied in strings, and they all were in chronological order. Thick sections from his years in Bolivia and Colombia. From his two trips around the world. At the end of the newest shoebox, the letters he'd sent from this most recent trip to El Salvador; it was the thinnest section of all, just a handful so far this year. She thought of the chaotic events Joe described—the abandoned crops and cattle, the approaching soldiers—and felt as sad and empty as she ever had. Her son was on a path toward personal catastrophe. There are things you feel as a mother, the danger that hovers over your son. I see this as a constant throughout his life. The way things catch him by surprise. At two years old: the boy who "didn't want to miss anything" and soiled his pants. Now he's thirty-nine, smoking a cigarette with an army in the valley below him. She closed her eyes and felt death lurking near him. Like being caught out in an open field in a Kansas tornado, the gray clouds boiling overhead, being wrung into a funnel. Nowhere to run.

LUCAS AND THE REBEL ARMY headed north, back into Morazán, protected from air attacks by rain and fog that clung to the undulating landscape. They were not going to march on San Salvador after all. Instead, they spent two weeks eating mangoes at the rebel base, and Joe met the head of the Ejército Revolucionario del Pueblo, Joaquín Villalobos, the theorist and thinker of the movement. His code name was Atilio, and he was long-jawed and clean-shaven and spoke with his hands, moving his joined thumb and index fingers before him as if his thoughts were a musical instrument he was playing for his assembled audience. Joe called him "the Juggler" in his journal. The commander in chief had marched down into Morazán through Honduras, after visits to Nicaragua and Cuba and Europe, and he brought an outsider's assessment of the military situation: The rebels were not yet strong enough to launch another "final offensive." Instead, they had to consolidate their presence in Morazán. Plans were drawn up. They were going to strengthen their position in the mountains by continuing to attack and occupy towns and cities. Larger ones each time. Weapons were cleaned and oiled, and ammunition gathered, and Lucas joined one of several rebel columns that moved out northward, through fields of prickly-pear cactus and white rocks, climbing steeply upward into a pine forest, toward the town of Perquín, population 3,500, located on an old Lenca Indian settlement, on the top of a hill overlooking the countryside below.

The rebel army quickly overwhelmed the National Guard detachment defending the town, half of whom surrendered immediately. The other half, about sixty men, retreated to the small barracks on one side of the oddly shaped polygon of the town's central plaza, and radioed for help. The army sent two hundred ground troops northward to rescue the Guardsmen, but the rebels held them off, and the Guardsmen in the town surrendered. Perquín was the biggest town the rebels had liberated in Morazán, and for several days Radio Venceremos broadcast from the plaza, and the Juggler later said these broadcasts were a kind of theater that was changing the balance of the war, because a war wasn't just troops on the battlefield, but what an entire country saw in its imagination and fears. A good radio drama carried the power of a rebel army all by itself, because it reached into the minds of thousands of people and occupied a space there as long as new dramas were broadcast. Radio Venceremos was a chortling, subliminal rebel with big teeth who lived in the relaxed space behind the eyes of everyone who hated the dictatorship.

Ten days after the assault on Perquín, Radio Venceremos announced another "triumphant withdrawal" of the revolutionary forces. The government casualties included eighty-three dead. The rebels took thirty-two prisoners and captured fifty-five M16s, and two machine guns and too much ammunition to count, and left four of their own compas buried in the grass of the town plaza, while the last rebel unit to leave the town covered the rattling retreat of the cooks and their arsenal of steel kitchenware with three hundred members of the Atlacatl Battalion bearing down on them.

WHEN THEY WERE BACK in La Guacamaya, Lucas asked Comandante Jonás if he could have some time to write, because there was so much that he had seen that he wanted to commit to pen and paper, and the comandante said yes, and he assigned Lucas to the radio crew again, because there he would have access to all the writing materials he needed. Over the course of five consecutive mornings, writing first in his notebook, and then using the radio station's typewriter, Joe composed the piece he had imagined himself writing during the Perquín campaign; it was a profile of Che, the idiosyncratic former army soldier who had become a rebel comandante.

Compañero Che is one of the old-timers, a guerrilla with half a dozen years of experience behind him. At present Che commands an entire guerrilla section; two platoons, or roughly 60 insurgent youths. As Joe typed, he occasionally endured the annoyed stares of the radio compas, many of whom resented Lucas for getting such special treatment: "Time to write, during a war," a compa said with a sneer. Joe filed his "Portrait" in his backpack, to use when he returned home to write his novel about El Salvador, a moment that couldn't come soon enough. *This war is going to drag on for years. I don't have years in me.* He needed solitude. He couldn't write with radio DJs and smart-aleck college-kid guerrillas looking over his shoulder.

The next day Lucas sought out Jonás. "Comandante, I have a suggestion."

"Tell me."

"It might be better for me to go to the United States. I might better serve the revolution there. Is there a mission I could do for you there?"

Lucas wanted to leave, which was not surprising. The comandante had been hearing complaints about the North American and his odd, solitary ways. "I need to talk to you because I can't deal with Lucas anymore," one compa had told him. "Lucas is completely out of line. He gets coffee when he wants, he gets cigarettes when he wants. And he acts like a child when he doesn't get what he wants." "Listen," Jonás had replied. "Lucas is a gringo loco who needs his cigarettes and his coffee. He works hard to get them. Keeping his own coffee beans doesn't make him an individualist. Let him be."*

TWO DAYS AFTER LUCAS made his request to return to the U.S., Comandante Jonás found him at the radio station and said, "In October. You can leave then. Through Honduras, probably. It's complicated. But it can be done." He suggested Lucas might organize a speaking tour in the United States when he got there. But first, before leaving, Lucas would work with the radio compas to prepare a series of reports on the war from his unique North American perspective. Jonás also gave Lucas permission to write to his family to tell them he would be headed home soon.

When Joe sat down to draft his next letter, it occurred to him that he might soon become a regular fixture on the rebel radio. The time had finally come, Joe decided, to be absolutely explicit about what he was doing in El Salvador.

---

*To my friends and fellow alumni of Radio Venceremos, let me say this: I loved you all and I know you loved me. Don't read too much into the Author's melodramatic descriptions of our "conflictos." I was just too old and too gringo to be there, among you, for so long.

1200. Dear Mom + Calhoun, Steven + Family—Now this is definitely a letter I've waited a long time to write. Looks like I'll be returning to the U.S. in about a month. Coming home! Some explanations are due, where I've been and what I've been up to. If Calhoun will get out his maps, you'll find MORAZAN DEPARTAMENTO (like a province) on the northeast side of El Salvador. I started out my trip months back from San Salvador, was first in Departamento Usulután, then La Unión, Morazán, San Miguel and now back in Morazán. He explained how he'd gone underground after being momentarily detained in Usulután. *About my friends, all those math scholars I've mentioned. It probably won't surprise you folks (nor the boys at the post office) nearly as much as it did me the day I discovered that these guys in the hills are all revolutionaries, and that the reason they carry guns is because they're guerrilla fighters. Not one to pass up a chance at some first-hand journalism, I quickly got out pen and paper and have been scribbling ever since. Kingston, Vietnam, Biafra, Bolivia—and now living with the insurgents of El Salvador. Whew! And busy I've been, day after day, writing like mad to keep a record of all that's been going on. Yet I don't want my jocular tone to give you folks a distorted impression of what it's like here in the mountains. Much of the misery and tragedy the people of El Salvador are presently enduring is identical to Vietnam. But this time I'm with the victims. When the bombs fall and the mortar shells start flying, I'm as much a target as they are. And I'm as angry as hell about the raw deal they're getting. U.S. bombs, bunches of U.S. military advisers, American helicopters, etc., etc. As a witness I couldn't be closer to the nightmare realities because I live exactly like the guerrillas, share their food + tents, travel with them in columns, and often even go along with them on operations and when they're shooting it out with enemy soldiers.* He said he'd written 138,000 words in his notebooks about the Salvadoran people and their struggle and all the tragedies and acts of resistance he'd witnessed since leaving Urbana last September. He told them about the broadcasts he expected to make and said, *Some of them will likely be reproduced in the U.S. and maybe excerpts*

will find their way into the U.S. newspapers. So if any reporters come knock-
ing on the door, either tell them the truth or say, "Joe who?" Just don't feed
them any of my pancakes! If all goes well a month from now I'll gladly grant
them interviews in person and scowl at their cameras (providing they spring
for beers). So set those cherry pies out to cool. All's well and I'm coming home!
Much love, J.

The letter was postmarked in Honduras on October 30, 1981, and it
arrived in Urbana on November 5, two months and two days after Joe dated
it. After twenty-two years, this would be the last letter Virginia received
from her youngest son on his bumming adventures.

BEFORE LUCAS COULD START working on the radio station, he became
seriously ill. An intestinal disorder. *The shits*, as it was known colloquially
back home. He was hammock-ridden for two weeks, and came to know the
rebel doctor quite well. The doctor was a Methodist from Northern Mexico
who liked to talk about religion and flying, and he was delighted to learn
that Lucas was a pilot—Joe showed him his license, which he still carried
in his wallet. Even after he'd recovered Lucas still felt wobbly, and he
confided to the doctor that he was worried that maybe all the drugs he had
done over the course of his life (the opium, especially) had weakened his
constitution, to which the doctor answered: "Possibly. But more likely it's
just that drug that brings all of us down eventually—old age."

By the time Joe felt fully himself the Radio Venceremos people had
forgotten about Jonás's instructions regarding the gringo Lucas: he would
not be going home. The rainy season was ending, and the comandantes
needed Lucas and every other man and woman who could be mustered,
and getting out via Honduras was practically impossible anyway, given the
troops massing in the north and the south. The rebel moles in the army had
learned of a major army offensive being planned for Morazán and word from
these spies soon reached the rebel comandancia: The army was preparing a

two-pronged attack to squeeze the guerrillas out of their bases, and clear them out of Morazán altogether.

LIEUTENANT COLONEL DOMINGO MONTERROSA landed amid a crazed downward wash of wind created by helicopter blades, along with many other whirling aircraft that brought several hundred of his men to Perquín, the same town the rebels had held and occupied four months earlier. The town's whitewashed buildings remained pockmarked with bullet holes, and the barracks the rebels had taken looked as if a Marxist giant had taken bites out of its cement walls. The paratroopers of the Atlacatl Battalion gathered on the grass of the town plaza, near the graves of the dead rebels and soldiers buried there in August; they absentmindedly stacked mortars and field packs near the patches of upturned soil. Their officers fanned out through the cobblestoned town and gave the local National Guardsmen lists of suspected subversives and subversive sympathizers, and these Guardsmen, in turn, pounded on doors. When they found men and women who were on the list, the Guardsmen briefly interrogated them and slapped them and pummeled them with their rifle butts, and they handed over the prisoners to the paratroopers, who took them to the edge of town and executed them with short bursts from their M16s, leaving their bodies to rot in the sun and the dry air, on a patch of highway between two cornfields. After a day of these operations, the officers of the Atlacatl Battalion took their lists, which contained the names of more people in other villages, and ordered their troops to set out on the march, southward, into rebel-controlled territory.

23.

El Mozote

"SEÑORA, MÁS RÁPIDO, POR FAVOR." Or should it be "señorita," since she's so young? But that would be sort of an insult too, because . . . Speed it up, young lady, yeah, I know you're carrying a load there. Hey, you, help her. Help her. Let me help you help her. Take her by the arm, and I'll take the other, up and over this mossy rock, así, así, if she falls she might have the baby right here. Freckle-faced mother to be, icy river water at her thin ankles, holding my wrist with her thin arms, barely twenty I'd guess. We guide her spidery form over the stream. A big belly at the center of her stringy limbs, and me and her and this boy at the center of a line of two thousand people stretched out over this canyon, climbing down one side, and up the other. The comandancia and assorted rebel columns up ahead; the civilians here in the middle, with the code-breaking kids from the school to help, and me, a bumming rebel named Lucas; behind us the radio station crew, burdened down with all their equipment, including the precious transmitter with its subversive transistors and diodes and dials. Very dangerous spot here, this river. Lucas and the pregnant girl reached the other side, and they stopped while the girl caught her breath, and Joe looked up to scan the high ground around them, and he worried the radio people might get ambushed here, and he yelled out, "Rápido, rápido, todos, rápido." He watched the children from the school bound across the rocks, unafraid, at play, and then one boy stopped, suddenly, and looked up at the sky, and the entire line of crossing children paused too, and turned their eyes upward, as if they were obeying a command the first boy had transmitted via telepathy. Look! Before he saw the helicopters, Joe heard the cardiac beat of their engines. Death up there, above us, and Lucas took two steps back into the stream, to order everyone out. The helicopters disappeared to the north. They were high up and in a hurry, headed northward, nothing to fear.

And now up the scrubby hillside. "Vos, vení," he calls out to a boy. "Vos, también," to a second boy. He appoints them personal escorts to the pregnant señorita. Help this young woman to the top of the hill and I'll give you a medal. The Illinois Medal of Valor. And the boys scamper down to grab the spider girl and guide her up the hill. Good, she'll move faster now, and finally Lucas joins the tail end of the column, the schoolchildren, and marches up behind them, and he thinks that this is an undeniably noble place to be, guiding children to safety. Saint Joe the Valiant, and if this isn't a character in a book . . . But who cares about literature now? Not Joe. No one. Everyone wants to live. To breathe.

THEY REACHED ANOTHER EXPOSED PLACE. The bald top of a hill. Here, the pregnant girl plopped down to the ground on her bottom, and Joe stopped to take in the view, the tops of pine trees and mango trees, and the villages below, and a rising drift of black smoke. "El Mozote," one of the boys called out. The enemy was setting fire to El Mozote. "¡Están quemando El Mozote!" At the sound of these words, the pregnant girl rose to her feet and saw the climbing black pillars of smoke, and she put a hand over her mouth and began to cry, and her weeping infected the older woman at her side, and the children too. Oh my God, oh my God, they are burning the village, and a boy of six fell to his knees, and closed his eyes, and began to pray. A murmured plea. Espíritu Santo. The boy was summoning the Holy Spirit and several adults fell to their knees around him. Joe wondered what forces the Holy Spirit could marshal, what brigades, what cannon fire. We have to keep moving, can't stay here, on this hilltop, visible to the aviation. "Seguimos," Lucas called out. Everyone to their feet, up, let's go, and the praying people completed their final signs of the cross, the tips of their fingers drawing the planks that held up the crucified prophet. Cross my heart and hope to die, yeah, yeah, let's go, let's get a move on. Back down, into another valley, and across the highway. The Black Street, they call it. Another dangerous spot, another potential ambush. Let's run across now. Quickly, back into the safety of the brush. We march at night. Easier for me now, because I have my night legs. A crescent moon rose above them.

They reached the safety of a silent hillside, 3:00 a.m. The spider girl rested on her back, and an older woman, one of the kitchen cooks, leaned over her to help, and the mother-to-be opened her legs, and in fifteen minutes of pushing and grunting and muffled screams, a boy slid out, covered with life juice, the thick umbilical cord slithered around his leg. Lucas handed over his knife for the older woman to slice said cord, and as she did so he saw the newborn's swollen scrotum. Totally normal. Joe had learned these things in Biafra. Boys come out with puffed-up genitals, announcing their gender with an exclamation of the flesh. Here I am, world! With all my testosterone loaded and ready to go. Look out, gimme some room! First born, primogénito. The girl is weeping and laughing at the sight of her child. A few minutes later a compa found Lucas and whispered in his ear: "The army captured the transmitter." He murmured the names of three dead compas. "The army caught them crossing the river. Ambushed them. And then crossing the Black Street too." Defeat. Radio Venceremos will be off the air. Escape and defeat. Santiago and most of the radio compas made it out. We've been squeezed by the army's pincers, but not squashed.

IN THE DAYS that followed the rebel columns engaged in a series of forced marches, and each night another group of civilians stayed behind or slipped away. To hide in the mountains, or to seek out friends in other villages. Until finally the Ejército Revolucionario del Pueblo became a lean military unit, unburdened by civilians, marching faster across rugged terrain. Across a field of sharp igneous rocks, up and over the side of a volcano. Southward, toward the lowlands. They crossed rivers and entered caseríos where they were fed tortillas and candy, and Lucas watched as two compas on the march argued over a cigarette for two hours, and then he listened to their whispered words of mourning. "He was shot in the head. He fell, we carried him." "Chilayo and Javier too." "No, no, it can't be." "We saw him turn white. So, so pale." They marched past coffee trees, and a peasant woman fed them fresh milk from the cow she was walking. In half moonlight they sprinted across the Pan-American Highway, between army patrols, trying not to make too much noise with their boots and their packs, tiptoeing over the asphalt, like children sneaking past their parents' bedroom. Often they slept during the day and marched at night, joining God's nocturnal creatures; the possums and the jaguars, the owls and the bats. We're headed to the sea, Lucas was told. To the Pacific and the southeastern front. No shit? We're going to walk all the way from the mountains to the coast? In four days? Yes. A new transmitter is waiting there for us. The air tasted wetter and hotter, and they walked through cotton fields and saw their first palm trees, and they watched the fronds catch powerful breezes, and they marched into these winds and one morning before sunrise their march ended at a ridge; the first light of the day revealed a vast plain before them, a gray looming mass, and several of the peasants in their group stared at this apparition as if they'd reached the end of the known world. They watched in wonder as the plain became speckled with reflected light. "¿Qué es eso?" "¡El Pacífico!" Joe was in the presence of young men who had never set eyes upon the expanse of the ocean, boys who knew only mountains and river valleys, and he watched as the knowledge of the existence of the sea fell upon their faces. We fought a revolution for you to know this, compañero, to bring you from the muddy milpa of your harvest to see this. The waves the conquistadors rode to reach this land across the curving planet. "It's like the biggest river you could ever see, all dammed up!"

The rebel unit walked one more day along the coast, and met another guerrilla band that lived and battled here, and there were embraces between old friends, and news from the north was shared. They stayed a day with the coastal fighters of the southeastern front, and heard from them of terrible happenings transmitted via CB radio from Morazán. The army had murdered many hundreds of people in the villages of what was once rebel-controlled territory. Word had come from the compas who covered the retreat: Not just one massacre, but many. El Mozote. La Joya. Arambala. All gone. Everyone. No puede ser. The boys who'd just seen the ocean for the first time began to cry, because these were their villages. After they wept, and after hours of quiet shock and mourning, a vengeful anger took hold of them, a desire to climb away from the ocean, back into the mountain fastness, and to fall upon the murderers. Soon enough the order came. We march northward again, back to where we came from. With a new transmitter now. A louder voice. They'll hear us in Mexico and Costa Rica with this.

Compañeros, we need to be back in Morazán by Christmas to start broad-casting. To tell the world what happened up there, in the villages. The next day Joe and the rebels marched again, from whence they came. A marcha forzada. What is a forced march? Just a fast march. That's all it means. Double-time, urgent, take no time to rub your weary feet, your abused ham-strings and calves. Upward, back into the battlefields of thinner air, home to good people. The baby boy born under my watch. Sweep out the evil that poisons his land. They marched back into the heights of Morazán, with a new radio transmitter that was riding first-class, as it were, on the back of a burro. And when the guerrillas stopped, it wasn't because they were ex-hausted (although they were); but rather because the radio-hauling burro needed to rest. On the slopes of a volcano, after crossing a river, after hoofing it across the Pan-American Highway. Good donkey, loyal four-legged compa. He did not complain, he only chewed, puffing his exhaustion through his nostrils, until the rebels reached the ashy landscape of their mountain home, assembling their armies again on high ground, to counterstrike at the gov-ernment troops waiting below.

ON CHRISTMAS DAY, the rebels reentered their abandoned camp at El Zapotal, and Radio Venceremos broadcast again. Santiago took to the mi-crophone to speak of the massacres that had taken place in Morazán, and promised more information in the days to come. Four days later, the rebel armies marched an hour to attack and quickly overwhelm the army troops occupying the rebels' old base at La Guacamaya. Turned tables. Joe in the rear, with Jonás. Now it's the army that runs, and we are their pursuers, chasing them away from the mango trees and the parapets of gathered stones. Ten army soldiers were killed, and seven surrendered, and Lucas stood next to Comandante Jonás as he interrogated them in the wake of the battle. "The lieutenant is the last one left back there," one of the soldiers said, his eyes cast down at Lucas's boots and the tops of his green socks. "He said you'd kill us all if we surrendered."

"No one in this army kills prisoners," Jonás said.

A short while later, Lucas and Jonás climbed over a barricade of rocks the army soldiers had built, and found the army lieutenant, with a red trickle oozing from the right temple of his clean-shaven head, and four flies feasting on the blood on his face. "Puta, he killed himself," Jonás whispered with reverence. The comandante kicked at the automatic pistol that was the instrument of the lieutenant's departure. Although death was common in this guerrilla war, suicide was not, and there was something otherworldly about seeing an enemy destroyed in this way.

"We weren't at El Mozote or La Joya. No." The captured soldiers insisted on their innocence. "It was the Atlacatl locos that did that." "They killed all those people." Joe had never seen army soldiers reduced to such a state. Groveling, begging, pleading, insisting. They're afraid we're going to execute them, take our revenge on their conscripted bodies. "No way. No, we didn't kill anyone." "But we saw all the bodies. Yes. Bodies everywhere." "The Atlacatl guys did it. They went crazy." "Please, believe us. I swear on my mother's grave. I wasn't there. I didn't do it."

The suicided lieutenant and the pleading prisoners spoke to the truth of the reports of the massacres and the next day the rebels marched with trepidation toward El Mozote, on a winding road through pine trees, toward an orderly village with no more than twenty houses, if Joe remembered correctly. Whitewashed adobe, a church, a store.

BEFORE THEY REACHED El Mozote the smell drifted over them. An assault on the olfactory senses. As if they were approaching a huge heap of rotting flesh. One hundred meters outside the town, the heavy, salty, sticky vapor reached into the gullet of the man next to Lucas, a compa named Rafael. He gagged, two desperate dry heaves, like a dog pleading, dying. "Controlate, hombre," Lucas said. The wind shifted, mercifully, but then it circled back, and the rot covered them again, poisoning the moisture in Joe's nose and in his eyes. They entered the town and found it smoldering. Or maybe they just imagined it was still burning, twenty days after the army had set fire to it, and that it would always burn. Joe's eyes were drawn upward by the muscular flapping of a low-flying vulture. More birds, black wings and red hoods over their heads, gliding in wide circles. Three, four, five, six . . . Zopilote is how they say vulture here. The white buildings facing the plaza were blackened, half-standing ruins, and on the street a set of ivory-and-purple vestments undulated and fluttered, as if a priest had been buried under the surface of the dirt roadway and was trying to crawl out. The bloodied and torn clothes of peasants nearby, cracked and soiled communal wafers tossed about. Joe approached one of the singed buildings and peered inside, and he saw bones and a burned denim shirt attached to them, and a skull with emptied eye sockets, yellow teeth locked in a grimace.

Lucas and the members of his unit drifted across the plaza. Remember, remember everything you see. "The church! The convent!" The locals called this building "el convento" but it was just a big room for the priest to change into his robes when he came to El Mozote. The convent vibrated with the loud buzzing of thousands of flies. Stepping closer Joe saw a tangle of blackened bones being squeezed underneath the charred beams of a collapsed roof. Many bodies, all miniatures. Like a small-scale reproduction of a charnel house. "¡Son niños!" a compa shouted. More insects in there feeding on the half-burned limbs of the children. The life span of a fly is four weeks. New generations of flies incubated in coagulating belly fat, and Joe turned away at the image of the machine legs of the flies, shoveling child fat into their clawed mouths. Joe was about to vomit on the red earth at his feet, and he stumbled toward the street facing the convent; he saw a pocket-size toy car. A toddler-size sandal, its toes pointing toward the convent pyre, a girl's shoe, the march of unseen children toward the flies and their aggressive, electrified buzzing. Something human here. The children and their murderers. Eternity. This will stay with me the rest of my days. The faces of my comrades, a nightmare we are all living together. Santiago in the middle of the plaza, setting up the mobile transmitter. Levelheaded SOB. He's going to broadcast from here. Of course. Joe drifted away, following the black soles of a compa's boots, out of the town square, into the surrounding fields, where there were more bodies. A family in a cornfield. Or rather, the leathery remains of a family. A man and a child, dried up, half-mummified skin. Blackish-brown beetles entered the space underneath the dried flesh of a woman's shoulders. Beetles, my father's beetles. Carrion beetles colonize a corpse at all four stages of decomposition, son: fresh, bloated, decayed and dried. "Mirá," Rafael called out to Lucas. He'd found a box of ammunition. "What does this mean?" he asked, pointing to the letters N-A-T-O. You gotta be fucking kidding me. Joe was too enraged to answer Rafael's question. (Eleven years later, when a group of Argentine forensic anthropologists came through El Mozote, they determined the ammunition used by the Atlacatl Battalion at El Mozote had been fabricated at the Lake City Army Ammunition Plant, in Independence, Missouri.) Boxes emptied of their cartridges and tossed as the soldiers stopped here, at this cornfield, to reload. After the killing, or before? The cornfield began to rustle. Something alive in there, moving. Rafael lifted his weapon and pointed at the stalks, which parted, revealing a half-crazed, living woman who stumbled out with her hands raised, as if surrendering; Rafael lowered his weapon and reached out to her, and as he did so she took his hand and fell to one knee.

A round-faced woman, a mother. Lucas and Rafael raised her to her feet and led her toward the town plaza, insisting, gently, because she seemed reluctant. They were taking her to the plaza, to see the radio people. "Compañeros, we have a witness." When she saw the faces of Mariposa and the women soldiers of the radio crew, she calmed down, as if she knew the first part of her nightmare had ended. She began to tell the story that she would repeat a half dozen times in the next few days. Rufina Amaya was the sole surviving resident of El Mozote, and her account of what happened there on December 11, and in the days before and after, would find its way first into the broadcasts of Radio Venceremos, and then into newspaper stories and human rights reports.

ONLY TWO HUNDRED PEOPLE lived in the score of houses of El Mozote and its surrounding farms on an ordinary day. But days before the massacre, with word of army troops massing nearby, the town began to fill with a few hundred more refugees. There was a debate outside the town's only store about whether everyone should leave, but the man who owned the store said he was friends with an army officer who had told him that the people had nothing to fear. So most of the residents and refugees stayed. When the soldiers came, they started banging on doors and ordering people out, and they were brutal and angry with everyone, even the elderly, and they made hundreds of people lie facedown on the ground, in the town's plaza and the surrounding streets, including Rufina and her husband, Domingo, and their four children. It was late in the afternoon, and it was turning dark, and they could hear shots being fired on the edge of the town, and the crackling of the flames consuming the store, and they were all very, very frightened. For the next several hours, the soldiers herded the men, women and children in and out of buildings, and slapped people and beat them with their rifle butts, and they took Domingo and the rest of the men out into the fields and began to shoot them, and to behead them with machetes, and they ordered the women and children into a small building where they were all squeezed in together, and through it all Rufina hoped Domingo wasn't suffering, and she resigned herself to the fact that he was dead, or would soon be dead. She described how helicopters landed in the town, bringing officers who gave orders. The soldiers began to separate out the older girls, and the soldiers took them away, and for the next hour the

women could hear the girls screaming as the soldiers raped them, and finally the soldiers began to kill the women and children in small groups,
and Rufina heard her own children being strangled and hacked to death,
and in a moment of desperation she escaped from the soldiers guarding her
and tried to reach her children, but she got lost in the dark. She saw the
bright glow of army flashlights, and hid behind a tree as a group of soldiers
guided the youngest of the town's boys and girls into the convent, which
was surrounded by other soldiers, who began to argue. One officer grabbed
another officer by the collar, and the two men half wrestled with each other,
and when the fight was over one of them shouted an order and the men began to fire their weapons into the convent, through its windows and its
front door, and Rufina slipped away, and ran into the fields and then into
the hills, and she spent many hours alone hearing laughter and shouts from
the town that were like those of drunken men. She listened, haunted by the
ghosts of Domingo and their four children, the youngest of whom was eight
months old, and after two days, when the soldiers were gone, she went back
into the town to look for her babies, but found only the corpses and the
vultures the compas had seen.

JOE FOUND SANTIAGO and spoke a few words he felt he needed to say to
someone, to anyone. "Why would they kill so many children?" And then,
"This is a Nazi thing." He remembered writing in his last letter home how
El Salvador was like Vietnam, and that night, by a campfire, in the long silence among his comrades, Joe gazed at the flames and saw the savage impulses at the center of human history. A fever that could sweep through a
group of men until they destroyed an entire tribe, a village, a people. How
do you write about such a thing and have people believe you? That men
could be so rabid as to gather children in a room and murder them, hack
them to death and set them on fire with their parents listening. His notes
that night were scribbles, incomplete sentences, words that stood for the

things he had seen. *Flies. Stacked bodies. Convent. Toy horse. Rufina. Son strangled. Sound of it.*

Lucas and his unit entered four more villages and caseríos the following day, and found a few more survivors of other destroyed villages. As at El Mozote, Lucas took his notebooks and joined a few other radio compas in trying to assemble a list and count of the dead, writing down what names they could find, looking for identification cards amid the corpses, reaching into the pockets of dead farmers, asking the survivors for more names, and after the second day Rafael told Lucas, "In these towns they say that when someone dies they enter the body of the first living person they find." Rafael placed his hand to his chest, as if he felt one or two or more spirits inside him, squirming and suffering. After a third day in the massacre zone, Lucas and Santiago and a few of the radio and intelligence comrades made sums and estimates, and they could say that somewhere between seven hundred thirty-three, and nine hundred twenty-six civilians had been murdered, and when word came that a North American reporter and photographer were on their way to the base at La Guacamaya, it was decided that these would be the numbers that would be reported to them. A few hours before the journalists' arrival, Jonás gathered the comandantes to tell them that anyone and everyone was to speak to the reporters and share what they had seen, and then Lucas stepped forward and said they should be very precise in what they said to the North Americans. "All these guns we have; they're all guns we captured. Right? These FALS, these AKs." Because of course not every weapon they had was captured, especially the new mortars and the big machine guns; firearms and ordnance were starting to arrive from Nicaragua and Cuba. That was all fine with Lucas, but it wouldn't be so cool with Joe Public back in Chicago and Peoria. "So let's exercise some discipline in the words we speak," Lucas said, and the compas looked at Jonás, who said, "Lucas is absolutely correct. Let's speak intelligently. Our weapons are all captured," and when the reporter for *The New York Times* and the photographer named Susan entered after two days of walking from Honduras, the rebels told them all their weapons were captured.

THE *NEW YORK TIMES* reporter was named Bonner and he regarded the blond rebel fighter named Lucas with curiosity, having heard much about him from the other rebels. "So you can't tell me your real name?" Bonner asked.

"No, absolutely not," Lucas said, and he grinned sardonically, a very American gesture, filled with hidden meanings known only to the individualist behind his blue Yankee eyes.

"Hometown?"

"Anytown, U.S.A."

"And your age?"

"That I can tell you. Thirty-nine."

"So why are you here?"

"I'm writing a book. Been here about a year. In the mountains since March. Started off in the city, hanging out with the students, going to the marches. Saw people killed. Horrific shit, really." Ah, it had been ages since he'd cussed in English to an English speaker who could appreciate it. "Eventually I hooked up with this outfit."

"And you're writing a book."

"Yeah. Sorta like John Reed in the Russian Revolution."

The photographer Susan Meiselas wandered through the camp as Bonner interviewed the rebels, and when she found Lucas he was leaning back in a hammock, an M16 draped across his lap, about to light a cigarette. She regarded him, an image of sun-kissed revolutionary machismo, his blond hair filled out, wavy, his sideburns robust and his mustache untamed. Must be at least fifteen years older than everyone here. Blue jeans, green socks, khaki shirt. She snapped his picture as he lit said smoke, the child-intelligence officers from the orphanage hovering nearby. What a shot. A grizzled gringo movie star amid the peasants. Something hard about him.

The photographer turned her camera to capture some of the young brown-skinned rebels lining up with bowls to eat lunch, and Rafael, who had been hovering nearby, sat on the ground next to Lucas and handed him a cigarette and Lucas lit it with the burning tip of his own.

"I know what it's like to have the dead inside you," Rafael said. He had small eyes that lit up when he heard funny stories and made ironic observations, and on an ordinary day he had the tragicomic look of an actor from the silent film era. "All those corpses we saw, Lucas. I feel them inside me all day. At night, they take over." The souls inside him wept, they pleaded, they laughed, Rafael said. They sang. They ate, they defecated when he did. "They're always in there. I am afraid. I think I'm losing my mind."

"Sorry, I am not an exorcist," Lucas said, and he blew a column of smoke from his mouth skyward, and looked into Rafael's eyes. And Rafael thought: Yes, Lucas is right. Smoke some tobacco, and the souls will get the idea and follow the smoke into heaven, and when he finished his cigarette, quickly, he asked Lucas if he could have another.

Joe did not feel the dead grappling inside him. Instead, their suffering circled in his thoughts. The toy plastic horse he'd seen in the grip of one of the skeletal hands inside the convent. Hard orange plastic, size of Joe's thumb, hooves rising in a gallop. He could feel the girl gripping the horse, as the pushing soldiers squeezed her into the convent. Toy, childhood. Separated from her mother, a toy with her as the soldiers open fire. Her grip on to it as the bullets pass through her. What a bullet does to flesh. If people knew. Orange plastic horse in her hand. They push her in. She grips it. Squeezes it. The soldiers push her into the convent and she holds on to her toy. They open fire, and a bullet cuts through her. Several. She squeezes, a reflex, she grips, she dies. The plastic horse melts in the fire just enough to stick to her fingers. The soldiers pushed her into the convent and she gripped her toy. Beloved toy, comforting toy. Joe's thoughts looped with the girl's, and maybe this was what Rafael was feeling. Looping thoughts, girl's final act. The orange horse. Flies probing her forearm, its carbonized skin. Lucas looked down at Rafael who had finished his second cigarette; he was working his jaw weirdly, like he had something stuck in his gums. Later, Joe went to the kitchen and chewed a tortilla with an odd, steely taste, and he wondered if the dead had taken control of his tongue, or was it just the smell of death from all the villages? He smoked another cigarette and the tobacco filled his mouth with a pleasant sting and the dead lost their grip on his tastebuds, and his thoughts returned to the hand of the girl and the orange plastic horse.

THE PHOTOGRAPHS SUSAN MEISELAS took of the rebel called Lucas did not circulate in the American media until some years later. Instead, it was her shots of withering corpses that illustrated Bonner's story on the El Mozote massacre in *The New York Times*, a report that appeared on the same day as the story written by another correspondent for an American newspaper, Alma Guillermoprieto of *The Washington Post*. Bonner also wrote a second *Times* article that described life in the rebel-controlled territories of El Salvador. This story mentioned the North American fighter "Lucas" in two sentences and included his age, thirty-nine, and his mission: to write a book.

If she had come upon Bonner's full story during her daily reading of El Salvador news reports, Virginia Colman might have recognized her son in "Lucas." But the wire-service version of Bonner's report that reached downstate Illinois was condensed, and redacted of any mention of an American guerrilla fighter. Instead, Virginia clipped out several stories about the massacre that had taken place in the mountain village of El Mozote, and she lingered over the disturbing details. In the absence of any new letters from Joe, she placed her son there, amid the smoldering ruins the stories had conjured in her imagination. Battlefield atrocities. *War crimes*, Joe would say. She could hear him saying it clearly, right there in her living room. *War crimes, Mother.* And it occurred to her that maybe Joe was right about El Salvador, and maybe he was right to be there, as dangerous as it was. To witness it all, to come home and tell her what he'd seen, to show her true things she would not have known otherwise.

24.

Yoloaiquín. San Francisco Gotera

29 Jan

Brother Steven:

Guess I better give up making predictions about when I'll be returning to the States. Just found out there will be still *another* delay. Could be a couple of weeks, could be three more months, so to hell with any more wild guesses. Just hope y'all and rest of family are doing okay. Damn near a whole year since I heard from anybody. But

so it goes. As for me—still punching in a 1200 and keeping fat and
healthy. Anyway—duty calls—so I best get cracking. Will continue to
keep in touch whenever possible. Let folks know I'm doing fine.
Love to all, J.

14 Feb
Morazan

Dear Papa:

4:30 a.m. Woke up to the sounds of shooting and grenades to the
north—the mountain lads bidding the soldiers "good morning."
Moon's on the wane, flashlight's on the wane, but wanted to scribble a
quick message Arizona-way since a pal of mine plans to do some
traveling in the next few hours. Been nearly half a year since I wrote
that I would "be home soon." Hmmm. So it goes. No indication even
now when I might be heading toward the bright city lights. Well over
2,000 pages of manuscript to date—rucksack quite heavy these days.
If you're interested in what's going on in this little corner of the world,
you might try catching back issues of *The New York Times* and *The
Washington Post* at the local library. Had a few visitors back in
January and have heard that their articles are causing quite a stir in
Washington these days. The weeks prior to Xmas were pretty grim
and with the help of U.S. military advisers the E.S. military went
from tactical massacres to a strategy of wholesale genocide. And that's
why I'm still in the mountains—to survey the aftermaths, collect data,
and try to figure out the reasons why. So here I be—still fat and
healthy on tortillas and beans, still grinning my grin, still ready to
swap my Salvadoran butterfly net for an Arizona fishing pole. By the
time we get around to splitting that bottle of wine, looks like we'll
have some real vintage stuff on our hands.
Love, J.

22 March

15:00-Limetree

> And a new phase begins. And with a little luck + good strategy and planning on our part + bad luck to the cuilios—even the last phase. Restless cold night, beaucoup fleas, up early to smoke + listen to radio. No coffee, so went patrolling after breakfast. Pan dulce, puros, coffee de palo. Village folks scared of recriminations with coming operations, keeping apart, but siempre nearby to undertake their daily ventas.

Joe wrote his letters in English, but every day more Spanish worked its way into his journal. Café de palo. A local coffee-like concoction made from roasted corn. When I write a novel, maybe it'll be bilingual. Will need footnotes to explain it all to Mom and Dad. Cuilios. What's the etymology on that one? An onomatopoeia? A peasant was being strangled by army soldiers, and a sound gurgled from his mouth. ¡Cuilios! And that's the word the peasants have used for soldiers ever since. In describing the coming battles between the rebels and the army, Joe wrote: *Vamos a ver quien es más vergón.* Verga = dick. Vergón = endowed with a big dick. Thus: We'll see who has the bigger dick. Compared to "dick," verga sounded so much more vulgar and penile. His favorite Salvadoranism was "pura paja," which translated as bullshit or lying. Pura = pure. Paja = straw. But, also: Paja = masturbation. In El Salvador masturbation was a synonym for falsehood. All the talk of democracy coming to El Salvador was pura paja. Half the leaders of the main opposition party had been murdered, and the other half were in hiding, and the junta scheduled an election. Pura paja. Instead of real democratic coitus, a simulation, a public jerking off.

On March 23, five days before a planned election, Lucas was assigned to a rebel column led by a new comandante he nicknamed Willy the Joker. He was an older San Salvador urban commando putting his gunfighter experience to work in the hills for the first time. *Pure talent and balls*, Joe wrote in his journal. His was one of several units that would lay siege to the provincial capital of Morazán, San Francisco Gotera, and to its airbase. But first the rebels captured the very small town of Yoloaiquín and occupied it, just north of San Francisco Gotera, giving chase to the small National Guard unit there, killing two soldiers. Lucas missed the fighting because he was on "ambush duty" on the high ground outside town, awaiting an army counterattack that never came. He fell asleep in the middle of the day, his forearm over his eyes, listening to the birds sending mating and warning calls in the tree-filled cemetery below their position. *Awakened from sunbaked siesta by the choppers machine-gunning area—troop carrier and a little round job that looks like a flying bathysphere*, he wrote in his journal. The flying craft disappeared to the south, toward the airbase at San Francisco Gotera. Otherwise, *it was a dull, tedious day for us here on the knoll.**

WHEN JOE OPENED his semiconscious eyes they were soothed by quiet yellow sunlight and he slipped back into a half wakefulness in which he was snoring while thinking about how tired he was. He was startled into full consciousness by the agitated voices he heard coming from the bottom of the hill, and he rose to his feet and walked down to investigate; the compas had detained a "suspicious civilian" trying to leave the town. *Suffering shakes, very quiet*, Joe would write in a small notebook later. *Willy the*

---

*Yeah, I know: This is starting to get a little repetitive. Me and my guerrilla pals enter a town, and then we pull out, and then we enter new ones, and pull out again. Fear not, my participation in this war will soon come to a close. In one month. Unfortunately, the fighting went on a lot longer for my pals. Nine years, eight months and sixteen days, to be precise. War is hell. And the hell is in the repetition of it. One terrifying thing after another, until terror itself is tedious. But the novel character that is me has to put up with another kind of tedium now. The boredom of waiting for my role in the battle to begin. The next battle, after the battle before.

Joker questioned him and the guy started contradicting himself right away. Willy soon concluded, "This guy is a cuilio, or an informer." The captured man was tall and muscular, and the rebel soldiers made him take off his shirt and found markings on the skin around his waist like those left by an ammo belt; they marched him out of the cemetery and up the hill for some further questioning. *Heard him holler once,* Joe wrote later. *About 30 minutes later cry went out: The guy was making a run for it. Willy the Joker yelled, "Don't kill him! Don't kill him!" By the time I reached the crest, a dozen compas were in hot pursuit. Eventually, one compa opened up with FAL from about 50 feet. Just got bored of chasing the guy. Saw the guy spin and seem to trip. No, he'd been hit by the burst. I was 200 meters away but he was still bleeding from carotid veins in his neck by the time I reached him. Half his head torn off too. The compas were already taking off his boots, and his pants (brown). "No photos," Willy said. Willy wasn't mad at the compa who shot him. Said the suspect had finally admitted he was a National Guardsman. The compas had him sitting on the ground, but he stood up and broke his wrist bindings. Willy said no one was much in the mood for prisoners. I guess not. Compas quite amused at the whole incident. "A fresh corpse? Garbage. Bury him, throw rocks on him so he doesn't stink."*

Joe felt a burst of wind blow across the hilltop and over the prisoner's stiff and unmoving form. His feet and chest, bare cinnamon skin, his arms limply at his side. Palms facing the sky, and in the bowl of each one Joe saw an eye. The bent line of his mouth, as if he were trying to keep the flies out. The insects explored the corpse's nostrils until the compas pushed him into the shallow grave they'd dug into the ground next to him. They tossed rocks and kicked dirt on his half-naked frame. *Strange to be watching a live person one moment, hearing him answer questions, then watch him get killed a few minutes later,* Joe wrote in his notebook.

After the death of the prisoner, more tedium followed, hours during which a few rebels amused themselves telling the story of the prisoner's lies and his brief sprint for life. There was nervousness in the compas' laughter, but with each retelling, a little less so. The next day, in his journal, Joe gave his psycho-tactical analysis of the incident. *Hard-nosed these kids. Definitely turning into soldiers. Yesterday's incident with the prisoner hardly pretty but the subsequent savagery, the general behavioral reaction, important to us winning this war.* After the December massacres, any cruelty inflicted on the enemy seemed justified. *Without the killer instinct, we probably don't have a chance.*

The rebel forces withdrew from Yoloaiquín that same day. Joe watched as a line of soldiers approached the town; but after two days of waiting, when the opportunity finally came to pounce on the army, the command came not to do so. *Sort of deflating to get the order to pull back.* Joe watched from above as the soldiers entered Yoloaiquín through the cemetery, a picturesque assemblage of stone crypts and small, teetering crosses of wood and steel. Army goblins with M16s, squat-running through a graveyard. A day later the rebels went back into the town following the same route through the cemetery; they crouched behind the stone monuments and the crypts with their pitched stone roofs, and crushed dried flowers under their boots, knocking over the few wooden crosses still standing. This time the battle lasted an hour and the army withdrew, both sides leaving shell casings amid the graves. Joe noted later in his journal that the taking of the town had not gone well for the rebels. *Bad intelligence. Our lads snuck into town and laid a charge on the wrong fucking building. It wasn't the army HQ we blew up after all.* A woman came screaming from the building carrying a bleeding child. "The guerrillas killed my son!" The boy was, in fact, very much alive, but she wouldn't allow the rebels' medics to treat him, and instead she climbed with him into the back of a pickup truck, to get a ride through the battle lines to the hospital in San Francisco Gotera. As the pickup drove off, a big man half dressed in civilian clothes ran and caught up with the pickup and jumped in the bed. "A soldier! He's escaping! Stop him!" But no one did. Instead, the rebels ransacked a store said to belong to an army informant, and Joe drank an orange soda and lit up a smoke from said store, enjoying these small comforts of civilization while they lasted. Fanta. Chesterfield. The rebels evacuated the town and allowed the army to take it back again, and Lucas found himself again on the top of No Ambush Hill, and of course he felt a sense of déjà vu. *Saw a line of soldiers down in the cemetery, where I'd been taking pictures earlier in the day.* Word came from the comandancia, which was communicating to its units with notes written on small pieces of paper carried by running little kids. "Army unit is preparing mortar attack on your position." A single shell fell well below his unit's position. Then two on either side of them. And then many, many shells all at once. *Crouched behind a tree when mortar slammed in only several meters away,* Joe wrote in his notebook afterward. *Went momentarily deaf. A dozen of us all covered with dirt. Like being inside the explosion. Rifles caked. Definitely a concussion. Jabs your fillings loose. Literally my teeth ached. No one hurt, everyone shaken.* The explosion had shattered a nearby rock, transforming its shards into stone daggers the size and shape of fingernails. *I picked up a few rock chips in right leg, blood soaking through blue jeans in several spots. Slight rock chip embedded in left hand. Comandante ordered me out, to the rear. I said, "No. I want to stay." "Why," he asked. "To fight," I said. So I went down to join the compas in the firing line. Chopper came by and strafed the shit out of us. But no casualties.*

THE BACK-AND-FORTH over the town of Yoloaiquín was a short prelude to the main event, the rebels' attack on San Francisco Gotera, the departmental capital, a town of fifteen thousand people with an airstrip that was the military's lifeline in Morazán. Just like the Juggler had prophesied, one town bigger than the last one. The army of massacring soldiers was waiting for the rebels there, protected by trenches and pillboxes lining the edge of the city and airstrip. Lucas's unit took a position on high ground near the army positions, and Joe watched as a C-47 troop carrier propellered over the city and landed. A day passed, and no attack took place. *Snoozing under shade tree getting gut ache over too many green mangoes,* Joe wrote in his journal. Several hours later he added: *Agonized with a gut ache + whooshing mango-peel shits—not helped by a cup of sweet milk last night.* The next morning: *Slept on firing line last night, at my position behind stone foxhole + small tree. Lots of movements, us and them, but in the end we left enemy alone, they left us alone. This a.m.? Awoke with slightly sore leg, rock frag wounds infected but no sign any chips remain inside flesh.* Two Fouga Magister jets swooped by on a bombing and strafing run. *Some really fancy flying, corkscrewing, pancaking in, standing on their noses. Had to be some of our gringo "advisers." Went out to the rock point to have a looksie and chat with the last compa on the rearguard. Soldiers opened up on us from Yolo (maybe 700 yards away) and holy shit they had us pegged. Then a chopper came and holy shit they knew exactly where we were too. Not much cover in the rocks. The bullets, as they say, came thick and fast. Sounded like little birds trying to whistle after eating cracker crumbs. Pfffittt! Pfffittt! Dozens and dozens of rounds came our way, all zinging in overhead. First time I've really gotten it from a chopper. But finally chopper left without dropping altitude and we ducked over the crest so the soldiers firing at us would get off our case.*

Joe and the rebels marched back to La Guacamaya and took stock of what faced them in a full assault of the city and the airstrip. After another day of preparations, they assembled in the dark, at 3:00 a.m. "This is the day we'll see who is who," Willy the Joker said, and Joe wrote later in his journal: *A real good feeling this time, watching the kids get ready to move out. We'll have a lot of activity today. Shoot and maneuver. Hit and run. Fire and Flee. Rough, select group of compas will be involved in our part of it. Compañeras too.* Boys and girls ready to murder and to maim. *Will most likely get our asses kicked today, but so be it.*

Radio Venceremos was planning to go on the air at sunrise with reports of the attacks in San Francisco Gotera; and also in Usulután to the south; in Chalatenango in the north, and many other places. Lucas was going to play a small part in a nationwide action, coordinated between different rebel factions, to disrupt the phony election scheduled to take place that day. That the many egos assembled, loosely, in the FMLN (or "the Fellow Merchants of Leftist Non-sequiturs," as Joe jokingly called it), could actually coordinate anything was a miracle in itself. But they had, using letters sent through the mail and notes hand-delivered by girl couriers, and coded radio messages. Lucas was assigned to provide security for a rebel comandante he called St. Pete, a former army officer with a fatherly disposition; Lucas had strict orders to stick to St. Pete and not move toward the firing line, and before they marched out, Joe swapped his mud-caked M16 for an M1 carbine, captured at Yoloaiquín. He called it "the Little Virgin" because it was brand-new, polished and beautiful. *I'm now with La Virgencita, and more than 150 shells, 2 packs of smokes, clean clothes, stitched boots, coffee + sugar, marching with St. Pete, who is the leader of one of two platoons led by El Che.*

They entered the town's outskirts at 4:00 a.m., with one of Che's platoons dispatched to capture a knoll five hundred meters from one of the enemy's positions, outside a barracks, while Lucas's platoon moved to a stone wall inside a farm, several hundred meters farther back. The forward platoon began to fire on the army positions, and soon the army soldiers were firing back with G3s, and Joe heard fire coming, too, from the airbase to the south. The rebels were close enough to the airstrip that Joe could see the air force markings on a plane taxiing on the runway, and the sight of the plane confirmed to Joe how momentous the coming battle would be. El Che peered into Lucas's agitated eyes, and saw the North American compa wanted to do something, anything, so he told him to enter the farmhouse and see who was inside. Joe found a family of trembling people. *Told the women to get their kids hidden under beds and to barricade the door with tables and bags of corn, whatever they had at hand,* he wrote in his journal later. *Couple of old folks, kids. Patted shoulders and tried my best to reassure everyone—difficult as the lead came flying into their yard.* Lucas rejoined El Che, who was ordering his troops to move out. *We didn't have much room to maneuver. Cuilios had us pinned down from their trenches. Got behind a woodpile, caught some lead, but didn't start firing until compas had all moved through the farmyard, to a grove of trees on the other side of a creek.* Lucas was covering his companions from behind with his M1, an instinctual act; no one had ordered him to do so. *Soldier on top of hill was firing at the compas; I could see he was an open target from the waist up. So I set my rear sight on 200 yards; the first shot fell way short. Went up to 250 and sent him scampering. Then he and his pals opened up on my woodpile; a burst from a G3, then shot by shot. Got my gear squared away to do some work. The soldier eased up on me, and started exchanging fire with Che and the compas, who were now another 50 yards forward and to the right. I opened up on the soldiers from the side.* Nothing better to disperse a group of human beings than spinning metal projectiles. *Cleaned off the hillside and started peppering their little pillbox with rifle shots. Finished a 15-round clip, switched to another, then zigzagged across the creek—stopping for a smoke and to get out camera along the way.* There were two women behind him, Sonia and Reina, and a handful of other "brigadista" medical support troops. Where the heck did they come from? All unarmed and hugging the ground to avoid enemy fire. *Yes, I'd say we were just about pinned down,* Joe wrote. *Found myself shin deep in a stinking bog, St. Pete nearby, not looking happy.* Lucas and St. Pete moved forward through the grove of trees, and finally Lucas got close enough to the front line to see El Che, crouched down behind one of the thicker trunks, his legs exposed to enemy fire. He motioned for Lucas to come to him. "I got a soldier firing at me," he told Lucas. "Get him off my back so I can concentrate on the radio." Lucas quickly gathered himself and studied the enemy position, which was near a clump of grass two hundred meters away, and started firing. *Wasn't getting any response,* he wrote later. Suddenly he spotted an army helmet directly in front of his position.

JOE WOULD REMEMBER this moment later as one of extreme lucidity. In his memory, the entire day would be illuminated more brightly than any he could remember. Some sort of brain impulse, perhaps. A way the mind has of keeping essential information in the foreground of one's thoughts. The events and the ambition that had brought him to this battlefield. His story assembled into something precise and powerful. He would remember the orange glint of the morning light on his American-made M1 carbine as he raised it, the sheen on the polished grain of its wooden stock. Brand-new. The Little Virgin. The hot bulb of sun rays reflected on the forest-green sphere of that American-made helmet (also called an M1, coincidentally), worn by a minion of the massacring army, right there in front of him.

FIRST ROUND LANDED short a few meters on dirt tailing below trench. Adjusted sights to 200 yards and continued. Next round splattered the soldier in the mug with dirt and rocks and the third creased his steel pot with a visible streak of sparks. The soldier falls, truly something to see. *His pal popped up and I started snap firing. Was all over the guy. He either ducked or got hit and never showed again. At least one other soldier kept firing on us from left side of trench. I started talking to him. "¡Cabrón de mierda! ¡Ya culero! ¡Venga pendejo!"* It was very bad Spanish, the voice of a foreigner heard suddenly in a battlefield in provincial El Salvador, and all who heard it never forgot it. *Cabrón de mierda* didn't mean anything, no Salvadoran would ever say that. Surreal. Comical. The accent you can't quite place. Lucas kept on firing. *Had the range down fine and kept on his case. Comfortably positioned, adequate stock rest. Would simply remain sighted in on trench line, take up trigger slack, and as I saw top of steel pot raising up, would swing over on him before he could get off a shot. Sometimes he'd literally jump* *into the air and fire off a wild burst in our general direction, but I rarely gave him time to aim. While I was switching clips, a compa to my left (from another squad several hundred meters away) would take over with FAL. Suddenly noticed a soldier moving, hunkered over, scampering across the knoll to the topmost enemy position, probably a pillbox. Didn't even readjust sights, just started blasting away. Was on him immediately. Soldier immediately went to his hands and knees as I kept on firing, maybe hit, maybe not, but disappeared. Shortly afterward another guy came from the same direction, also hunched over. Dropped him on the move. He never made it to the trench or pillbox. Seemed to have crumpled on his side, then on his back. "¡Ay Chihuahua!" I yelped. "¡Cayó uno! Mirá, por encima de este cerrito. ¡Hijue puta!"* Could see the body outlined on the ridge. Got out the AE-1 and its telephoto for a looksie. Soldiers in lower trench were leaving us completely alone. Hillside still obscure in the early a.m. light but could make out the form of not only the one body, steel pot lying upside down nearby, but what looked like a second body in the background several meters away. Reported what I saw to Che, took three pictures, put camera away, and reloaded clip to continue on soldiers in the trench. Didn't occur to me until later that the photo-taking was—I guess—something of a snuff-movie reflex. And I was not surprised many more hours later not to feel any qualms—such as I did during that first ambush where the chance of my actually having hit any of the soldiers was quite slim. I didn't feel elation, yet a sense of satisfaction, a job done. Felt better at having killed an enemy soldier than if I'd missed killing an enemy soldier. And maybe the slightest hint of anger. As if to say—all right, if I'm stuck here in Morazán, then goddamnit I'll be a guerrilla combatant and to hell with everything. Later on the compas would laugh and*

---

*The Author, following a recent fad for untranslated Spanish in American novels, doesn't think he should translate this. I'll do it for him. "One fell! Look, on this little hill. Sonofabitch!"

*joke about me hollering "¡Ay Chihuahua!" They said they could hear the
soldiers yelling back, "Come closer, you Cuban faggot!"*

AFTER LUCAS KILLED AT LEAST that one soldier, and probably the second, and maybe a third, he began to take fire from his right. The army had maneuvered some troops to attack his position, and to drive the guerrillas back from their assault on the hillside and its pillboxes. *One guy kept playing jack-in-the-box until I caught him on the spring. Pulled the trigger just as he reached the zenith of his jump. Either tickled his ribs or came damn close. But they were working on us again with real enthusiasm and I was down to 75 shells and suddenly enemy on the right really opened up on us. Squad to our rear positioned on the other knoll said the soldiers were making an advance from the barracks and breaking through. They couldn't cover for us indefinitely. Compas started to leave the firing line. Che told them to cover our right but they were rapidly losing interest.* A retreat was looming. Understandable but heartbreaking. The army of teenagers seeing it ain't gonna be so easy attacking a fixed position, a collective survival instinct kicking in. *One compa with an FAL even worked his way over to Che and said he was too shaken to keep fighting. Che was enraged and yelled at him to get his ass to the rear. I kept working on the trench, Che and a few other compas worked on the right flank, but it looked like we'd soon get boxed in. Che started pulling his compas off the line.* Lucas covered the retreat; he was the last man back across the creek, through the farm and back into the hills beyond.

JOE LEARNED LATER that an advance squad of the rebel army, led by Willy the Joker, had fought some fifty meters into the perimeter of the airbase. Facing stiff army resistance from about eighty soldiers, and a looming counterattack, they too were forced to withdraw. Another unit, carrying a brand-new rocket-propelled grenade, had attempted to fire it at an armored personnel carrier; but the RPG failed to go off. The column to which Lucas and El Che belonged assembled on the highway outside San Francisco Gotera, awaiting orders from Comandante Jonás and taking stock of their losses. *Modesto had been killed in Francis's group, Armando shot through the right arm (broken bones and bad hemorrhaging and pain). And Jacobo? Lost and presumed dead. Another compa fallen from GI Billy's lads. Edwin, Orlando wounded. Oscar shot through the foot. Revolutionary roulette was certainly turning up a lot of our numbers. But was Jacobo really lost?* "We should send someone to recover his FAL, at least," a compa in his unit said. No one stepped forward. There were signs of doubt and disorder. Several of the peasants detailed to stretcher duty and one of the local guides had disappeared: *Just went on down the road, never to be seen again.* When Comandante Jonás appeared, a compa approached him and said, "We're all here and ready to go. Send us anywhere but home." For Joe, given the carnage, the gung-ho rebel seemed a bit crazy. *A magnificent display of soothing solidarity and loyalty. Someday after the victory I'll recommend the lad as our Minister of Recovery Programs for Revolutionary Lunatics.* But El Che didn't see the sense in a new attack, and neither did Joe. *Suddenly, our army looked like what it was: a ragged bunch of 17-year-old farm boys, dressed up as guerrilla fighters. Che's children seemed an ill-prepared bunch to be going up against this fortress town. He wasn't going to send them back in as cannon fodder. This was the Che who other platoon leaders would speak of with admiration for his personal "concern" for his boys, that they always have fresh fruit and anything else available and would himself go and do the gathering if need be.*

Rather than turn back south for a renewed attack on the city, the rebels congregated in clusters in the riverine and hilly landscape north of San Francisco Gotera. Some descended into a grove of mango trees and emerged with sweet fruits to eat. *Che started eating mangoes, I started eating mangoes, we got into an interesting conversation about mangoes, and by the time we reached the creek and irrigation canal everybody was casually turning their backs on the war to eat mangoes. Our band of guerrillas didn't look much like soldiers anymore, but at least they didn't look like panic-stricken soldiers either.* Joe spotted the compa who had told El Che he was too scared to fight with a line of juice dripping down his chin, laughing with some other compas who were recounting their morning's exploits by drawing three-dimensional battlefields in the air with their sticky mango-juiced fingers. The army soldiers at the airbase fired some mortars in the rebels' general direction, even though by now they were out of range. *I guess they figured that they might get lucky and kill that "Cuban" they had heard earlier, and some of his friends.*

The rebel army moved on, to another creek and finally to open fields intersected with more irrigation canals, and populated with cattle. *Terrain strikingly similar to outskirts of Saigon, in the Gia Dinh area*, Joe would write later in his journal. They met a group of sugarcane farmers who had small ovens to make candies, *but the army had burned their cane fields and they had few sweets to offer us.* These farmers hated the army, but didn't seem to place much trust in the rebels either. An army helicopter flew very high overhead, speeding quickly northward. A Huey. UH-1. Workhorse of the bellicose skies. Another echo of Vietnam. That war, this war, many wars rippling across the lushest lands of the globe.

The cane farmers made coffee for the rebels. *While I chatted and smoked and swilled coffee with St. Pete, the brigadista girls promptly fell asleep. Reina, the little girl I fell in love with over Xmas, mouth open, shirt open, lavish cleavage open to the sweaty sunshine, little farmyard pigs rooting around, threatening to drag her off.* Wake up, little Susie, wake up. Time to get on the march again. The army was said to be advancing toward them, very half-heartedly and cautiously, having gotten their butts kicked pretty well too, but creeping northward nonetheless. Lucas's unit marched on a ridge above the "Black Street" roadway that ran from San Francisco Gotera to Honduras. *Thought I spotted a line of enemy creeping toward highway 400 meters to the rear. Advised Che and he said to open fire. Told him I still couldn't be sure of target. Turned out to be a column of black chickens. Soon complete disorder set in. There were stores on either side of the highway and the compas descended on them, one by one. St. Pete brought me cigs and warm Cokes, and I teased a lovely barefooted campesina maiden with a blond-haired child. She and neighbors said they wanted to do us up a batch of tortillas, and stores started giving away sodas and practically anything the compas requested. The day's battle was over and Che and the Whale better get used to the idea.* Moving northward, into rebel-controlled territory, Lucas and his column found a woman cooking beef in a caserío, as if she'd been waiting for their arrival. *Unburnt and juicy; the señora knows exactly what she's doing. Some flor de elote soup, while she ground me a ¼ lb. bag of coffee (20 centavos) and listened to me describe the battle we'd fought in Gotera. Finally stumbling in twilight back to camp through the arroyos, the kid next to me trying to bum a peso off of me, and recalling every "gringo" (i.e., European) who'd ever set foot in Morazán since he'd become an organized compa. He's maybe 14 or 15 and he says his brother is "too afraid" to join the guerrillas—but his brother is all of 9 years old! Meanwhile compas yelling and grab-assing, telling combat lies with lonesome radio-love songs in the background, and chirping crickets and frogs too. Some life. At this rate I'll turn 40 in a guerrilla camp in Morazán.*

As Lucas marched the final kilometer toward camp, a compa named Freddie marched behind him, still holding the FAL he had not put to good use at San Francisco Gotera, looking at the soles of Lucas's boots in the dying light. Freddie vowed that next time he faced the enemy he wouldn't be so afraid. He'd be as brave and focused as the American he'd seen firing at the pillboxes, screaming war yells that made everyone laugh.

FREDDIE WAS SEVENTEEN and he wanted to make it to the end of this war, doing his part to defend his family and the people of the mountains. In the

years that followed, he fought in many more battles, until the peace treaty
was signed and the hated National Guard and the Treasury Police and the
Atlacatl Battalion were all dissolved, and the rebel army disbanded too,
and he went back to his life on the plot of land in Morazán his family owned.
By then he was twenty-six, and he got married to a woman named Juana,
and started a family, and like most peasants in Morazán they were as poor
after the war as they were before it. Freddie's wife traveled to the United
States to find work and send back money, and she found employment in a
desert city called Phoenix, and for years she sent back pictures to Morazán
of herself standing in rocky desert gardens, and on the phone she said one
day the temperature was predicted to reach fifty degrees Celsius, and Freddie did not understand how human beings could live in such conditions. In
her phone calls, and her occasional letters, his wife described the United
States as a sterile and mean place. When Freddie tried to imagine what it
was like to live there he couldn't help but remember the gringo Lucas, and
the battle in which he had seen Lucas kill at least two soldiers.

Lucas, the good gringo. Who came to my country to kill people with
North American precision. Not to defend his family or his land, as Freddie
and his Salvadoran comrades did. For Freddie, the war made sense only as
a blood-fight between Salvadoran brothers. Why had Lucas come to fight?
What was his home like, how did he learn to shoot like that? Freddie borrowed a peso from Lucas once and never paid it back, and twenty-four years
later, when Freddie went to the money-transfer place in San Francisco
Gotera to pick up the dollars his wife had sent him (because by then the
U.S. dollar was the official currency of El Salvador), he stared at the gringo
presidents on the bills, and he worried about Juana being there, in that
country where people were born with guns in their hands, apparently,
learning to hit bull's-eyes with every shot. A country with so much wealth,
a country that held his wife as a prisoner-maid, because she could not simply travel back and forth to El Salvador at will; many years had gone by
without seeing her, and they were growing older, separately. Freddie wanted

his wife home, and despite the still-loving sound of her voice on the phone every two weeks, he was afraid she might never come back. And sometimes he wished that Lucas was still around, to explain this one last thing about his country, the United States of America. He'd ask Lucas: *Will your country ever let my wife go?*

JOE ARRIVED IN CAMP, CLEANED his rucksack and sorted its contents. *The usual post-op ritual, second only to the stream shower in importance.* The next day, after a cool river bath, he sat down to write in his newest journal notebook, the one he'd begun with the declaration, *A new phase begins.* He reflected on the battle at San Francisco Gotera and the performance of the two competing armies, government and rebel. *From what I saw, the army soldiers were badly trained, poorly prepared for combat. Overall strategic defense of Gotera was excellent, however. Somebody, maybe those crew-cut gringos, had spent time at the drawing boards. Defended well or not, really amazed that we still had so much room to maneuver on the killing ground. Communication and military coordination on our part was certainly adequate enough to prevent the compas getting massacred, but not good enough for effective offensive tactics and maneuvers. A decent showing that promises improvement with experience. I await the next operation with more confidence than I felt going into battle Sunday a.m.*

Joe added a description of his own role in the battle of San Francisco Gotera, and afterward he thought of the dead soldiers. Two. Or three. Saw the two through the telephoto lens, snapped the shutter. Snuff pictures. When he woke up the next morning, and the morning after that, Lucas wondered if the civilized version of Joe Sanderson was dying, because he'd slept like the big healthy Illinois man he was. Unbothered by images of corpses or sounds of gunfire, his happy slumbers were filled with a restful silence and a uniform blackness.

25.

San Miguel

TWO HUNDRED FOUR THOUSAND WORDS. In three filled-up notebooks since joining the rebel army, and one he'd hidden in the house in La Libertad. And the seventy pages of the new one he started before the attack on Gotera. About seven words per line, thirty lines per page, all in cursive. A numeral in a circle at the top of each page, the date and year and often the hour at the top of each entry. The text? A cast of characters that was as big and diverse as in a Tolstoy tome or a Cecil B. DeMille flick. Armies and villagers moving across the landscape. Comrades killed, babies born. New guys and gals always coming in. Juggler. Sebastián. Noodles. Doc Holliday. New towns and cities and the code names he gave them: Limetree, Borealis, the Big M., Ulster. As if El Salvador were the setting of a folktale or an epic poem.*

After a brief respite at the rebel base, Lucas was back on the march again. All the more reason to keep his load light. Fewer notebooks, more ammo. The three filled-up journals in his pack had become too heavy to carry into combat. He'd started the current one just before heading off to the battles in and around San Francisco Gotera. The previous volumes he gave to Yancy, the man now in charge of the Radio Venceremos archives: tapes, photographs, written articles, Santiago's daily broadcast journal. "Right, your book, your famous book. Am I in it, Lucas? I hope you make me handsome and smart." Yancy placed the gringo's notebooks in the wooden crate that stored other precious documents, and the weight of that paper did not burden Lucas on his new mission.

Through a series of orders in which one comandante had overridden another, Lucas ended up with El Che again, with fifteen misfit soldiers from other units, culled together to head southward to reinforce the southeastern front. Before leaving Limetree, Joe shot the breeze with the rebel quartermaster, and traded La Virgencita for an M16. *I am now master of a Sweet XVI I'm calling "La Cabrona,"* he wrote in his journal/manuscript. *Forestalk had been shot up in Vietnam, left over with the rest of the weapons tonnage from the GIs' hasty departure. Thanks to the ways of the world and its wars, it ended up here, in Morazán. But the innards work just fine, so now it's me and La Cabrona.* He wrote his next entry the following morning.

---

*My book was writing itself. The older and wiser voice in my head was taking over. I stopped being a numbskull trying to imitate James Jones or Hemingway and just told the story. Scene by scene, the adventures of Lucas and the guerrilla army. As if I were scribbling a letter home to Mom. I had to face death, and then kill someone, to see that my writing should be free and easy. The mass murder around me made me into a writer, finally, which is a completely fucked-up thing to say. But in my case, it's the truth.

*1 April. 08:15. Finally got the boots off after a hellish 12-hour march. Bottom of my feet feel like they've been massaged with a pile driver. Sore back, weak knees; hell, this poor old lonesome guerrilla is just six weeks short of turning 40. But Jesus, we covered a lot of ground.**

VIRGINIA HAD STOPPED clipping news stories about El Salvador. Something about the sight of those newsprint rectangles and squares piled up, and her inability to send them to Joe frustrated her. Joe wasn't receiving any correspondence from his family: that had been clear for several months now. After she stopped clipping, she wrote one or two more letters, and then she stopped, not out of spite, or from a sense of hurt, but rather because it seemed to be a wasted effort. Not writing to him made the distance between them wider. Then Steve got his letter; and Milt got his, which she heard about through Steve. A year since Joe's received a letter from us. Repeats what he said in the last one I got: He wants to come home. But can't. He apologizes for the delay but gives no explanation.

There was so much about her current life that was rewarding. Her granddaughter. A young woman whose life would extend deep into the twenty-first century. Calhoun said Kathy would live to see an era when women began to run the world. This is why I love Calhoun. The powerful, simple observation. He sees things in geologic time. The eons. Precambrian, Paleozoic, Mesozoic. Within those great passages of the millennia, the shortness of our lives. There was comfort in the reliable routines of life with Calhoun. The uncluttered orderliness of their apartment home. Calhoun's health a bit better. All good things are fragile and passing. How many good years left for us? Inflation 10.3 percent, we live on a fixed income. The accountant in her says: inflation will unravel us. Middle-aged men in unbuttoned shirts, women with short hair and long pants with high

---

*Like writing a letter home to Mom.

waists, a new kind of formality with rules I don't understand. Creeping sideburns, aluminum and plastic everything, shoddy. Once upon a time, the hearth fire, the iron skillet, a ticking wind-up clock. Now the march of digital minutes, glowing red hours, abstract and electric. The sense that each week, each year marches past more quickly. The open *Courier* on the table. A line of soldiers with polished helmets in El Salvador, and peasant people, walking on a road with their belongings.

JOE AND HIS COLUMN of rebel reinforcements skirted the San Miguel volcano in a slow curve of a march around its base, through the fields planted on its steep slopes by industrious peasants. On the higher elevations, the cornfields dissolved into the fog, as if they were standing below the entrance to a peasant heaven. The fog shifted around them, rising and drifting, taking the shape of migrating animals and spaceships as it slowly burned off. The day turned hot. Their boots kicked up dust from the path on which they walked, all day, and then the sun set to the west behind the cone of the volcano and they walked by starlight, reaching the edges of the largest city in eastern El Salvador. *Bright lights of San Miguel snuffed out in the hazy mountain dawn and rising blood-hued sun,* Joe wrote in his journal the next morning. Lucas and his fellow rebels reached an open plain where they met a peasant who was hauling a huge water tank inside an oxcart; they stopped to drink and rest, and finally they arrived at the camp Joe called "Coconut Grove" in his journal, the headquarters for a "front" of about one hundred soldiers. The compas in Joe's unit began climbing trees and whacking coconuts. They split open the globes with the same machetes they used to clear brush on the march, carving out white flesh on the blackened blades, and someone produced sugar and a bowl and they began mixing. Soon the young fighters were drinking coconut water from hollowed-out shells, looking like an army of Robinson Crusoes. One of the older rebels approached him. "Lucas, I have some bad news for you."

Seems my old pal and mentor Sebastián was captured, Joe wrote in his journal later. *Doing political work in La Unión, apparently unarmed. Disappeared, presumed tortured and dead. He and Máxima had patched up their quarrel and continued their companionship. She was with him in La Unión, likewise captured and presumed tortured and dead. They were on a hacienda when the army arrived; two other captured compas had fingered them, no doubt under extreme pressure.* On the long walk to Morazán, they were two silhouettes in the night marches, one in front of me, the other behind. All of us eating possum together on the march. Their relationship a story Sebastián told me with his New Jersey accent. Their unrecorded whisperings to each other, their promises, sucked into the void. What does love leave behind? Silence. What we tell, what we write down, what Sebastián told me. "I'm in love with that woman. Can you tell?" Yes.

LUCAS AND HIS COLUMN went back on the march, and they reached an ancient railroad track of sinuous steel and termite-ridden ties on the western outskirts of San Miguel. El Che said the army was using this old line to bring in supplies. Lucas watched as rebel sappers placed the charges on the track. They were going to blow up a train, which struck Joe as a wonderfully anachronistic thing to do, like stepping back in time to the battles fought by Lawrence of Arabia and bands of marauders in the U.S. Civil War. A platoon of swashbuckling swordsmen on horses should come riding through any minute now. Lucas and his comrades retired to a station platform a kilometer away, and waited. Several hours later, at 6:00 p.m., El Che said the piece-of-shit train wasn't coming, it probably broke down, so they went ahead and blew up the track anyway. Five minutes later the army train approached the broken rails, stopped, and set in reverse and withdrew. Mission accomplished. Sort of. Not really. The rebels made the station platform their base for the night, and Lucas set his plastic sleeping sheet on some remnants of cardboard boxes. There was something very familiar about the humid tropical air and his contented state. The dry season was ending. Déjà vu. It was going to start raining any day now. Joe opened his notebook and turned on a flashlight.

20:00. Hot muggy evening full of moonlight and mosquitoes and quiet voices along the railroad tracks in a dusty village. It was the kind of night when a seven-year-old boy would watch shooting stars burst through the night skies of America, slurp down bowls of homemade vanilla ice cream, capture sphinx moths hovering over the morning glory flowers, go frog hunting with his father and brother in the swamps. It was the kind of evening when a 14-year-old boy would ride on the dark, muggy streets of a Midwestern town on his bicycle, desperately wishing for a girlfriend to love. A night like the sultry, moon-drenched evenings along the Ohio River when he was 19 and found love amidst the sweat and the sweet taste of straight bourbon whiskey and French kisses. A night with a ring around the moon—a moon dog—that promised rain. A steamy night within which he roamed the streets of Kingston and Port of Spain, in the jungles of the Guianas, along the beaches of Arica, Ipanema, Guayaquil, evenings spent on the decks of boats, hotel rooftops, along a thousand roads and highways throughout the world when he was 23, 27, 35. The evening was hot and muggy, the voices quiet, and for a brief moment he fondled the taste of youthful dreams between his tongue and the roof of his mouth, and it held a long and familiar savor . . . *

*The Author is faithfully reproducing here what he found on pages 105, 106, and 107 of my war diary, now stored at the archive of the revolution Santiago assembled after the fighting was over. But here the Author has refrained from his somewhat annoying (to me) practice of snipping out my bad writing. He's keeping my "fondled" dreams and my somewhat confusing "long and familiar savor." What can I say? After all the battles and marching I was living a beautiful moment. I laid it on thick, but the Author is going to print it as is, so that you know it was really me who wrote it. So that you can imagine me there, the real person I was. Thankfully, however, he's going to spare y'all a bit of trouble, and summarize what I scribbled next.

As Joe wrote he became more sentimental, and also more confused and embittered, and the words he composed to express his thoughts were as muddled as his feelings. He wrote in the authorial third person, describing on the page a tortured soul who was him. *Another hot, muggy evening, moonlight and quiet voices, and a brief moment of contentment before he re-membered he no longer carried a butterfly net, but rather, an automatic rifle . . .* He was *nearly 40 years old*, and no longer had *the aching virgin hunger* he'd had as a boy, and he recalled the loss of his innocence after his *first, long overdue fuck*, and how unfulfilling that act was. The child within him was pure; the man was not. The man had killed a soldier, and felt a *deadening loss of innocence* afterward, and he had seen many corpses— *dead flesh . . . numb and useless.* Joe the author foresaw the death of his protagonist, Joe/Lucas, and the loss *of the last sanctuary of innocence that was his own flesh and blood—bullets coming his way like rosebuds of spin-ning lead*, that would strike him *for the first and last time.* Life was beauti-ful, and it was cruel, and the protagonist of Joe Sanderson's unpublished masterpieces had seen so much of it. Joe Sanderson the writer ("Joe") and Joe Sanderson the adventurer (now named "Lucas") were both prepared to bring their story to a conclusion. Here in El Salvador, if the muse called for it; or by driving down Race Street again, to his Mom's senior abode, for a book-concluding serving of Virginia Sanderson's macaroni and cheese.

LUCAS MET MORE of the local comrades, and in his journal Joe gave them nicknames: Heavenly Hope (a woman whose nom de guerre was Esper-anza), Sparky (for his bright eyes), and Danny Boy, who was a local com-mander born in the city of San Miguel, a middle-class university graduate who had the lively mustache and untamed hair of a Velasquez self-portrait. Danny Boy was Lucas's new squad leader, and he was familiar with these villages and towns where he now guided the guerrillas in a semi-aimless meandering around the countryside, eating watermelons and free tortillas in the daylight amid the local populace, like ordinary road bums. Danny Boy said their guerrilla-bumming was a military-political act—it proved to the locals how weak the army was. They visited a small pond where Lucas took one picture of the compas mingling with peasants and their oxcarts, and another of women washing clothes, and Joe had another flashback. *Setting reminded me of India or British Guiana, the surrounding countryside of flat fields and dusty roads the same.* They returned to the railroad line, and entered a settlement called San Carlos El Amate, and Danny Boy announced it was time to stir up the passions of the local villagers by gathering them up to explain why the FMLN had opposed the recent, farcical elections.

Instead of one big meeting, compas broke off in twos and threes and chatted informally with folks up and down the tracks. Everybody eating fruit, buying crackers, bumming tortillas. Sparky came through like a champ, bought me sausage, cookies and soda, and finally cigs and a whole bag of sweet bread. In another village they met with a group of peasant rebel collaborators who had been given some homemade grenades known as "papayas." *They told us they had succeeded in stopping an army tank by placing a papaya in the treads, but couldn't quite manage to blow it up.* In the town after that, there was a flurry of excitement that had nothing to do with the revolutionary cause. *Compas passing around tattered remains of a skin magazine, slathering over gringüitas,* Joe wrote, *while ignoring the half-naked, taut-breasted compañeras bathing only five meters away.* In Morazán, the rebel army was a disciplined fighting force; here in San Miguel the army was as mellow and naughty as a band of California musicians. Finally, Danny Boy gave an order with clear strategic purpose: they were to march off into the campo to blow up an electrical tower. Some of the squad leaders and fighters *bickered over who would haul the TNT brick, made in a Morazán workshop, apparently,* and Joe remembered a similar scene in the Hemingway novel *For Whom the Bell Tolls,* when an American helps a group of Spanish Republican guerrillas blow up a bridge. *Was imagining myself accompanying an elite commando squad of specially trained and disciplined sappers, off on a crucial mission, but my fantasy quickly got mushy around the edges.* To reach their target they walked through brush and through cotton fields, and sandy streambeds and finally they came upon four strands of wire, and they followed those cables for a kilometer. *We found some unfinished business. An operation in August had left the towers badly damaged, but not quite wrecked.* The wounded tower resembled a praying mantis that was struggling to rise on its hind feet. *Danny Boy did a little on-the-job training with the TNT and an ordinary industrial fuse and detonator rig.* A single charge brought down the tower-insect and they ambled over to the next town and heard complaints from a store owner: "The power just went out again. The government can't do anything right." The people in the town were *leery and edgy* of the guerrillas, Joe wrote, but they sold Lucas cigarettes—and a safety pin to keep the gaping fly of his pants shut, *the zipper having surrendered the night before.* That night, they reached a rebel camp with sixty combatants. Here, Lucas received new orders. *El Che will head south to pick up a load of clamshells and eat shrimp, while I participate in acts of revolutionary vandalism on behalf of the people. Sounds like a lousy deal to me. As the informal unofficial unauthorized chronicler of the El Salvador revolution and playboy gadfly of the Eastern Front, and member in good standing of the Fraternal Members of Leftist Non-sequiturs, I insist that my bones be buried in the wall of some McDonald's hamburger joint in San Salvador.* That night, they camped near a waterhole, ¾ *moon hazy from dust kicked up by the winds and the oxcarts.* The air was as muddy as the swamp fog in the Cajun towns where Joe Sanderson once slept in the back of his truck while painting flagpoles. *Mango trees here, cypress trees there. Close my eyes and I can see the Spanish moss casting moon shadows. Open my eyes, and it's Sunday evening, up late passing the time with the compas.* A fighter called Pepe gestured for Lucas to come over to the plastic sheet where Danny Boy and several compas were gathered. *"Hey, jodido! Come over here. No jodás hombre." By which they meant, Don't keep to yourself, Don't remain solitary, sad, isolated,* Joe wrote in his journal. He was aware of his growing apartness from the struggle for which he was risking his life, and he was grateful to Pepe for pulling him into the group of squad leaders who had assembled around Danny Boy to shoot the breeze.

"We're discussing the military-political situation, Lucas," Danny Boy said. "What do you think?"

So I offered my two centavos' worth, Joe wrote later. Lucas said he believed that more guerrillas should be sent down from Morazán to fight in the lowlands around the eastern cities of San Miguel, Usulután and La Unión. "The enemy has proven they're not strong enough to defeat us in Morazán. It's time to move the revolution down from the hills, southward. We should live in the larger population centers, operate more against the enemy here, show the people we can win." The assembled rebels, all reclined on the ground, nodded their heads in agreement.

"Yes, that would be the ideal strategy," Danny Boy said. "That would be our best chance to end the war quickly. Unfortunately, it's not for us to decide, Lucas. But rather for Atilio and for Jonás." The men at the top of the ERP would not risk what they had already built up by emptying Morazán of its best fighting units, Danny Boy explained, and suddenly Joe had a vision of the future. Of many, many battles more, and thousands more dead, and how the years of violence would age the faces of the young men and women gathered around him. Worry lines would spread across their smooth copper faces. Their cheeks and foreheads would grow grayer and less taut, until they resembled the weary road bum Lucas saw when he looked in the mirror at Joe. Years from now, they'll say, *The revolution took our youth from us.* Danny Boy, the oldest of the guerrillas present, also saw this future, and his shared thoughts echoed Joe's.

"We'll launch another big offensive, and then the army will hit us with a counteroffensive, and the killing will go on," Danny Boy said. "I'm afraid killing might become part of who we are, permanently. Like a poison in the soil. This is what happened after La Matanza, fifty years ago: forty thousand people murdered in a week, followed by generations of violence. We all want to think that the final victory will be like a huge pill of happiness. But after all this death it's hard to imagine peace could follow."

The next day, during their ordinary rambling through the San Miguel countryside, Lucas marched with Sparky, who related a story about Danny Boy. Three weeks earlier, Danny Boy's uncle had been murdered in San Miguel. *A death squad killed him, KKK style, in front of his store,* Joe wrote later in his journal. *Neighbors marked the spot with stones and flowers. Danny Boy has since taken care of the three orejas* who betrayed his uncle. Must still be spies on the loose, but not too active anymore. Apparently, now there's a price on Danny Boy's head.*

LUCAS AND HIS UNIT entered places that were as poor as any Joe had seen in El Salvador. *Villages all seem sad and defeated and in disrepair.* Mud-covered tin structures, rusty rebar holding up roofs. Globe bellies of children filled with swimming parasites. Nakedness everywhere. Naked boys, naked girls, genitals exposed to the dust, bare feet and blackened toes, and finally Joe wondered if it was the wet air eating away at the people's clothes, because his own wardrobe was also coming apart. *I'm once again a fairly shabby guerrillero. Knees ripped on my jeans shortly after the zipper and back pockets gave way. My National Guard T-shirt and khaki long sleeve won't last too many more ops.* Later that day, Lucas finally acquired another pair of pants. *Became the proud owner of a new pair of Jaguar blue jeans. Hate to part with the souvenir mortar rips in my old pants, but you can't have everything.* More than ever, he was ready to leave El Salvador. *Time to exit. 13 months here and bearing down hard on 40 years old. I feel ship-wrecked. Sometimes I think my physical as well as psychological strength is just plain giving out.* One morning he awoke from sleeping on the ground—as he had for most of the past thirteen months—to find his upper

---

*Informants. Literally, it means "ears."

back muscles completely seized up. *I was semi-paralyzed. I felt my vertebrae clicking and cracking when I moved my right arm. I wondered if it might be something psychosomatic. Definitely not in top fighting condition.* That day, he eschewed carrying a pack while on patrol and his seized-up back muscles relaxed. *I start to imagine how pleasant it would be to spend a few time-killing hours in the Midwest, let's say cruising the Champaign-Urbana junkyards on a Saturday p.m. with brother Steven—talking and drinking canned Cokes and looking for $5 tires.*

8 APRIL. 09:00 HRS. After breakfast, and without fanfare, it was announced that we're going to do some executing today. A family of army collaborators would be our first targets. Little reaction from the compas. Unlikely the first time for most of them. I was reminded of the eerie disclosure Sparky made to me not long ago: He and the compas W. and U. had been part of a special revolutionary death squad, full-time executioners. Some 50 deaths to their credit, Sparky said. W. had been traumatized by their very first hit—a 13-year-old girl for some reason unclear to me. W. became "psychopathic" toward the end—so the chiefs sent him away. They had gone from using guns to using knives, machetes, killing by hammering pegs into the skull, garroting, etc., etc. Grim business. "It's not difficult," Sparky said. "Splas! Splas! And it's finished." Later, Joe reflected: *Saw nothing to indicate such backgrounds in W. and U. Nor is it easy to imagine Sparky carrying out such tasks.* How will I react if I'm ordered to kill someone unarmed? Probably they won't ask. Doesn't look good, no, to have a foreigner bloody his hands that way.

14:00 HRS. Killing spree canceled pending further assessment of political situation. After scanning skin mags, Danny Boy and the politicos decided to cool it on the executions. Apparently, such killings are the domain of platoon leaders who have quite a bit of autonomy for such decisions. Didn't seem like much of a day for slaughter and killing. Lucas and Sparky went out to patrol for milk and chicken instead, joined by a new young fighter. A fourteen-year-old girl who looked so much like Sparky that Joe dubbed her "Sparkette" in his journal. She was quiet, not a little afraid, but her smile was bright and spoke to some grown-up pearl of secret wisdom she possessed. Her wordlessness was eerie, however, as if born from some deep trauma. Finally, after a day on the march, Sparkette began to tell a story. "I saw this American movie once, Lucas. It had people who look like you. They were going up and down the mountains. They carried packs and long ropes, and wore caps. They had pants tucked into their boots, just like you wear yours. And they had lots of tools. They looked just like guerrilleros, except they didn't have rifles."

Sparky was moved to hear the Sparkette speak for the first time. He felt the need to say something too.

"The other day I had a dream that was like a movie," Sparky began. "In the dream I'm walking toward a house. A house out in the fields like the one my tío has, but this house isn't my tío's, it's a stranger's house. I see a bunch of cuilios are standing nearby. I start shooting at them. Pah-pah-pah-pah-pah! But nothing happens. For some reason my bullets can't hit them, they just fall in front of their feet. And so they start to circle me. They have me surrounded. I keep on firing, and my bullets keep missing . . ." His voice trailed off, and Joe realized that was the end; it was an anxiety and vulnerability dream. But the Sparkette was waiting for more.

"And then what happened," she asked.

Sparky looked into the hopeful eyes of the Sparkette, and said something Joe knew wasn't in his dream at all. "I just started killing them all. And they fell like toys."

BEEN MOPEY AND MOURNFUL as I hobble around camp with my bad back, Joe wrote. *As a consolation prize I was allowed to turn in my Jaguars for a* *spiffy pair of Lee jeans with a 32-inch waist. Simple pleasures.* On April 10, the day after Good Friday, they entered a village near the railroad tracks that was home to a family of devoted supporters of the guerrillas, for what turned out to be an Easter Eve holiday party. *Compas in high spirits in anticipation of a few extra treats. "Una torta para los montaños!"** *On the way, we "ambused" a friendly truck driver, who supplied watermelons and big slabs of homemade sweet bread.* The compas listened to Latino rock on a transistor radio, and then to Radio Venceremos, sitting on the roadside. *Night had fallen and the guerrilleros once again controlled the countryside and the thousands of small villages where the soldiers of the army feared to tread.* Moses, Giovanni and Fidelito were some of the names of the rebels in this group. Fidelito was a comandante. When a group of children approached, Fidelito played the big uncle to them and told a series of nursery rhymes about birds and papayas and the final triumph of the revolution. Finally, they all ended up in the home of the family they'd heard about: a gray-haired patriarch with *arms muscular from endless labor,* and the matriarch, *his señora, the brains behind Pa, who stood behind the king at the table and wrapped her arms around him affectionately.* They offered the rebels some homemade moonshine, and for the first time in more than a year Joe took a swig of alcohol. The family patriarch then guided Lucas to a hammock he had on his porch, and invited the gringo rebel to "rest, relax," and Lucas did so, taking another swig of moonshine, which burned his innards pleasantly, and he clinked glasses with the old man, who sat on the ground next to him. After a few pendulum swings of the hammock, a reclining Lucas said the first thing that came into his head: "There are no mosquitoes here." The family patriarch responded with a long lecture on the mosquitoes of El Salvador, and of the spread of malaria locally. *It turned out he was the area* Anopheles[†] *expert. An amateur entomologist.* After an-

---

*A sandwich for the mountain men!

†That's a genus of mosquito. The one that transmits the malaria virus.

other drink the old man started talking about something beautiful he had for Lucas's enjoyment. "Something to delight and enchant any man after a long day of work." The old man grinned meaningfully in the moonlight.

I suddenly thought: "Jesus gawd, this character has a muchacha hidden away in the woodshed, and he's making with the old tribal hospitality. I wonder what she looks like, how old she is. Ohmygawd whatamIgonnado?" Didn't take me long to figure out what I was going to do, especially after another belt of moonshine. So Lucas followed the old man into the darkness, *only to discover my generous host was offering me the use of his brand-new latrine!* White porcelain, toilet paper on a roll and towel hanging on a rack. Luxury! Comfort! "Thank you, señor, thank you." And Lucas took his turn on the commode, with a couple of other compas soon outside waiting, and he had just finished a gloriously luxuriant bowel movement when he heard voices yelling outside.

A rebel sentry had raced up to report to Danny Boy that a thief had been captured by the compas. With that, Joe wrote in his journal, *We began A Rough Night in Jericho. The Good Saturday life-and-death saga of "The Nocturnal Guerrilla Theater."**

The Nocturnal Guerrilla Theater
by Joseph D. Sanderson

The culprit was hunkered in the road dust with his thumbs tied behind his back. Shirtless and shoeless, lanky, easily six feet tall, dirty-faced—yes, he even looked like a thief. He talked in a slow, slurred voice, pleading and whining and appropriately humble. "¡Yo

---

*At this point the Author is going to hand it over to me. Entirely. He's going to quote directly, and at length, from pages 160 through 181 of my journal—with just some minor editing here and there. Well, a lot of editing, actually. Nevertheless, we have reached an important milestone in my story. Because with the printed words that follow, I, Joe Sanderson, will become, after a mere half century of waiting, a published writer at last.

soy pobre! ¡Pobre! Soy un pobre pescador."* But he had been caught red-handed with a pilfered live duck and chicken. The villagers had complained to the compas often enough about local ladronismo.† Gangs of thieves, "mañosos," who had guns and machetes and kept the village folk terrorized. The compas were excited to capture him. A vigilante fervor spread quickly. We had the opportunity, now, to display revolutionary justice and power to the village, and to repay their hospitality and collaboration with us. In the countryside, especially by night, we were the law. The stolen poultry was confiscated, and the compas fashioned a hood for the "Fisherman" and consulted with Fidelito. "A delicate situation," Fidelito said. The Fisherman quickly put the finger on the three guys he lived with—an old man and his two sons. They were just borrowing the poultry, they said, and planned to pay for it later, etc., etc. Complicating matters was the fact that being a thief, in these parts, is synonymous with being an ear for the government. A crowd gathered, and even Señor Anopheles got into the act, blurting out, drunkenly, that bad blood ran in this family of thieves; such and such was a member of the hacienda police, another had wounded someone with a machete, another had fingered a compa to the National Guard. The vigilante fever spread and it looked like we had the makings of a necktie party.

I watched the compa Nero lead the Fisherman away from the railroad tracks, the purloined duck left on the platform—the chicken had fled. Figured Nero would chop the guy up with a machete and that would be the gruesome end of the whole incident. But instead they both reappeared, and we all started walking with the hooded man down the tracks toward his house. Moonlight and railroad tracks on the edge of town, and a tied-and-hooded thief and a dozen armed

---

*I am poor! Poor! I am a poor fisherman.
†Thievery.

silhouettes. My heart was pounding like it never did in combat. We reached the house in question, surrounded it at close quarters and shouted for the occupants to come out. Voices, whispers. One by one they emerged into the moonlight, one older man in his early fifties, two young men in their early twenties, all in their underwear. We ordered them up against the wall as the compas ransacked the house—a poor squatters' shack filled with the usual campesino clutter. Just four men living together, with no women present—all the more suspicious. The compas were brusque, harsh, no-nonsense, and though they often seemed on the verge of slapping the suspects, none did. The three men were led away from their house across the tracks and ordered to lie facedown along the railroad embankment. One by one their thumbs were tied behind their backs with twine, then later their upper arms with rope. The questioning commenced, the threats, and all they could respond was, "¡Por dios! ¡Somos pobres! ¡No somos ladrones!" About thirty minutes later all four were lifted and we began the return march to the station platform, myself guarding the prisoners along one flank. A group of compas took a separate path with the Fisherman, I felt for certain to kill him. Expected to hear a pair of shots or a burst of automatic rifle fire at any moment, or screams from the victim. The other three were questioned some more; no compas made any open threats; they weren't really necessary. The men knew the revolution had no way of imposing jail sentences. Freedom or death were the only options. One of the suspects picked up on the revolutionary context of the interrogations and began saying he wanted to get a gun and join the guerrillas. And suddenly all of them were in agreement with this. Up to that point, I was feeling sympathy for them. Feeling miserable. I figured we might be making a big mistake. And I still had no way of knowing if the comandantes had already decided the issue.

Now a fifth suspect was brought up. He said there was another house with thieves, with weapons, including a .38 rifle. I stayed quiet, I left it alone, it was all bigger than me. The compas told the Fisherman to guide us to this house, but he said he was afraid the people inside might shoot him when he approached; too bad, said the compas. I remained on rearguard as four compas surrounded the place. I led the Fisherman out of the direct line of fire and told him to sit down, but he claimed he had a bad leg. Too bad, I said. Sit down! He sat down and started mumbling, until I told him to shut up. I could hear Nero yelling at the people inside. Telling them to stop fucking around or we'd open up on them. The Fisherman tried talking again, and tried to get up, until I leveled La Cabrona at him. Soon enough the compas were inside the house, and I could hear them ransacking it. They brought out three young men, all in their underwear, Nero snorting and puffing and telling them all he was tired of their fucking around. Finally, Nero came out with their "arsenal"—the ".38 rifle," which was actually an ancient museum piece of a shotgun with a broken stock and attached cleaning rod. And the rest of the guns? "What guns? We don't have any more, just that one." Nero told them we were a right-wing death squad and would finish them off if they didn't produce the other weapons, and then an old woman came out of the house, bawling and wailing. Apparently, she was the mother of the young men; the sight of her sons kneeling in the dirt, arms and thumbs tied behind their backs caused her to fall to her knees too, begging. "Please don't kill my sons! My sons!" She pleaded to God, to the neighborhood, and to us not to lead her sons away into the night to be slaughtered.

We brought up the three newest captives to where the others were, and Fidelito recognized them immediately. He told us to set them free, and I helped to cut the ropes; he even allowed one of the three to sneak into the bushes for a nervous shit. Apparently, they were collaborators with the revolution; they had believed Nero's "death squad" talk, and had kept their mouths shut. But the fact was that, collaborators or not, there was "good" evidence that they had a long record as a family of thieves. Someone had the brainstorm to throw all eight of our suspects together, and we promptly did so—the mumbling and the glares between them seemed to implicate all eight of them as co-conspirators. Danny Boy at times seemed set on a mass execution, but not so much for crimes of theft, as for the threat they posed to the revolution if freed. They could blow the lid off the whole area scene, he said. So now the compas began to debate: kill all of them, kill some of them or let them all go? The revolution was at stake, some said, no time to get personal, feel compassion for the wretched scum of the earth. Fidelito seemed to have made up his mind. All that was left was how to go about it. Only hours remained until sunrise. He summoned the politicos for an informal meeting. During one of their lengthy reflective pauses Moses entered the discussion and suggested all eight be allowed to live, and be assigned revolutionary tasks as proof of their honesty and good faith, their love of the people and solidarity with the struggle. I walked away, afraid that the slightest thing I said might impact their decision, relieved that my only appointed task was to stand guard over the prisoners and watch and listen. From time to time a compa would speak out, saying the revolution meant to stop the spread of crime, which damaged the people, and how dictators used criminals against society; or a captive would speak in his own self-defense.

Finally, the compas on the platform fell asleep, and even Danny Boy and Moses took short naps, and when they woke up they seemed to understand what they had to do. Danny Boy and Moses began to speak to the captives, one by one, taking turns; talking about the revolution and justice, and all the people who had died in the name of

basic human rights and a better country, and their words were so
incredible I wished I'd had a tape recorder to get them all down
accurately. Listening to them, even the most callous of the suspects
must have felt stunned and slightly awed. It was the revolution in its
finest hour. The compas had not even finished their lecture before the
captives were lifted to their feet, their ropes cut, men and boys given
their freedom. None attempted to leave. They knew their lives had
been spared. They were told to make no mistake about the revolution
being soft—at the first sign of any recriminations in the village, or the
slightest theft, they would be held collectively responsible and dealt
with accordingly. Incredibly enough, some of the suspects began to
slouch and yawn, and at that point I lost any remaining doubt I had
about their guilt, and one compa stepped forward, to say maybe we
should execute them all anyway. But soon enough the suspects
started thanking the compas, blathering mealymouthed gratitude,
promising to be good. And the compas? Disgusted but resigned to
the outcome. With the lingering resentment that so many good people
had been murdered, and the good people continued suffering, and yet
these criminals would live, and the struggle would go on without any
concrete sign that the night's drama would bring us a single step
closer to victory.

The next morning—that is, a few hours later—as we returned from
sleeping in the hills, exhausted from our night of guerrilla theater, we
watched the villagers in their crisp white clothes striding briskly
toward their chapels, hymn books in hand, to sing out the glory.
Easter. Later, the gay blades and the village maidens would surely
head to a dance at somebody's home. The noonday sun climbed
overhead and covered us with sweat, and we rested and shared a
couple of watermelons among ourselves and laughed and made lame
jokes. One of the compas noticed the stolen chicken hiding nearby,
among some tree roots. Nero walked up and solemnly spoke to it.

"Buenos días, chicken. You can come out now. We saved your life.
You owe your life to the FMLN."*

THE REVOLUTION WAS a series of improvised and arbitrary acts resembling the "nocturnal guerrilla theater," one after the other. Every decision
taken by the movement made perfect Marxist sense, or made no sense at all.
When Joe asked up the revolutionary chain of command if and when he
might be allowed to leave, no one could give him a straight answer. Assorted comandantes said his fate was in the hands of the top movement
leaders in Morazán, who informed him, in turn, that it was the underground political chieftans in San Salvador who had final say. *Going through
another period of frustration over my blocked exit. Nearly 7½ months on the
catbird seat*, he wrote in his journal. *My present assignment has freedom
and mobility, and dramatic experiences and the promise of more to come.
Couldn't ask for more. Regardless, still time to go and has been for months.*

Instead, Lucas and his squad received another new mission: recruiting. They were to draft at least ten youths, from three villages. *Brief instructions followed on how to make getting shanghaied by the revolution
relatively painless for the victims. No rough stuff, but make sure you keep 'em
surrounded, cover the exits of the houses, don't take any back talk from those
punks loitering in front of the village store. And get them away from Ma and
Pa, especially if Ma's bawling or if Pa's going for his machete.* The spirits in
Lucas's squad lifted. Funny thing, Joe noted in his journal: *When it came to
twisting arms, most of the compas love their work.* The same man who could
be generous and considerate to a refugee or to his fellow fighters could truly
enjoy the harshness and sadism that come with dealing with a suspected
deserter, informer or thief. *I can't be critical of them, given the circumstances*, he wrote. *My attitude about these matters is different now.* The

*And now my writing soul can rest in peace.

numbness again. Will I feel it when I'm back home, when I'm with my own Ma and Pa? In the first caserío Lucas was assigned to a rearguard while Nero and his compas *rounded up the calves. Nero was pleasantly insistent as he drug some boy away from a very concerned and suspicious and quite large señora—Nero stands about 4 ½ feet high, a bow-legged gremlin with a Solzhenitsyn beard.* The compas rounded up a dozen or so youths more, *6 found playing cards (the drugstore cowboys at the local tienda), a few tugged from mommy's clutches in their own homes, and then a few more hard-core teenage loafers with rock music, sports and señoritas swirling in their brains.* They were all gathered on a soccer field (or was it a pasture?), to hear a speech to inspire them to join, to be delivered by the Sparkette—who wasn't there yet, but on her way.

Silence hovered over the soon-to-be-shanghaied boys as they sat among dirt clods and cow dung, and finally it became a vacuum that Joe felt compelled to fill with something theatrical, something optimistic and American, like a speech from a Frank Capra movie. *I found myself playing the pitchman, softening up the crowd before she appeared, The Star.* What to say? Well, the things he knew about. The Christmas massacres. Freedom. Justice. The Death Squads. International solidarity. Americans marching in support. Vietnam. The Christmas massacres again. *It was almost as if I, presenting myself to the assembled youths as a "representative of the international press," was the whole point of the meeting.* The rebel fighters and potential compa-draftees looked on with awe, bemusement, confusion and resentment. Nero thought: These village boys already think we're astronauts who've come from the moon, and now we've brought our own alien. Danny Boy thought: This is really too much. This man Lucas, as much as I love him, shouldn't be speaking; he's a foreigner after all. Fidelito thought: Now these peasant kids will see how vergón we truly are, as they listen to our blond giant talk about "the nobility of the popular uprising." And when the Sparkette finally arrived and caught the tail end of Lucas's remarks, his peroration as it were, she saw the youthful audience staring at him with open mouths and perplexed brows, and saw his jeans tucked into his socks, in the style of a rock climber, and she thought: He looks like one of the actors in that movie I saw!

After Lucas, the Sparkette's remarks were brief and to the point: The revolution needed men and women. If I, a fourteen-year-old girl whose father was killed by the fascists can join the revolution, so can you. Then Danny Boy spoke, and said a few words about defeating the army. When he was finished the village youths began to chime in. Yes, I'd love to join you, said the handsomest of the youths, but my girlfriend "está panzona," by which he meant not that she was fat, but pregnant. I have my studies in San Miguel to complete, said the smartest of the youths, who was the village college student. And we all have to work to support our families, said the others. Finally Danny Boy moved to the center of the field, and said, in effect, your excuses are not good enough. All of us want to go to school too, all of us have family responsibilities too, but there's a war going on and it's time for everyone who supports the revolution to put his body on the line. *He said individual decisions must be made immediately,* Joe wrote in his journal. *The subject is closed. Fall in and let's get on our way toward camp. All personal problems will be dealt with mañana.* Danny Boy ordered all the young men to hand over the corvo knives most of them were carrying. Only one refused to surrender his knife, and Danny Boy turned tough with him. "What are you, an oreja?" "No, no, absolutely not," the youth protested, and he fought back tears protesting his innocence, because to be called an informer was a death sentence. One of the compas snuck up behind him and disarmed him. The compa handed the corvo to Lucas.

Joe and his unit marched away with the conscripts, with Danny Boy and five other compas using the beams of their flashlights to guide the young men and keep them corralled. *We guarded them more closely than captured soldiers—because we knew it would be impossible to shoot them if they escaped. It was a long journey from town back into the hills. Upon arrival, the compas herded the youths into a house behind camp. At first light I went off on a milk run—I had a real hankering for some fresh cow's milk and sugar. Upon my return, a few hours later, all the recruits were gone. What had happened? It seems they started begging Danny Boy to return to their homes, and he got disgusted and told them,* "Leave, then. But we'll be back there one day." Joe later concluded his account of the shanghaied youths with these words in his journal: *The whole caper was a flop.* He sat with Danny Boy, who was the picture of a dejected and bitter bohemian. Around them, the compas were mocking the weeping mothers and whining young men from the night before, laughing. "We're trying to act the way we think we're supposed to act," Danny Boy told Lucas. "The way we've been taught by all the strongmen who've ruled over us forever: kick the peasants in the butt, humiliate them, bend them to your will. But it turns out we can't be that vergón. Maybe because trying to be vergón is the whole problem."

The next day Joe's unit met a rebel column marching in from the sea with a supply of weapons. A shipment of rifles and ammunition from the rebels' friends in foreign countries, and also an .81 mortar, and ten G3 rifles recently captured from the army. The leader of this unit had urgent orders to return to Morazán and to take a few of Danny Boy's men with him. New army offensives were expected in the mountains. Danny Boy later approached Lucas and gave him the news in guerrilla officialspeak: "We're going to reintegrate you into your former position of responsibility. In Morazán." That night, before he left, Lucas sat around with Danny Boy and his men and felt nostalgic, and he began to sing to his rebel friends. A song for the young men who couldn't bring themselves to kill the thieves or shanghai the village knuckleheads. In a revolution, you never know when, or if, you'll see your friends again. *Impulsively, I began dancing and strumming my M16, holding it by the sling like a concert guitar. A little Rod Stewart.* "Patti gave birth to a ten-pound baby boy, yeah! / Young hearts be free tonight, time is on your side." *Compas loved it; or at least they seemed to as they keeled over laughing. Delighted to discover I still have some Zorba the Greek left in my soul.*

Before he left for the mountains, Lucas traded away La Cabrona, his beat-up M16, *for a lovely if not exactly mint condition AR-15.* On the march around the base of the volcano, back up toward Limetree, a scattered beat of fat water drops fell on the dusty roads.

18 APRIL. 6:00. Morazán . . . Oh shit . . . What am I doing back here in Morazán? Presumably awaiting the revolutionary apocalypse. All right, so be it. April, May, June—how long? Until the infinity of victory.

26.

Crossing the Río Sapo

18 April. 18:00. It was a long 12-hour jaunt for the last stretch but felt good and did well. Bath, clean uniform, no foot trouble. Lungs ✔. Cigarettes ✔. No raging farts or the shits ✔. Enough starlight for the march ✔. Stopped off for cakes and bread fresh out of the oven that tasted like granny's sugar buns. One last 5-hour sleep on foot of mountains and at dawn we hijacked some trucks for the ride up here. Last downhill jaunt to free country was a breeze. Back in town, immediately went AWOL. Met up with old friends and we teamed up to terrorize the neighborhood: hot coffee, watermelon, scrambled eggs with onions, tomatoes, chili peppers. At the base in La Guacamaya he accompanied his squad of compas as they delivered their cache of new weapons. *Compas were all tired but their spirits were high.* The rebel army in Morazán had grown in his absence. *Literally everybody armed, no shortage of weapons anymore—most were carrying two weapons apiece. My ballpark guess is that we've doubled the ranks of combatants in a single year.* The next day he wrote: *Everybody awoke this morning jubilant, effervescent. Definitely the smell of victory in the air. You can cut it with a corvo. Compas are so happy that it all might finally be coming to an end; they're ready to die with few qualms. Myself included.*

His first days in camp he heard distant thunder but there were, as yet, no true rain showers. A helicopter flew over La Guacamaya and fired off a few desultory shots, and turned away, and the pulse of its engine grew dimmer and faded. Joe slept better than he had in the flatlands, waking up each morning covered with dew, *comfortably cold, with no mosquitoes!* he wrote. He marched from camp to camp on various assignments in his role as the "international press reporter" for Radio Venceremos, and tried to avoid actually being in the presence of the radio crew and their workspaces around the transmitter, because most of them were open in their disdain for him. They would get hold of some candies, or sweet bread, and share with everyone else but him. Go buy some with all those pesos you're carrying, they'd say. Or: Why don't you trade us from those cigarettes you're hiding. Petty indignities suffered by the outsider. Lucas was a norteamericano pebble in their revolutionary shoe. But he went about his work without complaint. He'd seen so much death, so much life. The rebel camps felt like dioramas constructed for him to walk through, like the perfect, heavenly landscapes behind the glass in natural history museums. Crimson sunbeams illuminated him when he marched between camps in the morning mist, and at night, hundreds of luminescent insects danced around him. *The lightning bugs were fantastic. The color of stars. "Ciérnegas." All blinking, like strobe lights.* New compas arrived, eager, disciplined and crafty, and he gave them nicknames. Silver Bullet (for his tooth) and Beaver (for his buck teeth). They were slimmer Salvadoran versions of the youngster he would have liked to be. *I dearly regret not having a camera when I met the compa with a special pouch on his ammo belt for carrying . . . a goddamn slingshot! He's got a 7.62 caliber Belgian FAL machine gun—and a slingshot! Ohmygawd!* All these young guys in a fighting peasants' paradise, with pretty young women there to share the adventure with them. Doris. Lucas took a photograph of her eating a mango and thought the image could become a guerrilla pinup. Later, Comrade Doris strolled through the camp lugging her M16—while wearing a new white dress. And the compas watching her squirmed, because she was beautiful and seventeen, and the top two buttons on said dress wouldn't stay hooked, and one of the compas whisper-moaned, "Eso, eso, eso."

The actual war was, for the moment, a series of stories he heard from other compas. *Apparently, we suffered a major reversal two weeks ago. Compas were attempting to seize the warehouse in Jocoatique. Seven dead including platoon leader and my old pal Diego, the ex-soldado captured in Guacamaya. Many others wounded. They were supposed to attack at 4:00 a.m., seize mortars, withdraw. When the shooting started at 5:00 a.m., the enemy was already in position. Compas were surrounded. Ventina died outside the town, Diego in our hospital.* Two rebel deserters, a man and wife who worked in the kitchen, had somehow ended up in San Salvador, and the army sat them behind a line of microphones at a press conference. *They said they had seen no Cubans or Soviets among the compas but that there was one North American, a combatant who went by the name Lucas. Ha. So much for my invisibility. The legend of Lucas spreads.* One of the new compas told him: "I heard you wasted a lot of ammunition in the battle at Gotera—and you wiped out an entire enemy squad." "Exaggerations," Lucas said, and later in his journal he wrote: *They think I'm a killer in the closet waiting to be unchained.* Planes had begun dropping leaflets in Morazán offering a reward for the capture of the top rebel outlaws. *3,000 pesos for Joaquín Villalobos, 2,000 for Jonás . . . 35 centavos for Lucas,* Joe quipped. He might be captured and become a war trophy for the government; or killed, his corpse put on display for the international media. *Gonna be a fine day,* he wrote the next morning, after a rebel dance at which he sang a bit, again. *Crashed out certain I was Bobby Dylan, and now I wake up convinced I am Hunter S. Thompson. Compa Lucas? Vanished without a trace.*

Lucas helped the radio crew dig a bomb shelter next to the rock escarpment that provided cover to the transmitter; a meter down into the soft ground they began uncovering bones. Very old bones. Hundreds of years old. A Lenca burial site. *Lovely, well-preserved pot with vegetable-dye color and Picasso-like drawings of human figures,* Joe wrote in his journal. The ground of Morazán. Burial grounds and battlefields. Out in the woods, not too far from the transmitter, one of the compas discovered an unexploded hundred-pound shell. *The boys at our bomb factory are excited. They say they'll fix small TNT charges to the side and use it to blow up a bridge, a radio tower, or fuck up an enemy convoy.* Lucas marched over to watch the rebel explosive experts take it apart, very much aware that he was close enough to be killed if they screwed up. *Isra deactivated the rear fuse, but just as I suspected there was a nose fuse as well. No problems, however. Helped lift the mother out of the hole we excavated around it. Rear stabilizer had markings that read:* an-m103a1. 100 lb. tritonal. explosive. U.S. bomb. *One of the compas shouldered it down the hill. Said we should paint FMLN on the nose and send it back to the store for a refund.*

While removing the unexploded bomb, one of the compas found a body decomposing in the woods, the skeleton of an enemy soldier. *Animals had drug the lower leg bones and attached foot bones off to one side. Well-preserved skeleton still inside army shirt and khaki pants. A stained handkerchief lay across the belly, where soldier had been shot and obviously attempted to staunch hemorrhaging. Compas started giggling and I cracked that he looked like he could use a few extra tortillas and beans. Immediately felt ashamed. Imagine the soldier died a lonesome death, cut off from his unit. A painful and lonely death. We left and the compas said that maybe we should go back and see if we could find his G3. I just wanted to get the hell out, get away from myself and my shameful mockery.* Joe thought later about the bodies at El Mozote, rotting into the soil. Eroded bones and eroded limestone, skulls decomposing in volcanic ash, wet earth, moisture, the tunnels carved by beetles and ants, insects eating away at flesh and fallen leaves. A man becoming compost. The rainy season was coming, and water would eat away at the soldier's clothes, and his exposed cranium and his wayward leg and foot bones would be covered in mud, and buried deeper with each rainy season, until they became archaeological artifacts. Near the spot where the Lenca buried their peaceful dead, by the rock overhang, a natural shelter and gathering place.

NO BOMBS FELL on the transmitter site after the trench shelter was dug, and the hole became an object of curiosity for the many foreign visitors to the Radio Venceremos camp. A French photographer arrived and stood inside it, and he asked Lucas to use one of his cameras to take a picture of him as he crouched inside, a playful smile on his face. The French photographer and Lucas shared stories of Srinagar and the lakes and snow-covered slopes of Kashmir. Next Lucas met a German leftist writer; in the portrait Lucas took of her standing over the new trench, she gave the camera the rueful look of someone contemplating a great tragedy. A Salvadoran compañera arrived from Nicaragua, after many years in exile there; she brought the five-year-old girl she had been raising among the Sandinistas, and now this girl jumped in and out of the trench, at play. Lucas and the Salvadoran exile talked about the crazy revolutionary scene in Managua, which had filled up with European and American fellow travelers. *She said lots of Europeans in Managua have taken to wearing T-shirts that say, "Yo no soy gringo." Guess I'll have to do up a T-shirt that says, "I'm a Yankee—eat shit baby."* The

Salvadoran exile, and the French photographer, and the German writer all sat around the campfire with Santiago and Mariposa and the radio compas, and they listened to political talks and they held another dance, with cumbias blaring from a Radio Venceremos tape recorder.

Yes, it was a guerrilla Woodstock up here in Morazán; the last days of hippie freedom before the bad trip of another army invasion. It was as good a time as any for Lucas to press his case with the comandantes. Will I be allowed to leave now? Can I return to the United States and serve the revolutionary cause there? St. Pete and Sweet Willy just left for Europe. Why can't I leave for Illinois? Yancy was the political officer Lucas had to ask first; Yancy would send his request back up the chain of rebel command, eventually up to Jonás and the Juggler.

I said, "Yancy, there's this old saying that in the revolution all comrades are equal, but some are more equal than others." And on that note our session began, Joe wrote later. *Hot and heavy from the get-go. "All right, I've been waiting 8 months for a salida, I assume the answer is still the same, but I believe I deserve an explanation. At this point, I'm more interested in the explanation than I am in leaving."*

Yancy could not look me in the eye. Seems my case had been on his mind. He said I was "personalizing" the issue. Other people and activities took priority. We were at war and circumstances sometimes prevented the orderly resolution of problems, etc. I said the administrative capacities of the FMLN left something to be desired. But more importantly, I highly resented the aura of desconfianza* that had settled over the situation. Yancy quite rightly rejected any blame for former treatment but insisted desconfianza did not exist. If for some reason I was under suspicion the question would have been settled long ago; interrogation, investigation, termination with a "tiro" (bullet). Unimpressed, I persisted. I played hard-core during the entire session and I believe he suddenly realized he was dealing with someone 15 years older, who

---

*Mistrust.

was totally disinterested in ass-kissing or power quests. I told him I was quite content with my new job as combat correspondent, and I wasn't even sure if I still thought I should leave, or be more useful afuera.* The party was happy with my work, he said. "No one else here can do what you're doing." I said I understood we were here to make a peasant revolution and that the headaches were enormous. Yancy said that if it was decided that I would have to stay permanently, he would have no hesitation to tell me so. He started playing the revolutionary tough guy again, not realizing I eat tough guys for breakfast. But I respect the guy—he's doing the best he can. In the end, I believe we cleared the air somewhat, and will have no future difficulties working together. Faith renewed.

Lucas ended by telling Yancy he wanted his manuscript back and returned to him, and that Yancy should have someone dig it up for him. Yancy said he would do so; privately, however, Yancy was a bit taken aback at the request. In the rebel army, no rank-and-file soldier ever gave a political officer an order. The gringo Lucas was very bold and direct, and it occurred to Yancy that his counterparts in the Salvadoran army suffered something similar when dealing with the U.S. advisers in their midst. What was that old saying? French is a language for talking to lovers, Spanish is a language for talking to God, and English is a language for talking to employees. Lucas speaks to me in Spanish that is like the English that has never left him. Lucas was also guilty of egocentrism: my journal, my cigarettes, my freedom to do as I wish. Now this bon vivant is inside our reality, our invention, our improvisation. He doesn't know we communicate our desires to each other with our eloquent silences, by that which is implied but unspoken, by forcing our adversaries to watch us suffer. It's our Salvadoran way of being that holds the movement together. Lucas can't see this, but I can't blame him for it. He gives of himself. He is a generous comrade.

---

*Outside, i.e., out of the war zone.

It would be so easy to let him go. Not my decision. We're keeping him here to be one more line in our Salvadoran poem, to be a punch line in our Salvadoran joke, a character in a Salvadoran nightmare. Poor Lucas. I would so much like to spend time with you elsewhere, outside this revolution. You would like me much more. And I could tell you everything I cannot tell you now.

APRIL 24. 9:00. Fascinating and exciting interlude with TNT last night. TNT was Joe's nickname for the explosive, articulate and self-proclaimed "incorrigible feminist" who had rejoined the guerrillas after a long speaking tour on behalf of the revolution in San Francisco, Amsterdam, Stockholm and other places. *Over thirteen months searching in vain for a free woman inside the revolutionary mentality to fulfill my impossible dream of mountainside companionship. She appears too late for me, I suppose, but not too late for the movement. Very strident, outspoken, utterly possessed by the idea of women's liberation within the revolution. She despises the blatant displays of revolutionary machismo, and she's the only woman I've met in the campo who views the achievements of North American and European women as having any meaning for the struggles of El Salvador. She has fun baiting me. "Gringo viejo, feo." And she gets back from me, "How ya doin' honey, brown sugar?" She was in Nicaragua during the revolution. Tells tales of macho belittling and scorn on the firing line and in marches there and here. After a 12-hour march, a woman might flop down to rest, only to have some compa ask her to wash his socks. "It doesn't matter that I'm a shrimp and half-blind, just because I'm a woman I have to carry double the load." Has she ever tried writing up such observations, getting something in print? "Are you crazy? There's no sexism in the revolution. Are you trying to get me shot?" She says she's clashed with the comandantes and they're the worst of all. "I talked to one comandante who said he didn't like seeing women on the firing line, because afterward they don't want to make torti-llas and wash clothes."*

ARMY TROOP MOVEMENTS were reported close to La Guacamaya. *April 24, 8:00 a.m. GI Billy and the lads off to keep an eye on the cuilios. Is it possible the enemy is in shape again to mount more invasions?* That afternoon Lucas made new inquiries about his manuscript, and finally received word from a compa named Israel. *Said he checked all the embutidos and couldn't locate MSS package. Perhaps my papers got burned along with part of Radio Venceremos archives during the March 27 troop reinforcements in Gotera. Had to get everything buried in two hours and be ready for a retreat. He didn't look much concerned, and a couple of the radio compas seemed delighted I'd finally gotten fucked over. Saw red and immediately felt destructive in my frustration.*

If his manuscript was lost, almost an entire year of his life was lost: from going underground in La Libertad to the days before the battle in San Francisco Gotera. Names, anecdotes, dialogue he could never recover. A literary catastrophe. He vented into his journal with red ink. *Even the possibility that people have been so irresponsible with something so valuable is a moderate final blow.* He was a crushed bum again. *Reminds me of Biafra. Something could easily snap inside the old skull. Nothing much I can do about the circumstances but wait out this sense of total vulnerability.* He still had the 308 pages on his back, plus a tiny notebook from the Gotera operation, and two more volumes hidden in the crawl space in his old house in La Libertad.

April 25. 11:00. No sign as yet of manuscript, but not feeling last night's trauma. All the compas were feeling bad about it; they did not hate him or wish him ill. He went back to his radio work, writing an article about the revolution's recruitment efforts, but soon he began to hear the sounds of gunfire and mortars coming from the south. *11:30. Mortars and machine gunning getting closer, definitely an enemy advance from Osicala area to-*

ward Cerro Pando. But no signs of any alert. 13:00: No MSS yet. Yancy says it will be looked into, probably tonight when other material gets burned. Seems like a medium-sized invasion or enemy incursion is underway. But we're still not on alert and compas appear to be holding the line at Río Torola. That night, word came down from the rebels' central command that an estimated 2,500 army soldiers were headed toward the town of Meanguera, in an attempt to recapture it, a month after it had been seized by the rebels. Lucas was ordered to roll out toward the battlefield as a combat correspondent. A comandante named Angel was leading the fight, and as Lucas left word came the fighting was already over: the rebels had forced the army to retreat. "There's a lot of dead cuilios out there, Lucas," Santiago told him. "Take the camera." He pointed to a new compa on the radio crew, a college student Joe had met before. "Go with Giovanni."

GIOVANNI GRABBED A TAPE RECORDER. As they left El Zapotal and marched to the battlefield another group of compas asked, "Where are you going?" "To the war!" Giovanni yelled back. *Just then, a mortar shell crashed behind us,* Joe wrote later in his journal. *Easy lope over the mountains to Angel's camp, blowing out a week's worth of tobacco on the way.* They arrived at Comandante Angel's field headquarters just after sunset to *great excitement.* The compas were sorting through booty recovered from the battlefield; several M16s and enemy rucksacks. Clothing, toiletries, cigarettes, the things the enemy carried into battle, *even a couple of pages of hard-core porno and a sheet of nine birth-control pills. And the usual pictures of girlfriends.* Dressed up and prim and proper, a young woman dressed for Sunday mass. Rosebud mouth, birthmark on her cheek. High collar, top button. Virginal. His querida. And the naked bodies of American women, open legs and pubic forests.

There were seventeen enemy corpses on the battlefield, Angel said. At first light, Lucas would go out to photograph them.

Angel's lads had fought well that day. Compa casualties? Lopez lay dead, tied to a litter and covered with captured uniforms, beside a table where Giovanni was reviewing enemy ID papers. The compas moved around Lopez's corpse but did not look at him, and Lucas went off to sleep; when he woke up he saw someone had placed a candle next to the dead man, and at 4:30 a.m. someone brought up a coffin. *The body lay in state, towel covering his face. He had been the primo of a rebel cook. A young campesina girl appeared in camp, perhaps his sister.* The girl stood over the fallen guerrilla and lifted the towel, and traced the sign of the cross on his forehead, and gave him a farewell kiss on the spot of this invisible crucifix, and Joe had the sense it was not the first time she had said goodbye to a relative this way. Joe closed his eyes to see if he could get maybe one more hour of sleep, but the fungus growing on his feet and groin itched, and his stomach ached from diarrhea, and instead his half-open eyes watched as the daylight began to erase the blackish gray from the sky and turn it magenta.

WITH GIOVANNI CARRYING A TAPE RECORDER, and Lucas carrying the camera and his M16, the combat reporters of Radio Venceremos marched through brush and dew toward the battlefield. Thirty minutes and they were there. They found several squads of compas searching the ground and the bushes around the Y intersection of two dirt roads where they had ambushed an army company the night before. The compas had been prowling through the night, looking for soldiers who might be hiding nearby. *No luck, but plenty of dead soldiers and captured weapons to satisfy everybody. Half the dead were all in one bunch, nearly side by side, suggesting they'd been executed.*

Lucas talked to several compas who described the strange events that followed the firefight. Several soldiers had played dead, taking cover among corpses until the compas were within a few meters. Then they stood up and started firing; Lopez was cut down by an M16 burst. Compas opened up on them and left them all for dead. Now Lucas walked up to an enemy corpse, *arm upraised in rigor mortis*, he would write later in his journal. He placed his own M16 next to the dead man, to replace the one the compas had confiscated: he snapped a photograph. *Just then the compas started yelling, "¡Cuilio vivo! ¡Cuilio vivo!" Everyone took cover. Turned out that a compa had spotted a wounded soldier, just meters away from us, on the other side of a hedge, still alive.* The soldier had been shot in the hip, and was still armed, and the compas quickly disarmed him and Lucas grabbed him under the arms and around the waist to help him stand up. *He trembled for nearly five minutes and was yelling, "I didn't fire my weapon, not a single shot at you people. Check my rifle, look at my ammo belt."*

The soldier's bloody pants were swarming with ants, a crawling mass of exoskeletons and microscopic teeth literally eating him alive, but he was too numb to feel them. As Lucas helped guide the soldier away from the ants, Giovanni conducted an interview with the soldier; and then Giovanni took Lucas's camera and took a shot of the captured man, while Lucas gave him water and a cigarette. Giovanni returned the camera to Lucas, saying, "I took out the old roll," and Lucas proceeded to take a series of photographs of the battlefield. The captured soldier, older than most of his dead companions, puffing on the cigarette Lucas gave him, smoke curling from the tip in front of his panicked face. The corpses on the battlefield and the compas standing over and around them. Government-issued olive uniforms, clean-shaven faces stained with blood and tissue, spotted with *Musca domestica*. Rebels in informal T-shirts, faded maroon and orange, and unshaven chin hairs, their fingers searching the pockets of the dead. A compa found a corvo knife on the body of one of the soldiers, and spat out the oath *¡hijueputa!* and he marched toward the captured soldier, and showed it to him. "Is this what you and your buddies used to carve up the little children?"

"No. Never. I never."

Lucas approached the prisoner. *I asked him if he knew what had happened in these cerros at Christmastime. He said he hadn't been in the army then; that he'd just been drafted during a recruiting drive that came through his village. He seemed sincere. The compas had no empathy for him; I usually wouldn't but now I did.* There was something different about this soldier. He had landed in a medieval tableau populated by teenage rebels who kicked and prodded the bodies of his dead friends. The soldier told Lucas he wanted to join the guerrillas. Some weeks later, after his gunshot wound had healed, the captured soldier did in fact join the guerrillas, and he fought alongside them for the rest of the war, becoming involved in literacy programs, and having a child with one of the villagers. But he was never able to see the photographs the blond rebel named Lucas had shot of him on the day of his capture.

As Lucas discovered when he reached the end of the roll, a nervous Giovanni had opened the camera to remove the completed roll, but had neglected to put a new one in. *Turns out I was shooting blanks the entire time,* Joe wrote later. When he returned to Angel's camp Lucas asked the comandante if the guerrillas were going to bury the bodies of the dead soldiers. "Maybe. Not sure. We might just let the vultures take care of them." Maybe the corpses were being left as bait, to see if the cuilios would risk an ambush to retrieve them. Lucas wanted to return to the Y intersection to see if he could get pictures of the fallen soldiers, but Angel said it was too dangerous. Lucas insisted and Angel finally let him go. He saw *bodies beginning to bloat beneath the buttoned army shirts that none of the compas wanted. Intestines slipping from open wounds. No creative satisfaction in these photos. It looked like a car wreck.*

Word came that the Atlacatl Battalion was on its way to recover the dead. Joe could see soldiers on a distant hill. *But they don't fire on us, even though we're in range. Just don't seem interested in advancing on us.* Moments after Joe wrote those words a new mortar and artillery barrage began.

APRIL 27. 6:00. No report yet whether compas held their fire long enough last night for the cuilios to recover their dead. Long discussion about enemy corpses and the demoralizing effect on the army, military honor. Reminds me of the Trojan Wars, whole armies perishing in the attempt to recover some heroic leader's body, surrenders negotiated on the return of the remains of the dead, bodies drug back and forth in plain view of the enemy, behind chariots, to destroy their fighting morale . . . Last night we had our own dead to care for. Compañero Mejano was dead almost the moment he was carried in. Shrapnel from a .105 in left thigh. Gaping wound the size of a cantaloupe. Doc J. checking body for heartbeat, breath, pupil dilation, muscle firmness in jaw, as I took flash photos. Nothing. A few minutes later it was medically official.
No one in the vicinity of the body wept, Joe noted in his diary. A few compas came to inspect the wound; the platoon led by the compa Crazy Willy was tasked with burial duty.

Watched the grave digging while nodding off. Could hear compas murmuring. How tranquil for the dead. All their worries are over. Mission completed. Compas empathizing with the dead, yet laughing and joking as they dig. Then literally dumping body in ground by flashlight, searching bloody clothing. (Scarlet, blood-soaked pants.) Billfold with 3 pesos, 35 centavos, a few scraps of cloth, stray buttons, pieces of string, a list of the compas in his squad (he was a squad leader) and a crumpled package of Kool-Aid. Turned over the money to Crazy Willy. Dirt shoveled quickly over the dead. My film was used up, my reserve of energy was used up. I returned to camp to sleep

Lucas awoke at the radio camp at El Zapotal, and Joe wrote his morning journal entry for April 27 there. He had reached the top of a new page, and wrote the number 332 above these lines and circled it. The notebook was more than three-quarters full. Every ruled line and piece of paper was a precious and limited resource; he did not leave big blank spaces in his war journals and often started new entries on the same lines as old ones, with two short parallel lines, or an asterisk as a marker. He wrote the last two words on the fifth line of page 332, and didn't bother putting a period at the end of his final sentence. He placed his journal inside his rucksack, and closed the straps.

Just before noon the sound of artillery fire to the south moved the Radio Venceremos crew to action again. Lucas marched to the south, this time with Santiago, to cover the battle between the Atlacatl Battalion and several units of the rebel army.

THEY REACHED A REBEL POSITION on a hill above the same road intersection the rebels and the army had fought over the day before. The idea was to force the enemy to attack the guerrillas on this high ground, a pattern that had been and was repeated again and again in Morazán, in this battle and battles before and after. Lucas looked down and saw the vultures gliding over the unburied enemy dead, and as he looked at their circling paths, which were roughly at his eye level, a sound was born from that patch of sky. "Artillery!" a voice yelled, and Lucas and Santiago dove for cover into a nearby trench, and a shell exploded higher up the hill. Santiago had fallen on his face jumping into the trench, and now he crouched up, with feces smeared over his cheek. "¡Puta!" Some nervous rebel had used this trench as a bathroom just minutes earlier. Lucas saw he was covered in shit too. "Puta, Santiago, esto es una mierda," Lucas said, the figurative and the literal meanings being exactly equal, because war was always shitty, no matter how you looked at it.

Two other compas joined them in the trench. "They're firing on us from Osicala," one of them said. About three kilometers away. To soften up the ground before an army advance. Firing shells at their own corpses, and maybe their own wounded too, because the army had tried to advance through there earlier, again. To recover their dead and to capture the field of battle. There were compas down there too, taking cover from the shelling, which now stopped. A pause before the army advance, surely. Word came that the compas on the front line had suffered some wounded, and that they had also captured a 90-mm anti-tank gun. A real prize.

"I'm going to take some pictures," Lucas said, and before Santiago could stop him, Joe was up and out of the trench with his rifle and his camera, running downhill, toward the crossroads where the compas had ambushed the army soldiers, again, because there was a wounded comrade and an enemy gun down there. He felt the drug of combat coursing through his aging body. His comrades were down there, bleeding, and there was a war prize down there too, and at this moment he was not Joe anymore, or even Lucas, but instead he was a compañero; he was the entire unit, a single body made up of himself and all his Salvadoran brothers and sisters, and as he squat-ran from the sloping hill into the flat battlefield he felt he was doing some small thing, or maybe a big thing to save his friends, or to win a great victory for their cause; they would live and fight again, with that 90-mm in their hands, that ferocious weapon that was like a cannon. Lucas found the wounded compa, who had been hit with shrapnel in the foot, and he helped him stand, and carried him away from the crossroads, and having done this, Lucas turned around and went back, because he had seen the precious 90-mm weapon, and he ran toward it, its barrel pointed up at the hill where Joe had sought protection, and where the rebels were waiting in ambush. Only an army corpse was nearby, and Lucas approached this corpse, and reached into the dead man's pocket and retrieved his identification; he was a member of the Atlacatl Battalion, and with that card and name Santiago could announce on the radio that the rebels had beaten back the hated murderers of that unit. Next Lucas moved toward the priceless weapon, and he was about five yards away when he felt an explosion, and he had time to think that he hadn't heard the fall of the shell, the whistle announcing its arrival. A mortar shell, fired from not too far away, maybe by the army troops on the next ridge, looking down at him. Joe felt the hot metal cut through his insides, and he fell, and his numbed eardrums heard faint voices calling to him. "Lucas! Lucas!" Saying something in Spanish. "¡Cayó Lucas¡ ¡Ayúdenlo¡" and in his wounded state, Joe's Spanish momentarily left him, it was all gibberish, and he tried to rise to his feet, but could not. He felt two compas lifting him up, and carrying him away from this deadly crossroads, up to higher ground. To safety.

JOE SAW HIS OLD FRIEND, the head of the radio station, one of the few men in the rebel army who was as tall as he was. "Puta, Santiago, I've been wounded," Lucas said. Joe's Spanish had returned to him and he handed Santiago the ID of the dead soldier from the crossroads, and also the coins and bills in his pocket. "Here, buy yourself some cigarettes," he said to Santiago, because even now Joe knew he might soon die. He might be the next compa to go in a hole dug by a burial detail. One of the rebels came up alongside him with the 90-mm gun, and showed it to him. See, Lucas, we got it. A wound to his side, just above the groin. He might not make it. No, no, no, I have to get back home. He might not make it, and this thought caused the water to evaporate from his mouth. "Agua, por favor, agua." But they won't give him water, he sees the doctor shaking his head. No water. Instead dabs from a wet rag on his parched lips, his reaching tongue. Más, más. And now they were carrying him, and he could feel meaty and taut biceps and triceps and wrist muscles holding him up, and he wished they could just lay him down, because the act of being carried was sending waves of pain from his wound. Into his groin, and into organs inside and below his ribs, and up his neck and into his head.

Soy Lucas. My name is Joe. Time lost its meaning and his existence was a wound, jagged flesh, severed tendons, the pulse of singed nerve endings. How long had they been carrying him? Two minutes, five, ten? They placed him on a litter. The same one the corpse was on yesterday? The same one? The Mexican doctor, Doc J, was over him. Eduardo is his nom

de guerre, but I call him Doc J. "This isn't too serious, Lucas. Not at all."
The doctor knew that if he was back in his native Monterrey, Mexico, in the
fully supplied emergency rooms and hospitals where he'd been a resident
not too many years ago, they would sew up Lucas and drip blood into him,
and he would almost certainly live and recover fairly quickly. But here there
was no blood to give him, only a little plasma, and this made Lucas's pros-
pects very poor. He was so big, this man. Twice the size, it seemed, of the
average compa. Doc J had a basic surgery kit, a few surgical clamps, and
now he looked down at his patient, who was alert, not yet in shock. And the
patient said, "Don't worry, doctor. Don't worry. I know you're going to do
your best to save me." At that moment, and in the years that followed, the
doctor understood that his wounded patient wanted him to be free of any
guilt or remorse. The younger compas died afraid and confused, gritting
their teeth and weeping, but this older man, this North American, he had
seen as much life as a platoon of child compas. The doctor worked, and
when he was done and looked back at the wounded patient, he remembered
their camp conversations. The intelligent feel of those talks. About reli-
gions and about the science of flight. Chess matches. The bombardment
began again, followed by the rain-sound of distant gunfire. The enemy
was advancing toward them. "¡Alerta! ¡Alerta!" Time to move out. Joe
heard the gunfire too, and the doctor's words, "Move this one as delicately
as you can." Joe looked down across his body as he was lifted into a type of
portable hammock. Two long bamboo poles holding up a net. He had seen
many wounded compas carried in this way. An old man, very short, carried
one end. And looking up over his legs, he saw another old man holding the
other end. Peasants. Campesinos. Porters. They aid the revolution with the
gnarled muscles of their shoulders and backs, and they carried the gringo,
uphill and downhill, and he could hear them grunting. This one is too big.
Too big for us. Yes, I'm five eleven in my socks. Too tall. They had tied the
bag of plasma to one of the bamboo poles. "Keep it high," the doctor said.
But now they were marching downhill, and the bag slipped down. It was

resting on Joe's legs, and he slipped into shock and could not speak, and could barely see. He was very afraid. The burial detail. Darkness coming. The blanket of soil over me. Darkness here, darkness forever. In my room alone in the dark, afraid, Mom and Dad on the other side of the door. Mom and Steve and Dad. He was slipping away, but his mother became a lucid thought: the desire to write her one more letter. One more letter. Explain everything. The tip of a pen scratching words on paper, his words, to Mom. He would stay awake to write that letter, to tell her why he always left home, even though he loved her more than all the roads and all the countries he'd seen. Mom, it's me, Joe.

He heard water splashing around him. They were crossing a river. The rainy season hadn't truly started yet. The river was low. The feet of the porters were plunking into deeper water. The two old men carrying him made it to the other side. They stopped to rest. And they set Joe down, and Joe rested too, because being carried was exhausting him. He listened to the trickle of water. He could not open his eyes, but he could hear the river, and then distant explosions, and then quiet, and then the river again. Flowing. If he could write a letter home, he'd say, *Mom, Dad, I hear the river. Trees too. A gust blowing through the crackling leaves. I can feel the branches of a tall tree moving, its sway, all its leaves catching wind. Swish, swish. The water. Moving, trickling, just like home. Like the Sangamon. Insects drawn to the moisture. I can feel them.* The music of water squeezing through paths between the rocks, the sound reaching his ears, turning dimmer. The music of the water.

WITH THE ARMY UNITS advancing toward them, the burial detail worked very quickly. They interred Lucas on the banks of the Río Sapo, still wearing his glasses. They tossed dirt over the arms folded across his torso, and saw dirt fill up the space between his fingers; but, as they did with other corpses, they looked away when it was time to cover his face. With shells beginning to fall nearby, they took a last look at the upturned dirt of the grave, crossed themselves and retreated eastward and upward, to higher ground and to parapets made from stacked stones.

LUCAS'S RUCKSACK, and all the written words inside, ended up in the possession of Santiago. The Venezuelan radio man looked at the words in black, blue and red ink. An entire book. Lucas's story. On May 6, more than a week after he was buried, and when it was clear the army's advance into the heart of rebel territory had been defeated, the rebels broadcast the news of Lucas's death. One more compañero who gave his life for the revolution. Santiago had also retrieved Joe's passport and was looking at it when he read Lucas's real name over the airwaves for the first time. Joseph David Sanderson. The United Press International reporter monitoring the broadcast in San Salvador was a bilingual salvadoreño who had never heard the name Sanderson before. In the modulated distortion of Santiago's transmitted voice, he heard "Joseph David *Anderson*," and it was with that name that the death of the American who had joined the ranks of the rebel FMLN army was first reported in English.

OF THE PEOPLE in Urbana who were closest to Joe, it was his friend Jim Adams who heard the news first. Read out by an announcer on CNN. Jim called Steve, who telephoned the CNN headquarters in Atlanta. "I think my friend just heard a report about my brother being killed." A very kind intern read Steve the text of the wire service dispatch from El Salvador: "*Rebel radio reported yesterday; an American fighting alongside Salvadoran guerrillas; killed by government troops; Joseph David Anderson; age and hometown not available; died in the village of Poza Honda; first came to*

El Salvador in 1980; participated in the January 1981 'final offensive,' before moving to rebel camps in Morazán province." The first and second name together, the dates. It had to be Joe. Oh little brother, what happened to you? Joe, what have you done? I have to tell Mom. And call Dad. I have to tell Mom in person. Drive over there. Bring Carol and Kathy too, for support, to give her a hug. Steve drove across Champaign-Urbana in a daze, his family with him, and when Virginia opened the door and saw her older son, his wife and their daughter standing there, unannounced, on a Friday afternoon, with grim expressions on their faces, she knew it could only be one thing.

"Joe," she said.

"Now, well, Mom, nothing has been confirmed."

Nothing was ever confirmed. Joe's rebel friends did not write to her, she received no official statement from her own government, or from the United States Embassy. The most eloquent and convincing evidence of Joe's death was the absence of his letters. Joe had always written home from his travels. Funny letters, bawdy letters. Letters in which he spoke of being lonely, hungry. Describing sunsets in Laos, babies in Africa, house fires in Peru, hurricanes in Florida. Letters telling her when he would be home. In the days and weeks that followed she looked at the mail carrier as one looks at a mortician. Instead of a new message from Joe, the mailman brought condolence letters. From old friends of Joe's, from friends here in Urbana. A nice note from Roger Ebert, the dear. At dinner, she silently clasped hands with Annabel. But she never held a funeral for her son, or a service, how could she, without his body, without him. She never learned how he died or where he was buried. The local newspaper called, but she could not speak to them. Steve did, and the newspaper ran a picture of Joe that Steve gave them; in Nicaragua, a smiling tourist shot. The hunk in the sunshine. "Local Man Dies Among Leftists in El Salvador." When Virginia finally talked to her ex-husband on the phone about it, the old tensions between them returned. He blames me. How could he? He doesn't say it, but the tone of his voice implies it. "Well, now we won't have to worry about Joe anymore," she answered back, because for years she had lived with the daily suffering, the idea that he might not return home, and now that nightmare had come true. Her baby boy. Smart and curious. Needing protecting. Needing to be fed. Let me cook for you, Joe, the things you like. Sitting at my table. A boy, eating hearty, growing. The man he became, rudderless but with so much joy, fighting off his loneliness by moving, one place to the next. Years, decades. His life of discoveries, and his desire to share them with me. He went to all those places so he could tell me stories. Beautiful boy I dressed in blue overalls that matched the color of his eyes. The man he became. Storyteller. I was his most loyal reader, it made him happy to write to me. I can feel it in these letters. My shoeboxes filled with his envelopes. Letters to me. Courageous boy, setting off on his own down the Sangamon River, across the oceans. I accepted it, I saw the beauty in his wanderings. I understood you, son.

I loved you.

I love you.

The unshakable, recurring thought that he might be alive, somewhere, out there. That it would all turn out to be one last, big prank. That he might walk up to the door. That a letter from him might arrive in the mail. One more envelope, the address in his handwriting, and the words on the first page. *Dear Mom.*

SANTIAGO STORED THE CONTENTS of Lucas's rucksack in a safe place: Joe's journal, and a few pages ripped from a small notebook, and a few articles he had written. When the rainy season had set in and the army's latest offensive had ended, he entrusted Lucas's writings to a compa courier. Santiago was looking ahead. He was building the archive of the revolution every day. Tapes of their broadcasts, photographs, typed-up scripts, and news articles. Lucas's writings would be gathered into this larger archive, stored in a safe place, far from the war. The young man carried the pack on his back, following routes Lucas and many other compas had followed, away from Morazán, around a volcano to the flatlands of San Miguel, around and through army checkpoints, hiding the notebooks under mangoes and plantains, and then to the coast, and finally the Gulf of Fonseca. The courier handed the package to a fisherman who was sympathetic to the revolution, and that fisherman, who had ferried many messages and weapons and people across this waterway for the rebels, launched his skiff at night, hidden by mangroves, and made the quick trip across the ocean waves to Nicaragua.

For the years that followed, Joe's writings remained in a file cabinet in Managua. In a proto-archive kept by friends of the Salvadoran revolution. Lucas's writings were stored in a protected place, as were the letters Joe wrote to his mother, which she filed and moved to plastic boxes. Joe's accounts of his travels endured in these pages. All the wondrous and weird incidents he had seen, and his memories of the rivers and the mountain ranges he had crossed, and the suffering and the human resilience he had witnessed during his two decades bumming. In these pages, Joe remained the living man he was, the writer who hoped to make art from it all. The sentences he scribbled, the metaphors he crafted, the people he met and described. Rants, anecdotes, soliloquies, observations, translated words, scenes. Preserved in his Illinois cursive, on sheets held together with staples and steel spirals, or folded inside envelopes. On paper resisting humidity, fungi, moths and silverfish. His words, waiting to be read.

A Few Closing Thoughts
from the Author

AFTER HER SON'S DEATH, Virginia Colman preserved and cataloged the letters Joe sent her during the twenty-odd years of his bumming adventures around the globe. She prepared index cards listing his various journeys away from Urbana. (*Crossed the Pacific, Feb. 1968–Apr. 1969*; *Back to El Salvador for last time, Sept. 1980 to Apr. 27, 1982.*) When she died of a heart attack in 1986, her son Steve Sanderson inherited those letters. Steve, in turn, assembled an archive of Joe's writings and life, which also included mementos from his life and travels, and the boxes of his brother's unpublished novels.

Steve didn't quite believe me when I told him, in a series of e-mails and phone calls from Latin America in 2008, that I had discovered Joe's diary in El Salvador. But once he saw a few sample pages from that journal, and confirmed they were in Joe's handwriting, he opened his home and archive to me as I began to write about his brother's life. Eventually, after conducting interviews in El Salvador and Mexico, I was able to tell him the exact circumstances of his brother's death, details Steve had been waiting to hear for more than a quarter century. "The first time I was ever convinced that there was no possibility that Joe could come knocking at my door," he told me, "was when I talked to you."

AS A WRITER, and as a centroamericano and a California Yankee, I am so grateful to Steve and to his wife, Jenny Bloom, for their friendship and their help with this project, and for their patience with me during the eleven years it took me to complete it. Steve introduced me to Jim Adams in Urbana, and to his daughter Kathy, and insisted I speak to his father, Milt Sanderson, which I did not long before Milt died in 2012. He also introduced me to Mafalda.

Mafalda had learned of Joe's death from a story in *Mother Jones* in 1984, two years after he was killed in El Salvador; she saw Susan Meiselas's photograph of Joe looking up at her from a copy of the magazine lying open in a college-town café. Like Joe's mother, she preserved her letters from Joe, and I am so grateful to her for sharing them with me, and for the conversations with her about Joe and the time she shared with him.

WERE IT NOT FOR ALEX RENDEROS, and his professionalism and dedication to El Salvador and its history, I would never have learned of Joe's contribution to the Salvadoran revolution, and of the existence of Joe's war journals, as preserved at the Museo de la Palabra y la Imagén in San Salvador. Alex and I worked for the *Los Angeles Times*, and as I prepared to write a story about Joe for that newspaper, he conducted interviews with a pair of former rebel fighters who'd played key roles in Joe's entry into the rebel army: the fighter "Fito" and the man known as Comandante Jonás. Just as important, Alex introduced me to Carlos Consalvi, aka "Santiago," who preserved Joe's wartime writings, and so many other documents and artifacts produced by the Salvadoran revolution. The memories Consalvi shared with me, and his book *Broadcasting the Civil War in El Salvador: A Memoir of Guerrilla Radio*, proved indispensable in my reconstruction of Joe's time in eastern El Salvador with the Ejército Revolucionario del Pueblo. And so did a two-day tour of the rebel-controlled areas and battlefields Consalvi gave me in 2008. Similarly, I owe thanks to "Eduardo," the Mexico City doctor who was with Joe when he died, and to all the former rebel soldiers and medical workers I met in Morazán during my visit there, who shared their stories about Joe with me.

In writing this novel, I also consulted Mark Danner's excellent 1994 book *The Massacre at El Mozote*, and the 1984 piece on Joe written by Peter Canby and Jay Dean for *Mother Jones*—a remarkable work of journalism they reported while the war was still being fought. Thanks, also, to the courageous Susan Meiselas, the photographer who documented so many Latin American struggles and who captured the iconic photograph of Joe as a guerrilla fighter.

THIS BOOK IS A WORK OF FICTION created from many sources. It's a product of my imagination, and also a work inspired and informed by the real life of Joe Sanderson. I quoted Joe's letters, for the most part, with few edits, and I can't vouch for the veracity of everything he wrote in those letters. And Joe and every other real person in this book would say they can't vouch for the truth of all the passages I made up. I know that in trying to re-create the dreamscape of Joe's life, I surely got some facts wrong.

Many writers are quoted and paraphrased in the text, including Claude McKay, James Joyce, W. S. Merwin, Denis Johnson and Cathy Linh Che. I also consulted the work of Christopher Okigbo and Chinua Achebe on Biafra and the Nigerian Civil War, and Mohamed Choukri's memoir about growing up in Morocco, *For Bread Alone*.

WHEN YOU WRITE A BOOK, your family lives it with you, as my wife, Virginia Espino, can attest. I thank her for her patience and support during the years I worked on this book, and also everyone in the Tobar–Espino clan, including my father, Héctor E. Tobar, who read all the early drafts of this work. My son Diego offered a critical insight into an early version of the prologue, and my son Dante gave me Funkadelic and assorted advice on matters scientific and literary; and I thank my daughter, Luna, for her repeated, dutiful notetaking while I dictated words and sentences as we drove on Los Angeles streets and freeways.

At the University of California, Irvine, I owe so much to Vicki Ruiz, Louis DeSipio, Barry Siegel, Michael Szalay, and to all the great faculty there who've accepted me into their family. And to my former colleagues at the University of Oregon, Gabriela Martínez and Julianne Newton, and to the many faculty members who wandered into my office in Eugene as I was writing this book, including Torsten Kjellstrand (for some basic lessons on firearms), Gretchen Soderlund (for insights into Champaign-Urbana, the "Center of the Universe,") and the late Alex Tizon.

And finally, thanks again to my longtime literary collaborators Sean McDonald and Jay Mandel; their faith in me and my work has sustained me for many years.

Héctor Tobar is a Pulitzer Prize–winning journalist and novelist. He is the author of the critically acclaimed *New York Times* bestseller *Deep Down Dark*, as well as *The Barbarian Nurseries*, *Translation Nation* and *The Tattooed Soldier*. Tobar is also a contributing writer for the *New York Times* opinion pages and an associate professor at the University of California, Irvine. He has written for the *Los Angeles Times*, *The New Yorker* and other publications. His short fiction has appeared in *The Best American Short Stories*, *Los Angeles Noir*, *ZYZZYVA* and *Slate*. The son of Guatemalan immigrants, he is a native of Los Angeles, where he lives with his family.